epic

# BRIGHT FAMILY

WRITTEN BY
## MATTHEW CODY
WITH
## CAROL KLIO BURRELL
ART BY
## DERICK BROOKS
COLORS BY
## WARREN WUCINICH

Andrews McMeel
PUBLISHING®

Andrews McMeel Publishing
a division of Andrews McMeel Universal
1130 Walnut Street, Kansas City, Missouri 64106

www.andrewsmcmeel.com

Epic! Creations, Inc.
702 Marshall Street, Suite 280
Redwood City, California 94063

www.getepic.com

21 22 23 24 25 SDB 10 9 8 7 6 5 4 3 2 1

Paperback ISBN: 978-1-5248-6773-7
Hardback ISBN: 978-1-5248-7079-9

Library of Congress Control Number: 2021931719

Design by Dan Nordskog

Made by:
King Yip (Dongguan) Printing & Packaging Factory Ltd.
Address and location of manufacturer:
Daning Administrative District, Humen Town
Dongguan Guangdong, China 523930
1st Printing — 5/31/21

**ATTENTION: SCHOOLS AND BUSINESSES**

Andrews McMeel books are available at quantity discounts with bulk purchase  for educational, business, or sales promotional use. For information, please e-mail the Andrews McMeel Publishing Special Sales Department: specialsales@amuniversal.com.

FOR STAN LEE AND JACK KIRBY--
EXPLORERS OF THE BEST KIND
**M. C.**

FOR THE CABIN CREW
**C. K. B.**

MANY THANKS TO MY BRILLIANT
WIFE, LAUREN, AND OUR FAMILY
AND FRIENDS: THIS BOOK
WOULDN'T EXIST WITHOUT YOU.
TO JONISE, DESTINY, NIYA, AND
DA'REL: NEVER BE AFRAID TO
STEP THROUGH A PORTAL AND
HAVE AN ADVENTURE!
**D. B.**

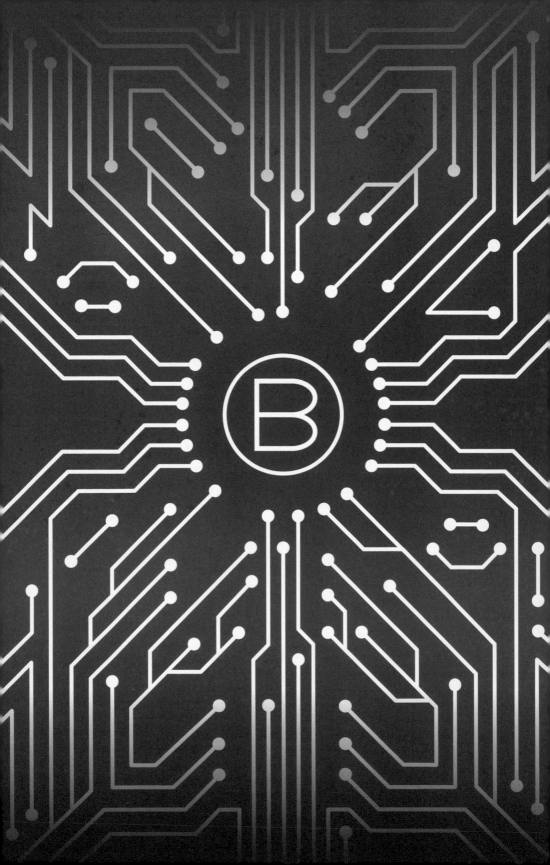

## CHAPTER 1

# VERSUS THE MULTIVERSE

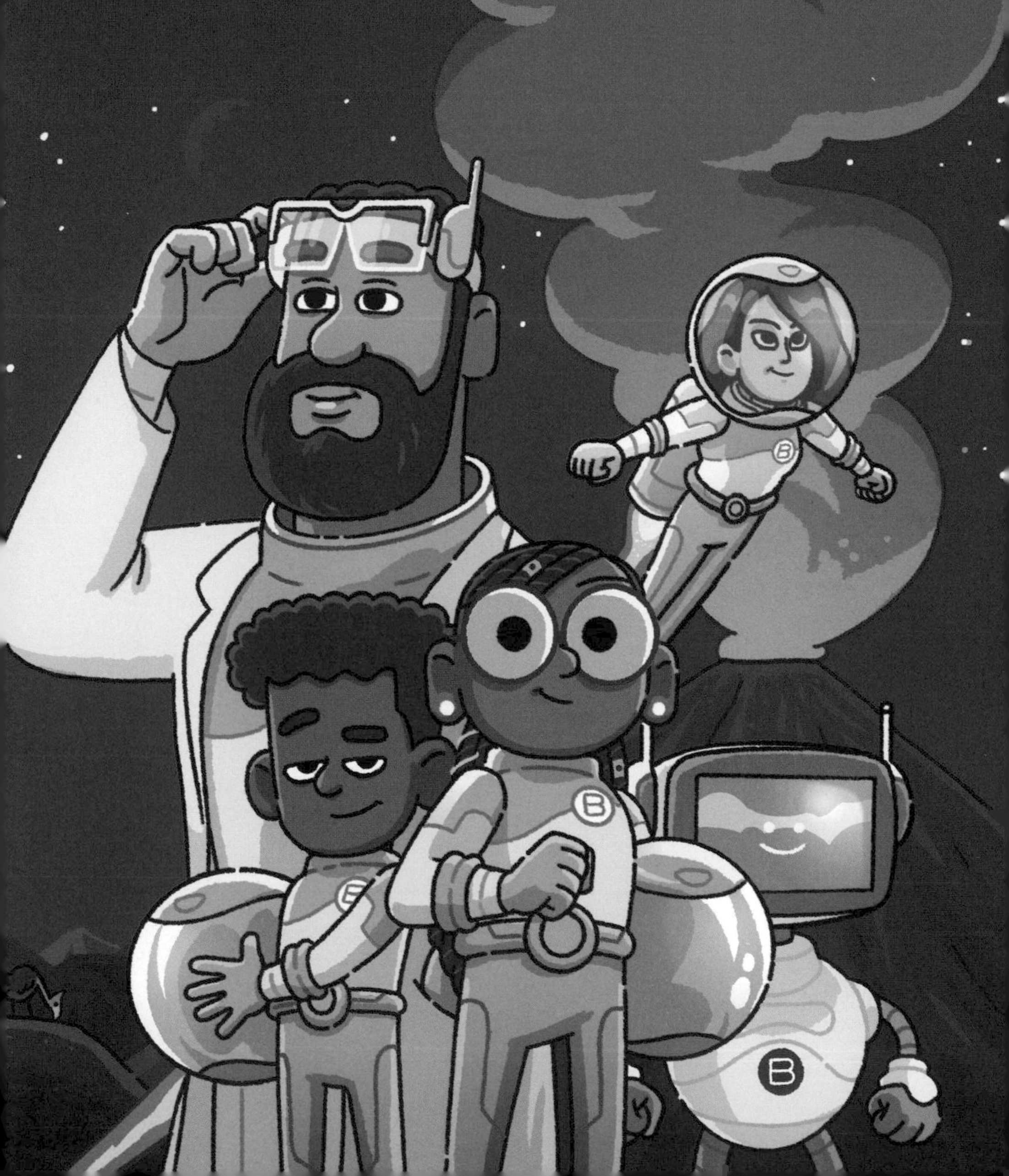

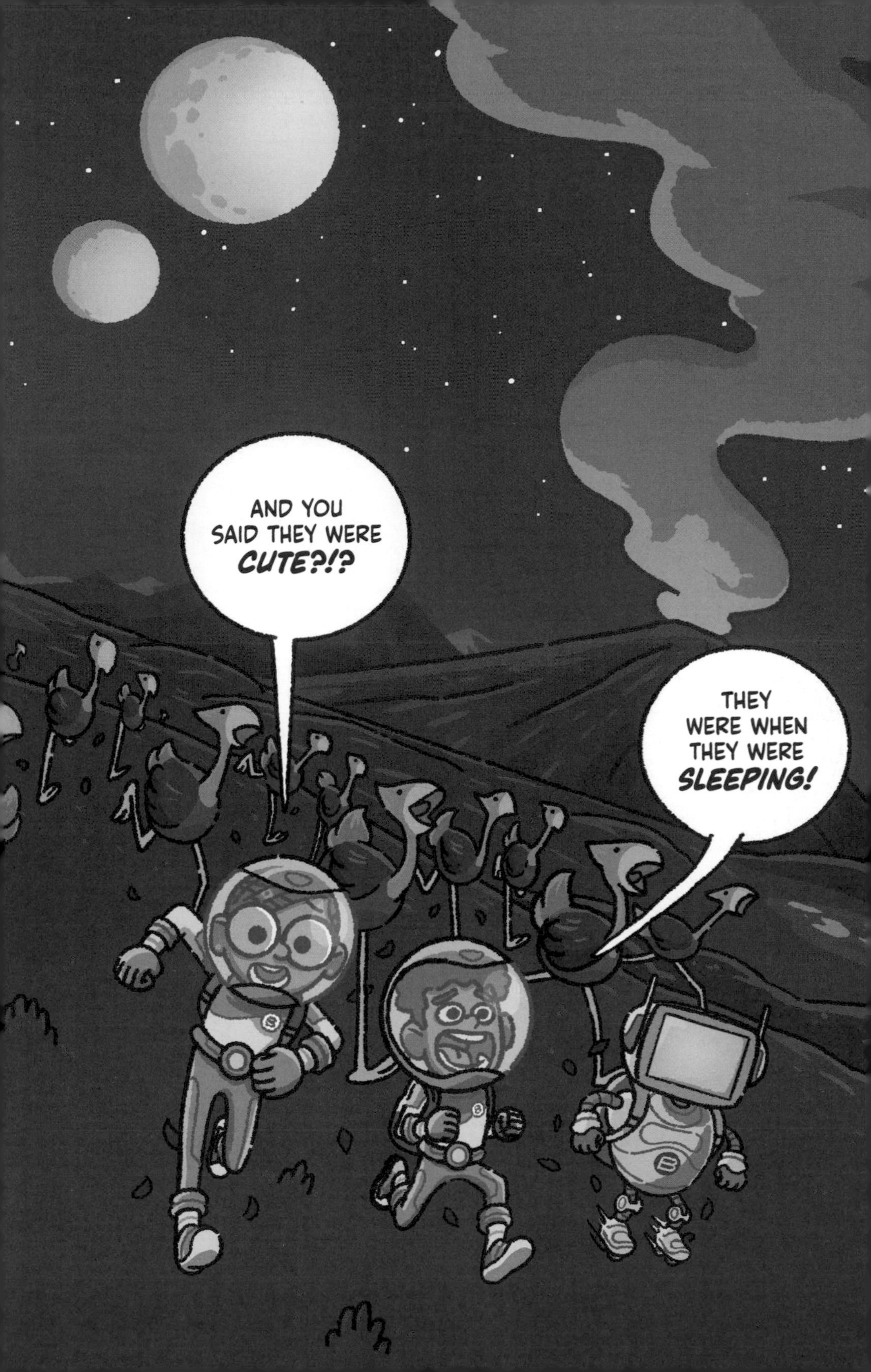
AND YOU SAID THEY WERE *CUTE?!?*
THEY WERE WHEN THEY WERE *SLEEPING!*

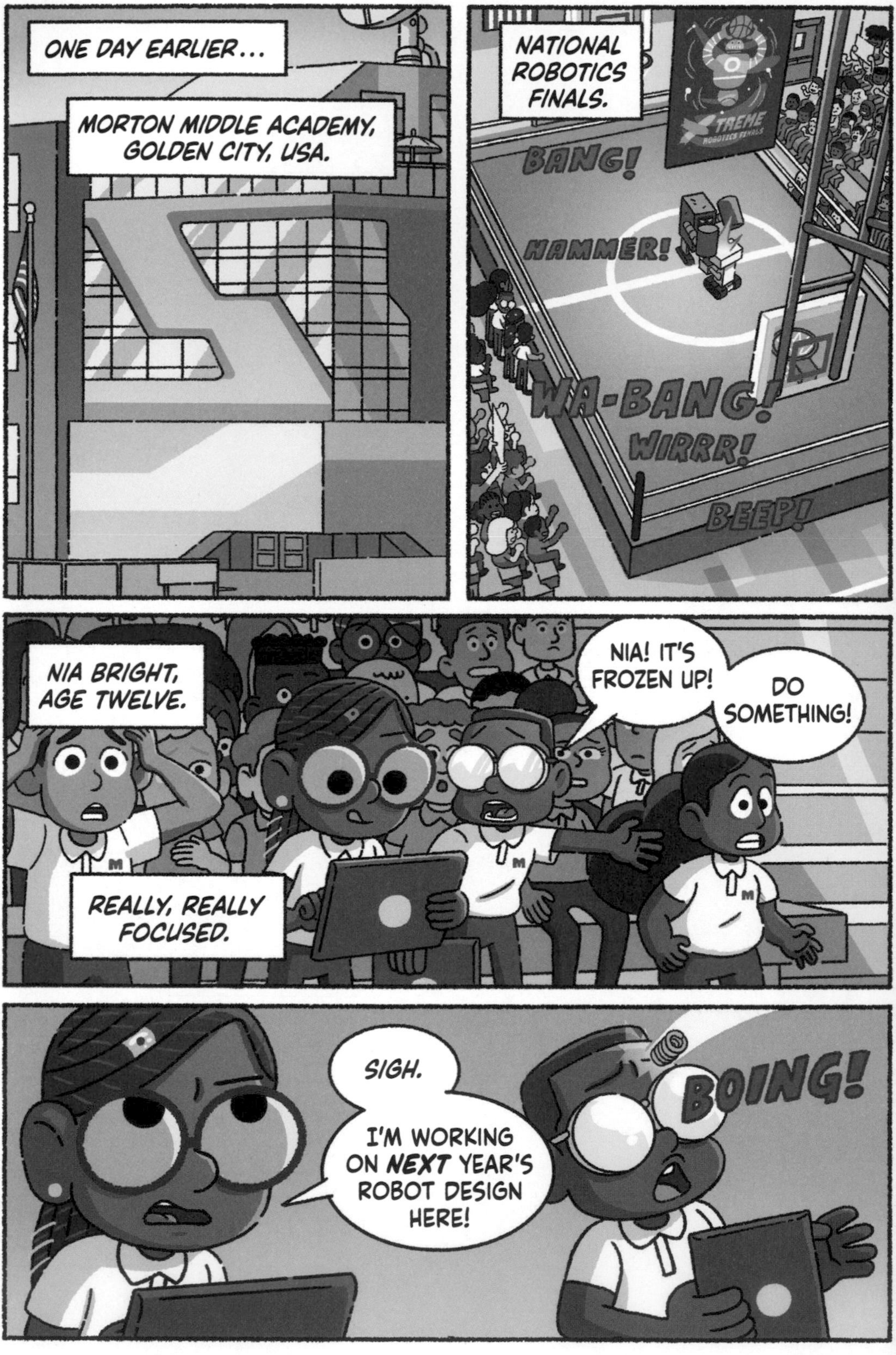
ONE DAY EARLIER...
MORTON MIDDLE ACADEMY, GOLDEN CITY, USA.
NATIONAL ROBOTICS FINALS.
BANG!
HAMMER!
WA-BANG!
WIRRR!
BEEP!
NIA BRIGHT, AGE TWELVE.
REALLY, REALLY FOCUSED.
NIA! IT'S FROZEN UP!
DO SOMETHING!
SIGH.
I'M WORKING ON *NEXT* YEAR'S ROBOT DESIGN HERE!
BOING!

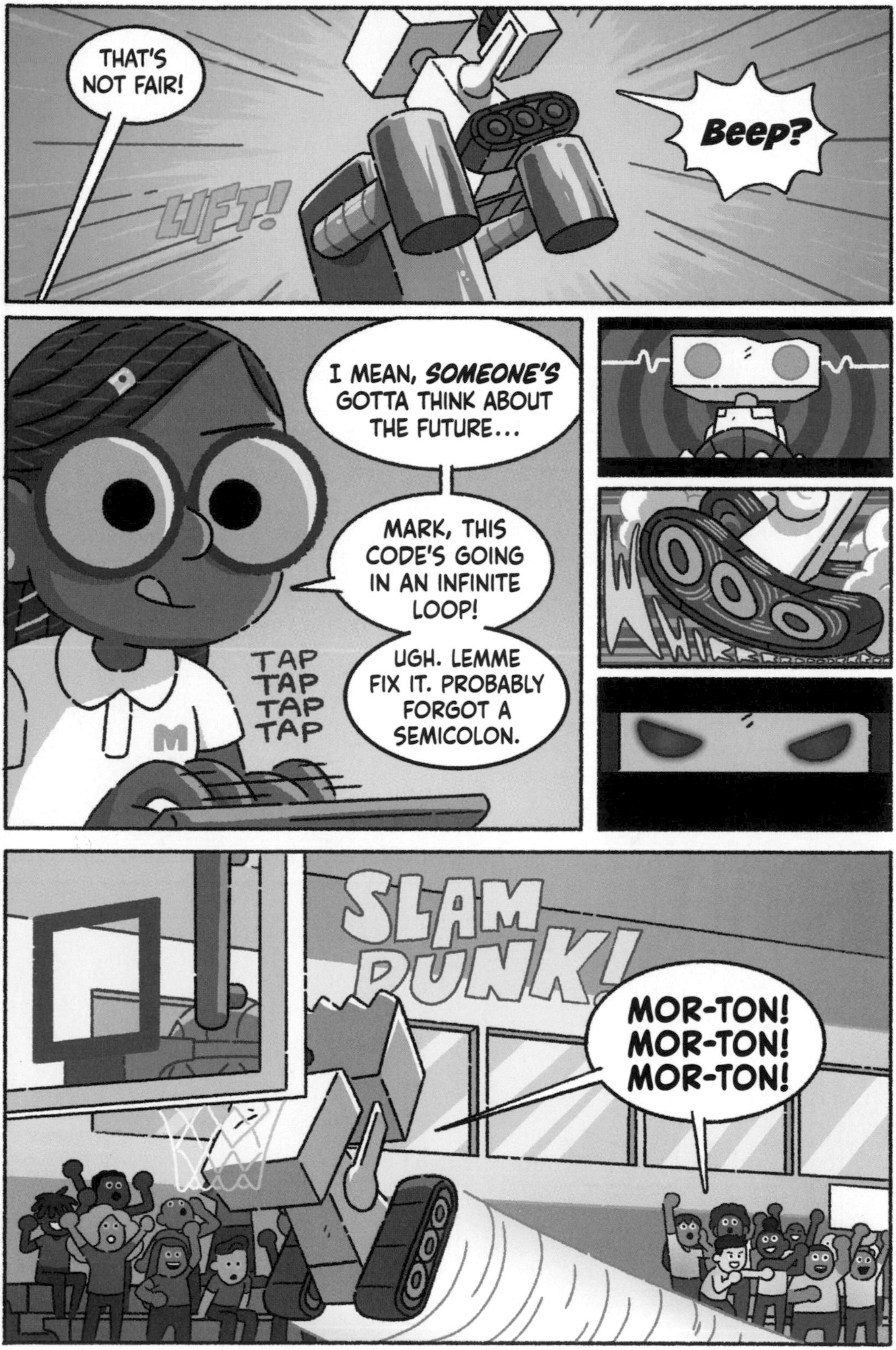
THAT'S NOT FAIR!
LIFT!
Beep?
I MEAN, SOMEONE'S GOTTA THINK ABOUT THE FUTURE...
MARK, THIS CODE'S GOING IN AN INFINITE LOOP!
UGH. LEMME FIX IT. PROBABLY FORGOT A SEMICOLON.
TAP TAP TAP TAP
SLAM DUNK!
MOR-TON! MOR-TON! MOR-TON!

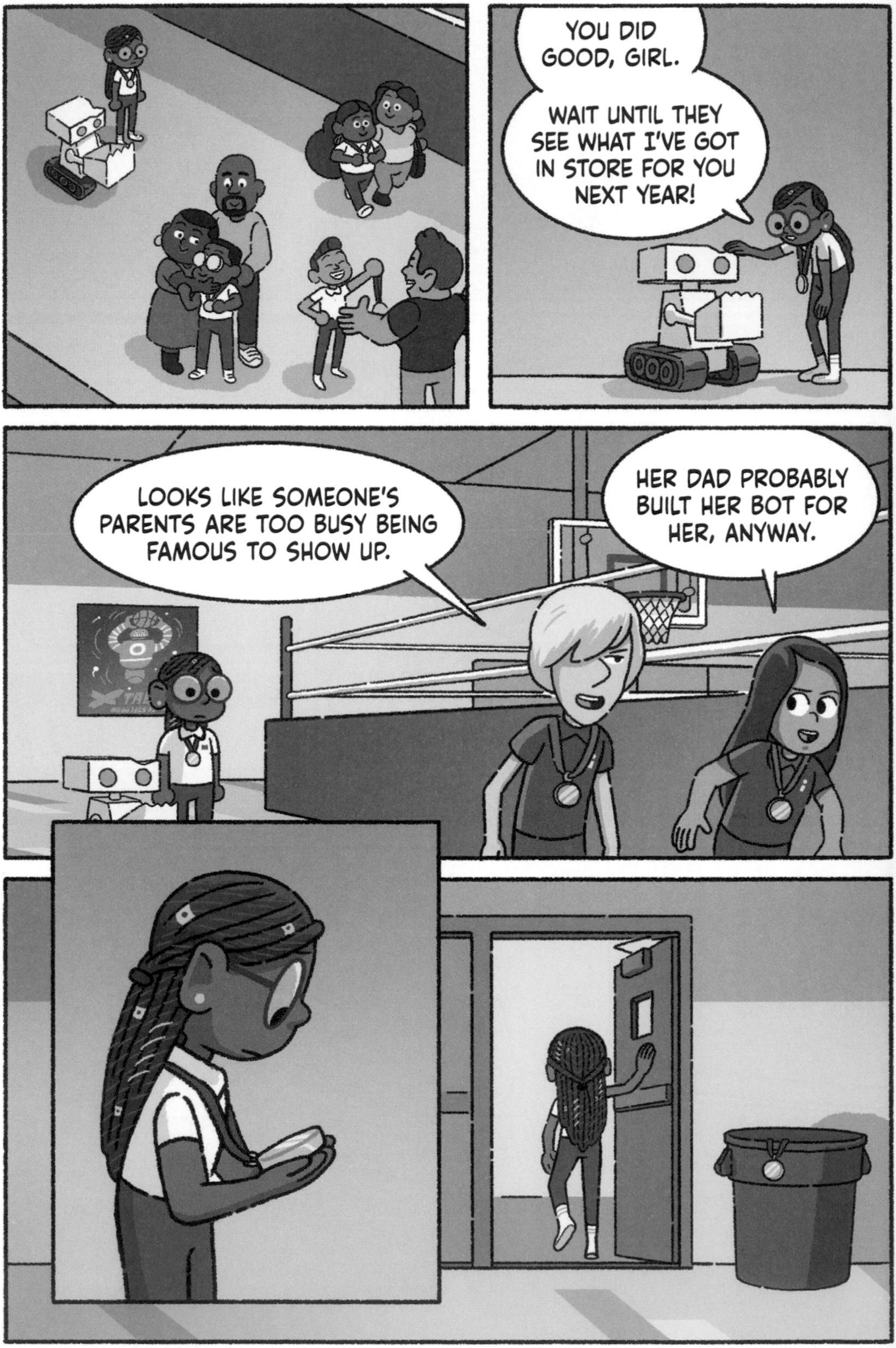
YOU DID GOOD, GIRL.
WAIT UNTIL THEY SEE WHAT I'VE GOT IN STORE FOR YOU NEXT YEAR!
LOOKS LIKE SOMEONE'S PARENTS ARE TOO BUSY BEING FAMOUS TO SHOW UP.
HER DAD PROBABLY BUILT HER BOT FOR HER, ANYWAY.

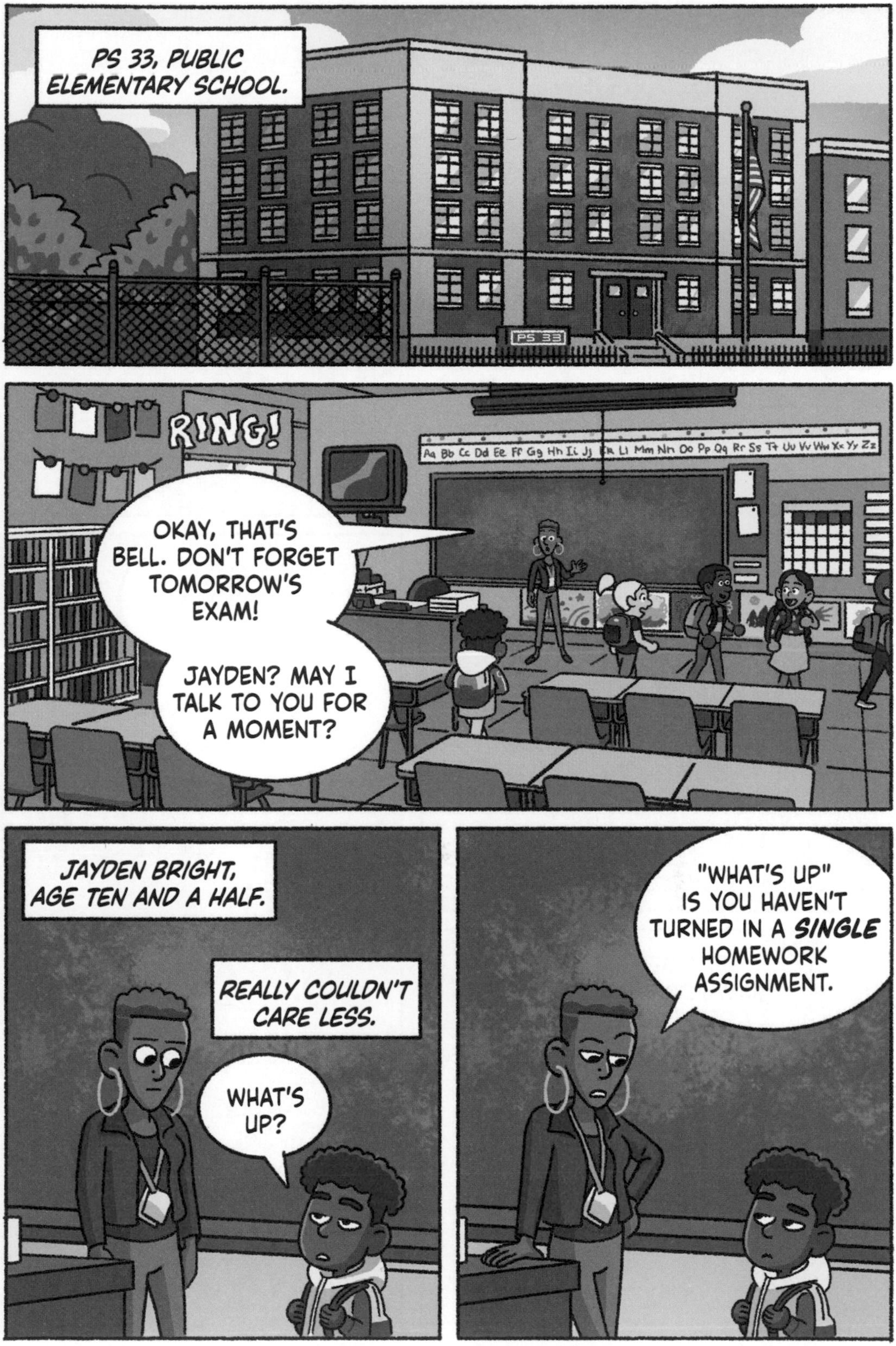
PS 33, PUBLIC ELEMENTARY SCHOOL.
PS 33
RING!
OKAY, THAT'S BELL. DON'T FORGET TOMORROW'S EXAM!
JAYDEN? MAY I TALK TO YOU FOR A MOMENT?
JAYDEN BRIGHT, AGE TEN AND A HALF.
REALLY COULDN'T CARE LESS.
WHAT'S UP?
"WHAT'S UP" IS YOU HAVEN'T TURNED IN A *SINGLE* HOMEWORK ASSIGNMENT.

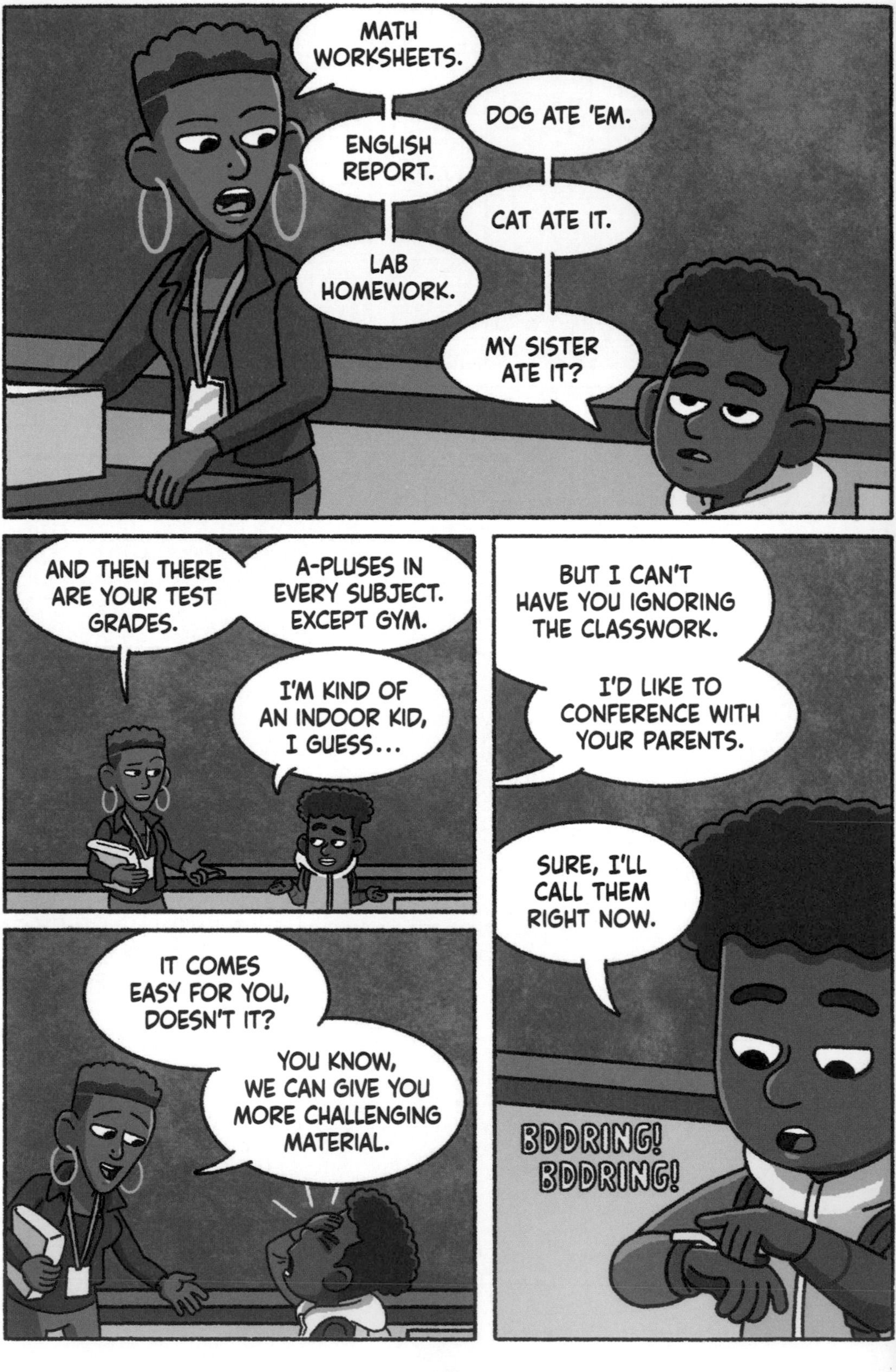
MATH WORKSHEETS.
ENGLISH REPORT.
LAB HOMEWORK.
DOG ATE 'EM.
CAT ATE IT.
MY SISTER ATE IT?
AND THEN THERE ARE YOUR TEST GRADES.
A-PLUSES IN EVERY SUBJECT. EXCEPT GYM.
I'M KIND OF AN INDOOR KID, I GUESS...
IT COMES EASY FOR YOU, DOESN'T IT?
YOU KNOW, WE CAN GIVE YOU MORE CHALLENGING MATERIAL.
BUT I CAN'T HAVE YOU IGNORING THE CLASSWORK.
I'D LIKE TO CONFERENCE WITH YOUR PARENTS.
SURE, I'LL CALL THEM RIGHT NOW.
BDDRING! BDDRING!

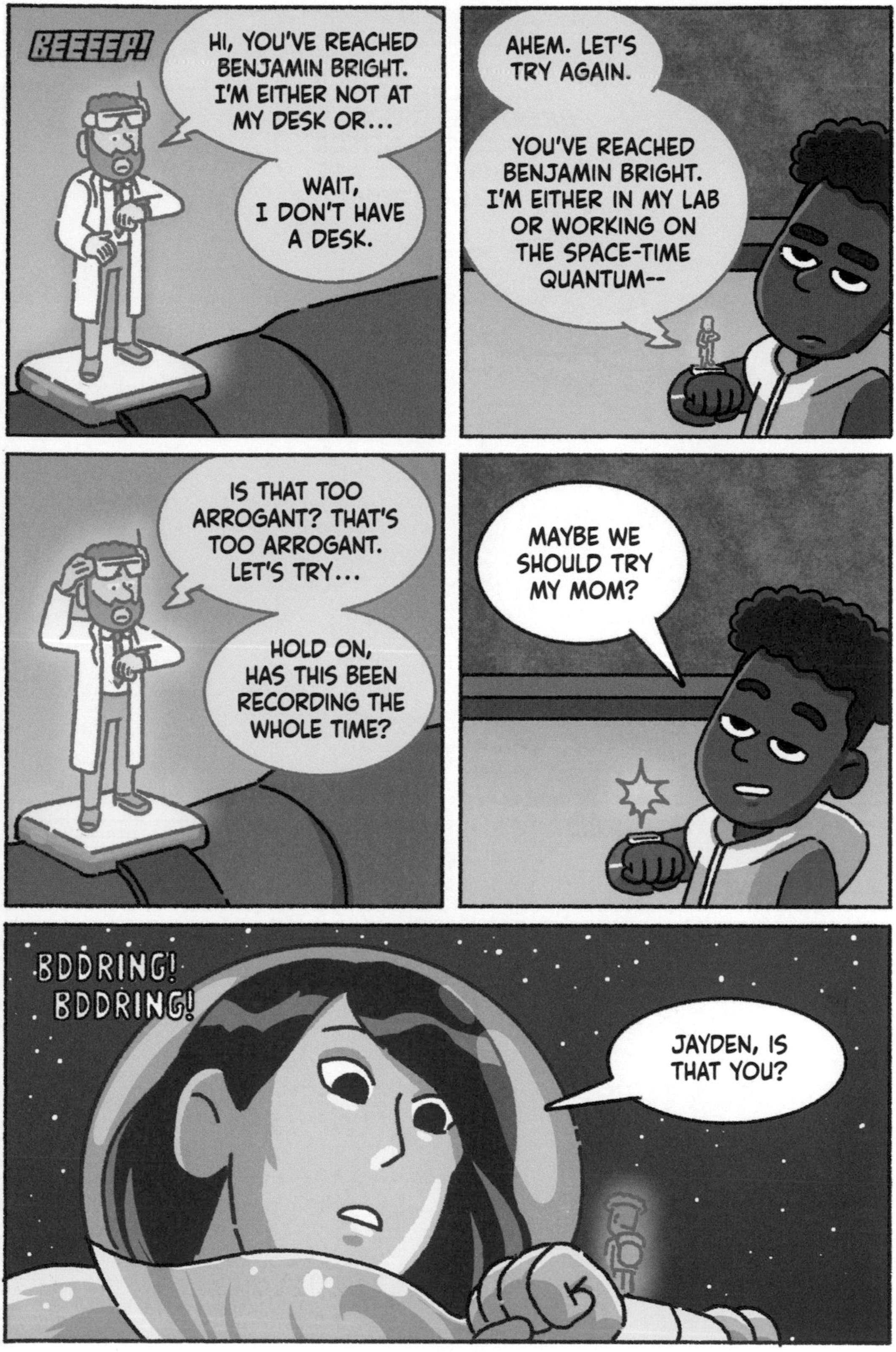
BEEEEEP!
HI, YOU'VE REACHED BENJAMIN BRIGHT. I'M EITHER NOT AT MY DESK OR...
WAIT, I DON'T HAVE A DESK.
AHEM. LET'S TRY AGAIN.
YOU'VE REACHED BENJAMIN BRIGHT. I'M EITHER IN MY LAB OR WORKING ON THE SPACE-TIME QUANTUM--
IS THAT TOO ARROGANT? THAT'S TOO ARROGANT. LET'S TRY...
HOLD ON, HAS THIS BEEN RECORDING THE WHOLE TIME?
MAYBE WE SHOULD TRY MY MOM?
BDDRING! BDDRING!
JAYDEN, IS THAT YOU?

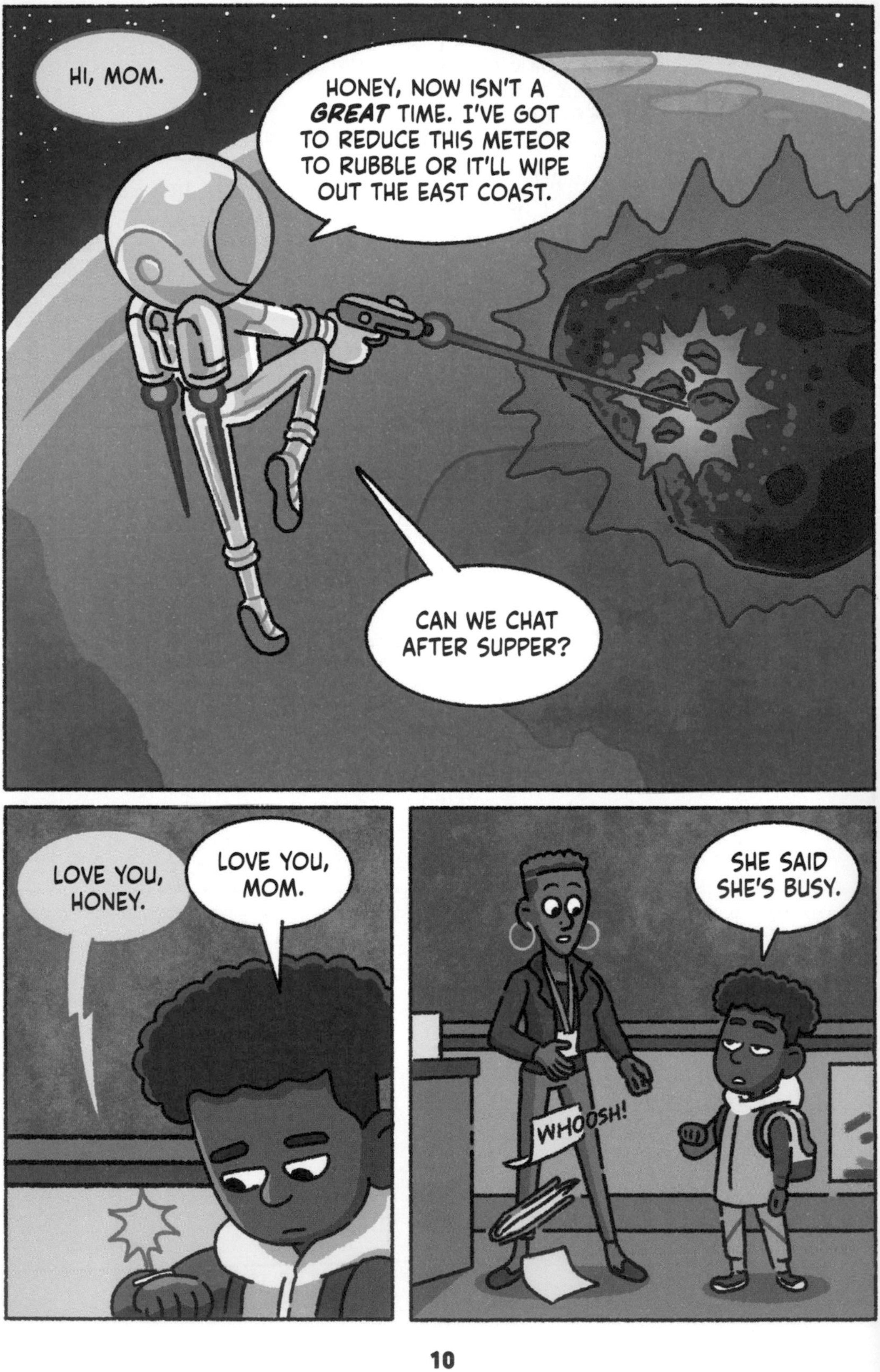
HI, MOM.
HONEY, NOW ISN'T A *GREAT* TIME. I'VE GOT TO REDUCE THIS METEOR TO RUBBLE OR IT'LL WIPE OUT THE EAST COAST.
CAN WE CHAT AFTER SUPPER?
LOVE YOU, HONEY.
LOVE YOU, MOM.
SHE SAID SHE'S BUSY.
WHOOSH!

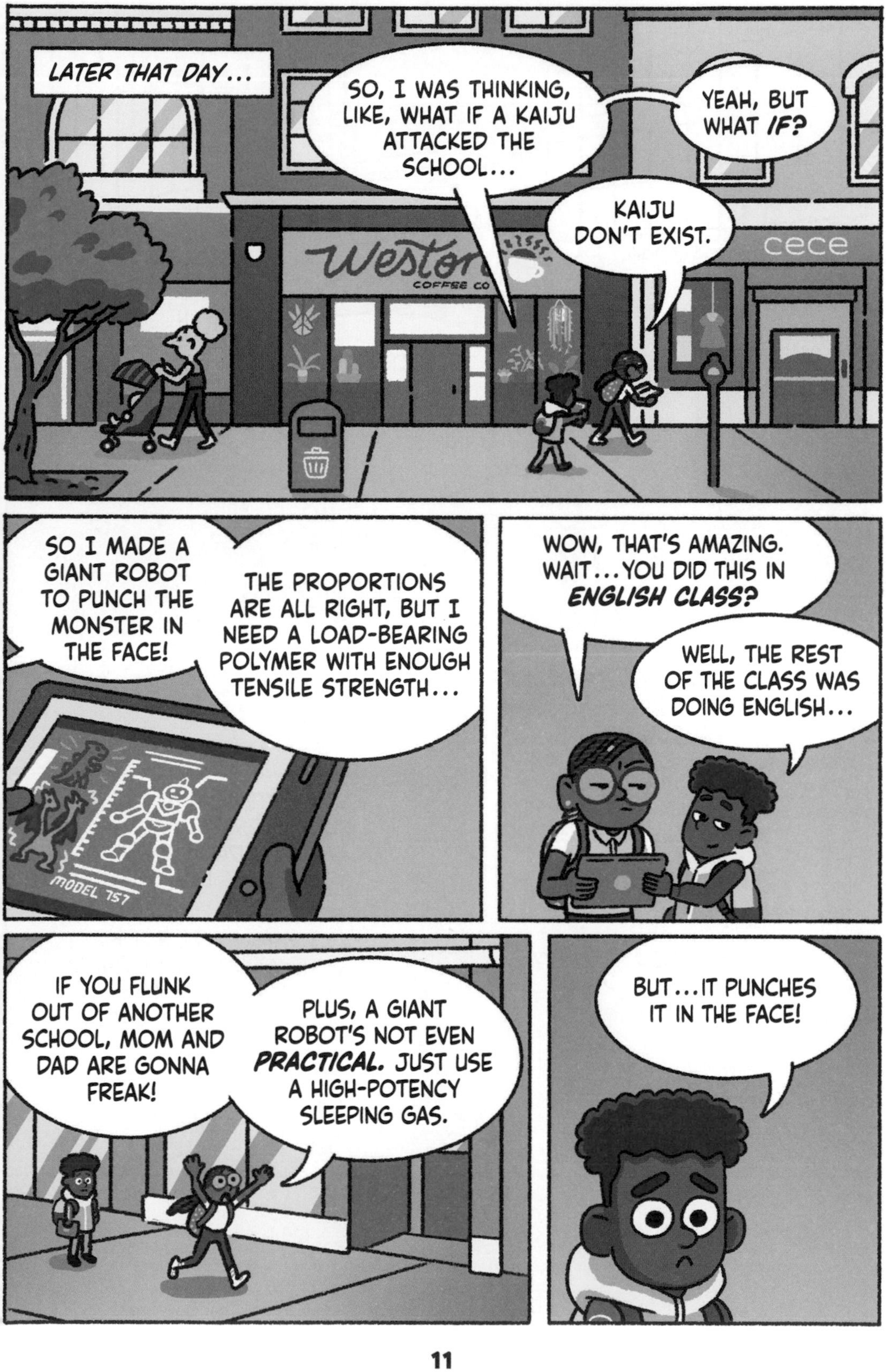
LATER THAT DAY...
SO, I WAS THINKING, LIKE, WHAT IF A KAIJU ATTACKED THE SCHOOL...
KAIJU DON'T EXIST.
YEAH, BUT WHAT *IF?*
Weston COFFEE CO
cece
SO I MADE A GIANT ROBOT TO PUNCH THE MONSTER IN THE FACE!
THE PROPORTIONS ARE ALL RIGHT, BUT I NEED A LOAD-BEARING POLYMER WITH ENOUGH TENSILE STRENGTH...
MODEL 757
WOW, THAT'S AMAZING. WAIT...YOU DID THIS IN *ENGLISH CLASS?*
WELL, THE REST OF THE CLASS WAS DOING ENGLISH...
IF YOU FLUNK OUT OF ANOTHER SCHOOL, MOM AND DAD ARE GONNA FREAK!
PLUS, A GIANT ROBOT'S NOT EVEN *PRACTICAL.* JUST USE A HIGH-POTENCY SLEEPING GAS.
BUT...IT PUNCHES IT IN THE FACE!

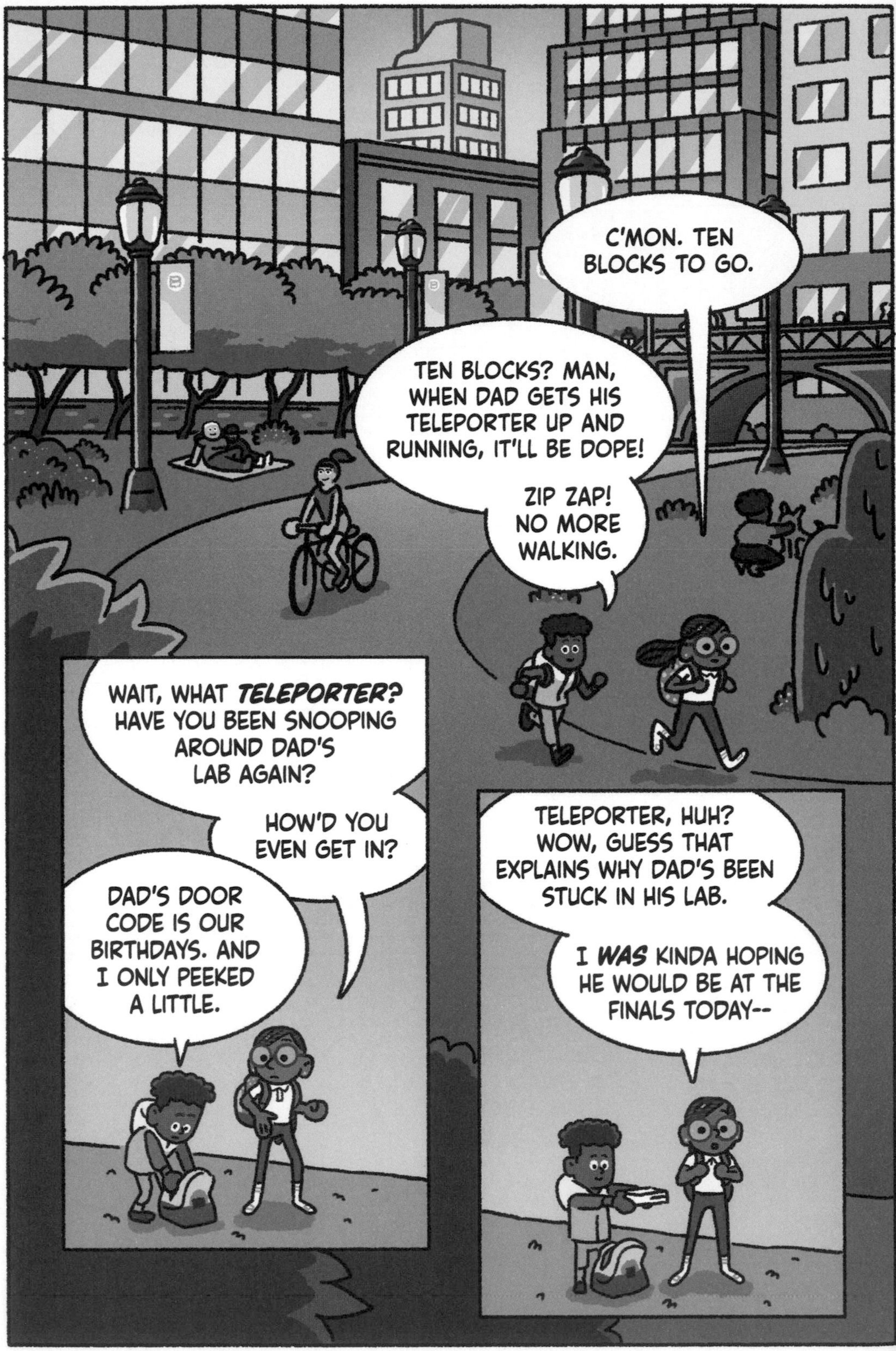
C'MON. TEN BLOCKS TO GO.
TEN BLOCKS? MAN, WHEN DAD GETS HIS TELEPORTER UP AND RUNNING, IT'LL BE DOPE!
ZIP ZAP! NO MORE WALKING.
WAIT, WHAT *TELEPORTER?* HAVE YOU BEEN SNOOPING AROUND DAD'S LAB AGAIN?
HOW'D YOU EVEN GET IN?
DAD'S DOOR CODE IS OUR BIRTHDAYS. AND I ONLY PEEKED A LITTLE.
TELEPORTER, HUH? WOW, GUESS THAT EXPLAINS WHY DAD'S BEEN STUCK IN HIS LAB.
I *WAS* KINDA HOPING HE WOULD BE AT THE FINALS TODAY--

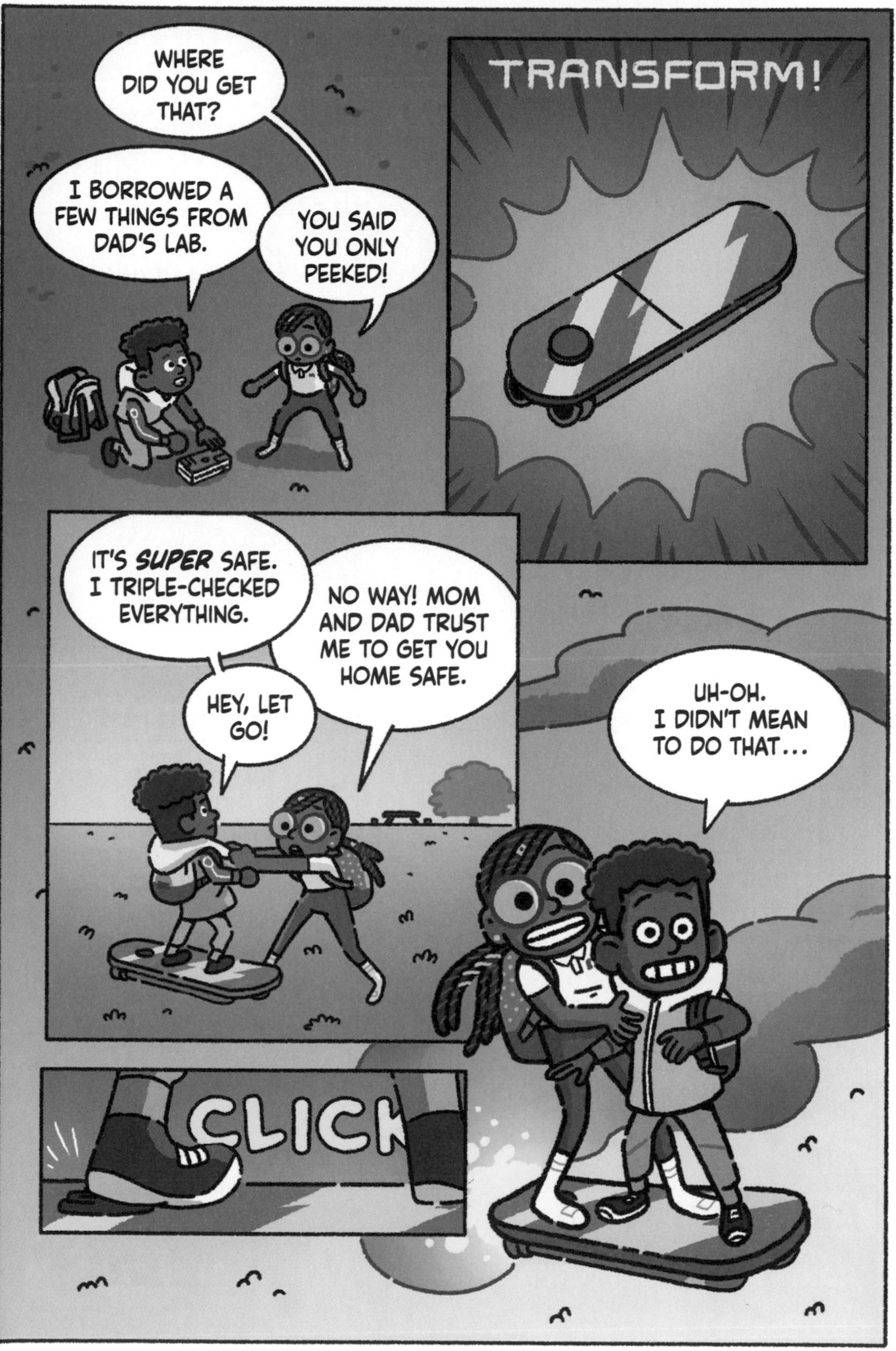
WHERE DID YOU GET THAT?
I BORROWED A FEW THINGS FROM DAD'S LAB.
YOU SAID YOU ONLY PEEKED!
TRANSFORM!
IT'S SUPER SAFE. I TRIPLE-CHECKED EVERYTHING.
NO WAY! MOM AND DAD TRUST ME TO GET YOU HOME SAFE.
HEY, LET GO!
CLICK
UH-OH. I DIDN'T MEAN TO DO THAT...

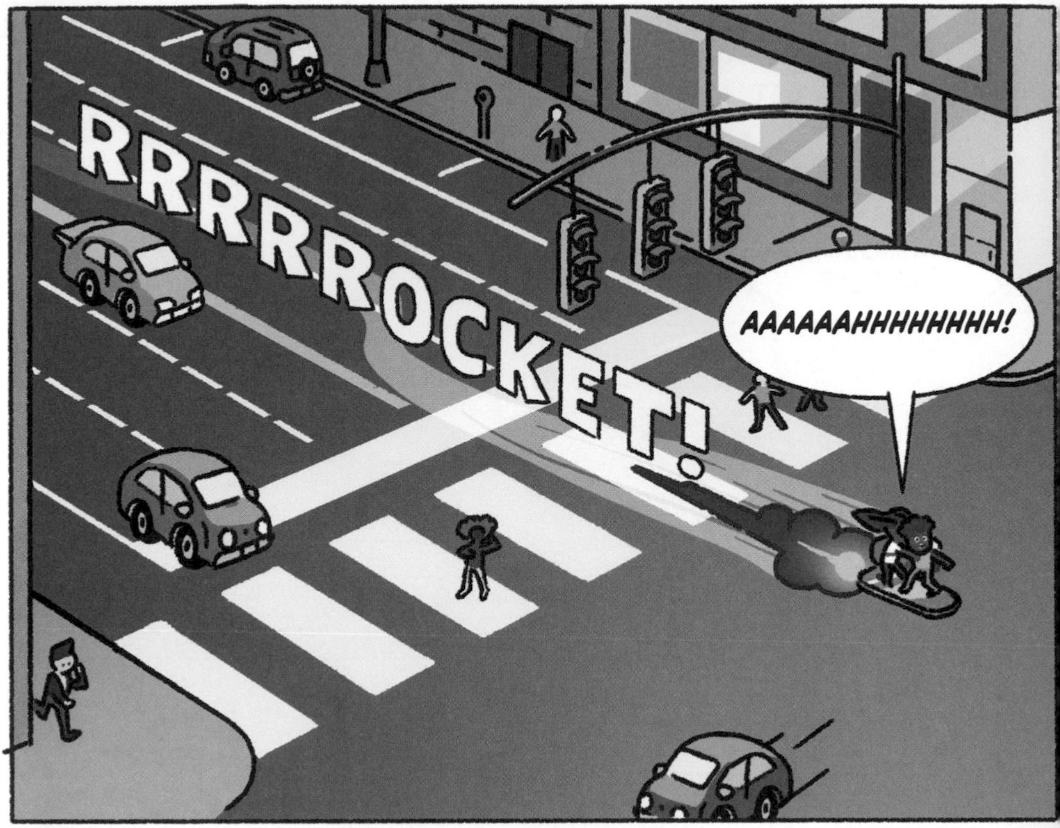
RRRRROCKET!
AAAAAAHHHHHHHH!

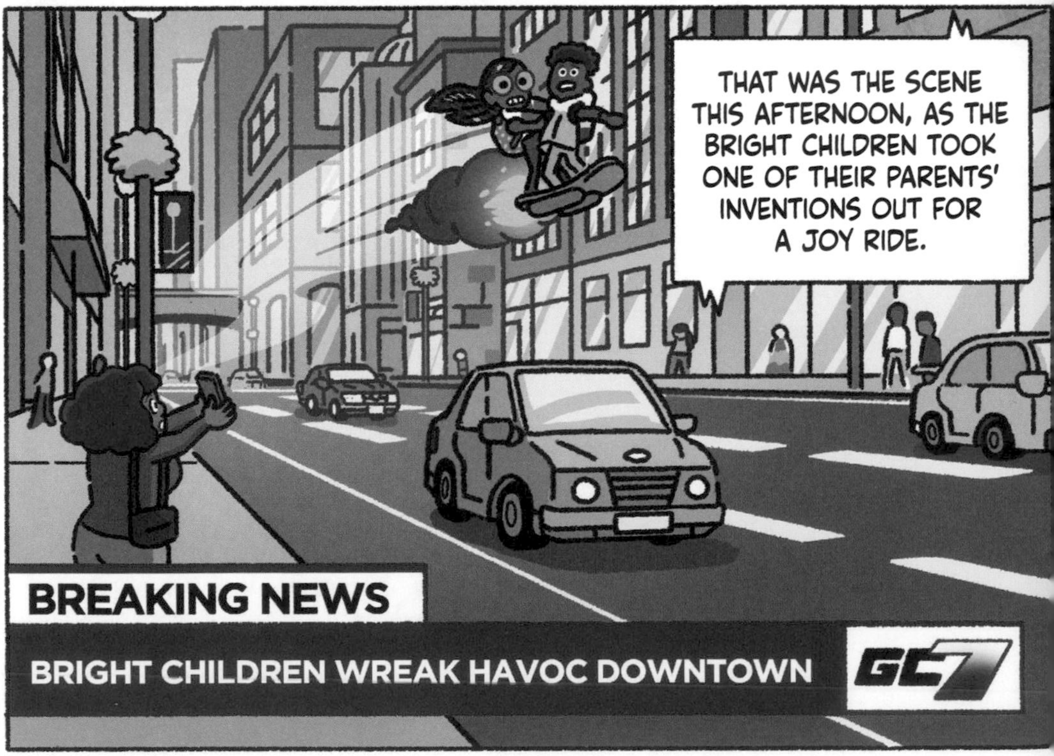
THAT WAS THE SCENE THIS AFTERNOON, AS THE BRIGHT CHILDREN TOOK ONE OF THEIR PARENTS' INVENTIONS OUT FOR A JOY RIDE.
BREAKING NEWS
BRIGHT CHILDREN WREAK HAVOC DOWNTOWN
GC7

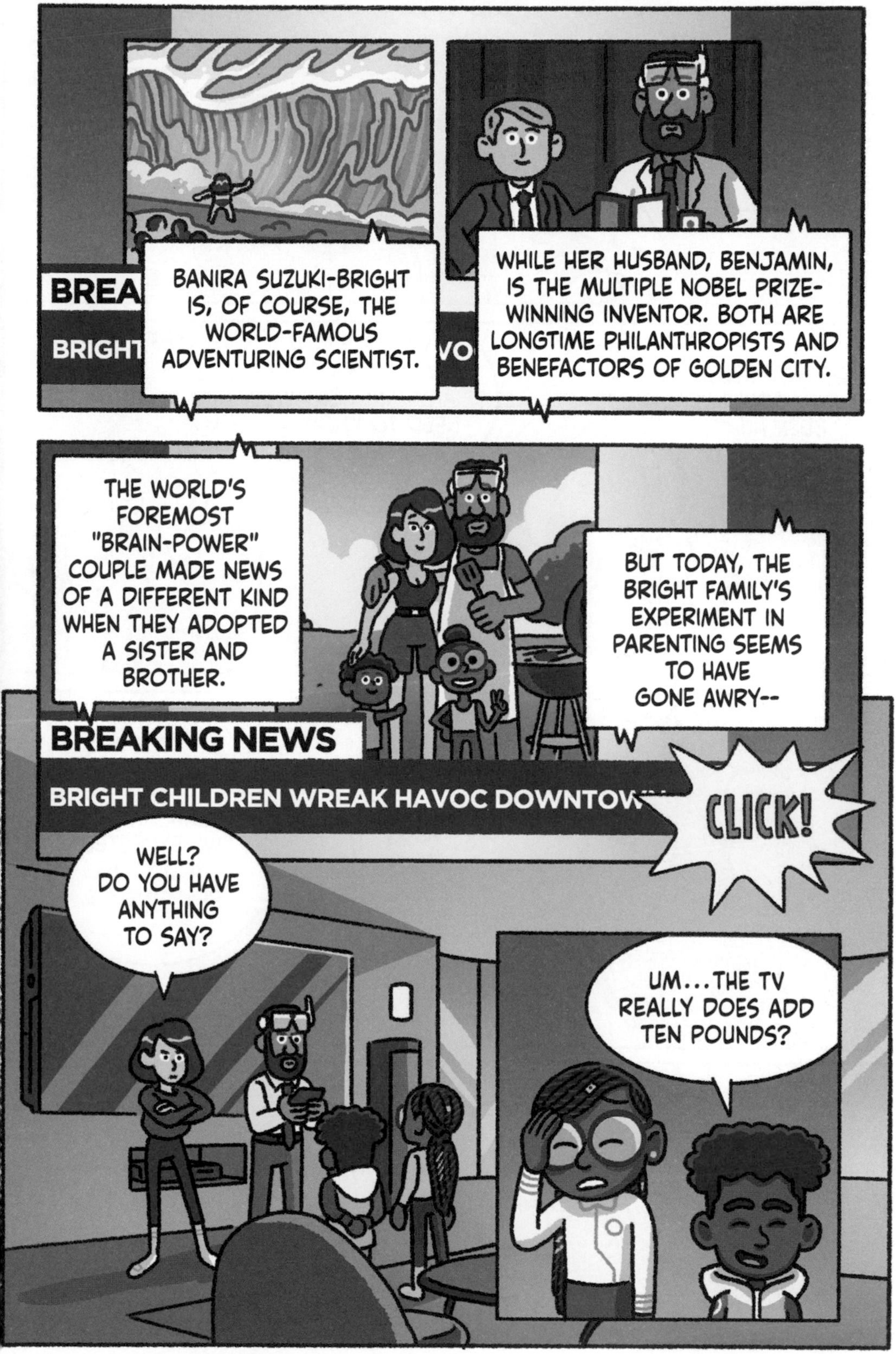
BREAKING NEWS
BRIGHT CHILDREN WREAK HAVOC DOWNTOWN
BANIRA SUZUKI-BRIGHT IS, OF COURSE, THE WORLD-FAMOUS ADVENTURING SCIENTIST.
WHILE HER HUSBAND, BENJAMIN, IS THE MULTIPLE NOBEL PRIZE-WINNING INVENTOR. BOTH ARE LONGTIME PHILANTHROPISTS AND BENEFACTORS OF GOLDEN CITY.
THE WORLD'S FOREMOST "BRAIN-POWER" COUPLE MADE NEWS OF A DIFFERENT KIND WHEN THEY ADOPTED A SISTER AND BROTHER.
BUT TODAY, THE BRIGHT FAMILY'S EXPERIMENT IN PARENTING SEEMS TO HAVE GONE AWRY--
CLICK!
WELL? DO YOU HAVE ANYTHING TO SAY?
UM...THE TV REALLY DOES ADD TEN POUNDS?

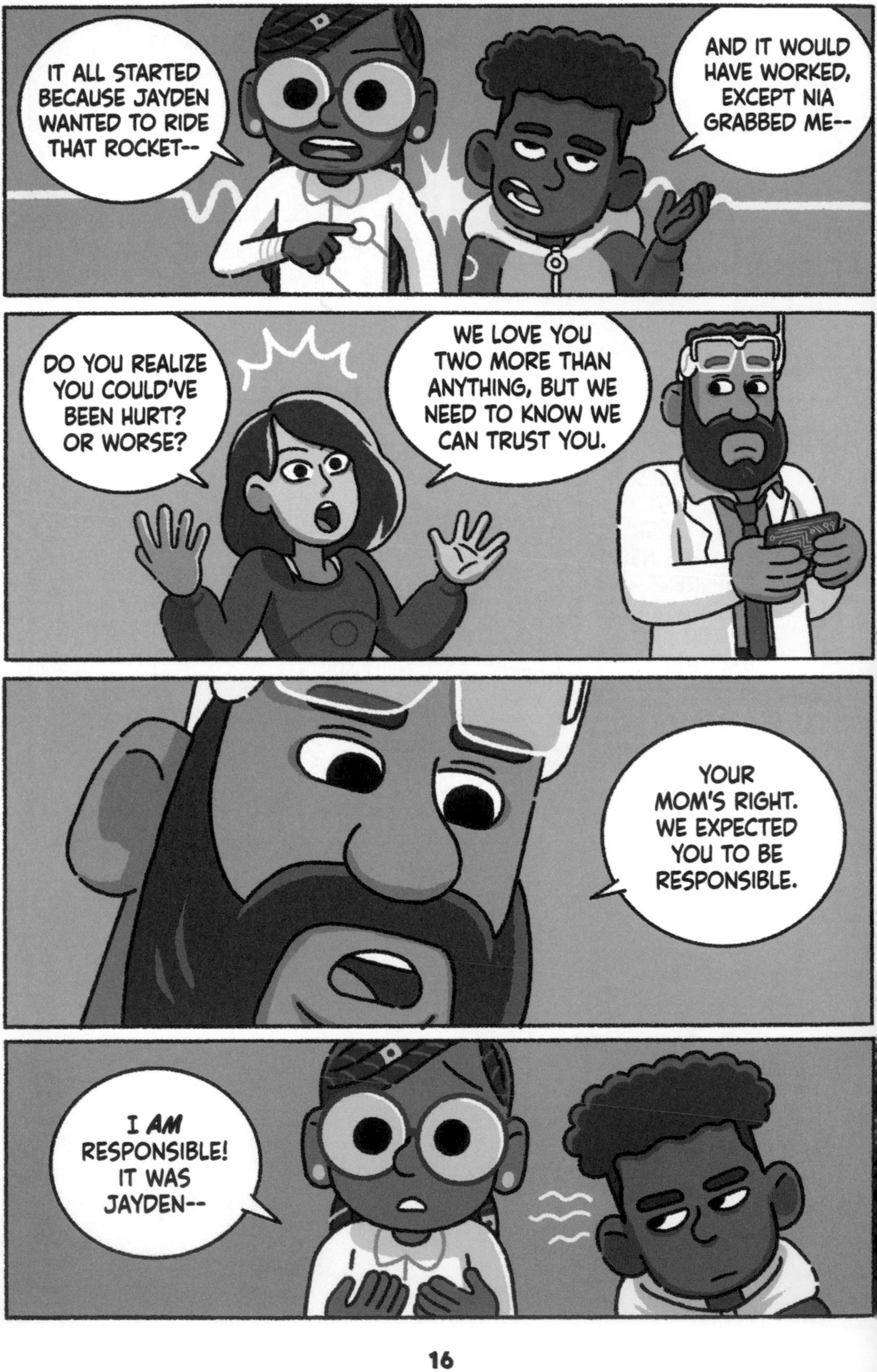
IT ALL STARTED BECAUSE JAYDEN WANTED TO RIDE THAT ROCKET--
AND IT WOULD HAVE WORKED, EXCEPT NIA GRABBED ME--
DO YOU REALIZE YOU COULD'VE BEEN HURT? OR WORSE?
WE LOVE YOU TWO MORE THAN ANYTHING, BUT WE NEED TO KNOW WE CAN TRUST YOU.
YOUR MOM'S RIGHT. WE EXPECTED YOU TO BE RESPONSIBLE.
I *AM* RESPONSIBLE! IT WAS JAYDEN--

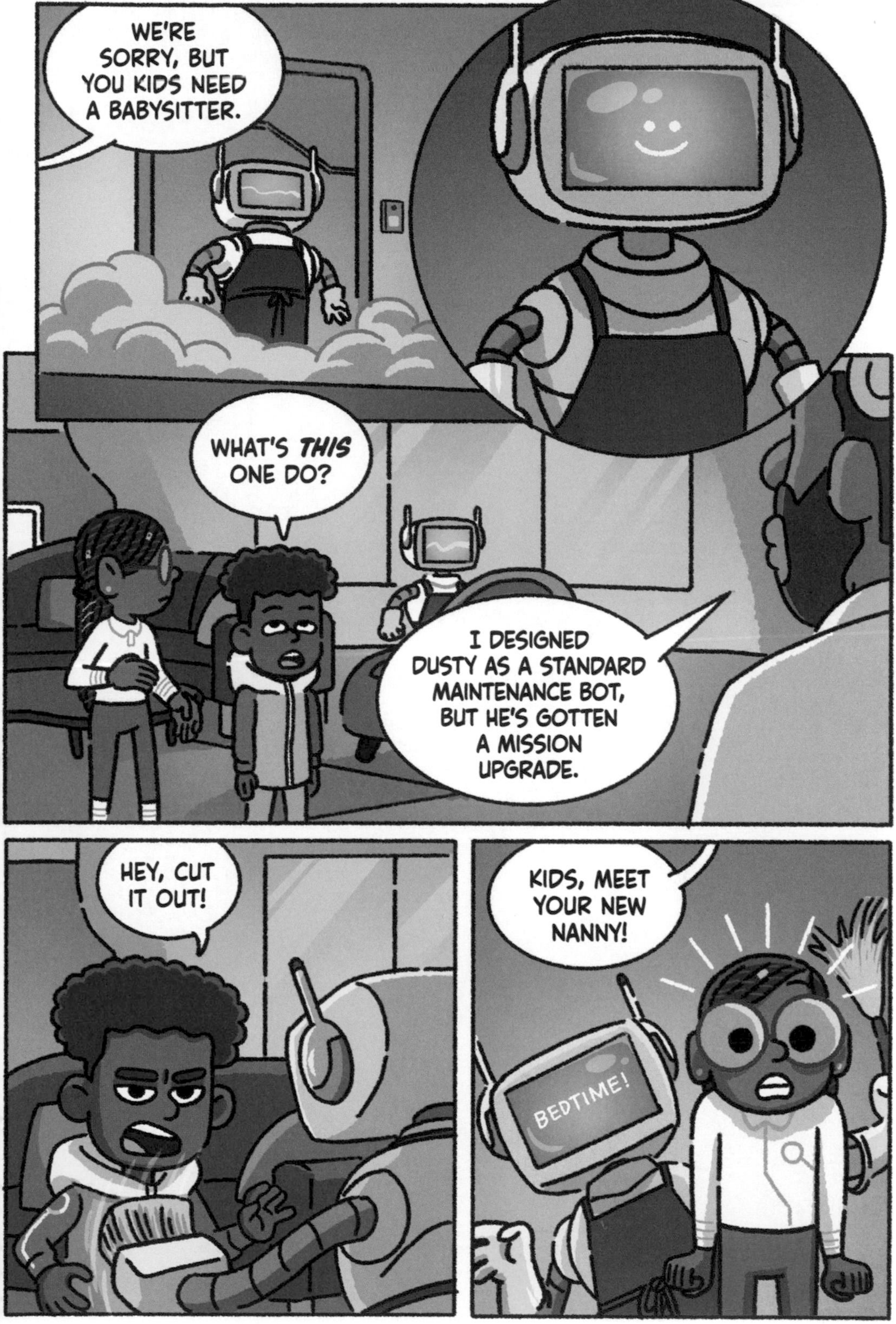
WE'RE SORRY, BUT YOU KIDS NEED A BABYSITTER.
WHAT'S *THIS* ONE DO?
I DESIGNED DUSTY AS A STANDARD MAINTENANCE BOT, BUT HE'S GOTTEN A MISSION UPGRADE.
HEY, CUT IT OUT!
KIDS, MEET YOUR NEW NANNY!
BEDTIME!

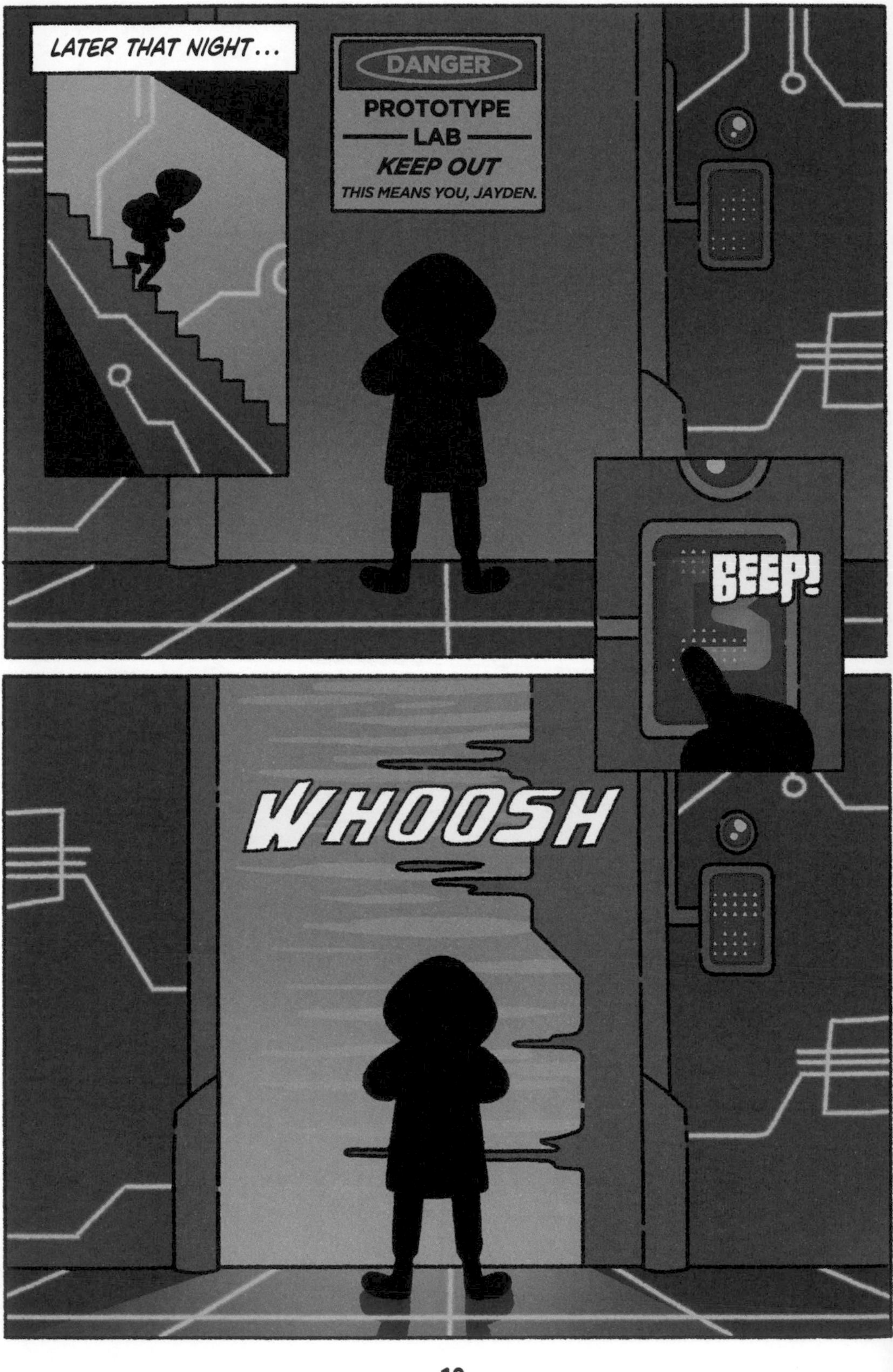
LATER THAT NIGHT...
DANGER
PROTOTYPE
LAB
KEEP OUT
THIS MEANS YOU, JAYDEN.
BEEP!
WHOOSH

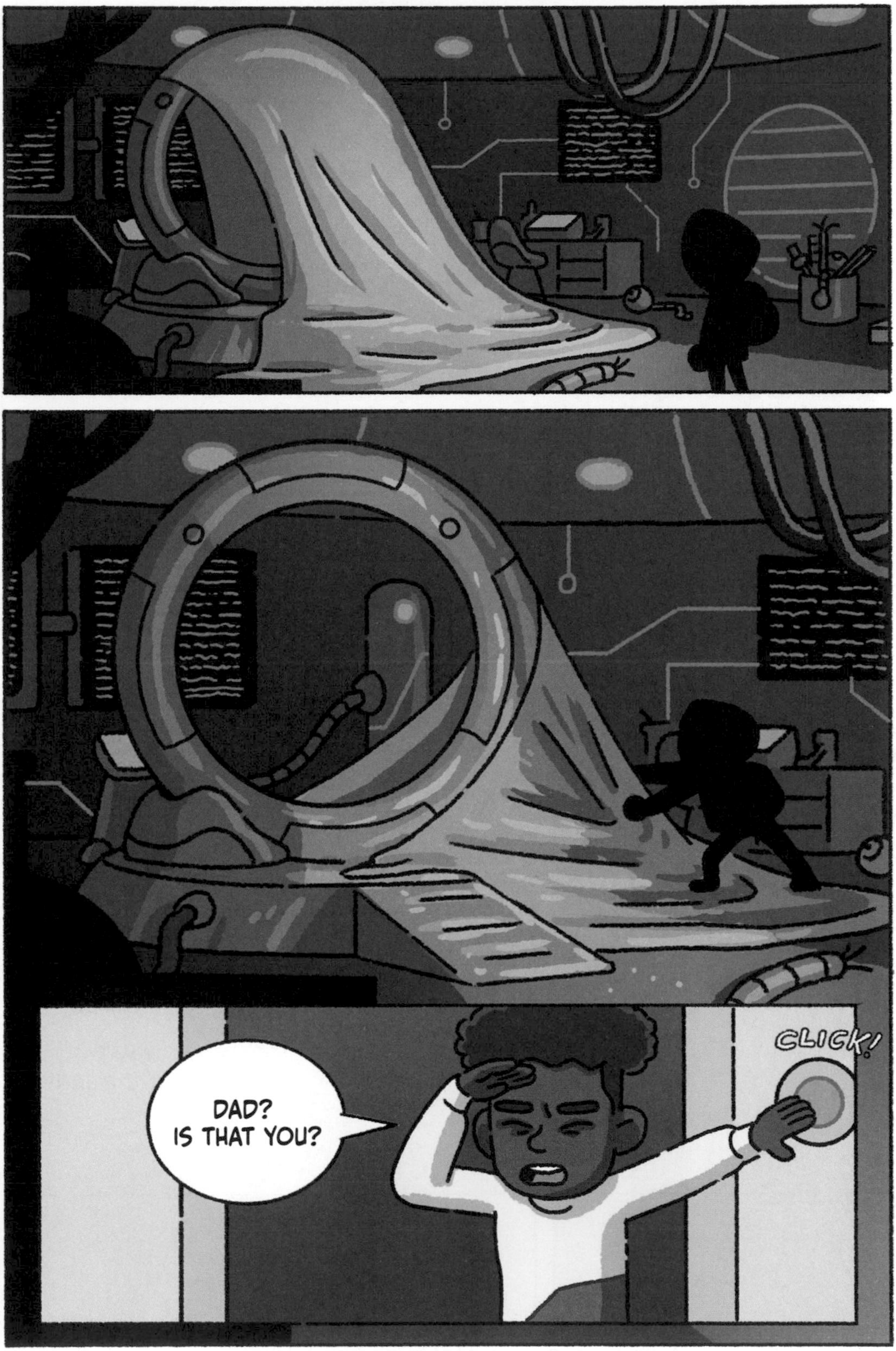
DAD?
IS THAT YOU?
CLICK!

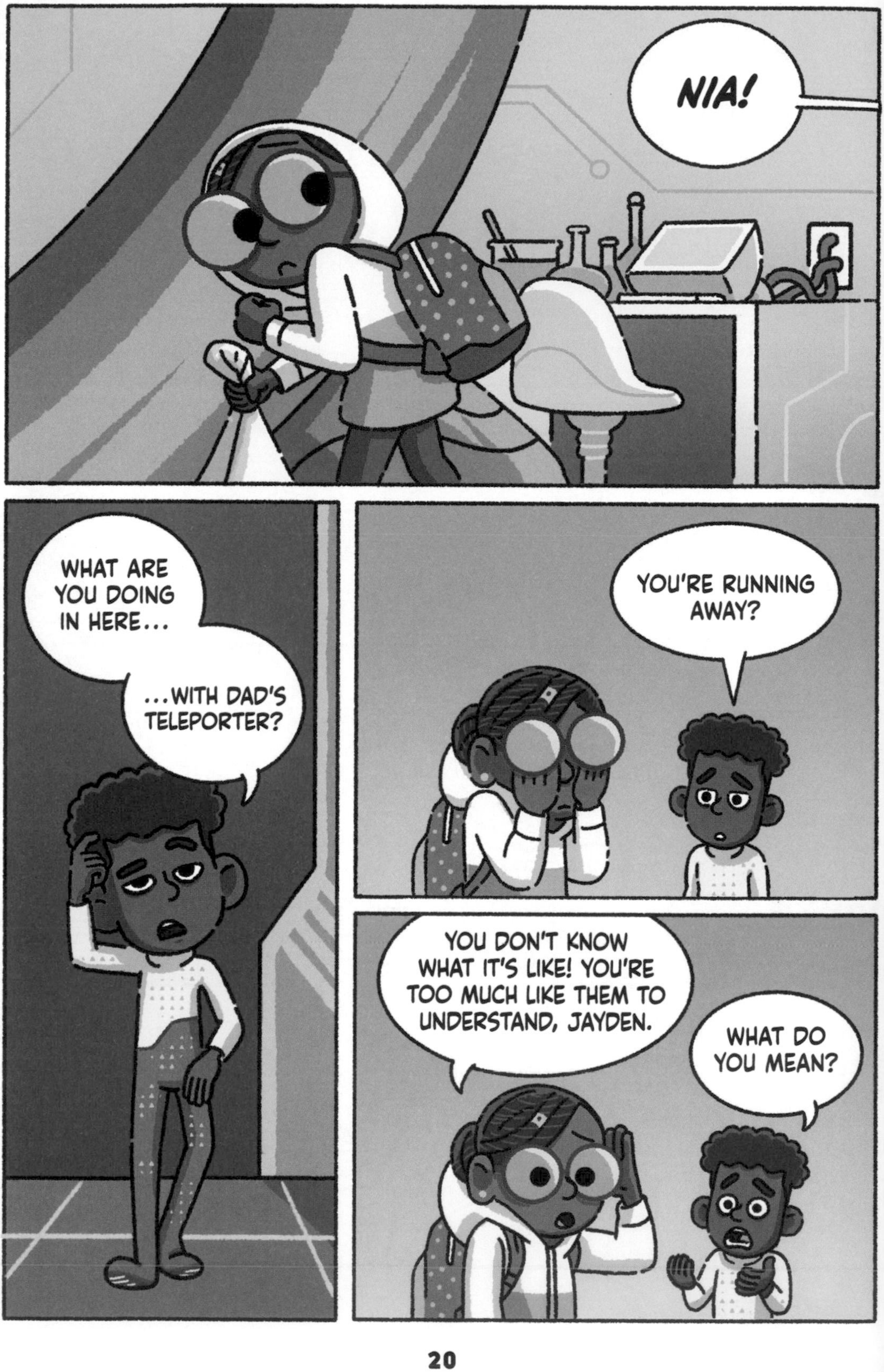
NIA!
WHAT ARE YOU DOING IN HERE...
...WITH DAD'S TELEPORTER?
YOU'RE RUNNING AWAY?
YOU DON'T KNOW WHAT IT'S LIKE! YOU'RE TOO MUCH LIKE THEM TO UNDERSTAND, JAYDEN.
WHAT DO YOU MEAN?

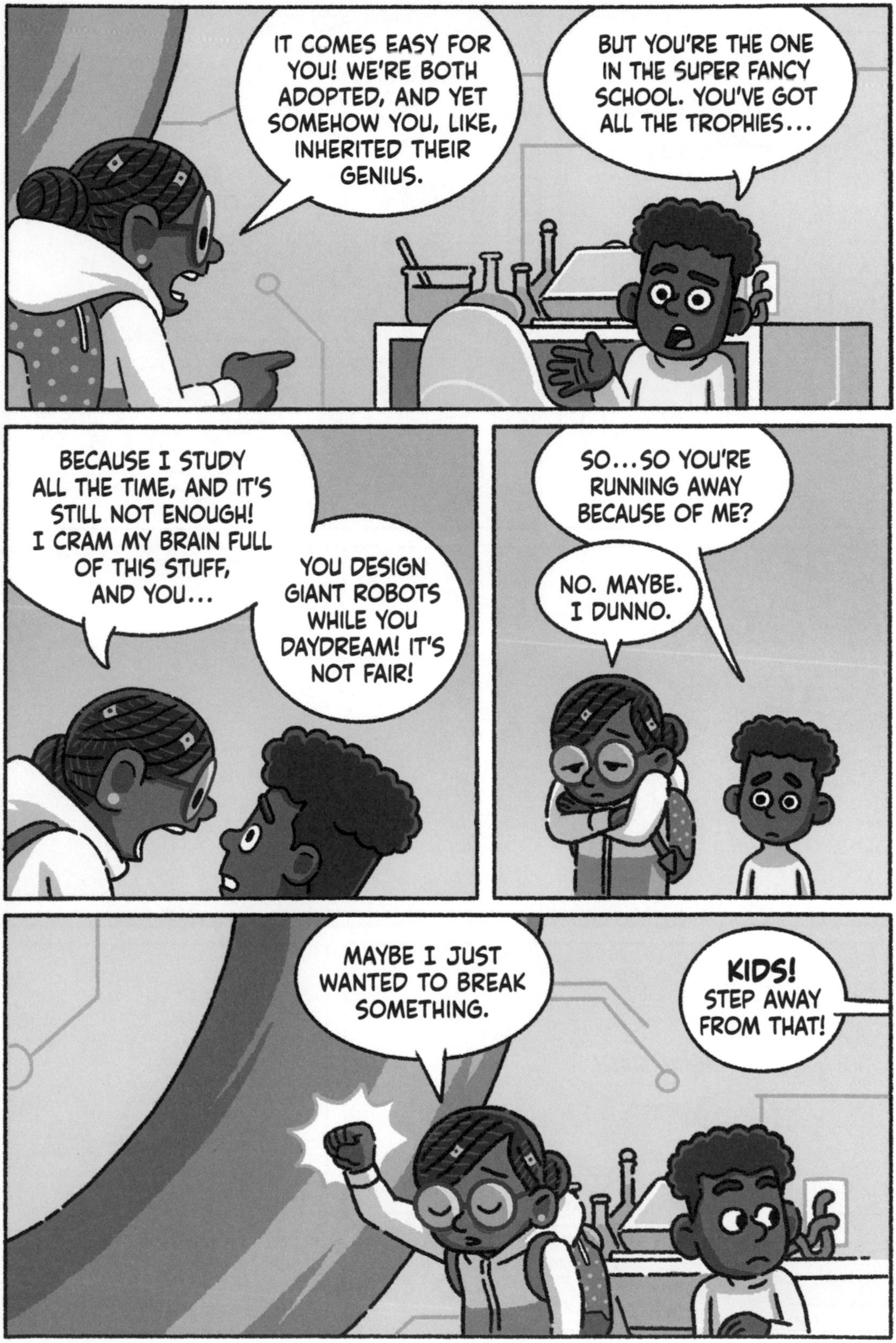
IT COMES EASY FOR YOU! WE'RE BOTH ADOPTED, AND YET SOMEHOW YOU, LIKE, INHERITED THEIR GENIUS.
BUT YOU'RE THE ONE IN THE SUPER FANCY SCHOOL. YOU'VE GOT ALL THE TROPHIES...
BECAUSE I STUDY ALL THE TIME, AND IT'S STILL NOT ENOUGH! I CRAM MY BRAIN FULL OF THIS STUFF, AND YOU...
YOU DESIGN GIANT ROBOTS WHILE YOU DAYDREAM! IT'S NOT FAIR!
SO...SO YOU'RE RUNNING AWAY BECAUSE OF ME?
NO. MAYBE. I DUNNO.
MAYBE I JUST WANTED TO BREAK SOMETHING.
KIDS! STEP AWAY FROM THAT!

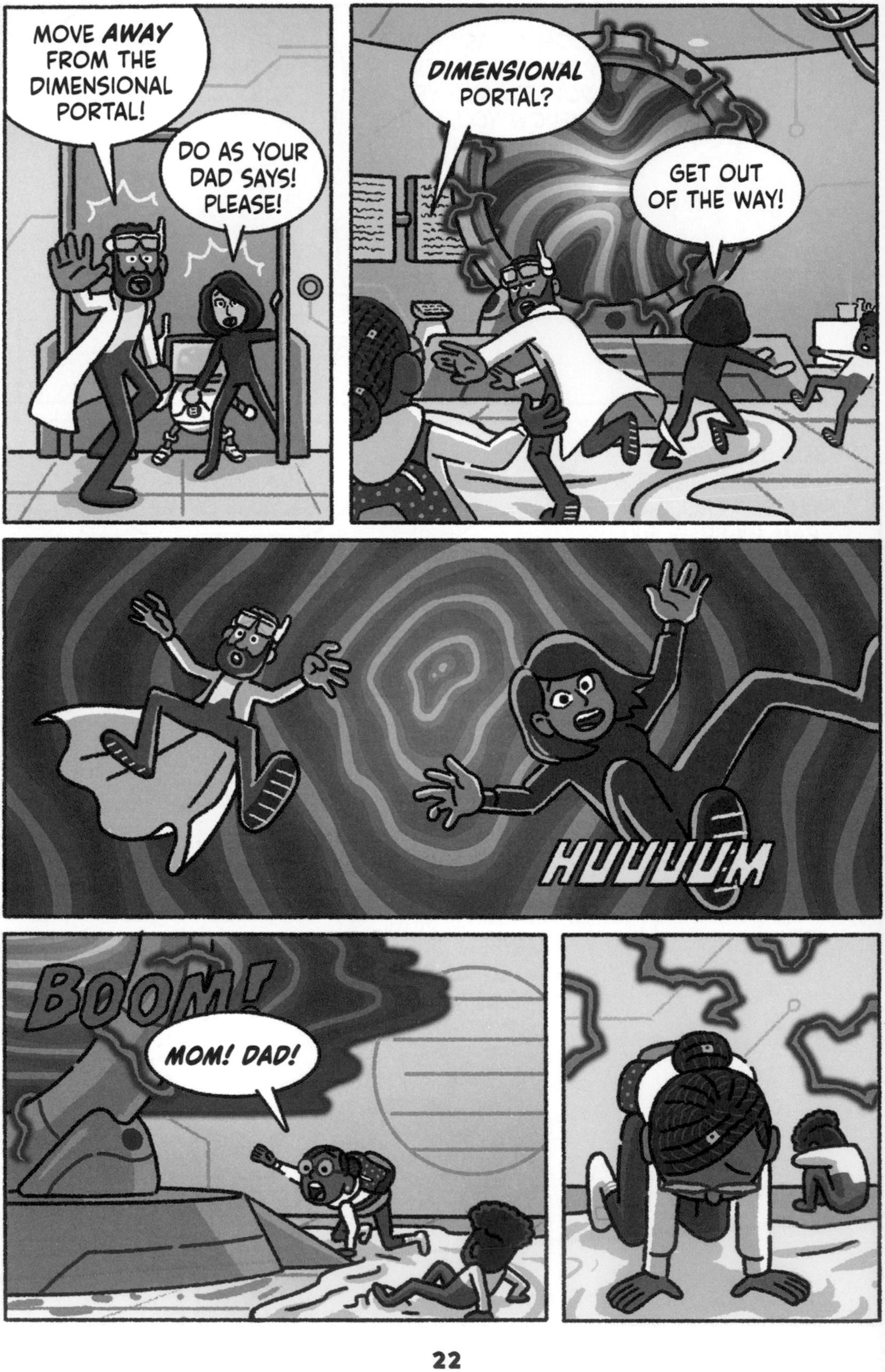
MOVE AWAY FROM THE DIMENSIONAL PORTAL!
DO AS YOUR DAD SAYS! PLEASE!
DIMENSIONAL PORTAL?
GET OUT OF THE WAY!
HUUUUM
BOOM!
MOM! DAD!

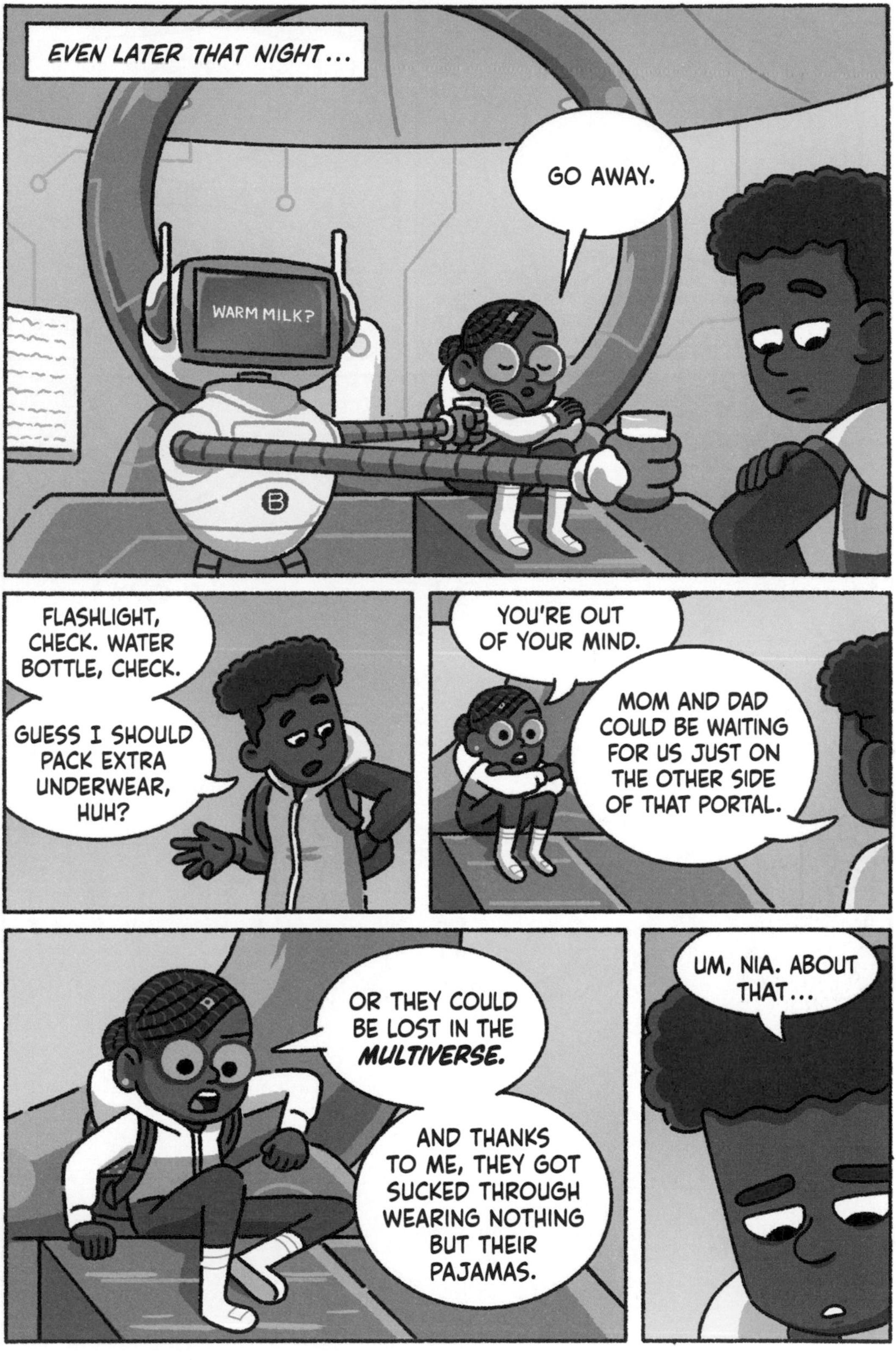
EVEN LATER THAT NIGHT...
WARM MILK?
GO AWAY.
FLASHLIGHT, CHECK. WATER BOTTLE, CHECK.
GUESS I SHOULD PACK EXTRA UNDERWEAR, HUH?
YOU'RE OUT OF YOUR MIND.
MOM AND DAD COULD BE WAITING FOR US JUST ON THE OTHER SIDE OF THAT PORTAL.
OR THEY COULD BE LOST IN THE *MULTIVERSE.*
AND THANKS TO ME, THEY GOT SUCKED THROUGH WEARING NOTHING BUT THEIR PAJAMAS.
UM, NIA. ABOUT THAT...

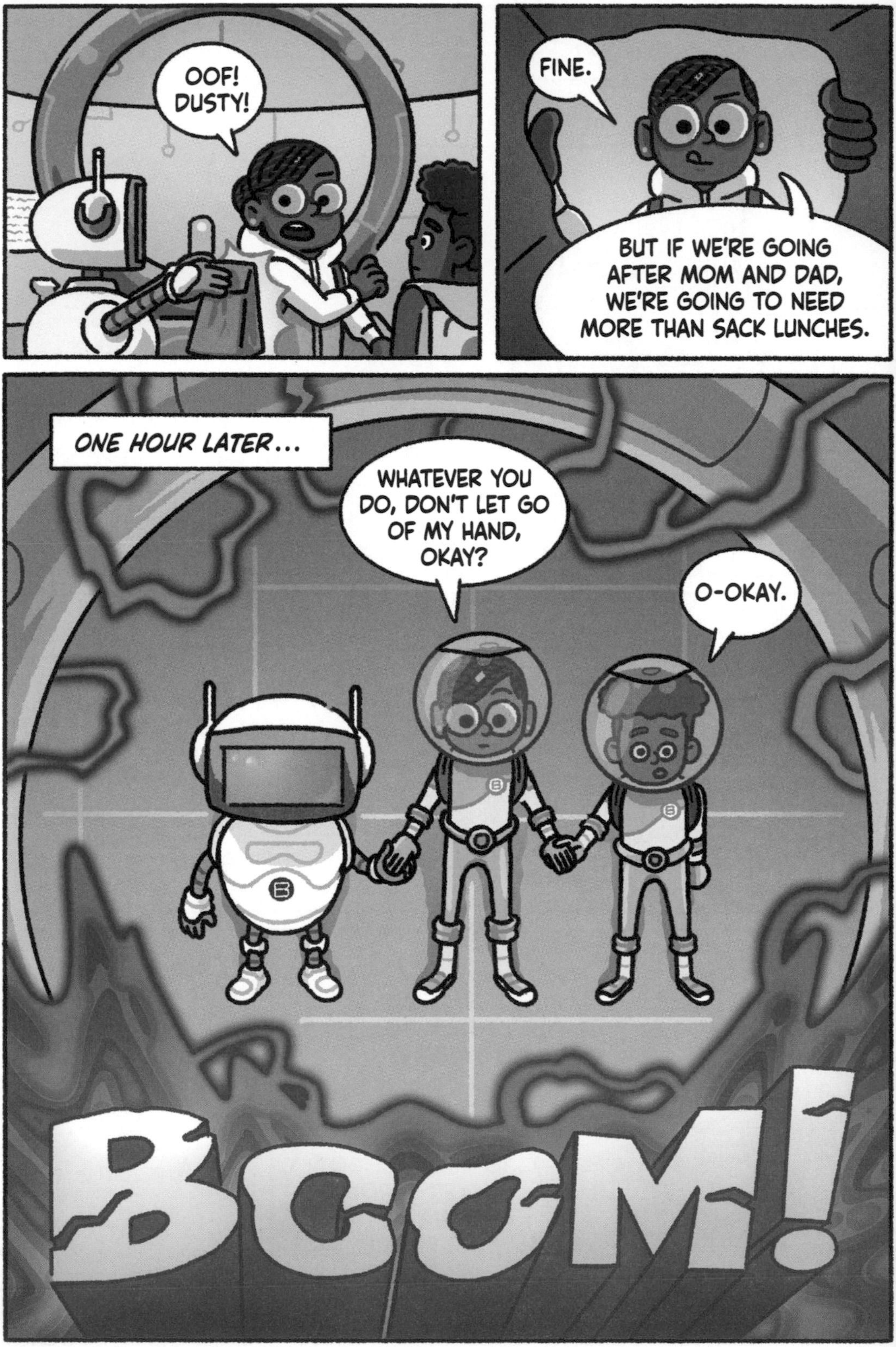
OOF! DUSTY!
FINE.
BUT IF WE'RE GOING AFTER MOM AND DAD, WE'RE GOING TO NEED MORE THAN SACK LUNCHES.
ONE HOUR LATER...
WHATEVER YOU DO, DON'T LET GO OF MY HAND, OKAY?
O-OKAY.
BOOM!

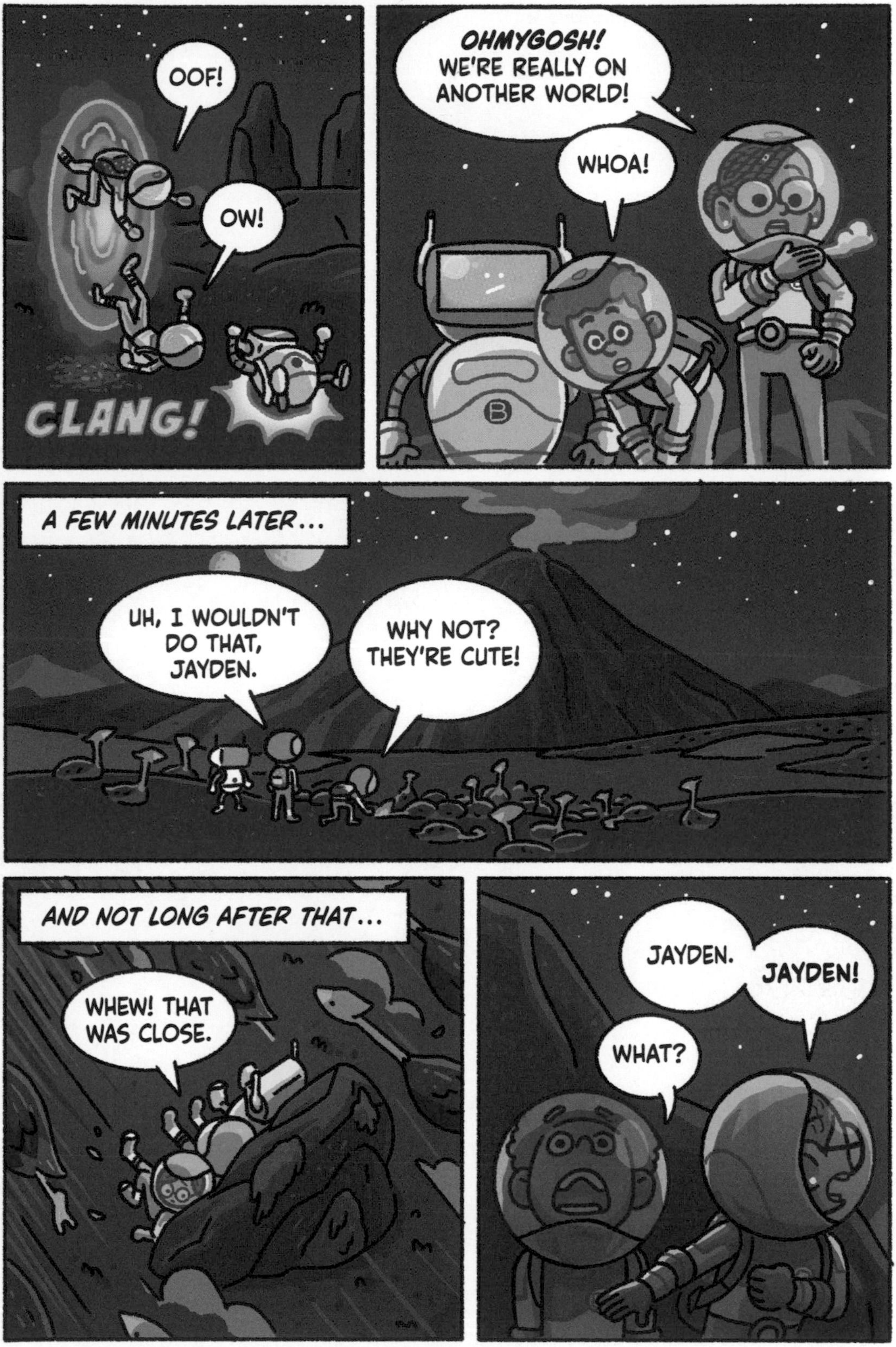
OOF!
OW!
CLANG!
OHMYGOSH! WE'RE REALLY ON ANOTHER WORLD!
WHOA!
A FEW MINUTES LATER...
UH, I WOULDN'T DO THAT, JAYDEN.
WHY NOT? THEY'RE CUTE!
AND NOT LONG AFTER THAT...
WHEW! THAT WAS CLOSE.
JAYDEN.
JAYDEN!
WHAT?

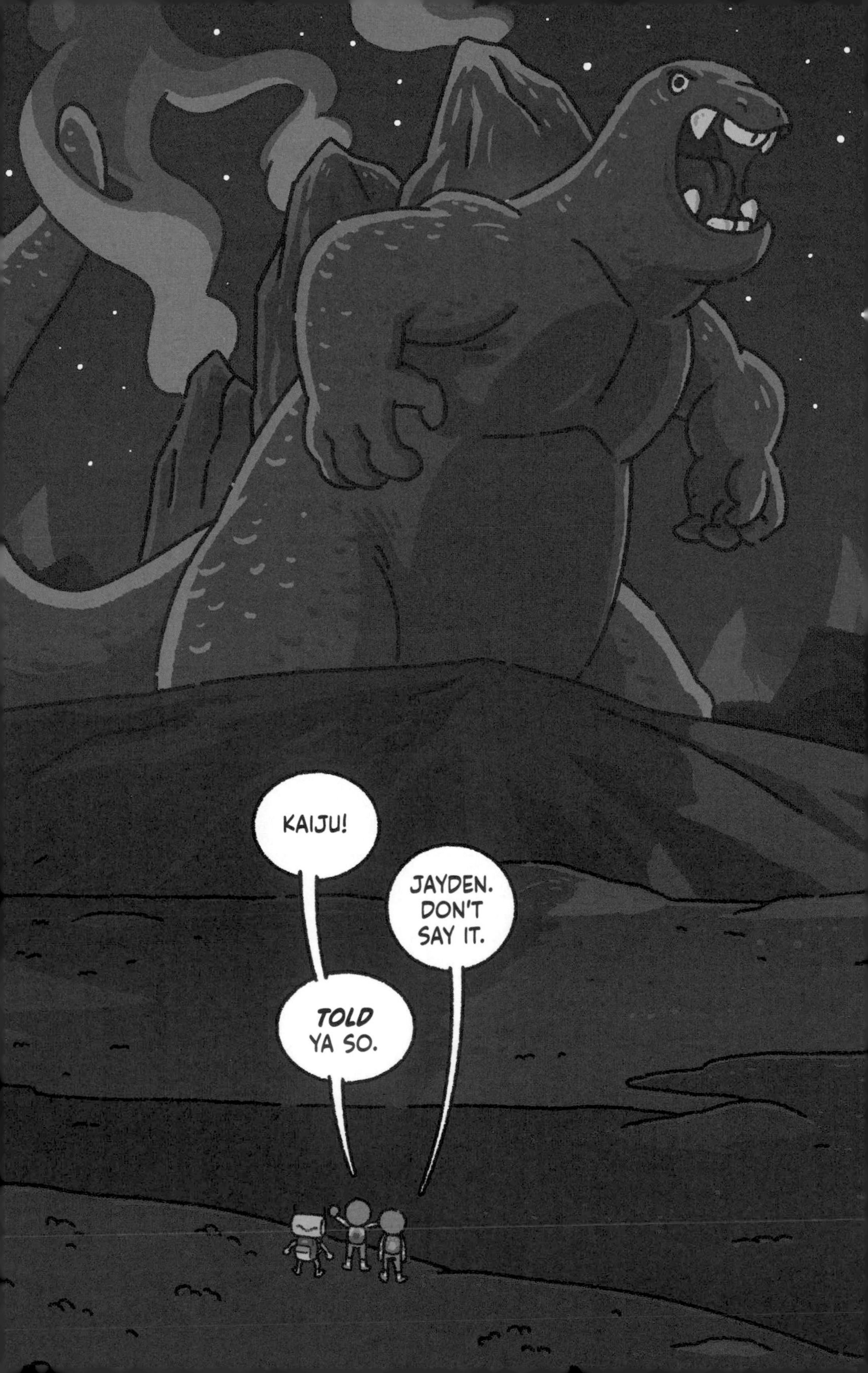
KAIJU!
JAYDEN. DON'T SAY IT.
TOLD YA SO.

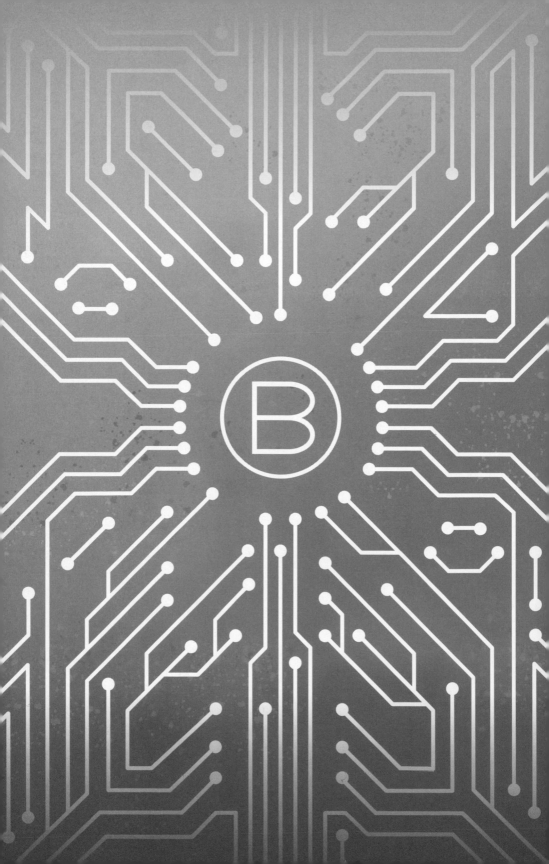

## CHAPTER 2
# PLANET OF THE KAIJU

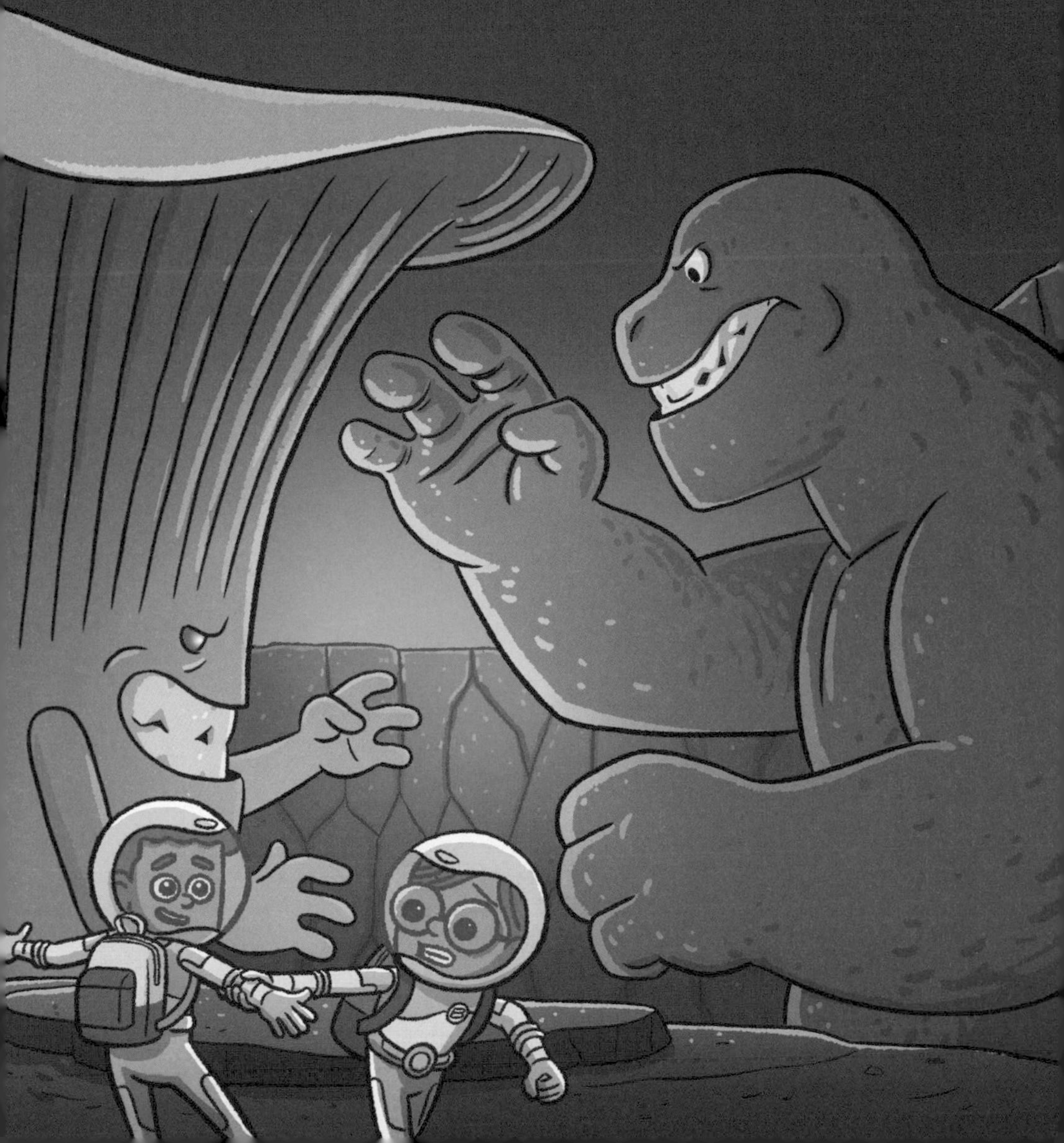

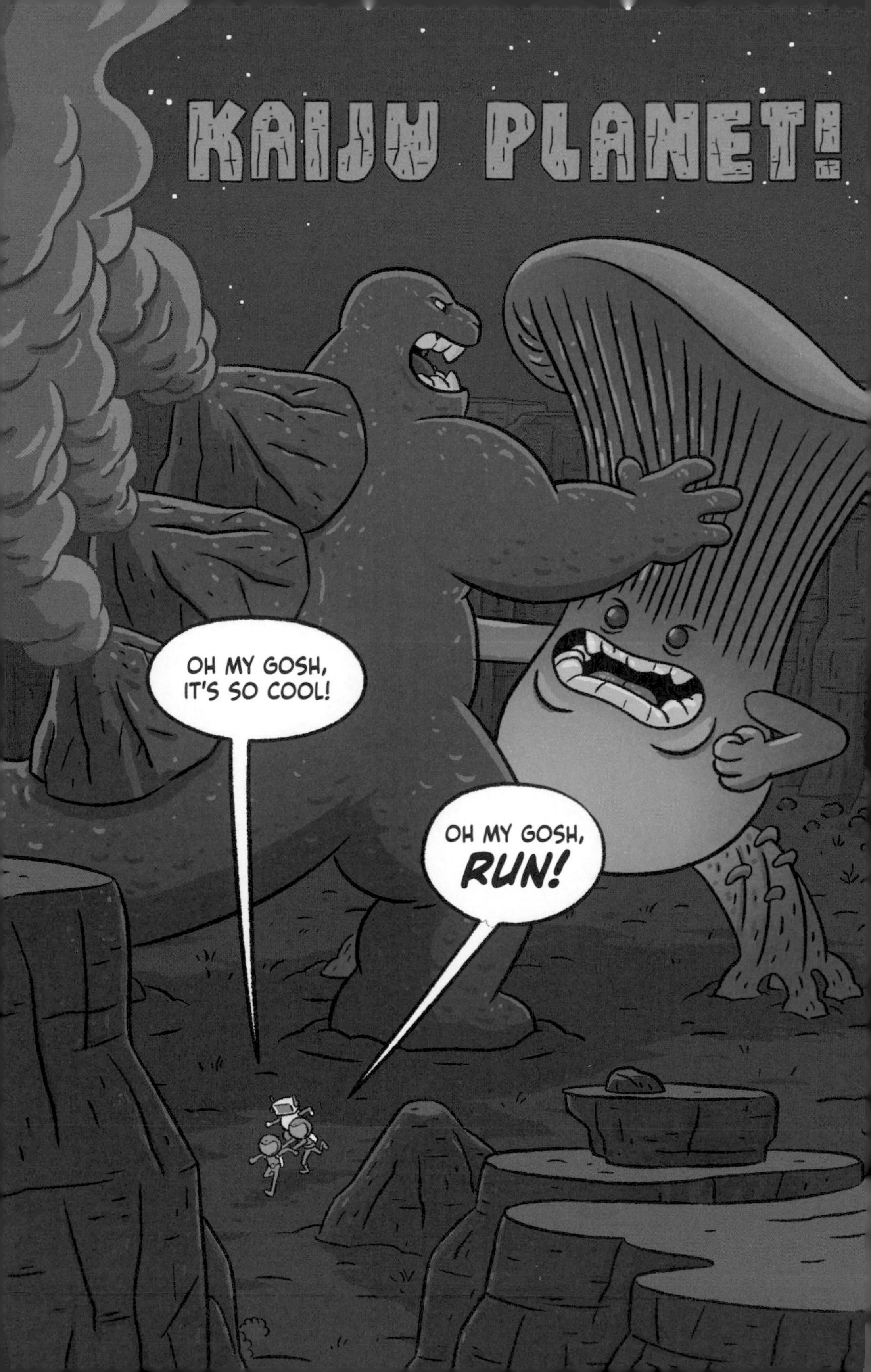
KAIJU PLANET!
OH MY GOSH, IT'S SO COOL!
OH MY GOSH, RUN!

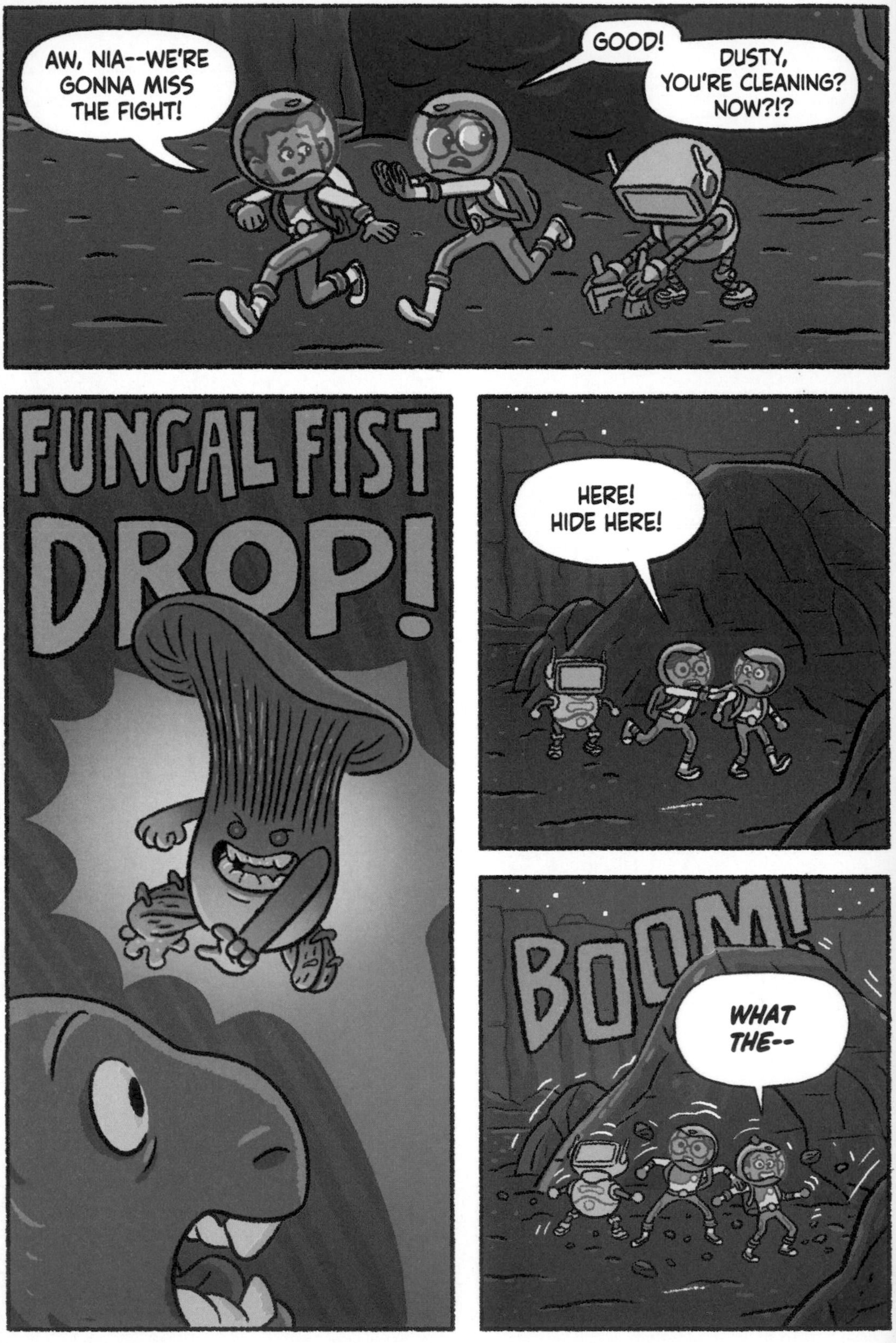
AW, NIA--WE'RE GONNA MISS THE FIGHT!
GOOD!
DUSTY, YOU'RE CLEANING? NOW?!?
FUNGAL FIST DROP!
HERE! HIDE HERE!
BOOM!
WHAT THE--

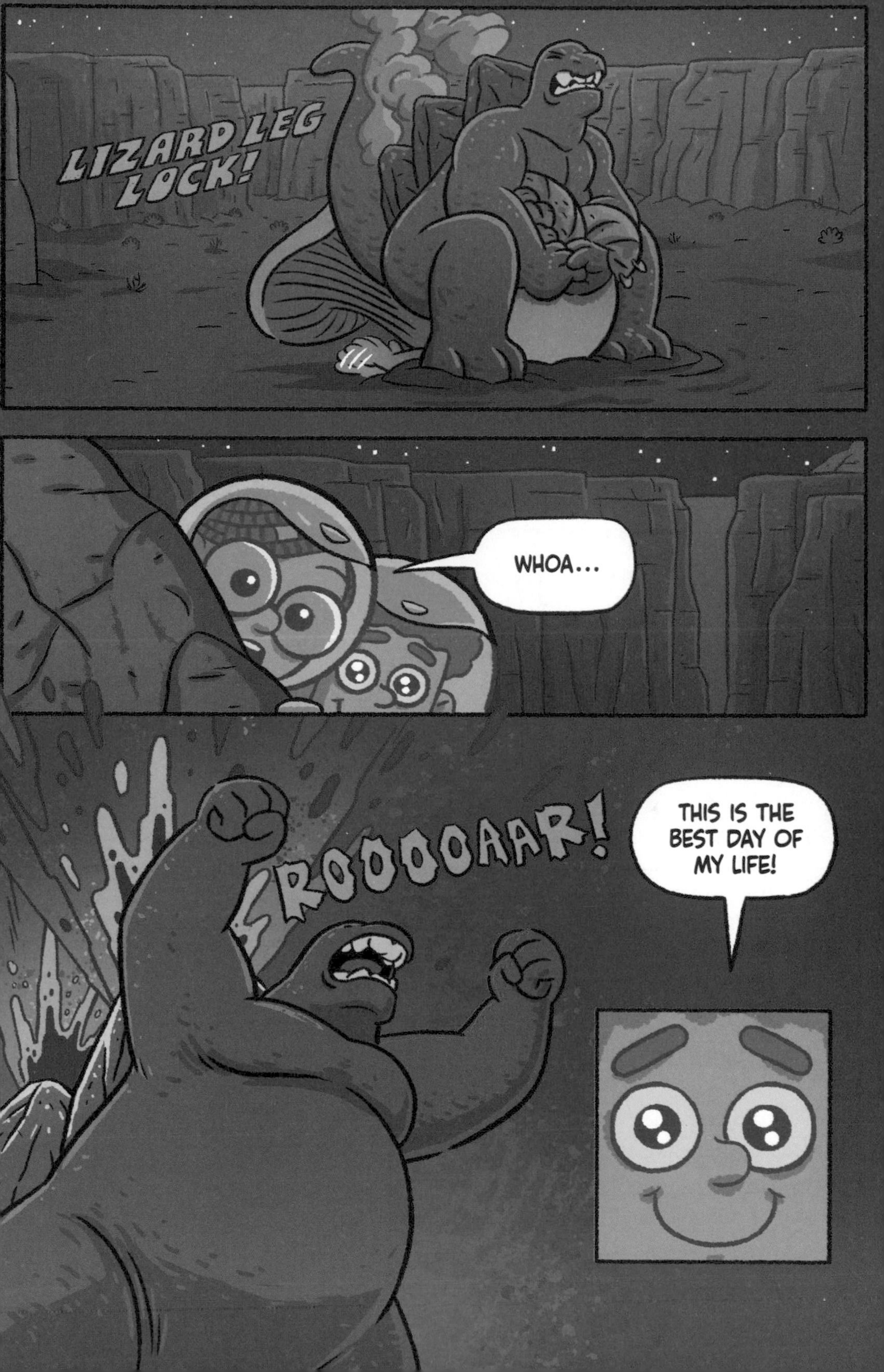
LIZARD LEG LOCK!
WHOA...
ROOOOAAR!
THIS IS THE BEST DAY OF MY LIFE!

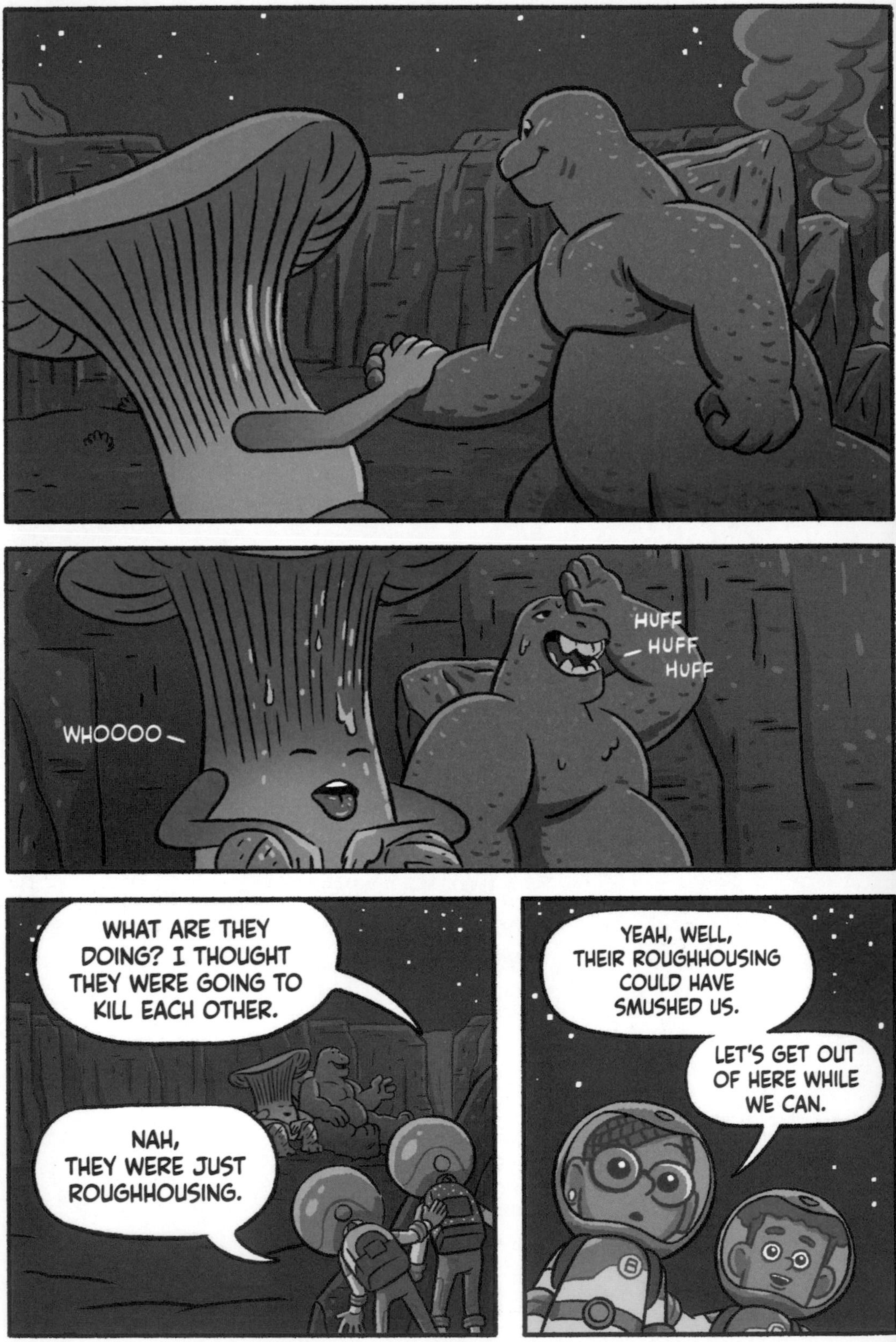
HUFF
HUFF
HUFF
WHOOOO
WHAT ARE THEY DOING? I THOUGHT THEY WERE GOING TO KILL EACH OTHER.
NAH, THEY WERE JUST ROUGHHOUSING.
YEAH, WELL, THEIR ROUGHHOUSING COULD HAVE SMUSHED US.
LET'S GET OUT OF HERE WHILE WE CAN.

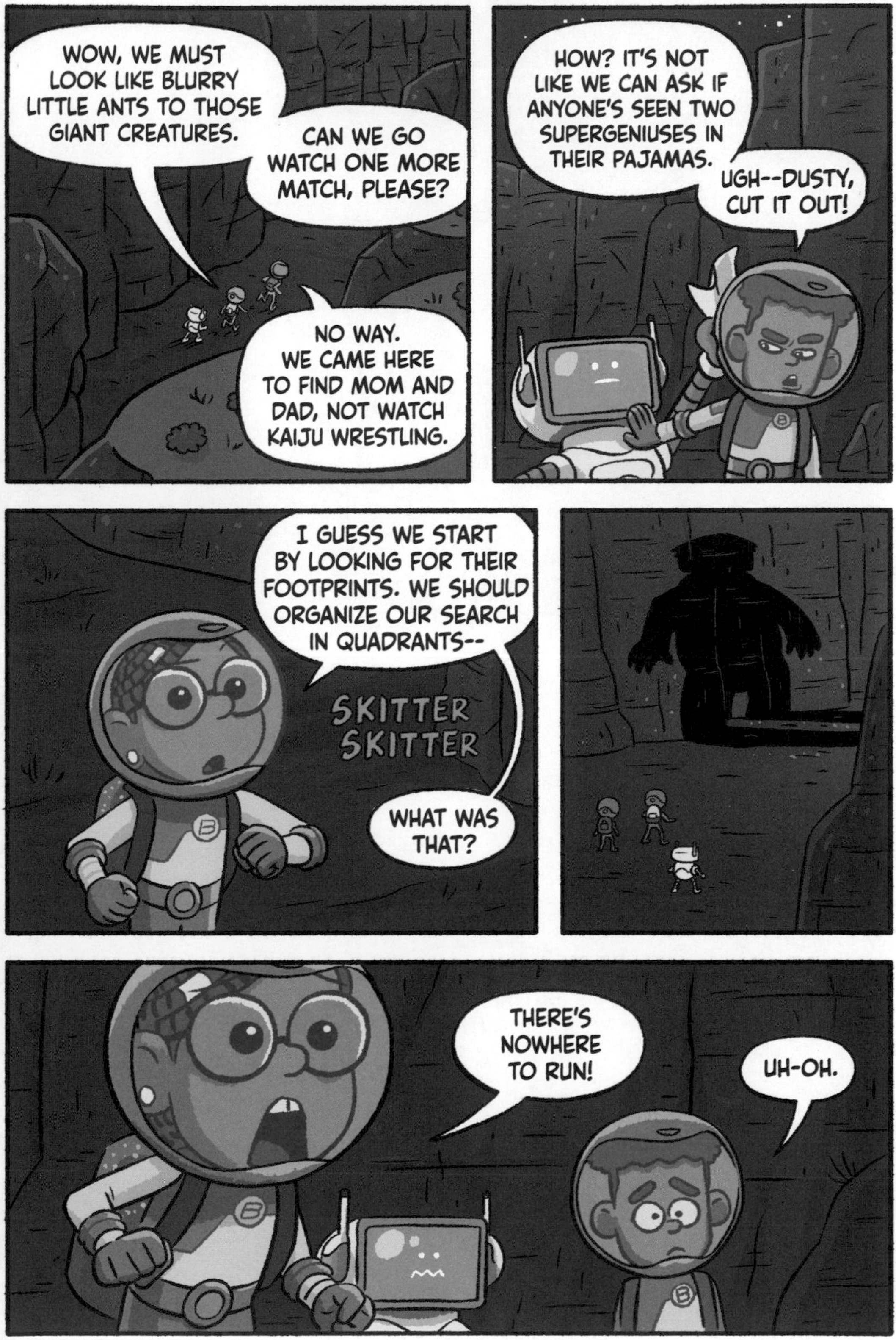
WOW, WE MUST LOOK LIKE BLURRY LITTLE ANTS TO THOSE GIANT CREATURES.
CAN WE GO WATCH ONE MORE MATCH, PLEASE?
NO WAY. WE CAME HERE TO FIND MOM AND DAD, NOT WATCH KAIJU WRESTLING.
HOW? IT'S NOT LIKE WE CAN ASK IF ANYONE'S SEEN TWO SUPERGENIUSES IN THEIR PAJAMAS.
UGH--DUSTY, CUT IT OUT!
I GUESS WE START BY LOOKING FOR THEIR FOOTPRINTS. WE SHOULD ORGANIZE OUR SEARCH IN QUADRANTS--
SKITTER SKITTER
WHAT WAS THAT?
THERE'S NOWHERE TO RUN!
UH-OH.

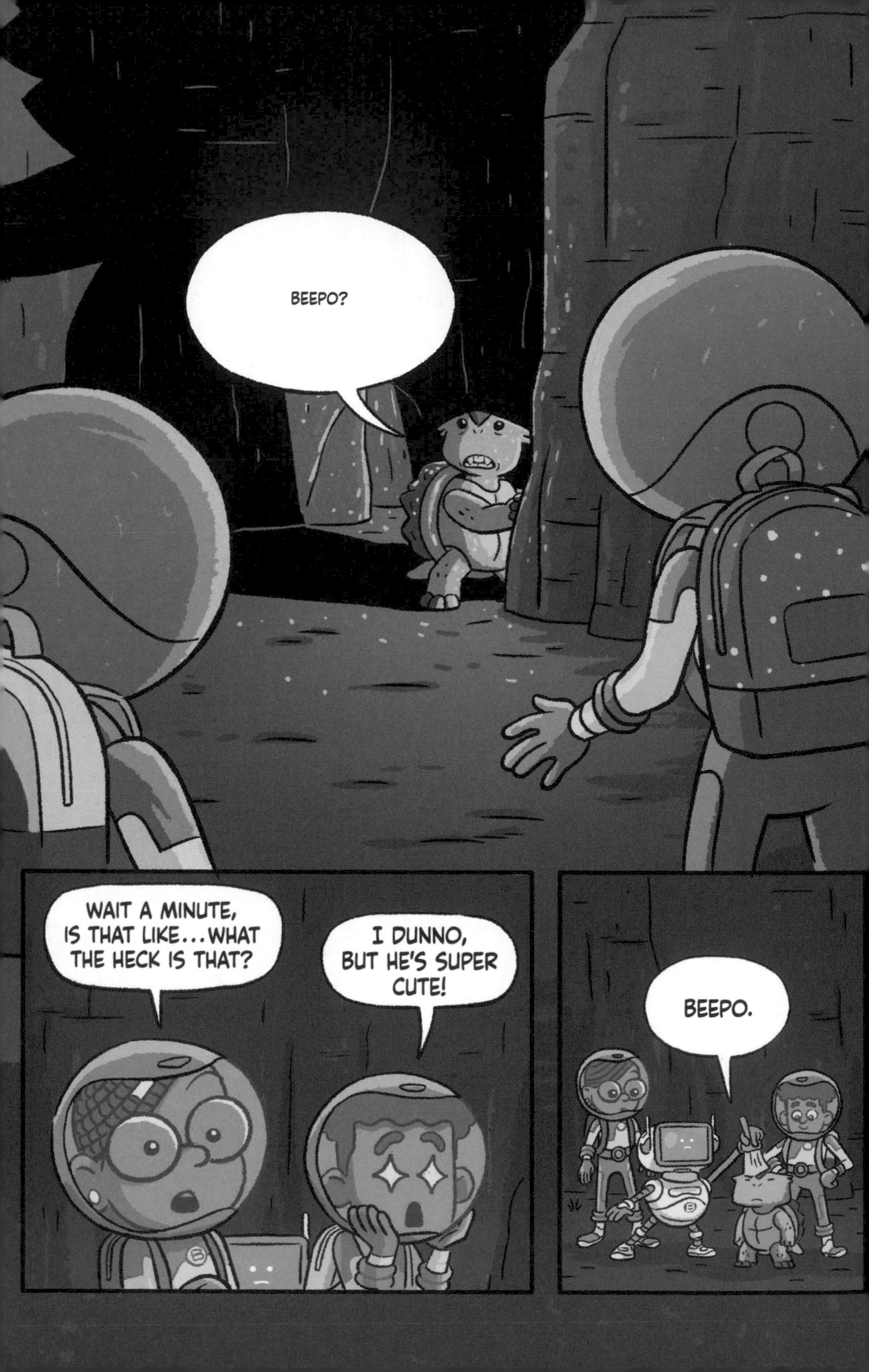
BEEPO?
WAIT A MINUTE, IS THAT LIKE...WHAT THE HECK IS THAT?
I DUNNO, BUT HE'S SUPER CUTE!
BEEPO.

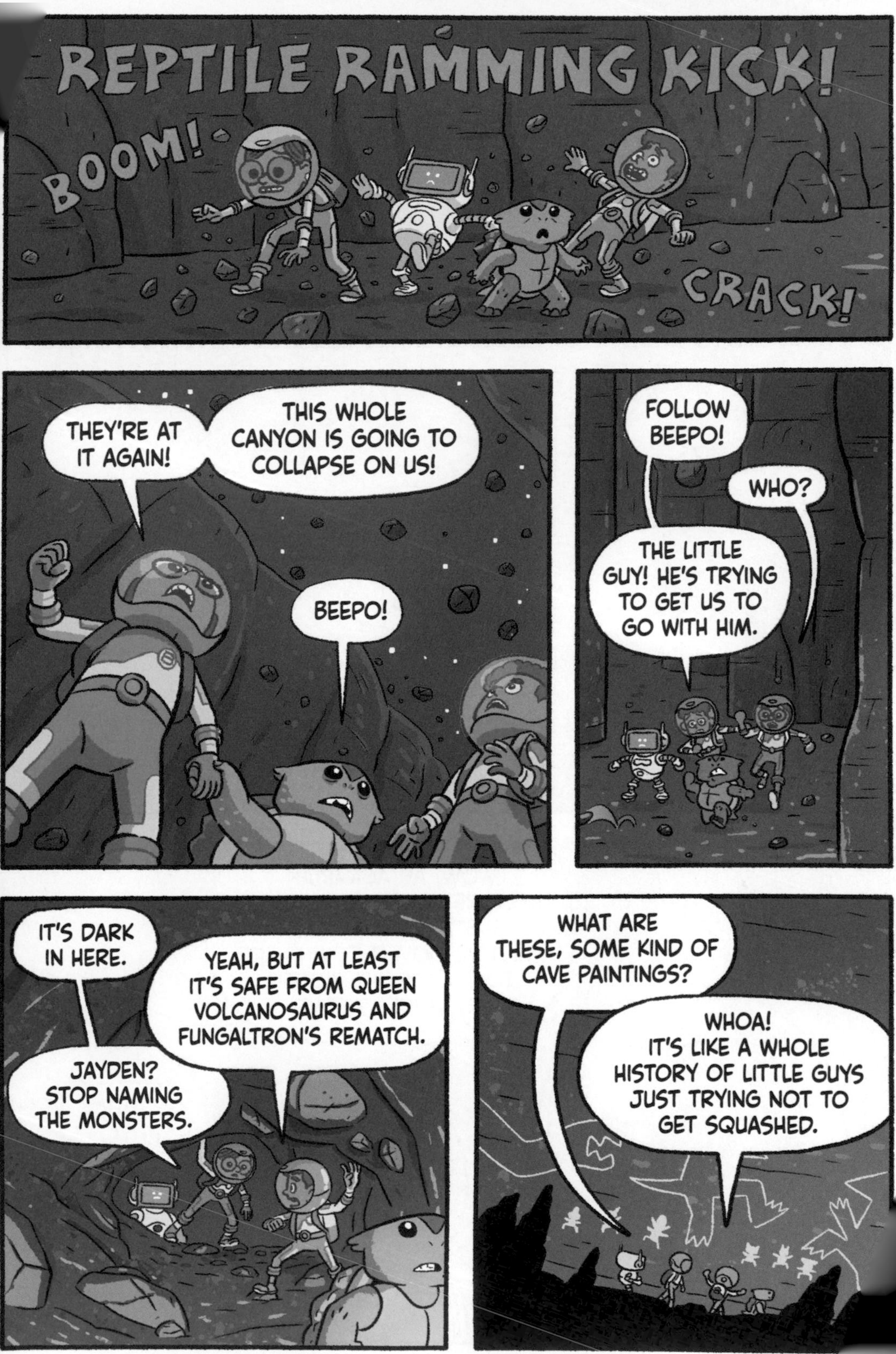
REPTILE RAMMING KICK!
BOOM!
CRACK!
THEY'RE AT IT AGAIN!
THIS WHOLE CANYON IS GOING TO COLLAPSE ON US!
BEEPO!
FOLLOW BEEPO!
WHO?
THE LITTLE GUY! HE'S TRYING TO GET US TO GO WITH HIM.
IT'S DARK IN HERE.
YEAH, BUT AT LEAST IT'S SAFE FROM QUEEN VOLCANOSAURUS AND FUNGALTRON'S REMATCH.
JAYDEN? STOP NAMING THE MONSTERS.
WHAT ARE THESE, SOME KIND OF CAVE PAINTINGS?
WHOA! IT'S LIKE A WHOLE HISTORY OF LITTLE GUYS JUST TRYING NOT TO GET SQUASHED.

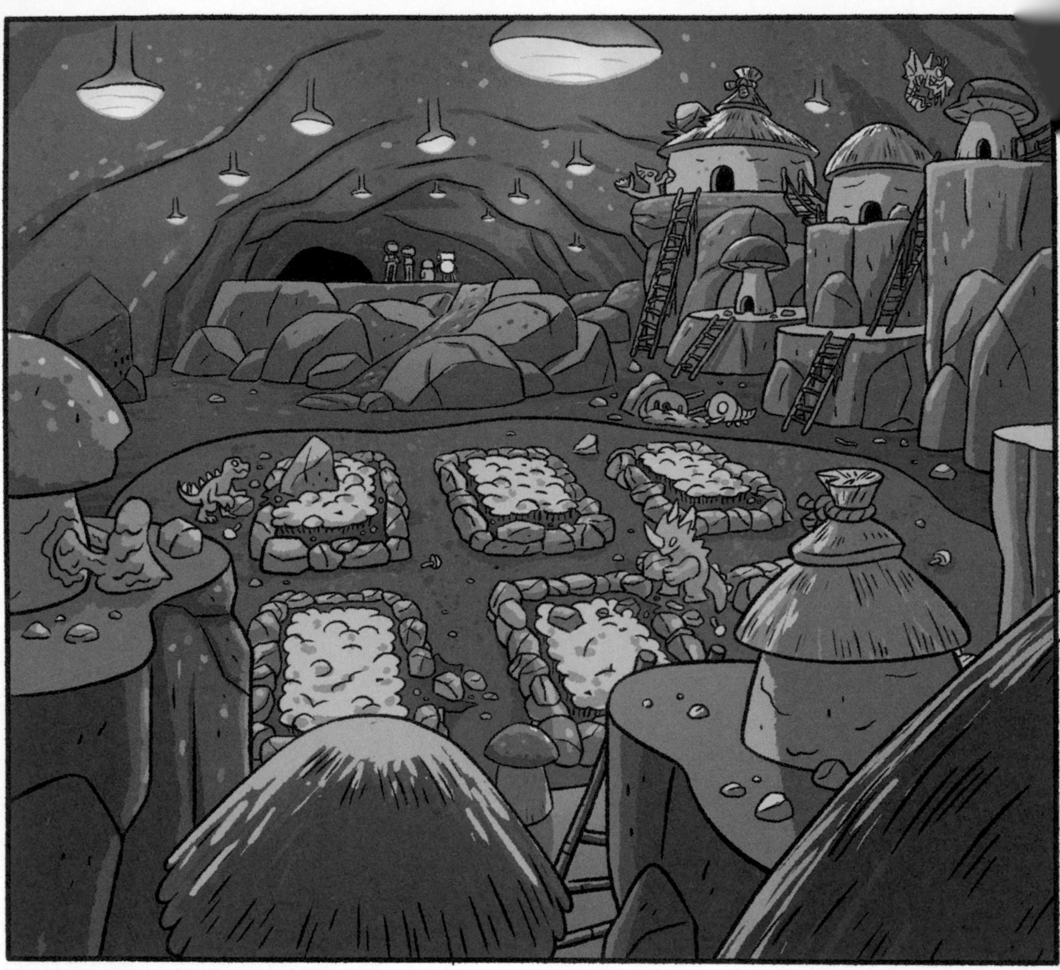

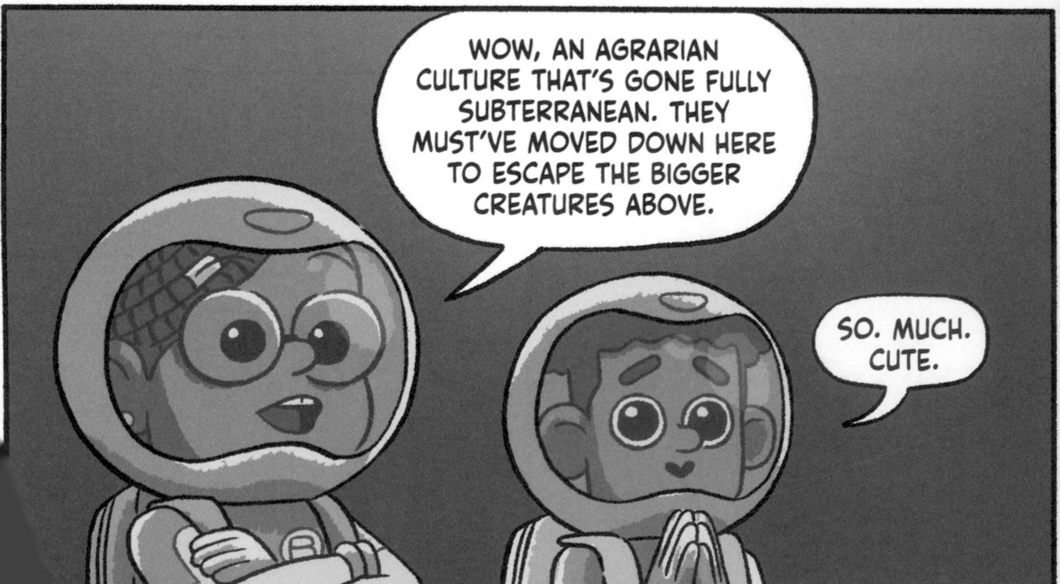
WOW, AN AGRARIAN CULTURE THAT'S GONE FULLY SUBTERRANEAN. THEY MUST'VE MOVED DOWN HERE TO ESCAPE THE BIGGER CREATURES ABOVE.
SO. MUCH. CUTE.

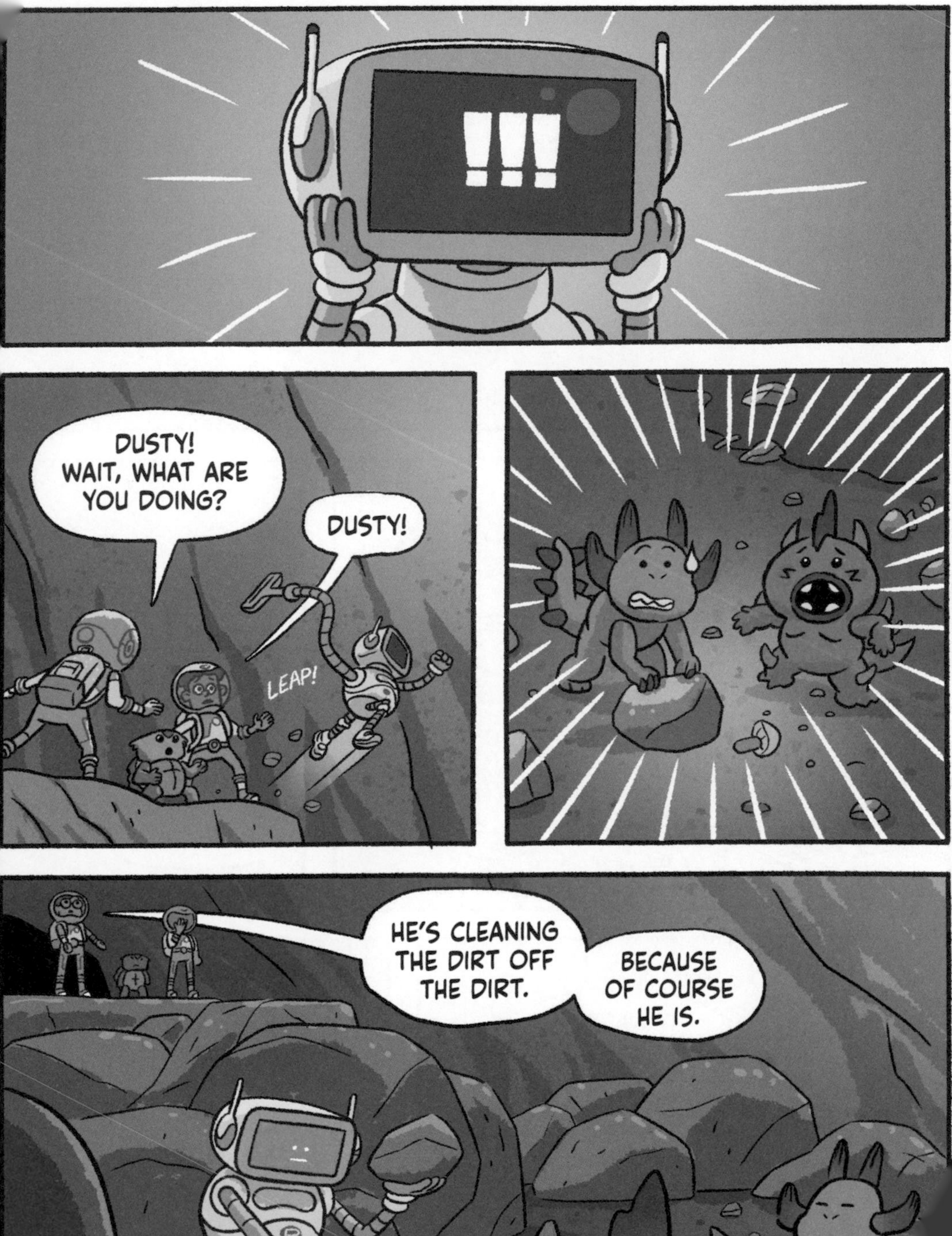
!!!
DUSTY! WAIT, WHAT ARE YOU DOING?
DUSTY!
LEAP!
HE'S CLEANING THE DIRT OFF THE DIRT.
BECAUSE OF COURSE HE IS.

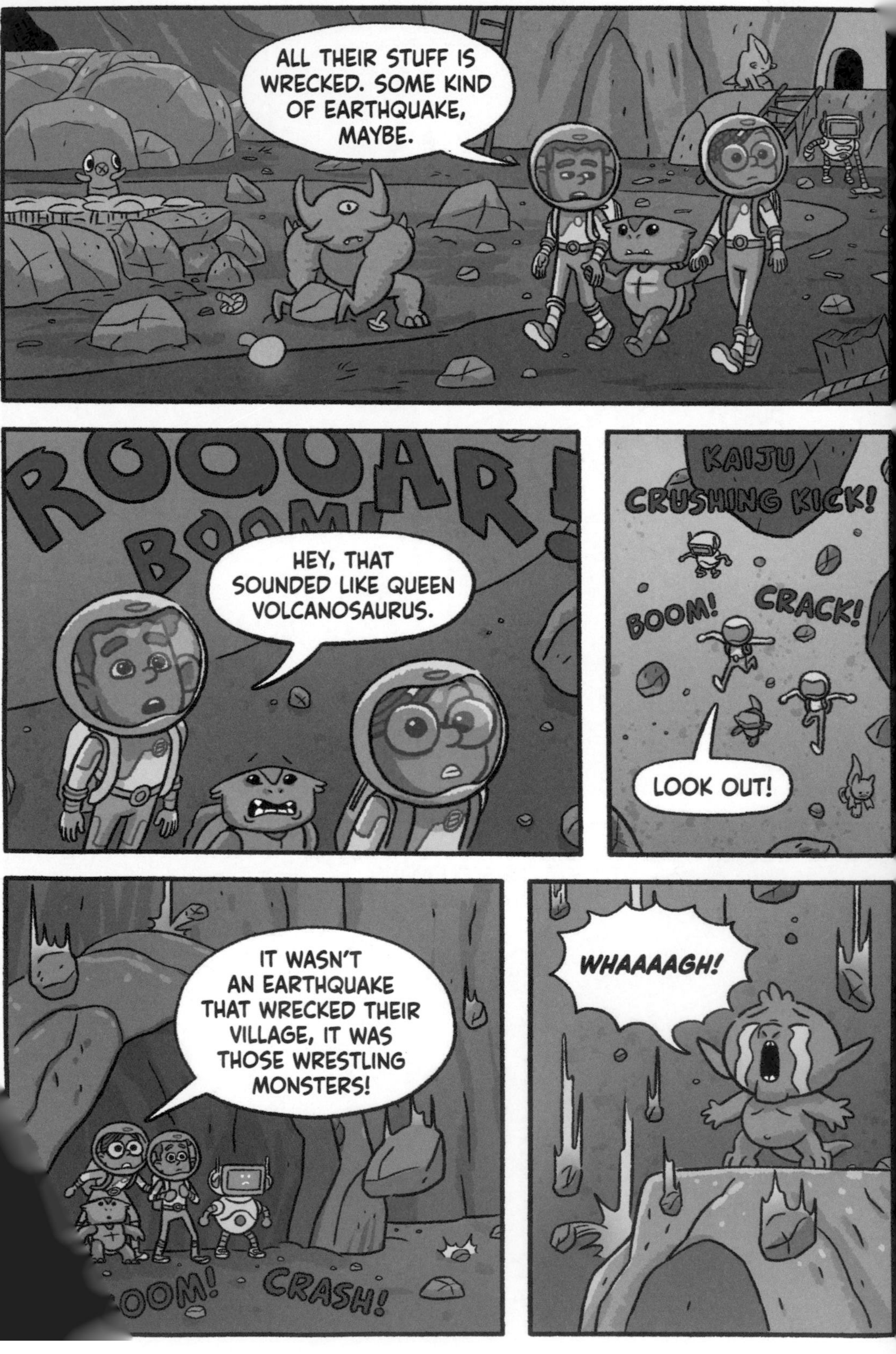
ALL THEIR STUFF IS WRECKED. SOME KIND OF EARTHQUAKE, MAYBE.
ROOOAR!
BOOM!
HEY, THAT SOUNDED LIKE QUEEN VOLCANOSAURUS.
KAIJU CRUSHING KICK!
BOOM!
CRACK!
LOOK OUT!
IT WASN'T AN EARTHQUAKE THAT WRECKED THEIR VILLAGE, IT WAS THOSE WRESTLING MONSTERS!
CRASH!
WHAAAAGH!

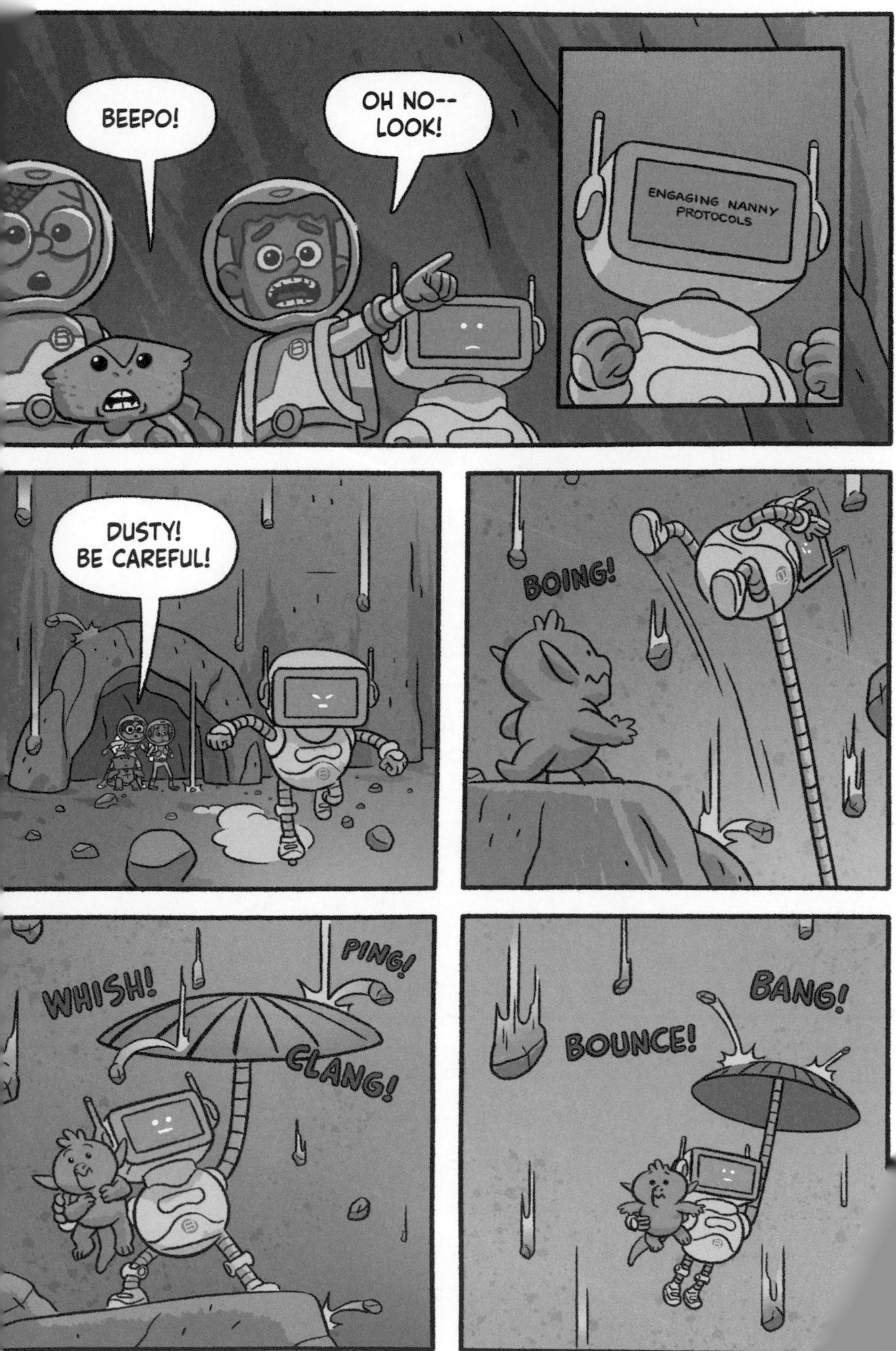
BEEPO!
OH NO-- LOOK!
ENGAGING NANNY PROTOCOLS
DUSTY! BE CAREFUL!
BOING!
WHISH!
PING!
CLANG!
BOUNCE!
BANG!

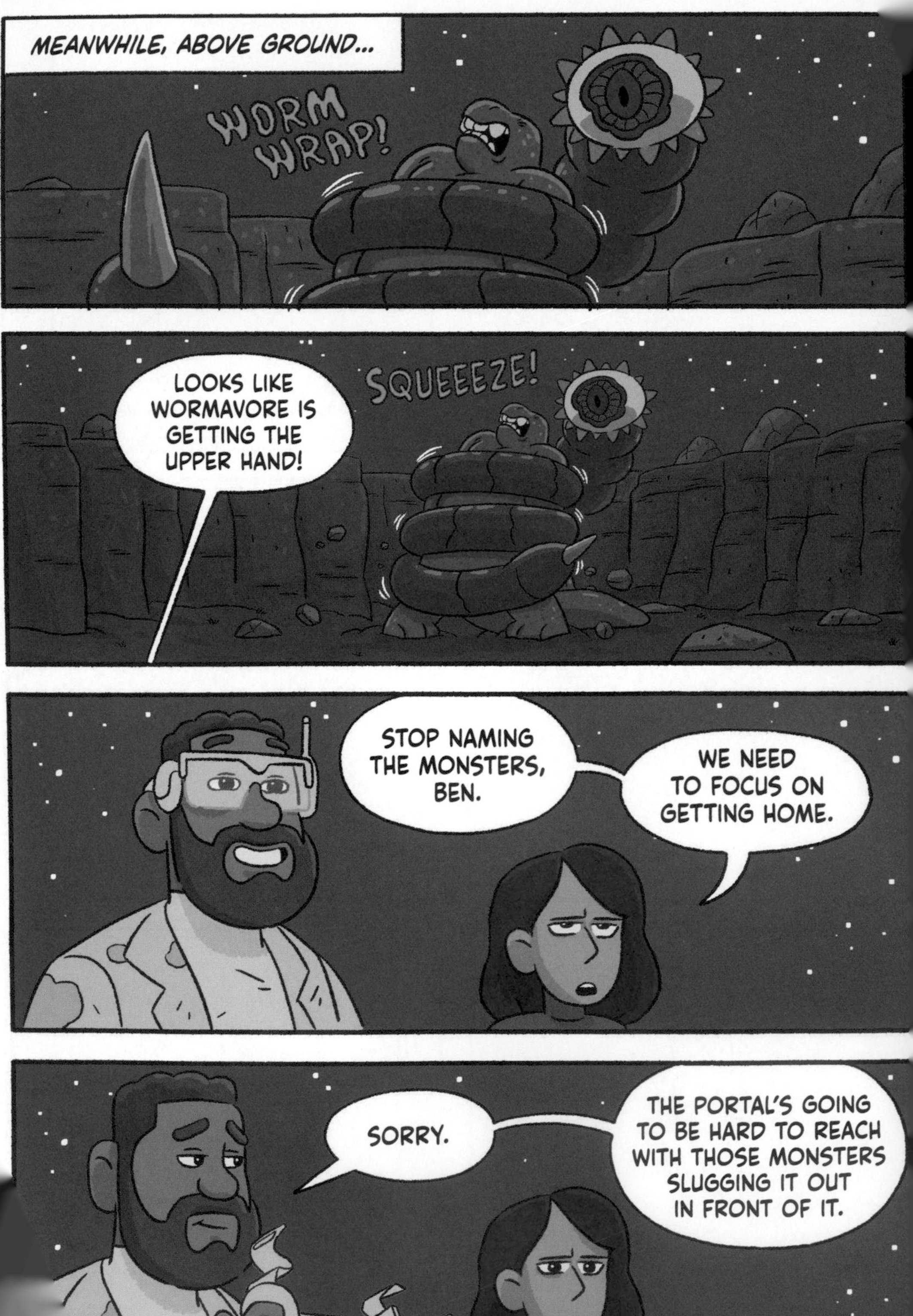
MEANWHILE, ABOVE GROUND...
WORM WRAP!
LOOKS LIKE WORMAVORE IS GETTING THE UPPER HAND!
SQUEEEZE!
STOP NAMING THE MONSTERS, BEN.
WE NEED TO FOCUS ON GETTING HOME.
SORRY.
THE PORTAL'S GOING TO BE HARD TO REACH WITH THOSE MONSTERS SLUGGING IT OUT IN FRONT OF IT.

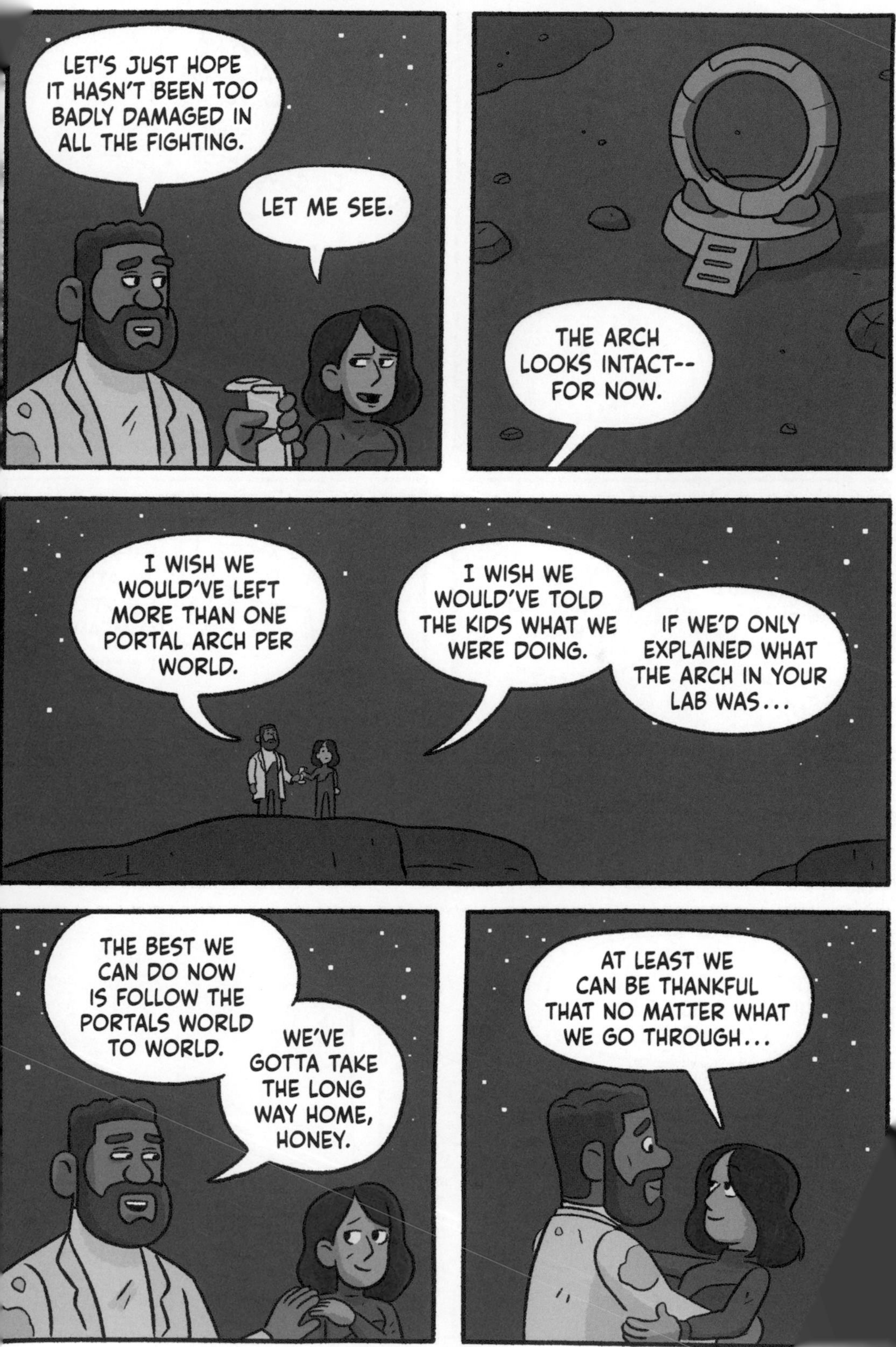
LET'S JUST HOPE IT HASN'T BEEN TOO BADLY DAMAGED IN ALL THE FIGHTING.
LET ME SEE.
THE ARCH LOOKS INTACT-- FOR NOW.
I WISH WE WOULD'VE LEFT MORE THAN ONE PORTAL ARCH PER WORLD.
I WISH WE WOULD'VE TOLD THE KIDS WHAT WE WERE DOING.
IF WE'D ONLY EXPLAINED WHAT THE ARCH IN YOUR LAB WAS...
THE BEST WE CAN DO NOW IS FOLLOW THE PORTALS WORLD TO WORLD.
WE'VE GOTTA TAKE THE LONG WAY HOME, HONEY.
AT LEAST WE CAN BE THANKFUL THAT NO MATTER WHAT WE GO THROUGH...

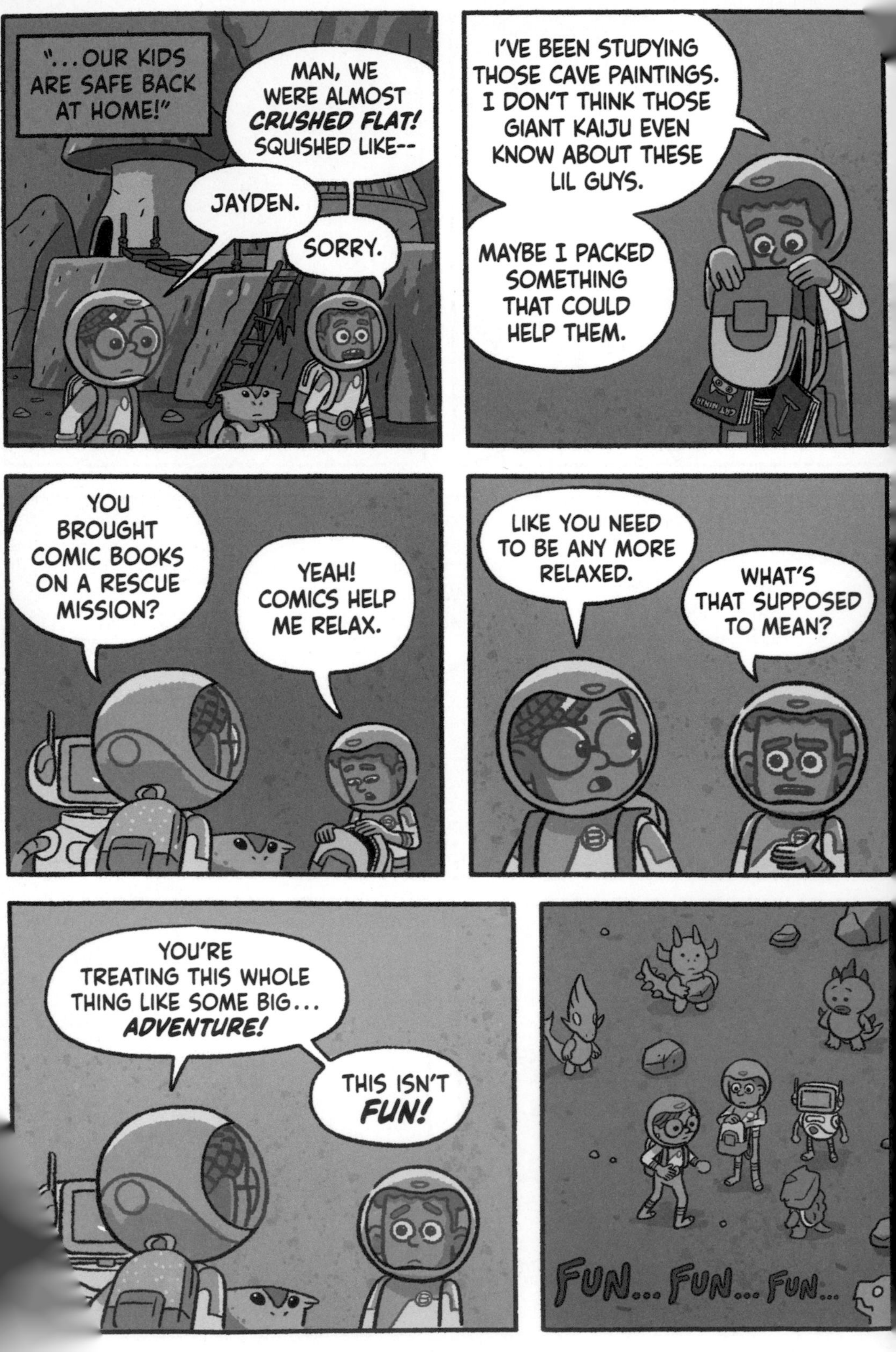
"...OUR KIDS ARE SAFE BACK AT HOME!"
MAN, WE WERE ALMOST CRUSHED FLAT! SQUISHED LIKE--
JAYDEN.
SORRY.
I'VE BEEN STUDYING THOSE CAVE PAINTINGS. I DON'T THINK THOSE GIANT KAIJU EVEN KNOW ABOUT THESE LIL GUYS.
MAYBE I PACKED SOMETHING THAT COULD HELP THEM.
CAT NINJA
YOU BROUGHT COMIC BOOKS ON A RESCUE MISSION?
YEAH! COMICS HELP ME RELAX.
LIKE YOU NEED TO BE ANY MORE RELAXED.
WHAT'S THAT SUPPOSED TO MEAN?
YOU'RE TREATING THIS WHOLE THING LIKE SOME BIG... ADVENTURE!
THIS ISN'T FUN!
FUN... FUN... FUN...

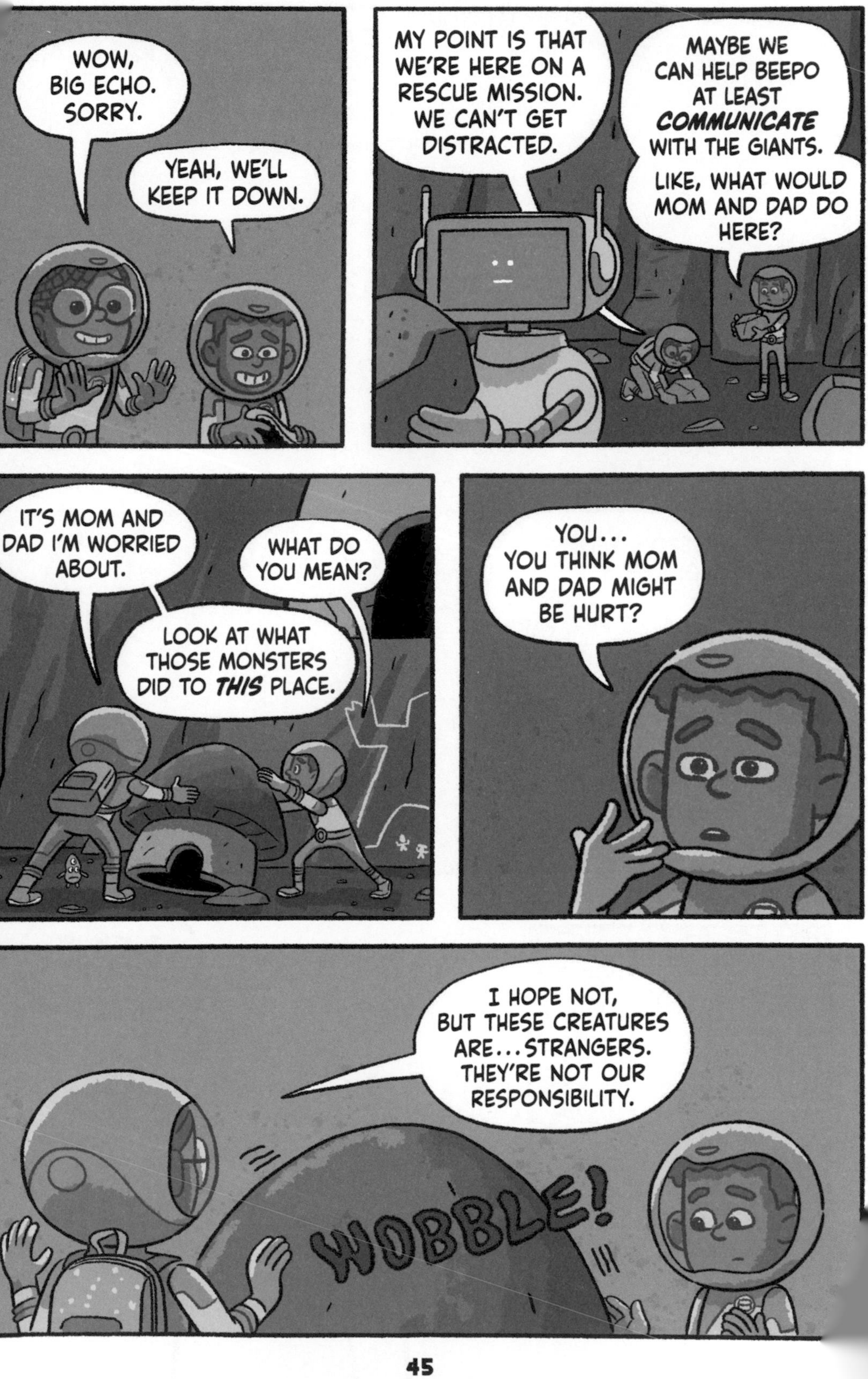
WOW, BIG ECHO. SORRY.
YEAH, WE'LL KEEP IT DOWN.
MY POINT IS THAT WE'RE HERE ON A RESCUE MISSION. WE CAN'T GET DISTRACTED.
MAYBE WE CAN HELP BEEPO AT LEAST COMMUNICATE WITH THE GIANTS.
LIKE, WHAT WOULD MOM AND DAD DO HERE?
IT'S MOM AND DAD I'M WORRIED ABOUT.
WHAT DO YOU MEAN?
LOOK AT WHAT THOSE MONSTERS DID TO THIS PLACE.
YOU... YOU THINK MOM AND DAD MIGHT BE HURT?
I HOPE NOT, BUT THESE CREATURES ARE... STRANGERS. THEY'RE NOT OUR RESPONSIBILITY.
WOBBLE!

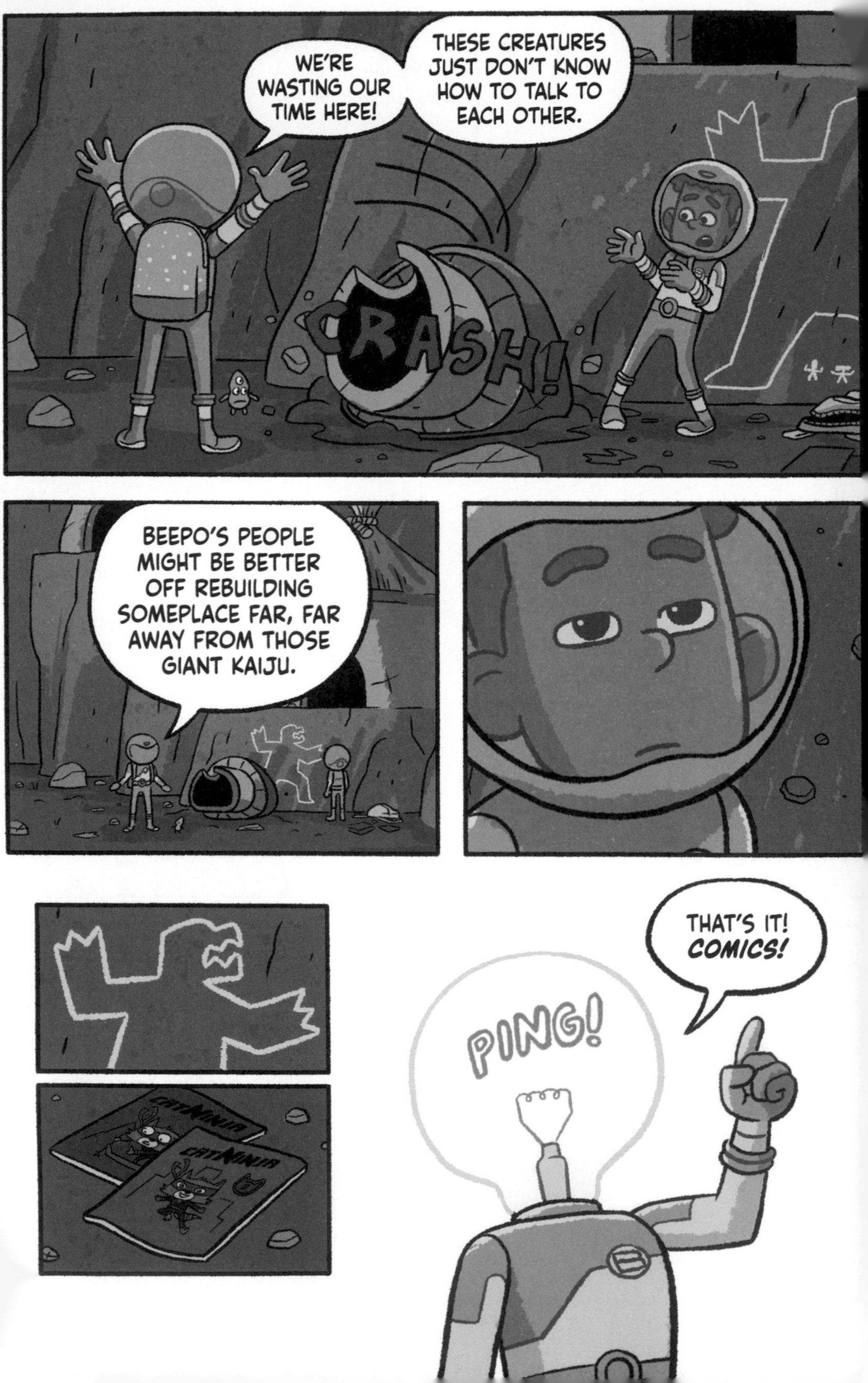
WE'RE WASTING OUR TIME HERE!
THESE CREATURES JUST DON'T KNOW HOW TO TALK TO EACH OTHER.
CRASH!
BEEPO'S PEOPLE MIGHT BE BETTER OFF REBUILDING SOMEPLACE FAR, FAR AWAY FROM THOSE GIANT KAIJU.
CAT NINJA
CAT NINJA
PING!
THAT'S IT! *COMICS!*

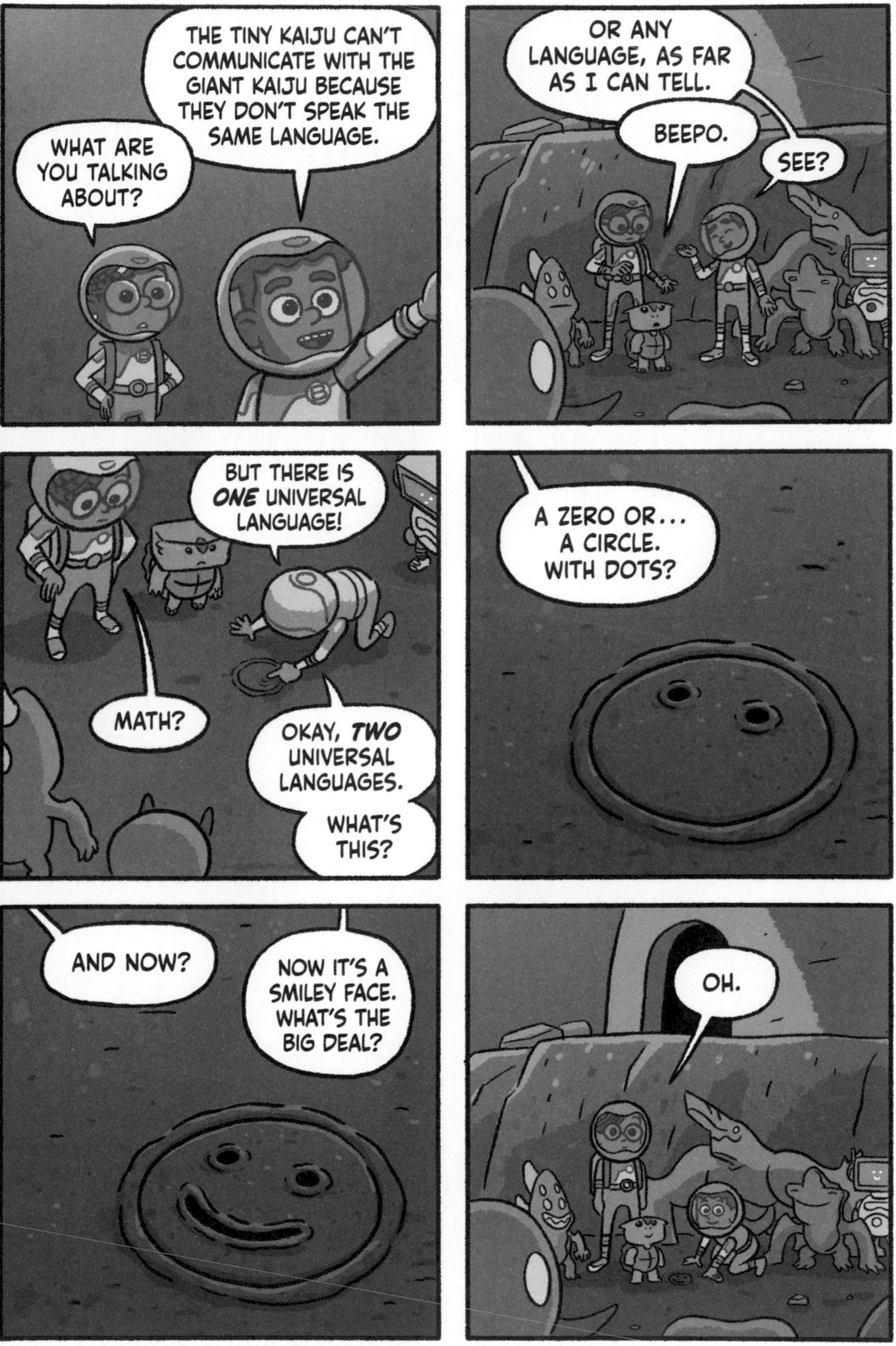
WHAT ARE YOU TALKING ABOUT?
THE TINY KAIJU CAN'T COMMUNICATE WITH THE GIANT KAIJU BECAUSE THEY DON'T SPEAK THE SAME LANGUAGE.
OR ANY LANGUAGE, AS FAR AS I CAN TELL.
BEEPO.
SEE?
BUT THERE IS *ONE* UNIVERSAL LANGUAGE!
MATH?
OKAY, *TWO* UNIVERSAL LANGUAGES.
WHAT'S THIS?
A ZERO OR... A CIRCLE. WITH DOTS?
AND NOW?
NOW IT'S A SMILEY FACE. WHAT'S THE BIG DEAL?
OH.

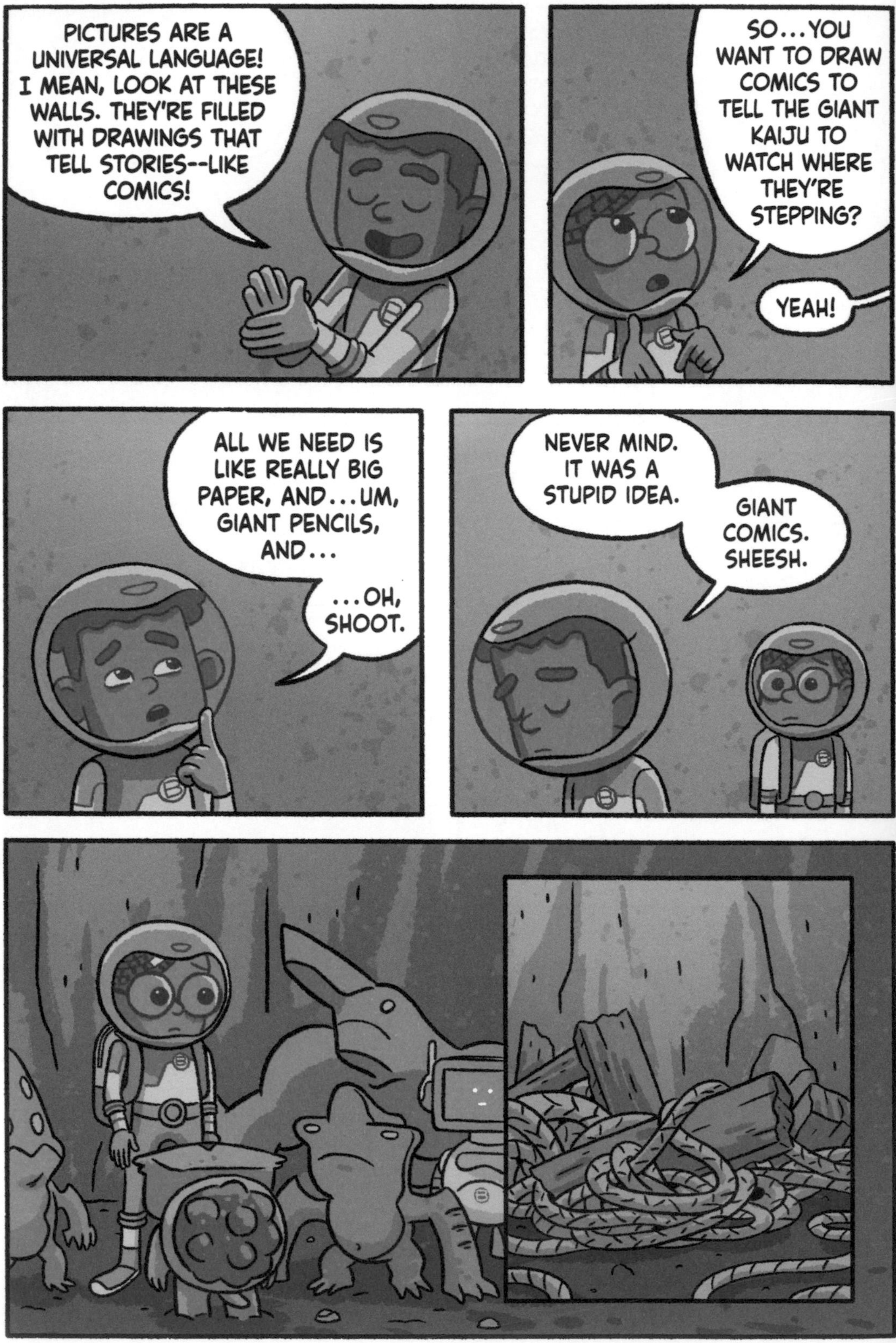
PICTURES ARE A UNIVERSAL LANGUAGE! I MEAN, LOOK AT THESE WALLS. THEY'RE FILLED WITH DRAWINGS THAT TELL STORIES--LIKE COMICS!
SO...YOU WANT TO DRAW COMICS TO TELL THE GIANT KAIJU TO WATCH WHERE THEY'RE STEPPING?
YEAH!
ALL WE NEED IS LIKE REALLY BIG PAPER, AND...UM, GIANT PENCILS, AND...
...OH, SHOOT.
NEVER MIND. IT WAS A STUPID IDEA.
GIANT COMICS. SHEESH.

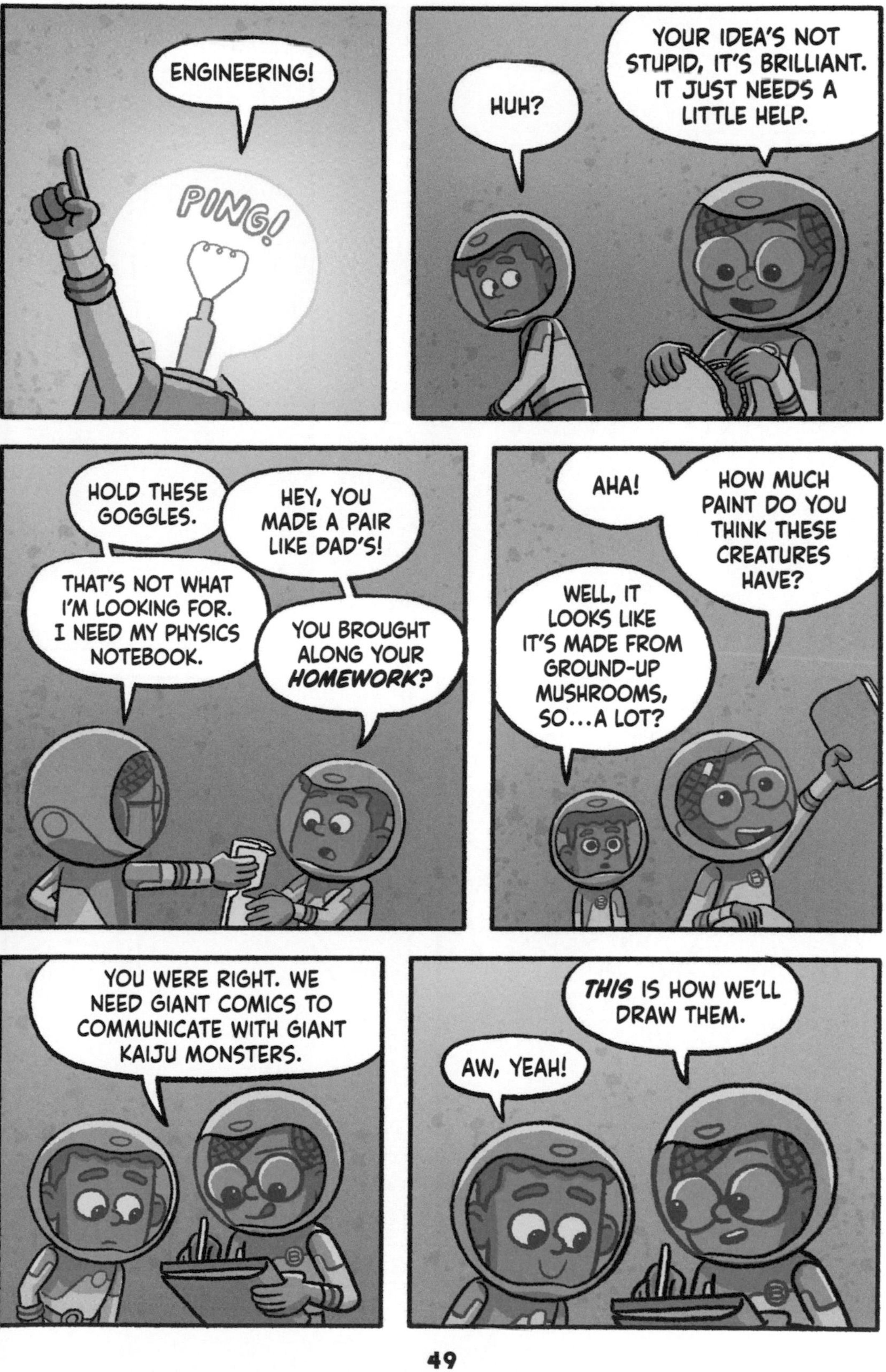
ENGINEERING!
PING!
HUH?
YOUR IDEA'S NOT STUPID, IT'S BRILLIANT. IT JUST NEEDS A LITTLE HELP.
HOLD THESE GOGGLES.
HEY, YOU MADE A PAIR LIKE DAD'S!
THAT'S NOT WHAT I'M LOOKING FOR. I NEED MY PHYSICS NOTEBOOK.
YOU BROUGHT ALONG YOUR *HOMEWORK*?
AHA!
HOW MUCH PAINT DO YOU THINK THESE CREATURES HAVE?
WELL, IT LOOKS LIKE IT'S MADE FROM GROUND-UP MUSHROOMS, SO...A LOT?
YOU WERE RIGHT. WE NEED GIANT COMICS TO COMMUNICATE WITH GIANT KAIJU MONSTERS.
*THIS* IS HOW WE'LL DRAW THEM.
AW, YEAH!

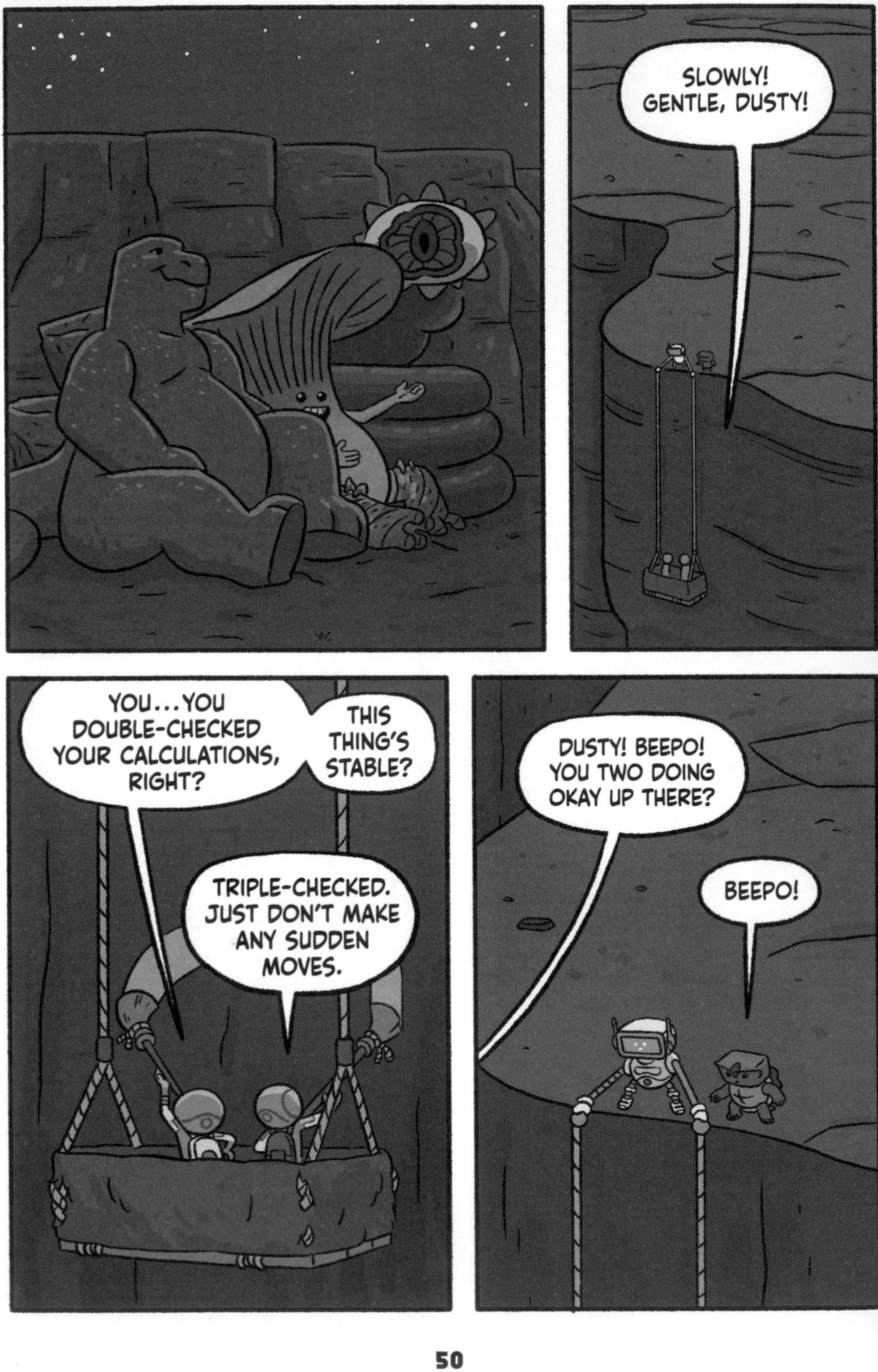
SLOWLY! GENTLE, DUSTY!
YOU...YOU DOUBLE-CHECKED YOUR CALCULATIONS, RIGHT?
THIS THING'S STABLE?
TRIPLE-CHECKED. JUST DON'T MAKE ANY SUDDEN MOVES.
DUSTY! BEEPO! YOU TWO DOING OKAY UP THERE?
BEEPO!

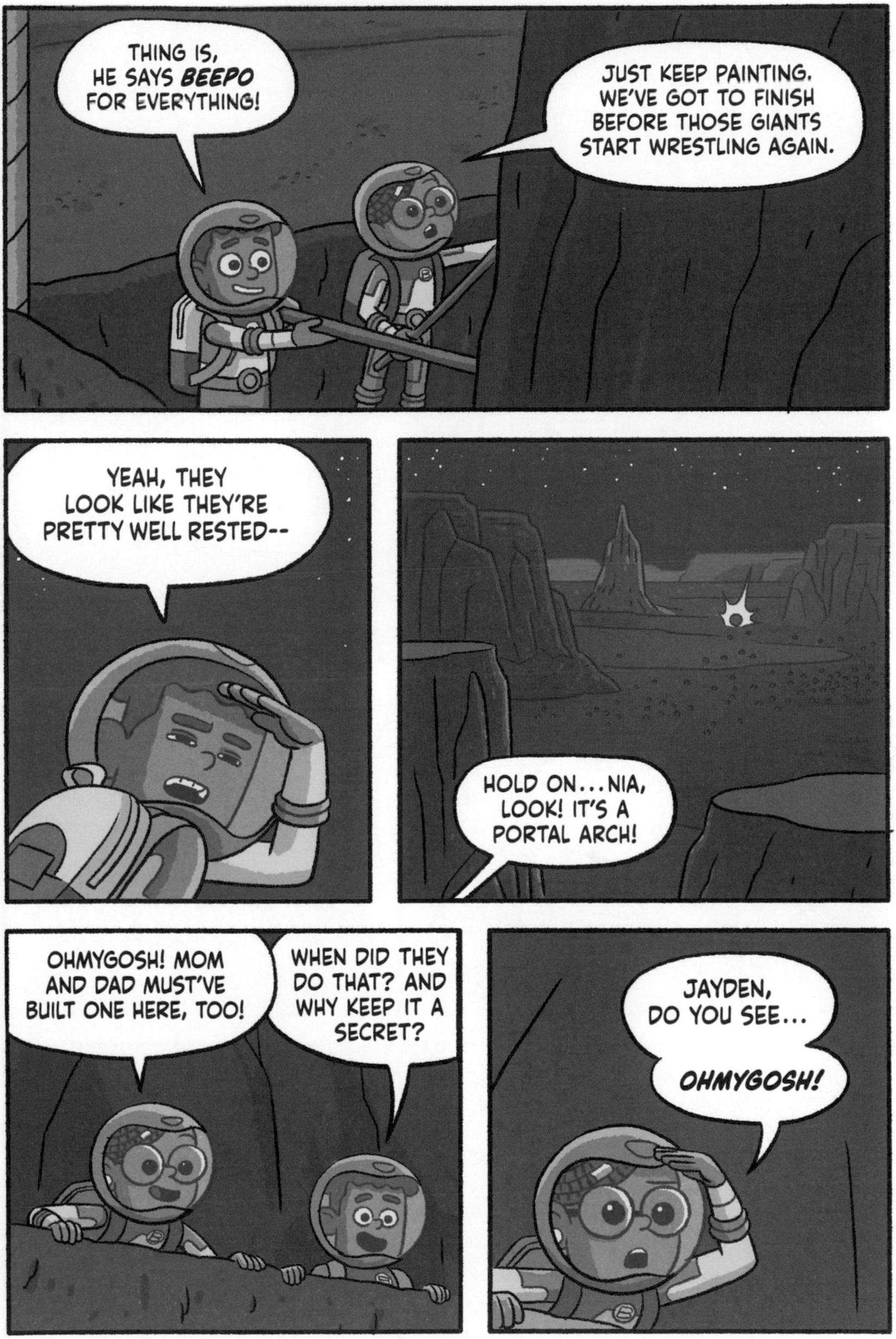
THING IS, HE SAYS *BEEPO* FOR EVERYTHING!
JUST KEEP PAINTING. WE'VE GOT TO FINISH BEFORE THOSE GIANTS START WRESTLING AGAIN.
YEAH, THEY LOOK LIKE THEY'RE PRETTY WELL RESTED--
HOLD ON...NIA, LOOK! IT'S A PORTAL ARCH!
OHMYGOSH! MOM AND DAD MUST'VE BUILT ONE HERE, TOO!
WHEN DID THEY DO THAT? AND WHY KEEP IT A SECRET?
JAYDEN, DO YOU SEE...
*OHMYGOSH!*

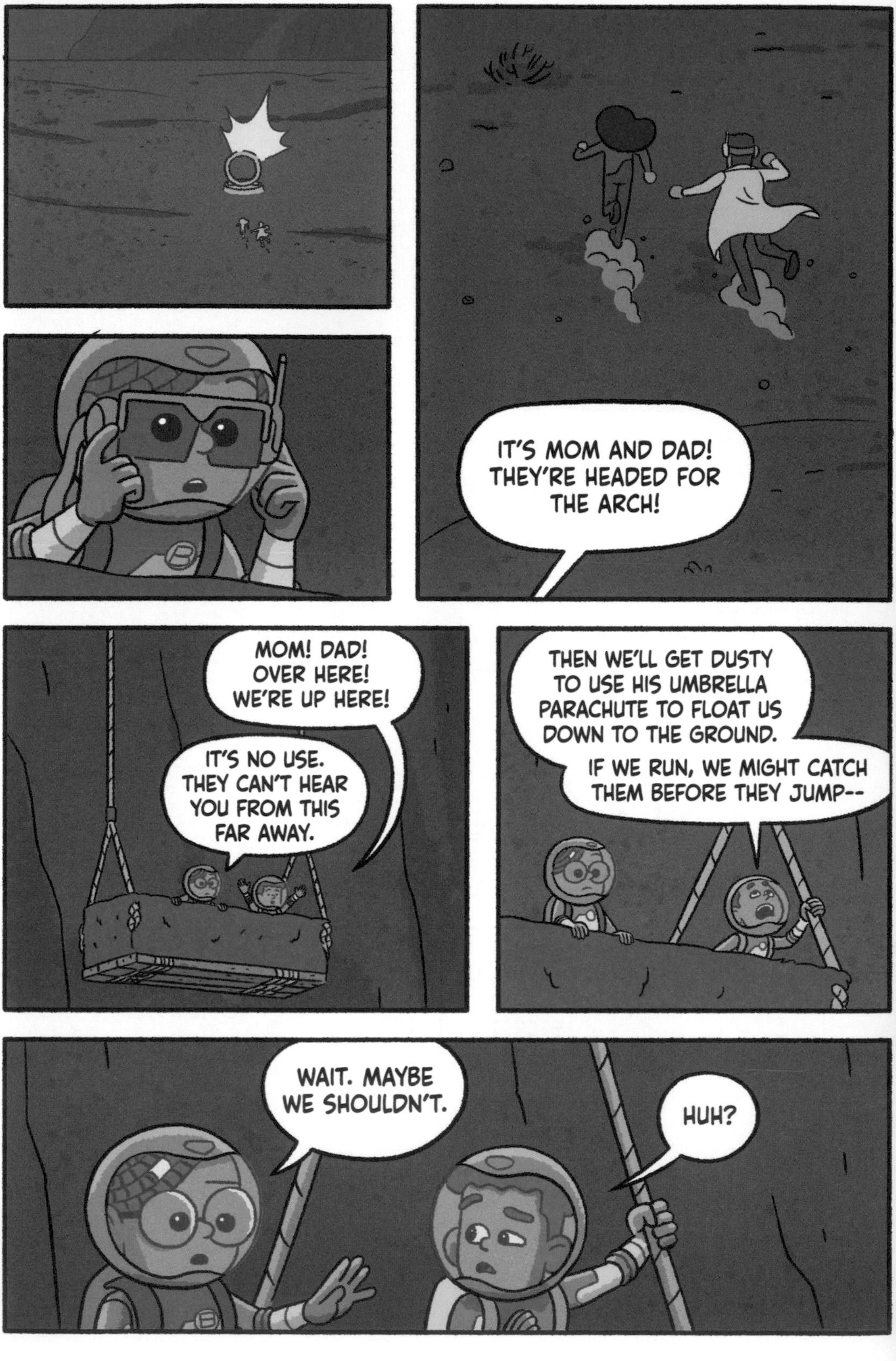
IT'S MOM AND DAD! THEY'RE HEADED FOR THE ARCH!
MOM! DAD! OVER HERE! WE'RE UP HERE!
IT'S NO USE. THEY CAN'T HEAR YOU FROM THIS FAR AWAY.
THEN WE'LL GET DUSTY TO USE HIS UMBRELLA PARACHUTE TO FLOAT US DOWN TO THE GROUND.
IF WE RUN, WE MIGHT CATCH THEM BEFORE THEY JUMP--
WAIT. MAYBE WE SHOULDN'T.
HUH?

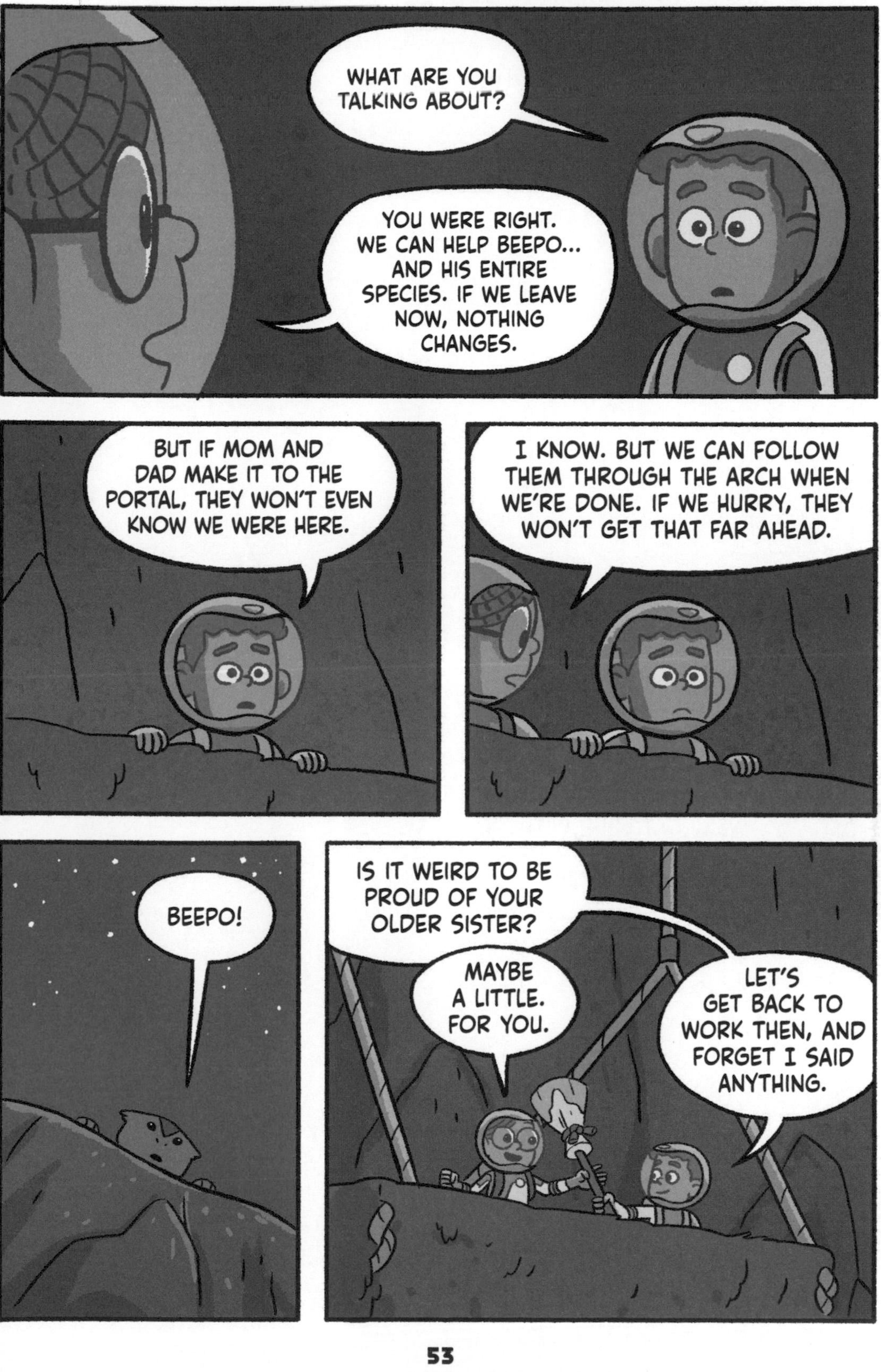
WHAT ARE YOU TALKING ABOUT?
YOU WERE RIGHT. WE CAN HELP BEEPO... AND HIS ENTIRE SPECIES. IF WE LEAVE NOW, NOTHING CHANGES.
BUT IF MOM AND DAD MAKE IT TO THE PORTAL, THEY WON'T EVEN KNOW WE WERE HERE.
I KNOW. BUT WE CAN FOLLOW THEM THROUGH THE ARCH WHEN WE'RE DONE. IF WE HURRY, THEY WON'T GET THAT FAR AHEAD.
BEEPO!
IS IT WEIRD TO BE PROUD OF YOUR OLDER SISTER?
MAYBE A LITTLE. FOR YOU.
LET'S GET BACK TO WORK THEN, AND FORGET I SAID ANYTHING.

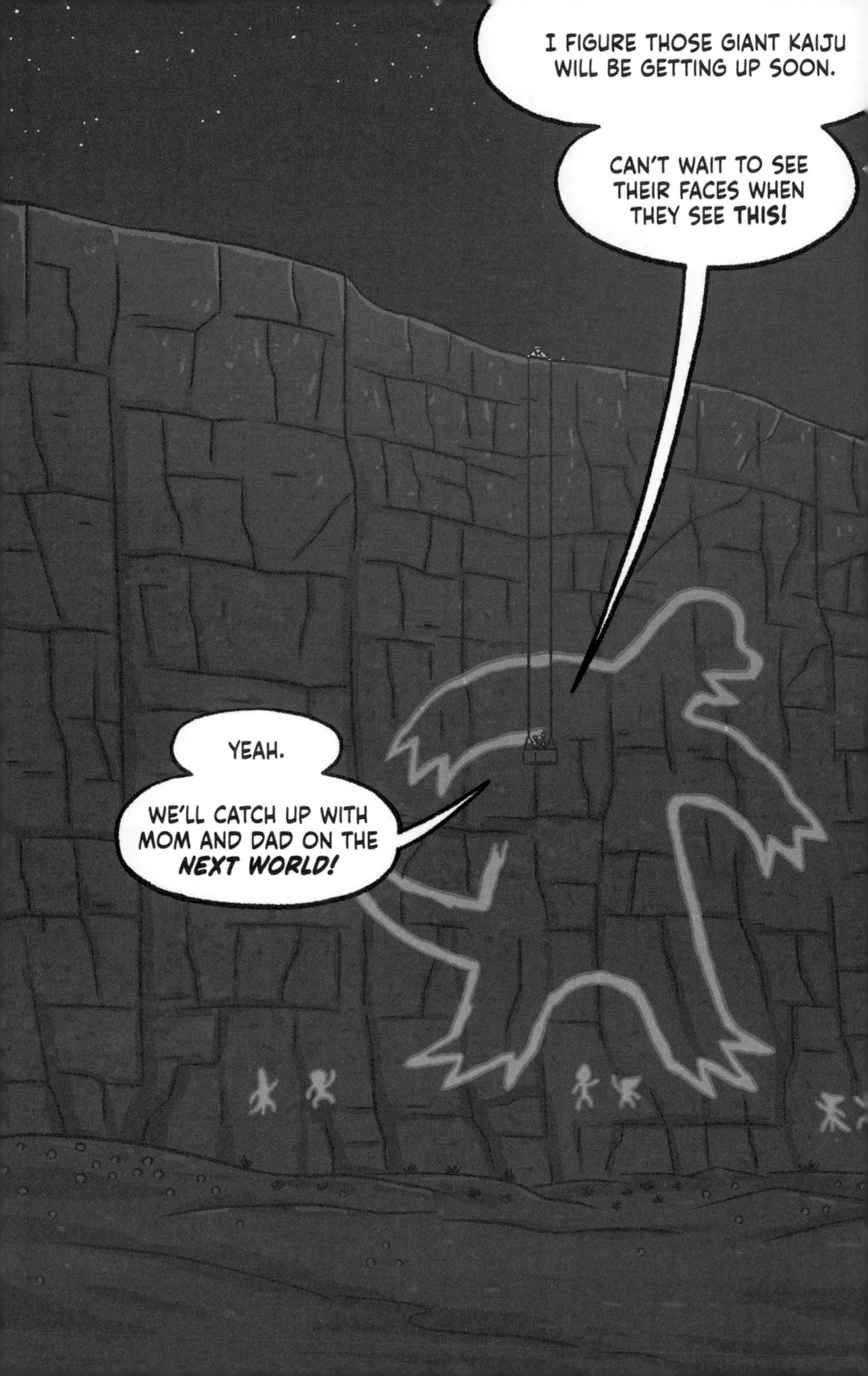
I FIGURE THOSE GIANT KAIJU WILL BE GETTING UP SOON.
CAN'T WAIT TO SEE THEIR FACES WHEN THEY SEE THIS!
YEAH.
WE'LL CATCH UP WITH MOM AND DAD ON THE NEXT WORLD!

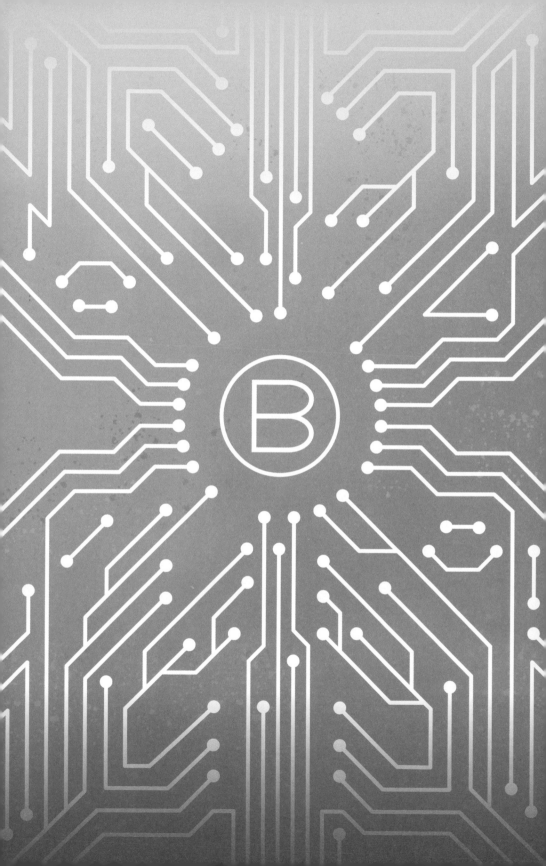

CHAPTER 3

# NIGHT OF THE LIVING SQUISHES

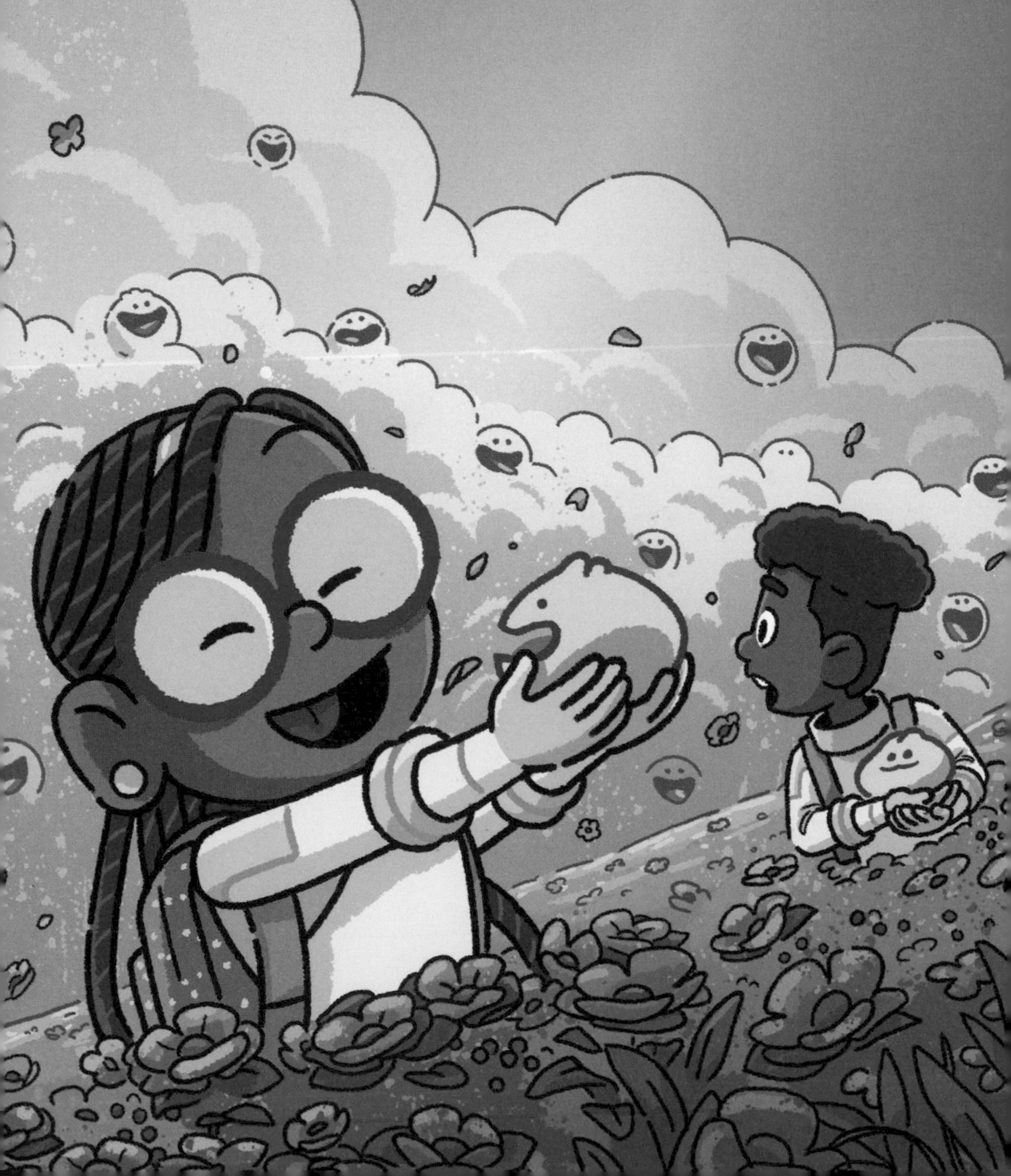

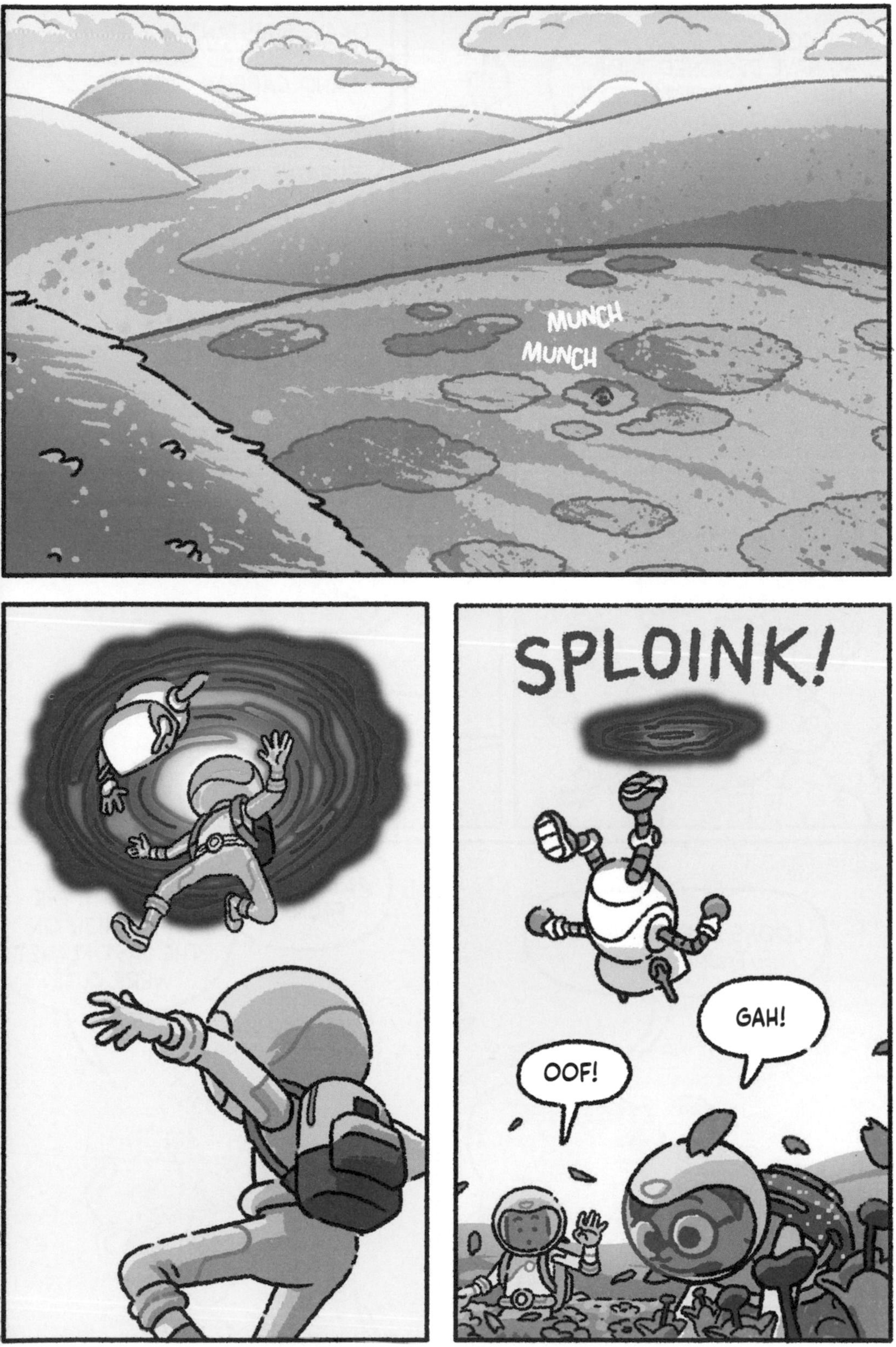
MUNCH
MUNCH
SPLOINK!
GAH!
OOF!

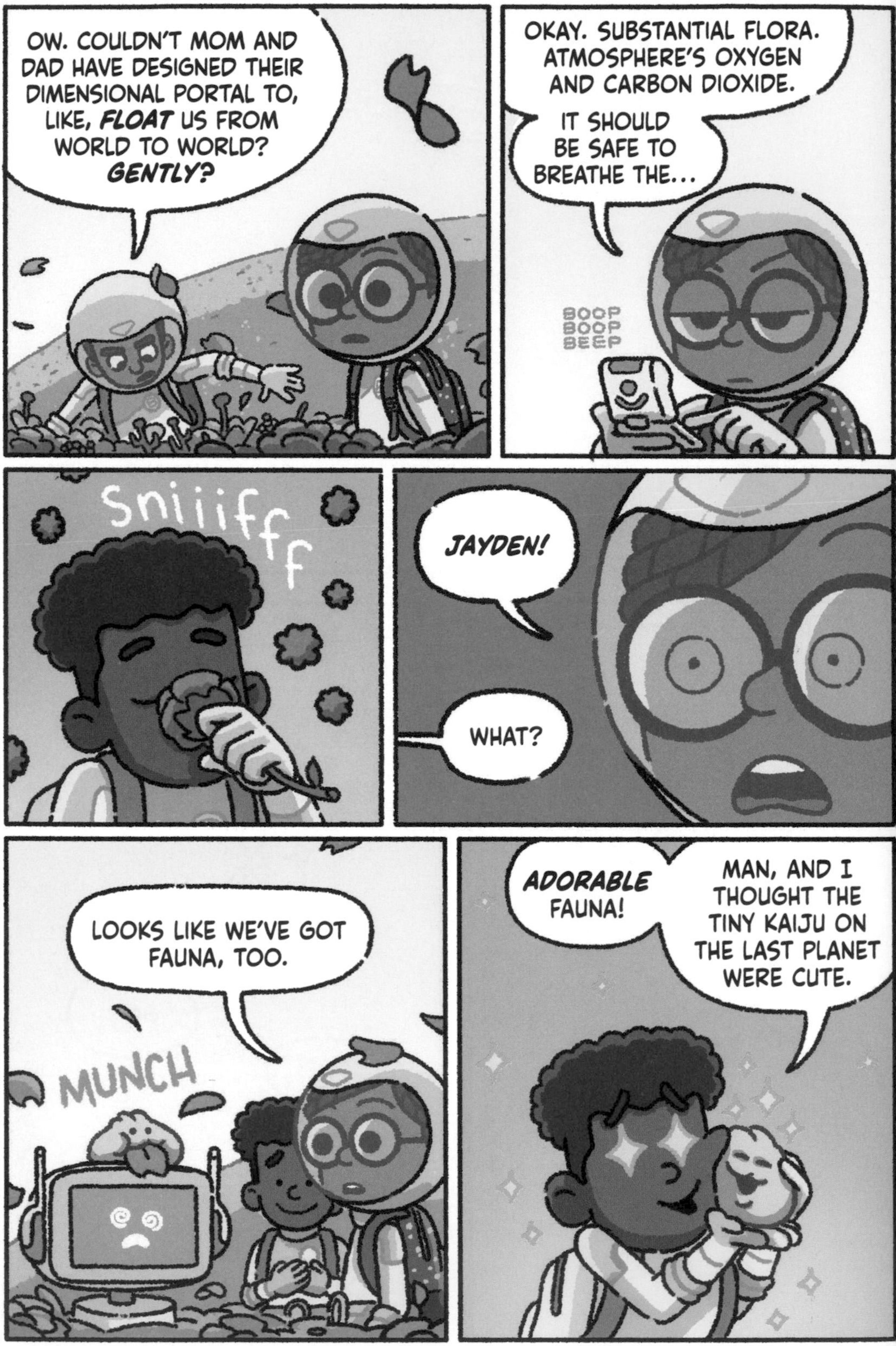
OW. COULDN'T MOM AND DAD HAVE DESIGNED THEIR DIMENSIONAL PORTAL TO, LIKE, ***FLOAT*** US FROM WORLD TO WORLD? ***GENTLY?***
OKAY. SUBSTANTIAL FLORA. ATMOSPHERE'S OXYGEN AND CARBON DIOXIDE.
IT SHOULD BE SAFE TO BREATHE THE...
BOOP BOOP BEEP
Sniiifff
***JAYDEN!***
WHAT?
LOOKS LIKE WE'VE GOT FAUNA, TOO.
MUNCH
***ADORABLE*** FAUNA!
MAN, AND I THOUGHT THE TINY KAIJU ON THE LAST PLANET WERE CUTE.

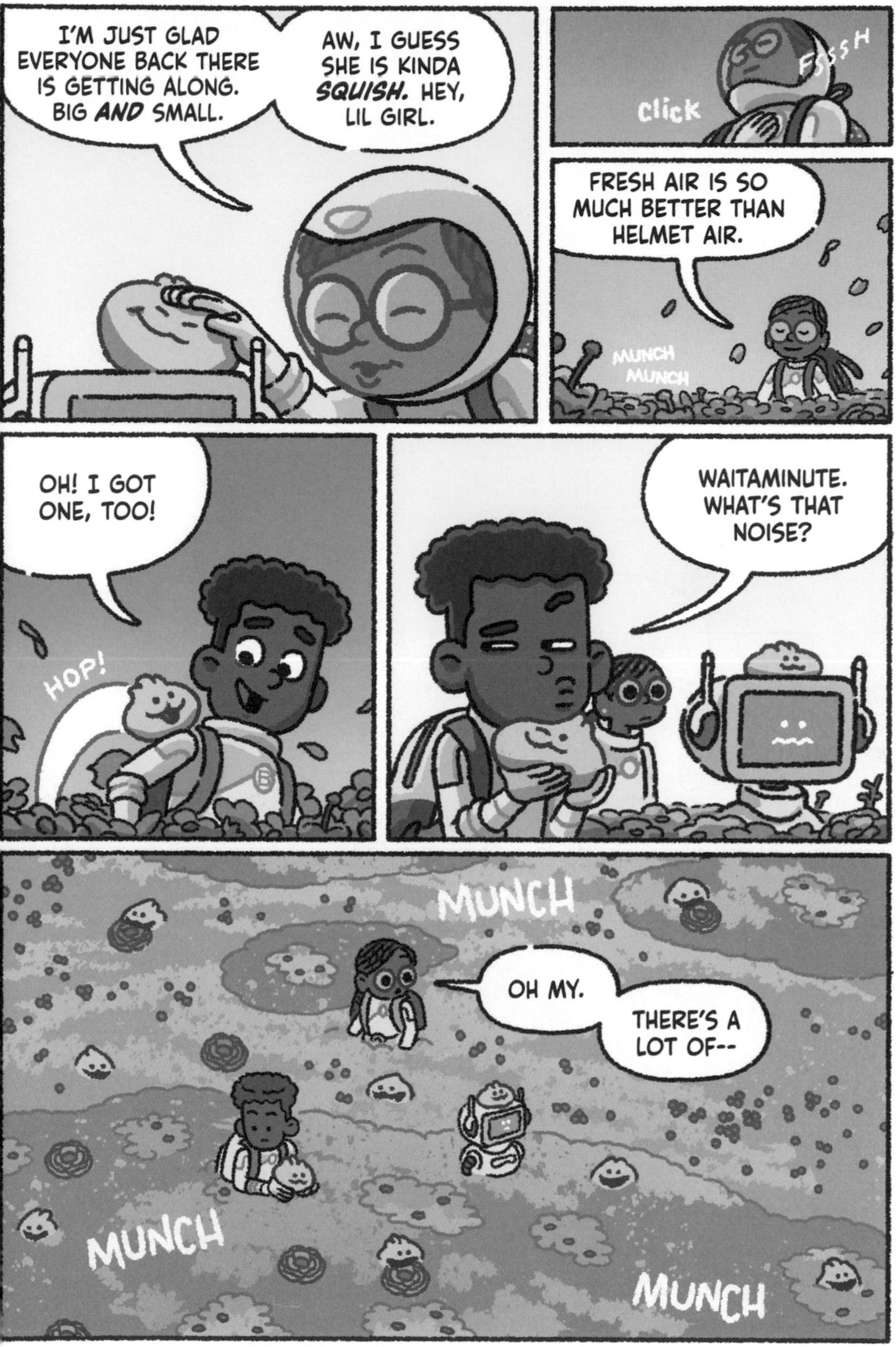
I'M JUST GLAD EVERYONE BACK THERE IS GETTING ALONG. BIG AND SMALL.
AW, I GUESS SHE IS KINDA SQUISH. HEY, LIL GIRL.
CLICK
FSSSH
FRESH AIR IS SO MUCH BETTER THAN HELMET AIR.
MUNCH MUNCH
OH! I GOT ONE, TOO!
HOP!
WAITAMINUTE. WHAT'S THAT NOISE?
MUNCH
OH MY.
THERE'S A LOT OF--
MUNCH
MUNCH

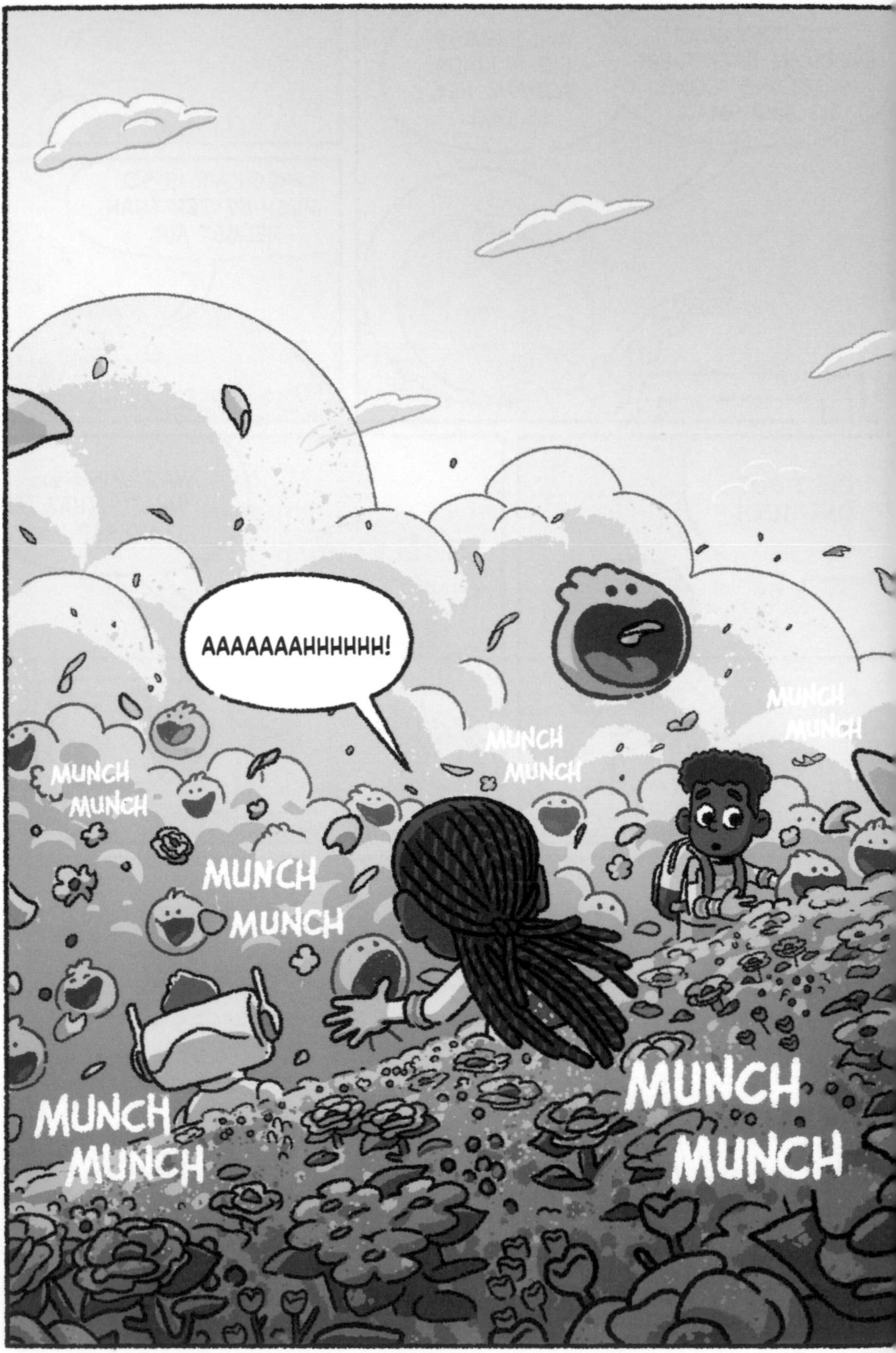
AAAAAAAHHHHHH!
MUNCH MUNCH
MUNCH MUNCH
MUNCH MUNCH
MUNCH MUNCH
MUNCH MUNCH
MUNCH MUNCH

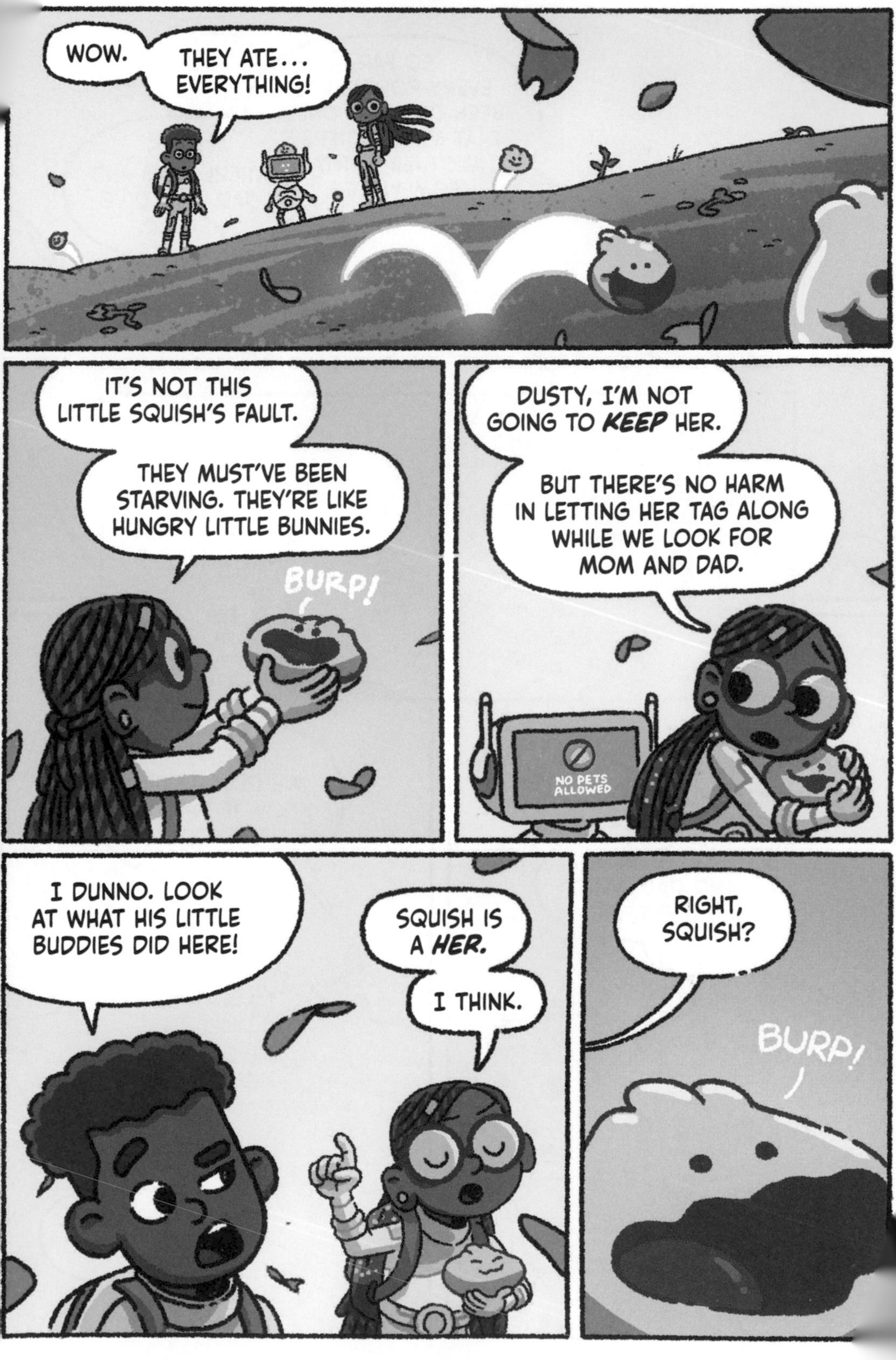
WOW.
THEY ATE... EVERYTHING!
IT'S NOT THIS LITTLE SQUISH'S FAULT.
THEY MUST'VE BEEN STARVING. THEY'RE LIKE HUNGRY LITTLE BUNNIES.
BURP!
DUSTY, I'M NOT GOING TO ***KEEP*** HER.
BUT THERE'S NO HARM IN LETTING HER TAG ALONG WHILE WE LOOK FOR MOM AND DAD.
NO PETS ALLOWED
I DUNNO. LOOK AT WHAT HIS LITTLE BUDDIES DID HERE!
SQUISH IS A ***HER.***
I THINK.
RIGHT, SQUISH?
BURP!

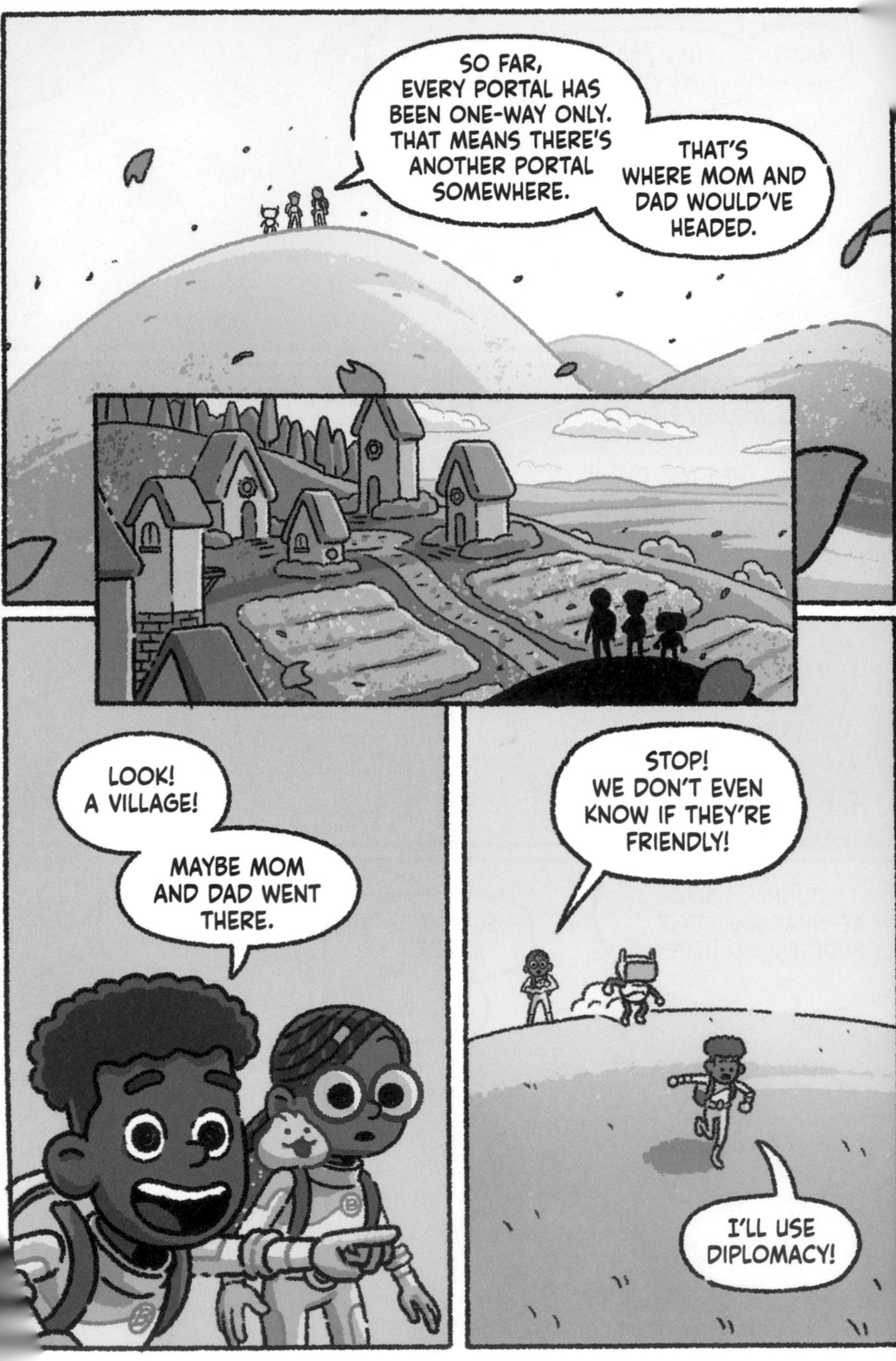
SO FAR, EVERY PORTAL HAS BEEN ONE-WAY ONLY. THAT MEANS THERE'S ANOTHER PORTAL SOMEWHERE.
THAT'S WHERE MOM AND DAD WOULD'VE HEADED.
LOOK! A VILLAGE!
MAYBE MOM AND DAD WENT THERE.
STOP! WE DON'T EVEN KNOW IF THEY'RE FRIENDLY!
I'LL USE DIPLOMACY!

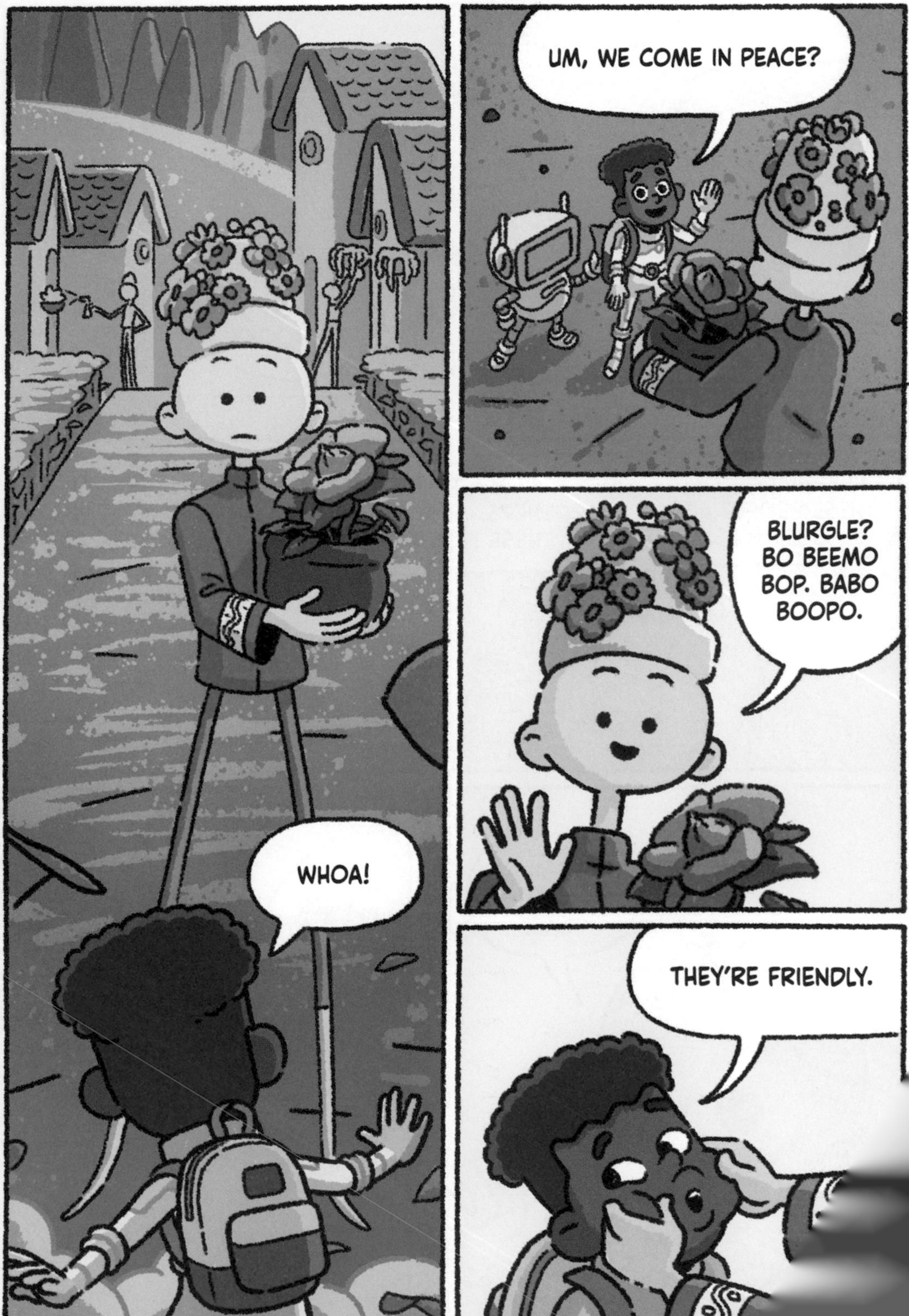
WHOA!
UM, WE COME IN PEACE?
BLURGLE? BO BEEMO BOP. BABO BOOPO.
THEY'RE FRIENDLY.

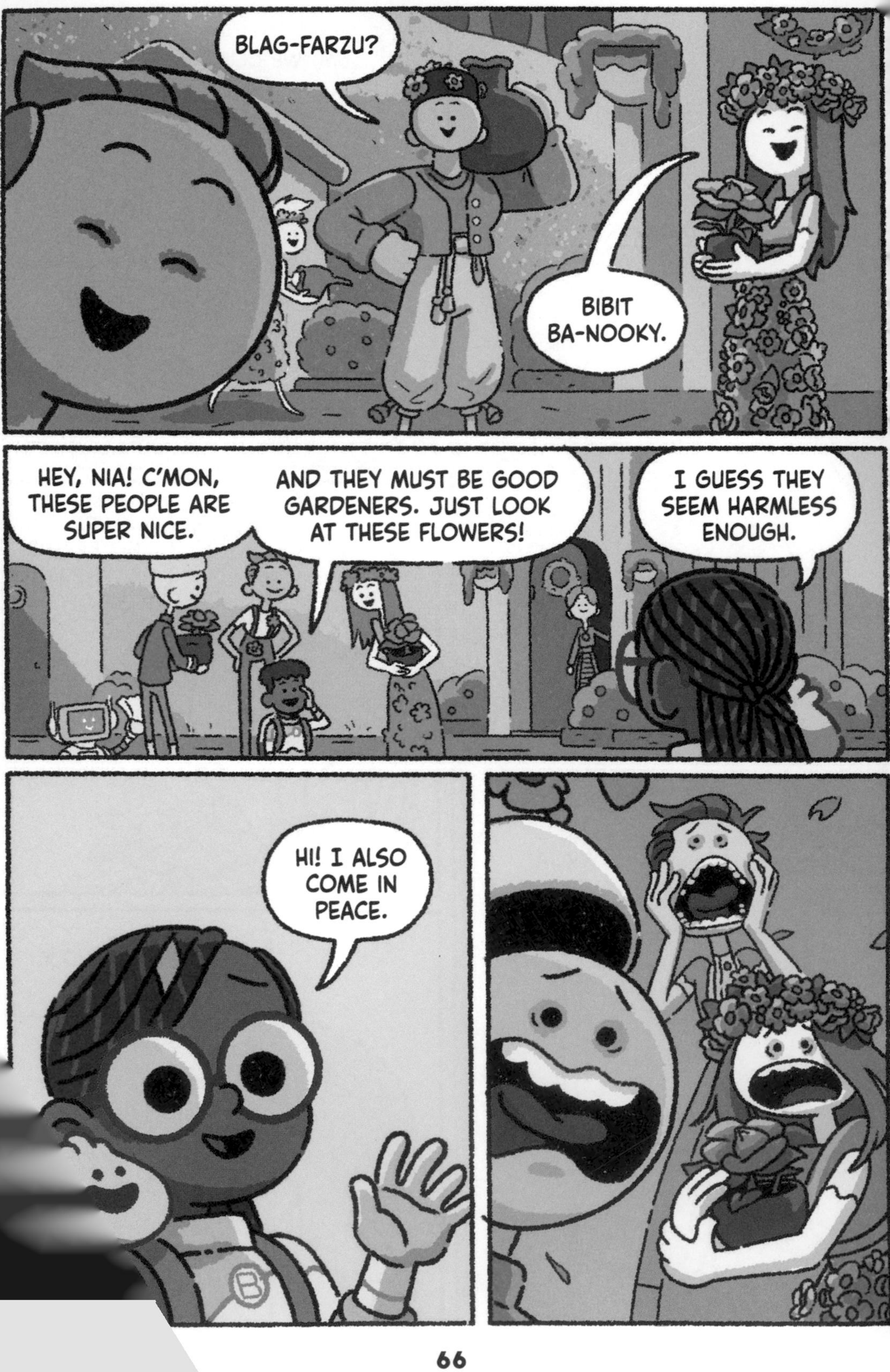
BLAG-FARZU?
BIBIT BA-NOOKY.
HEY, NIA! C'MON, THESE PEOPLE ARE SUPER NICE.
AND THEY MUST BE GOOD GARDENERS. JUST LOOK AT THESE FLOWERS!
I GUESS THEY SEEM HARMLESS ENOUGH.
HI! I ALSO COME IN PEACE.

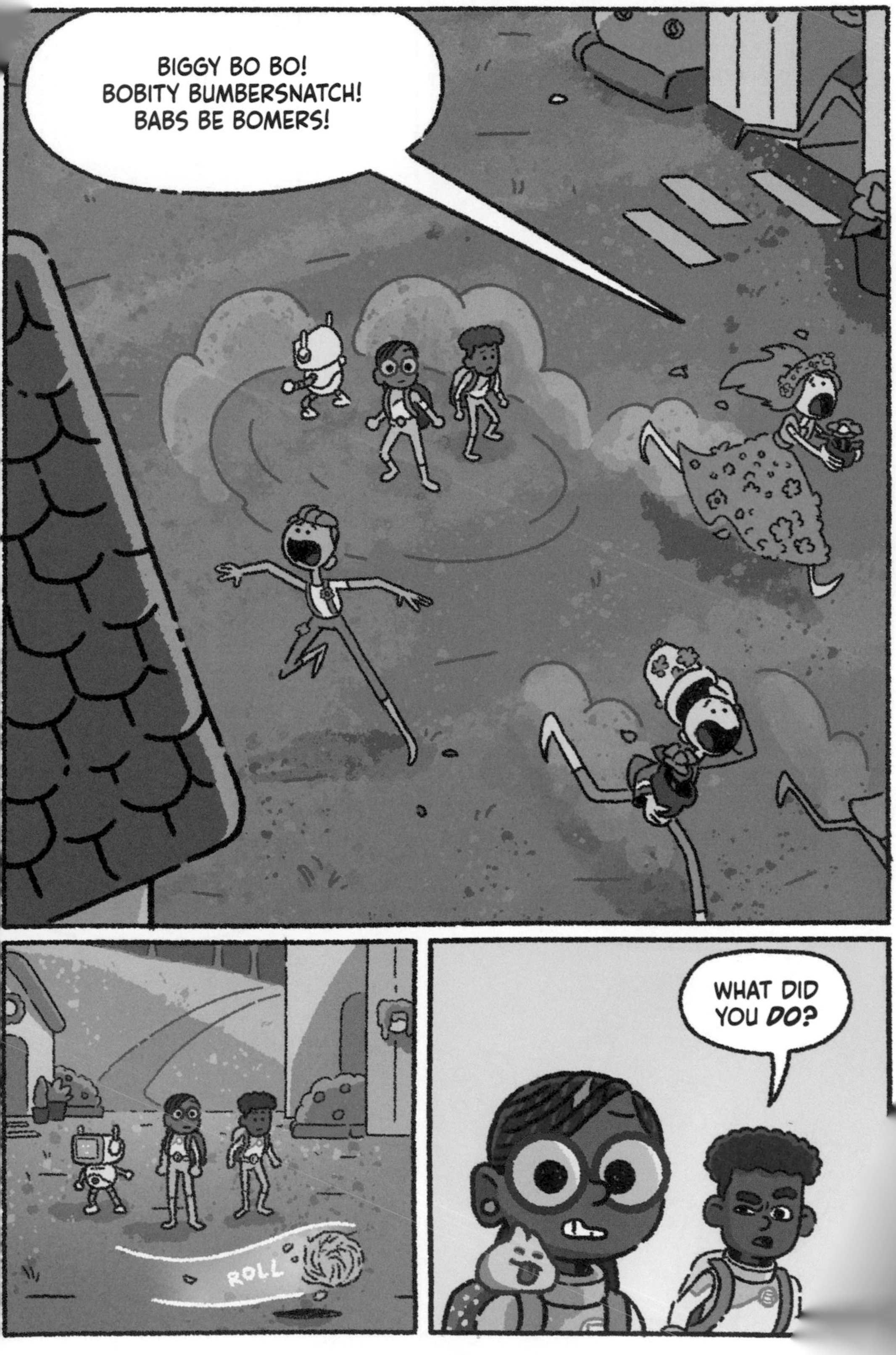
BIGGY BO BO!
BOBITY BUMBERSNATCH!
BABS BE BOMERS!
ROLL
WHAT DID YOU *DO?*

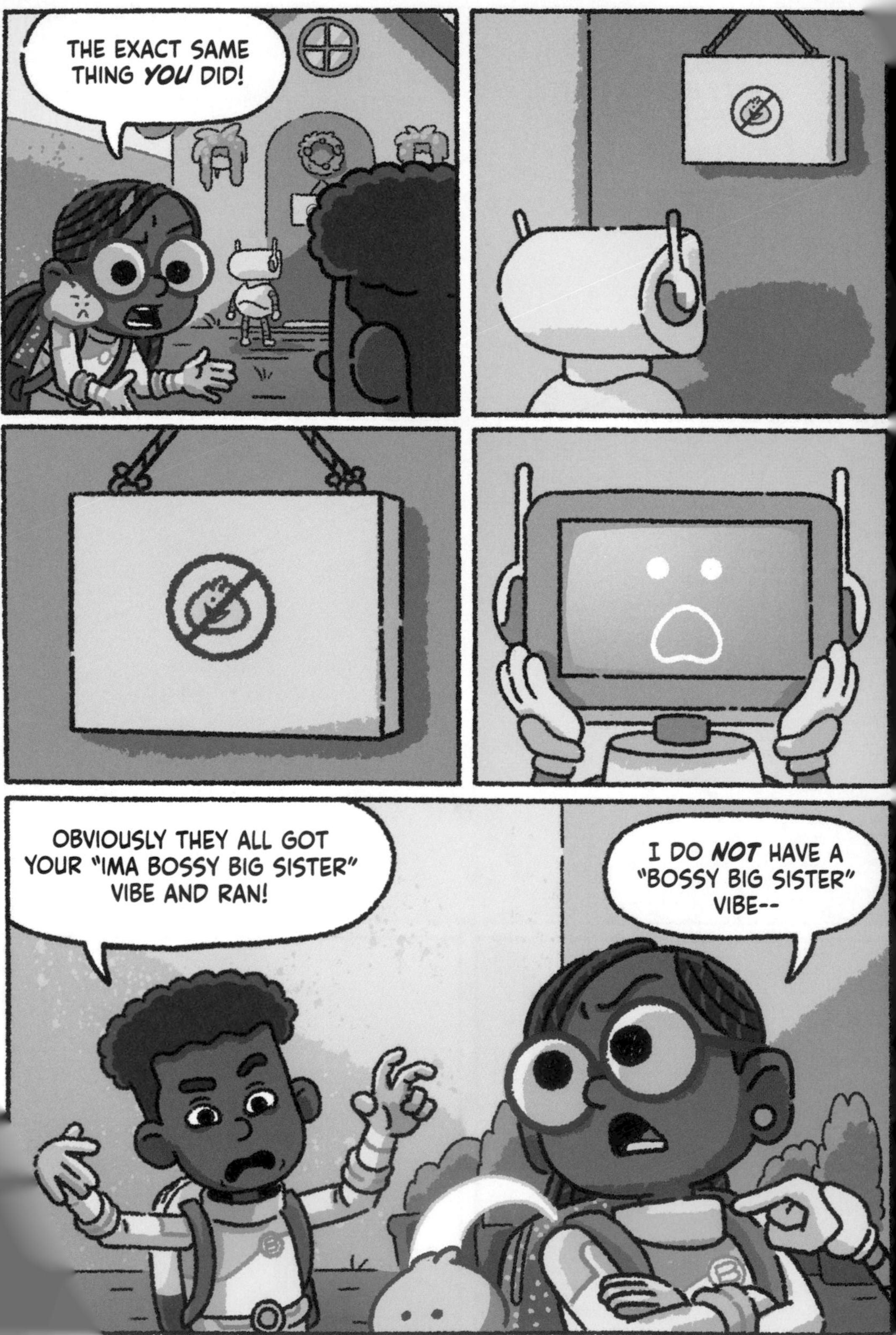
THE EXACT SAME THING *YOU* DID!
OBVIOUSLY THEY ALL GOT YOUR "IMA BOSSY BIG SISTER" VIBE AND RAN!
I DO *NOT* HAVE A "BOSSY BIG SISTER" VIBE--

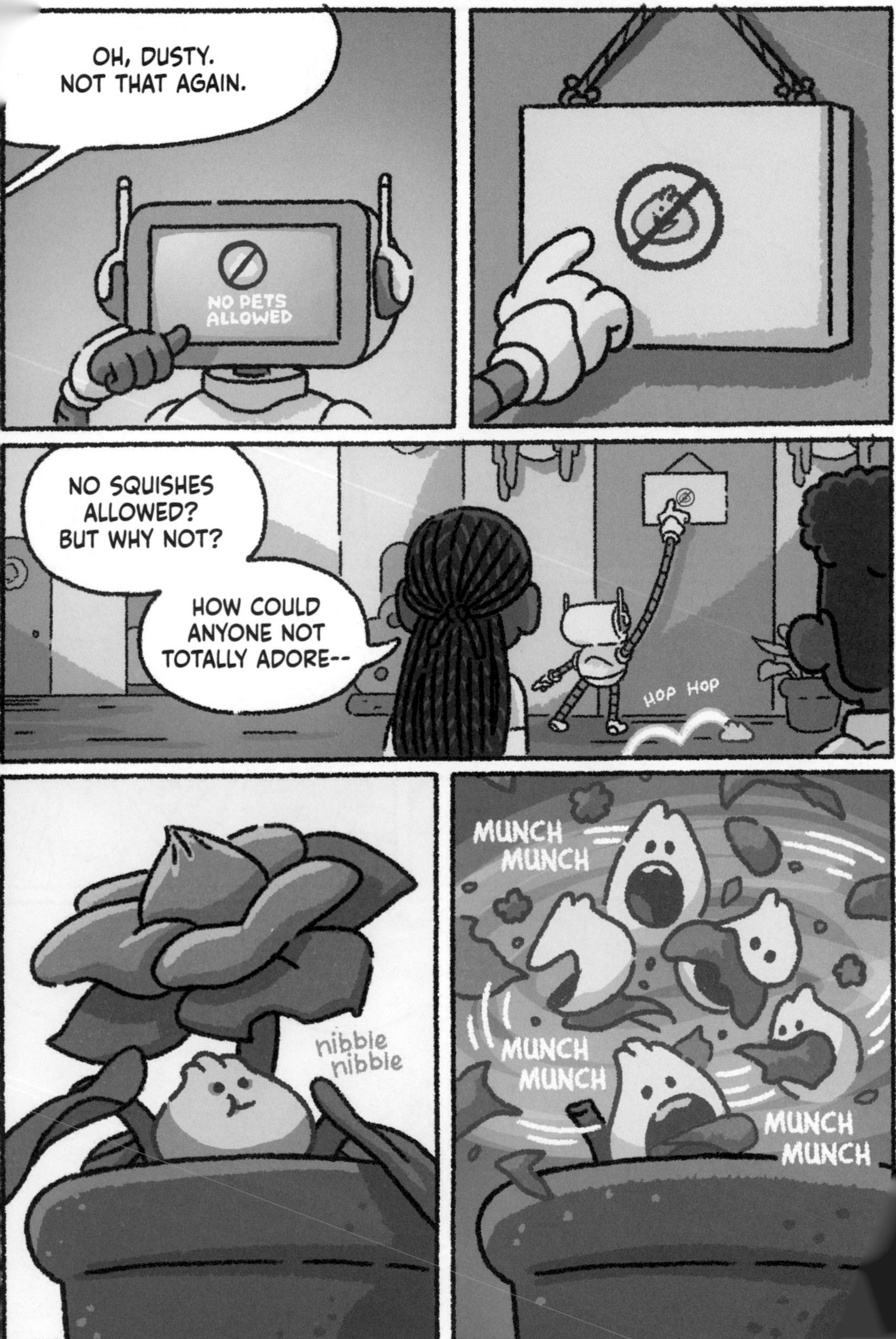
OH, DUSTY.
NOT THAT AGAIN.
NO PETS
ALLOWED
NO SQUISHES
ALLOWED?
BUT WHY NOT?
HOW COULD
ANYONE NOT
TOTALLY ADORE--
HOP HOP
nibble
nibble
MUNCH
MUNCH
MUNCH
MUNCH
MUNCH
MUNCH

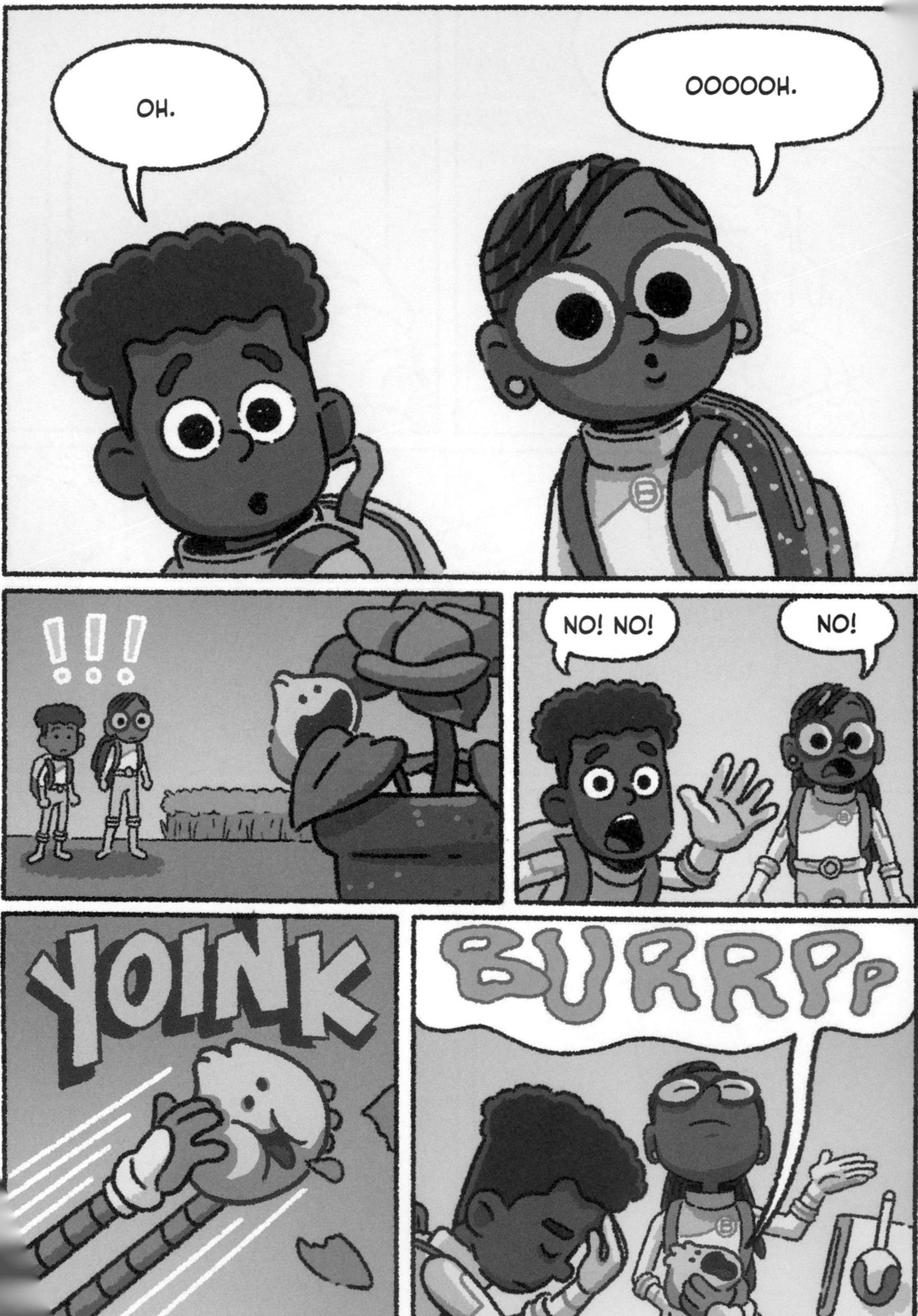
OH.
OOOOOH.
!!!
NO! NO!
NO!
YOINK
BURRPP

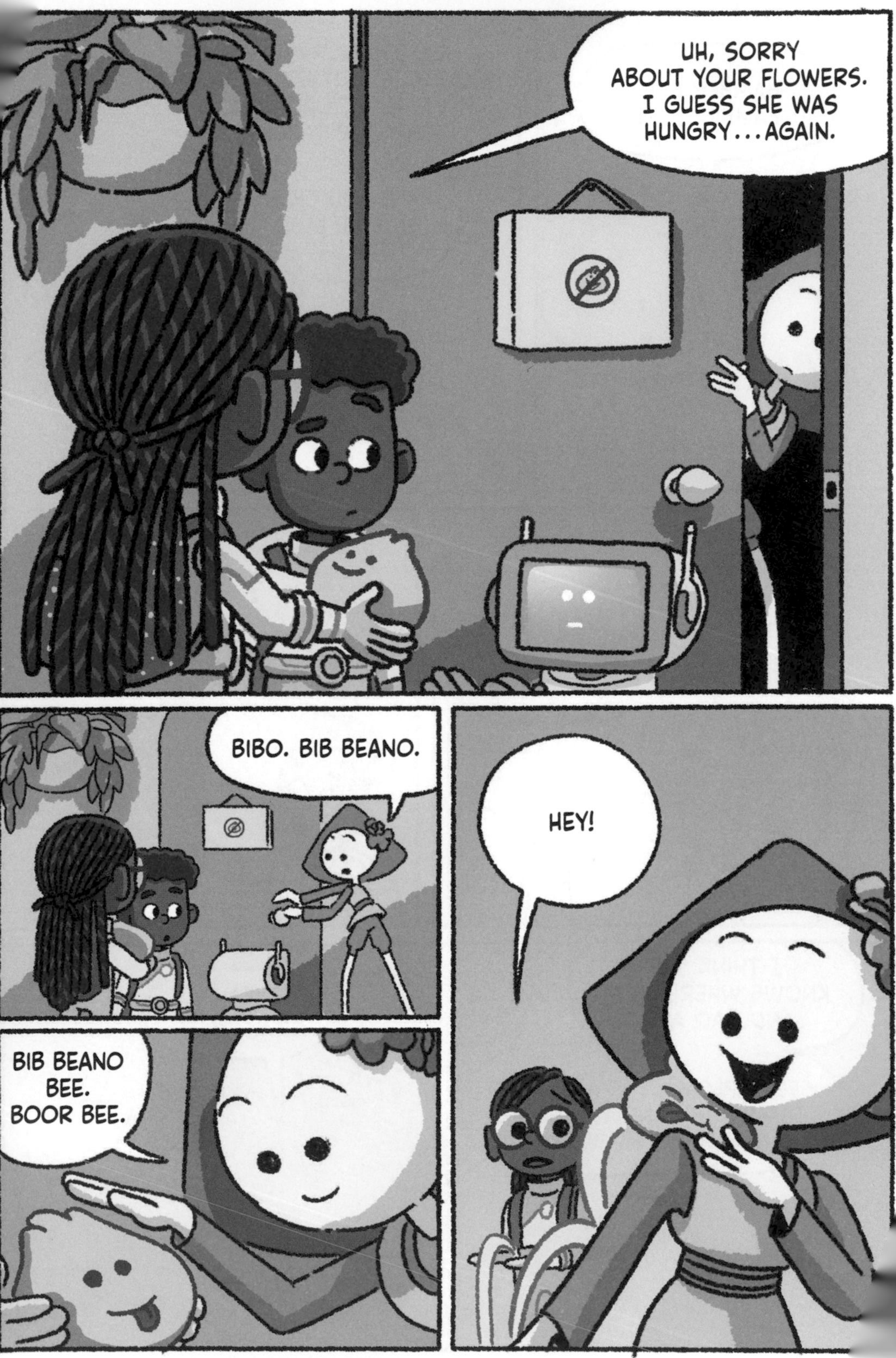
UH, SORRY ABOUT YOUR FLOWERS. I GUESS SHE WAS HUNGRY...AGAIN.
BIBO. BIB BEANO.
BIB BEANO BEE. BOOR BEE.
HEY!

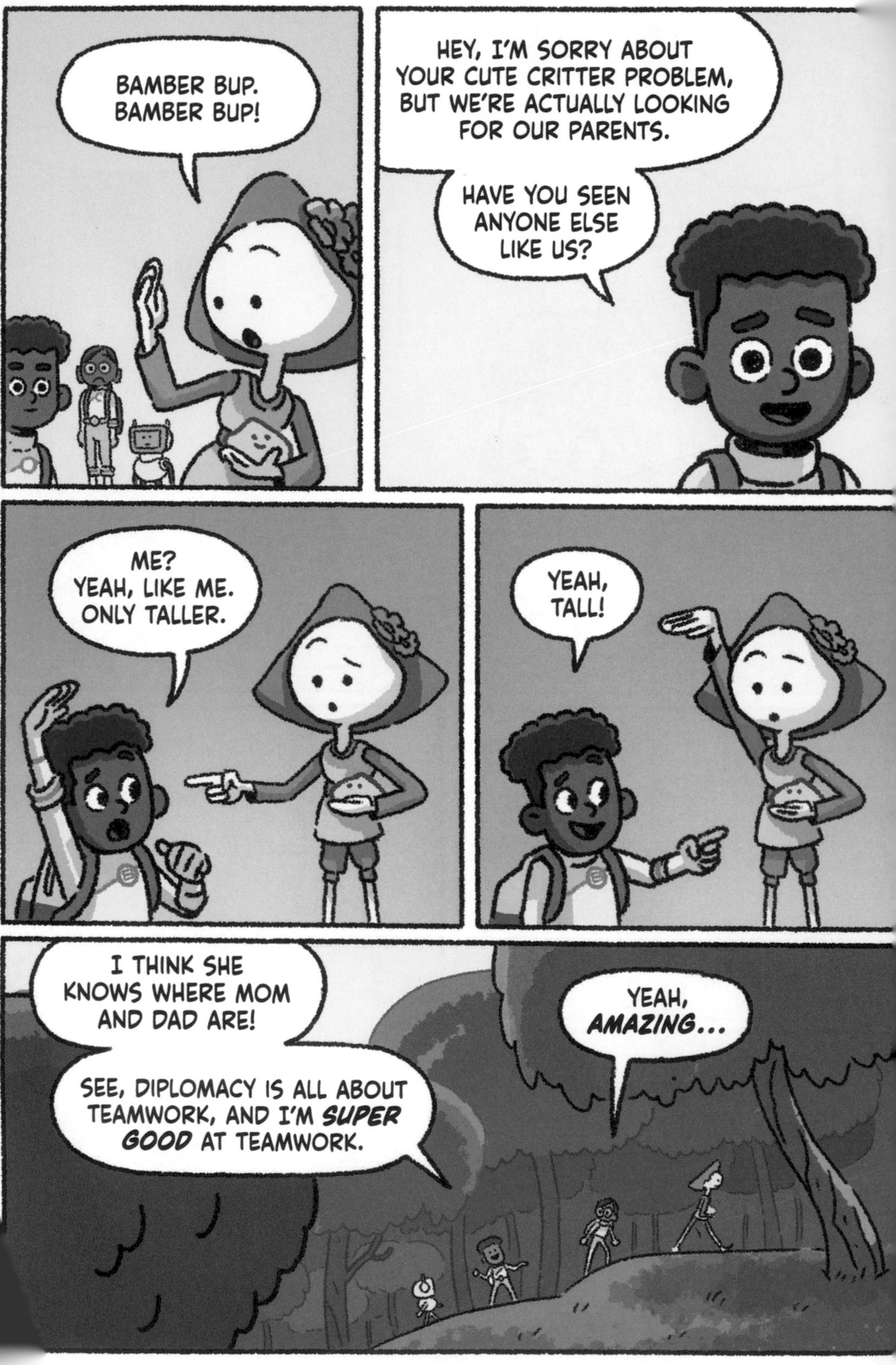
BAMBER BUP. BAMBER BUP!
HEY, I'M SORRY ABOUT YOUR CUTE CRITTER PROBLEM, BUT WE'RE ACTUALLY LOOKING FOR OUR PARENTS.
HAVE YOU SEEN ANYONE ELSE LIKE US?
ME? YEAH, LIKE ME. ONLY TALLER.
YEAH, TALL!
I THINK SHE KNOWS WHERE MOM AND DAD ARE!
SEE, DIPLOMACY IS ALL ABOUT TEAMWORK, AND I'M ***SUPER GOOD*** AT TEAMWORK.
YEAH, ***AMAZING...***

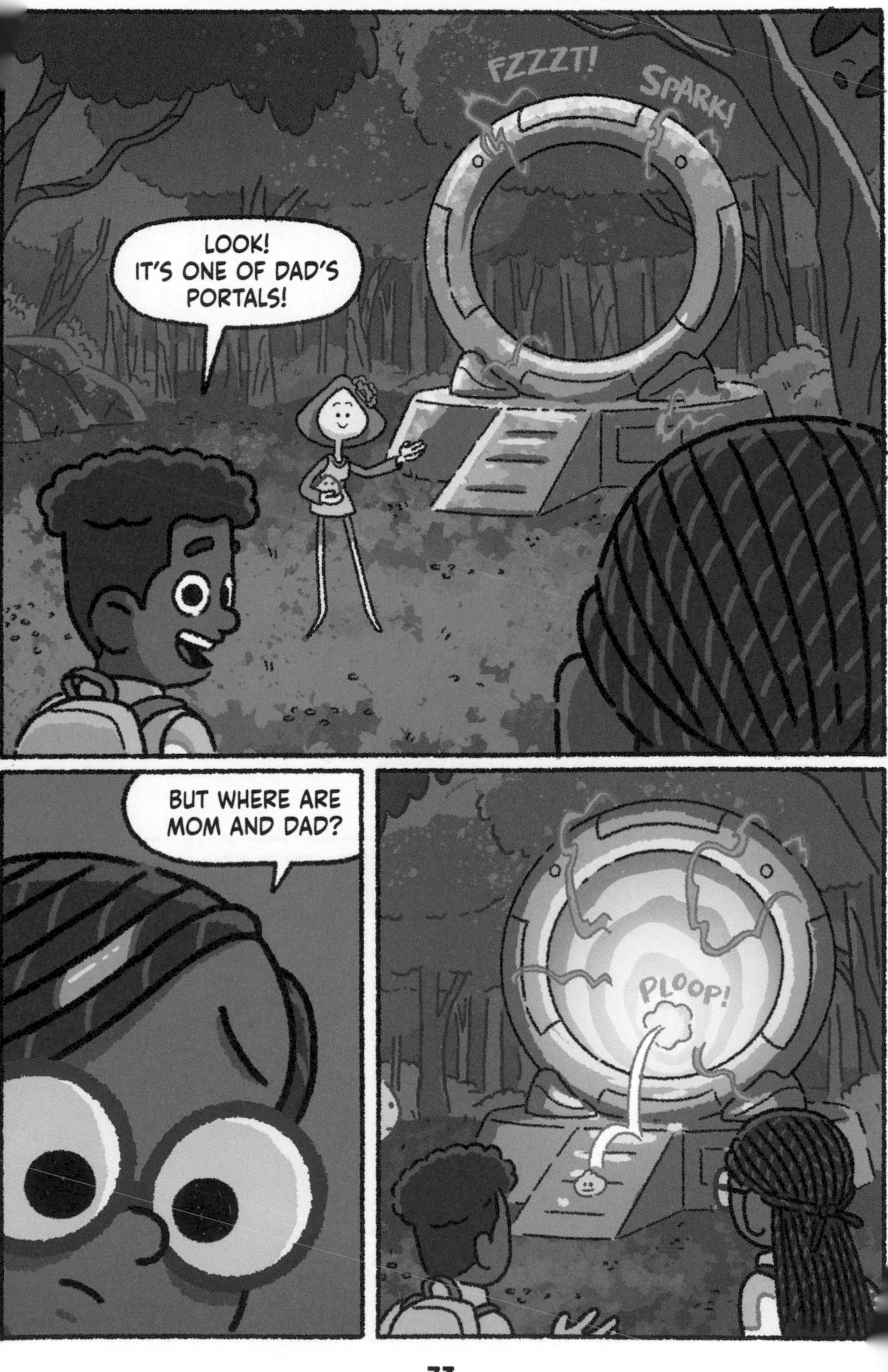
FZZZT!
SPARK!
LOOK! IT'S ONE OF DAD'S PORTALS!
BUT WHERE ARE MOM AND DAD?
PLOOP!

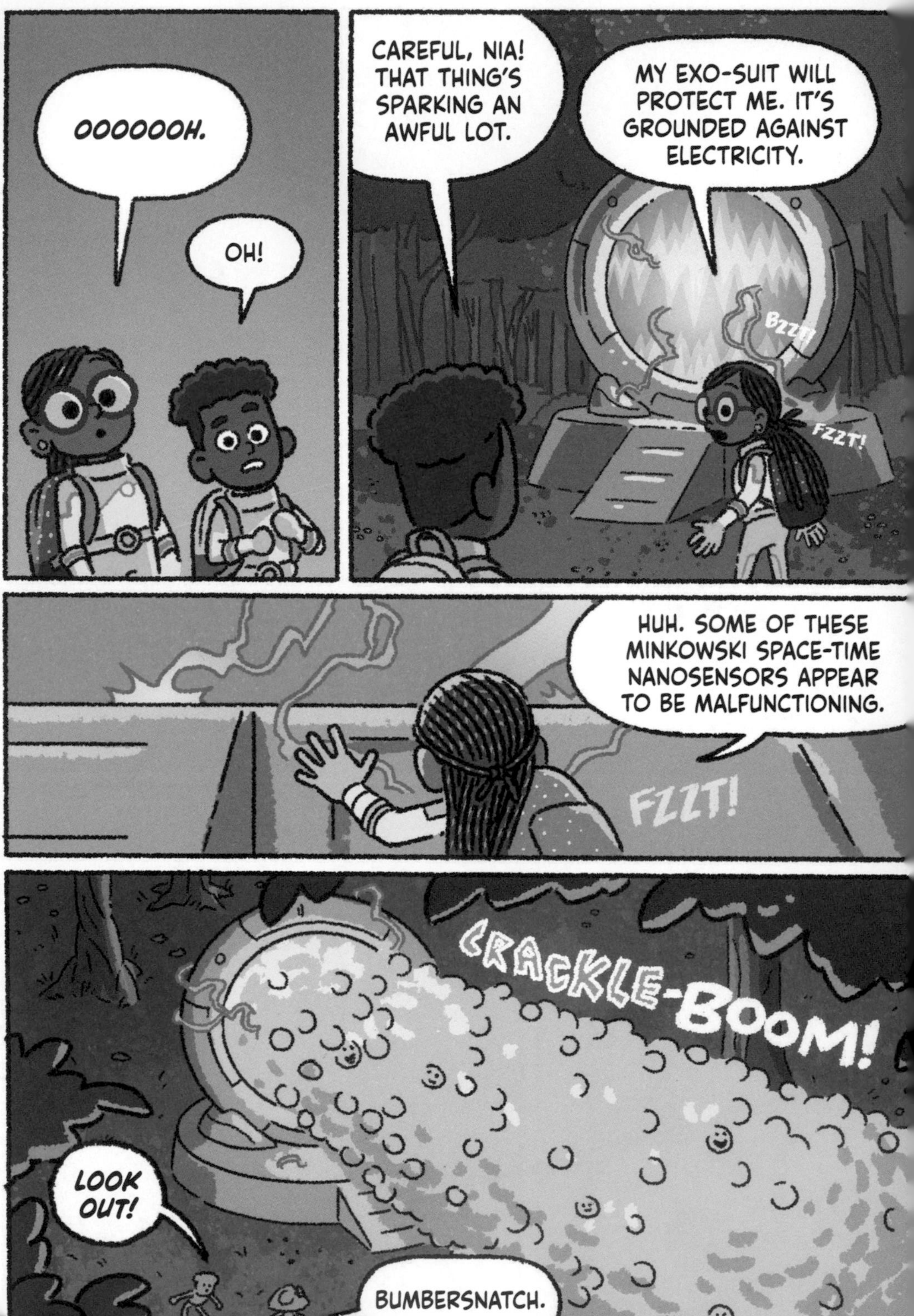
OOOOOOH.
OH!
CAREFUL, NIA! THAT THING'S SPARKING AN AWFUL LOT.
MY EXO-SUIT WILL PROTECT ME. IT'S GROUNDED AGAINST ELECTRICITY.
BZZT!
FZZT!
HUH. SOME OF THESE MINKOWSKI SPACE-TIME NANOSENSORS APPEAR TO BE MALFUNCTIONING.
FZZT!
CRACKLE-BOOM!
LOOK OUT!
BUMBERSNATCH.

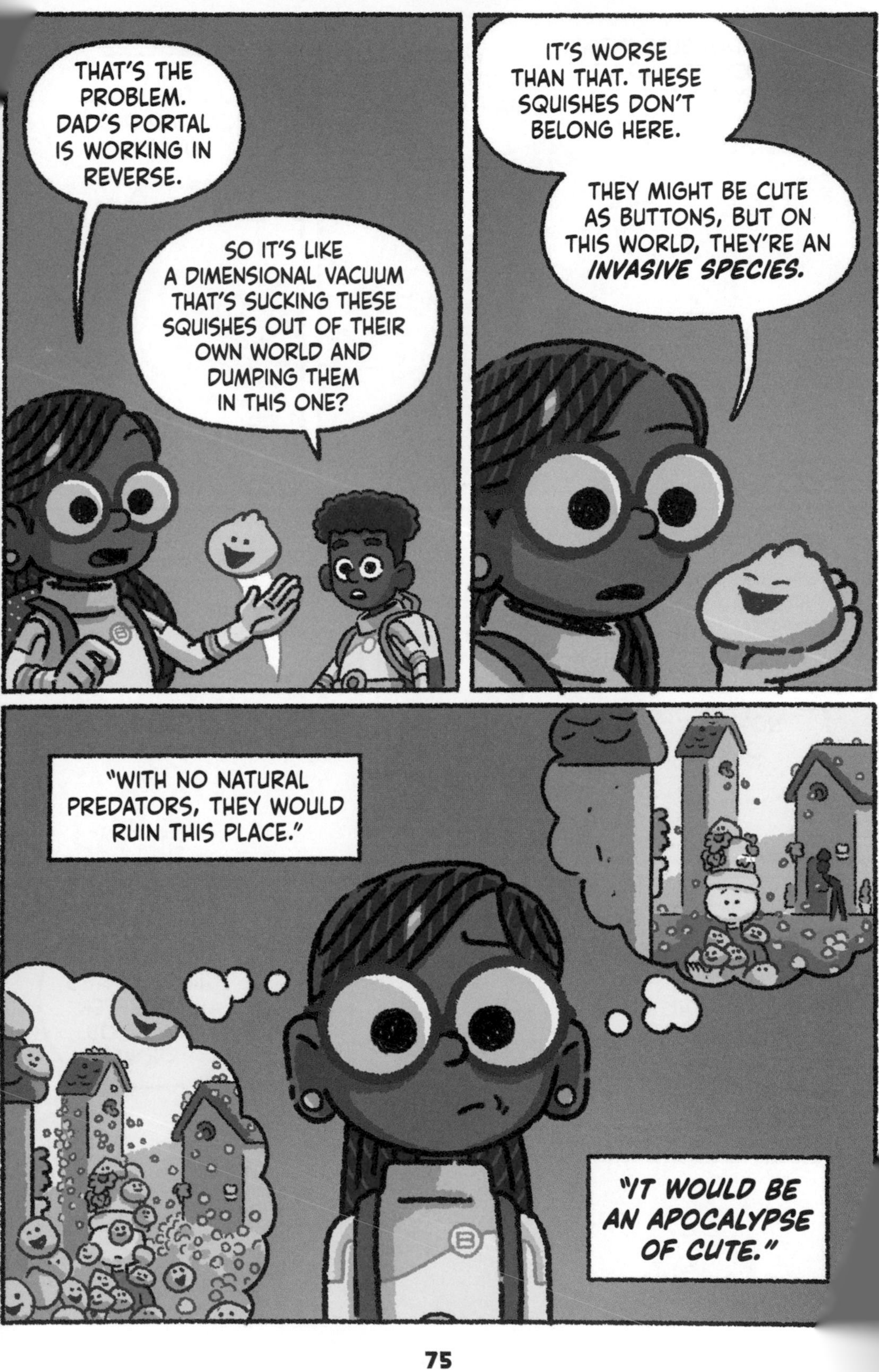
THAT'S THE PROBLEM. DAD'S PORTAL IS WORKING IN REVERSE.
SO IT'S LIKE A DIMENSIONAL VACUUM THAT'S SUCKING THESE SQUISHES OUT OF THEIR OWN WORLD AND DUMPING THEM IN THIS ONE?
IT'S WORSE THAN THAT. THESE SQUISHES DON'T BELONG HERE.
THEY MIGHT BE CUTE AS BUTTONS, BUT ON THIS WORLD, THEY'RE AN *INVASIVE SPECIES.*
"WITH NO NATURAL PREDATORS, THEY WOULD RUIN THIS PLACE."
*"IT WOULD BE AN APOCALYPSE OF CUTE."*

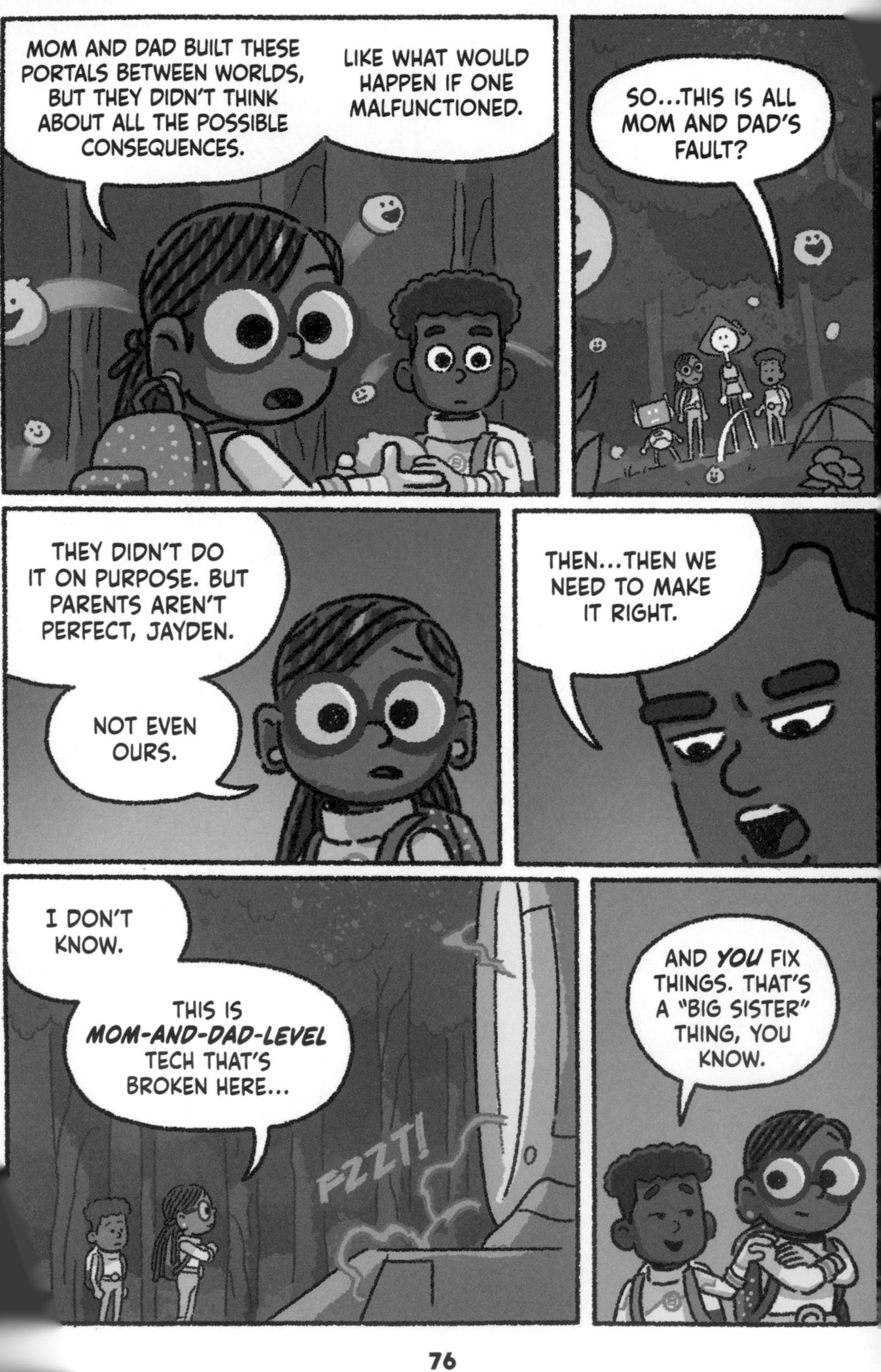
MOM AND DAD BUILT THESE PORTALS BETWEEN WORLDS, BUT THEY DIDN'T THINK ABOUT ALL THE POSSIBLE CONSEQUENCES.
LIKE WHAT WOULD HAPPEN IF ONE MALFUNCTIONED.
SO...THIS IS ALL MOM AND DAD'S FAULT?
THEY DIDN'T DO IT ON PURPOSE. BUT PARENTS AREN'T PERFECT, JAYDEN.
NOT EVEN OURS.
THEN...THEN WE NEED TO MAKE IT RIGHT.
I DON'T KNOW.
THIS IS ***MOM-AND-DAD-LEVEL*** TECH THAT'S BROKEN HERE...
FZZT!
AND ***YOU*** FIX THINGS. THAT'S A "BIG SISTER" THING, YOU KNOW.

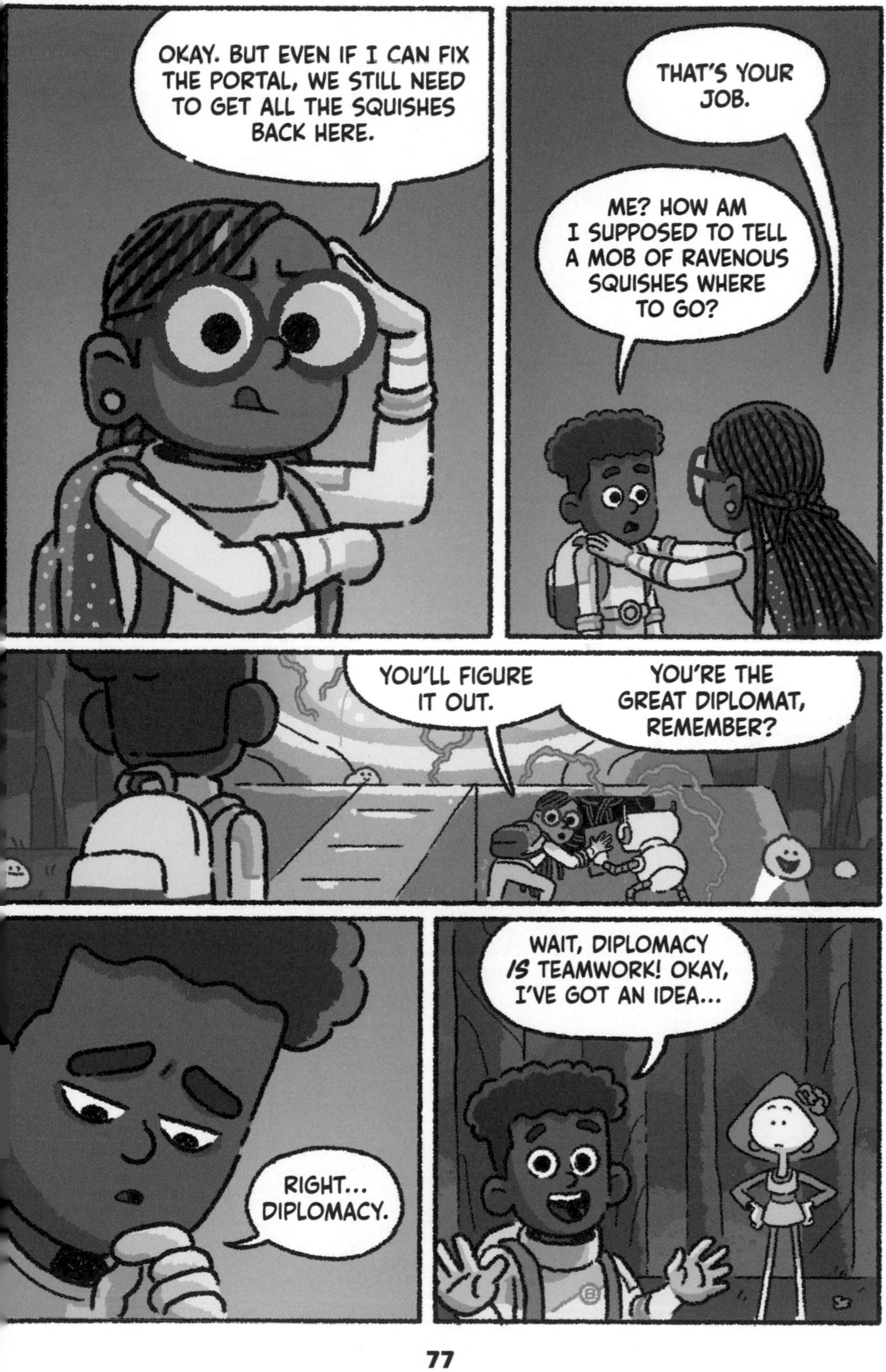
OKAY. BUT EVEN IF I CAN FIX THE PORTAL, WE STILL NEED TO GET ALL THE SQUISHES BACK HERE.
THAT'S YOUR JOB.
ME? HOW AM I SUPPOSED TO TELL A MOB OF RAVENOUS SQUISHES WHERE TO GO?
YOU'LL FIGURE IT OUT.
YOU'RE THE GREAT DIPLOMAT, REMEMBER?
RIGHT... DIPLOMACY.
WAIT, DIPLOMACY *IS* TEAMWORK! OKAY, I'VE GOT AN IDEA...

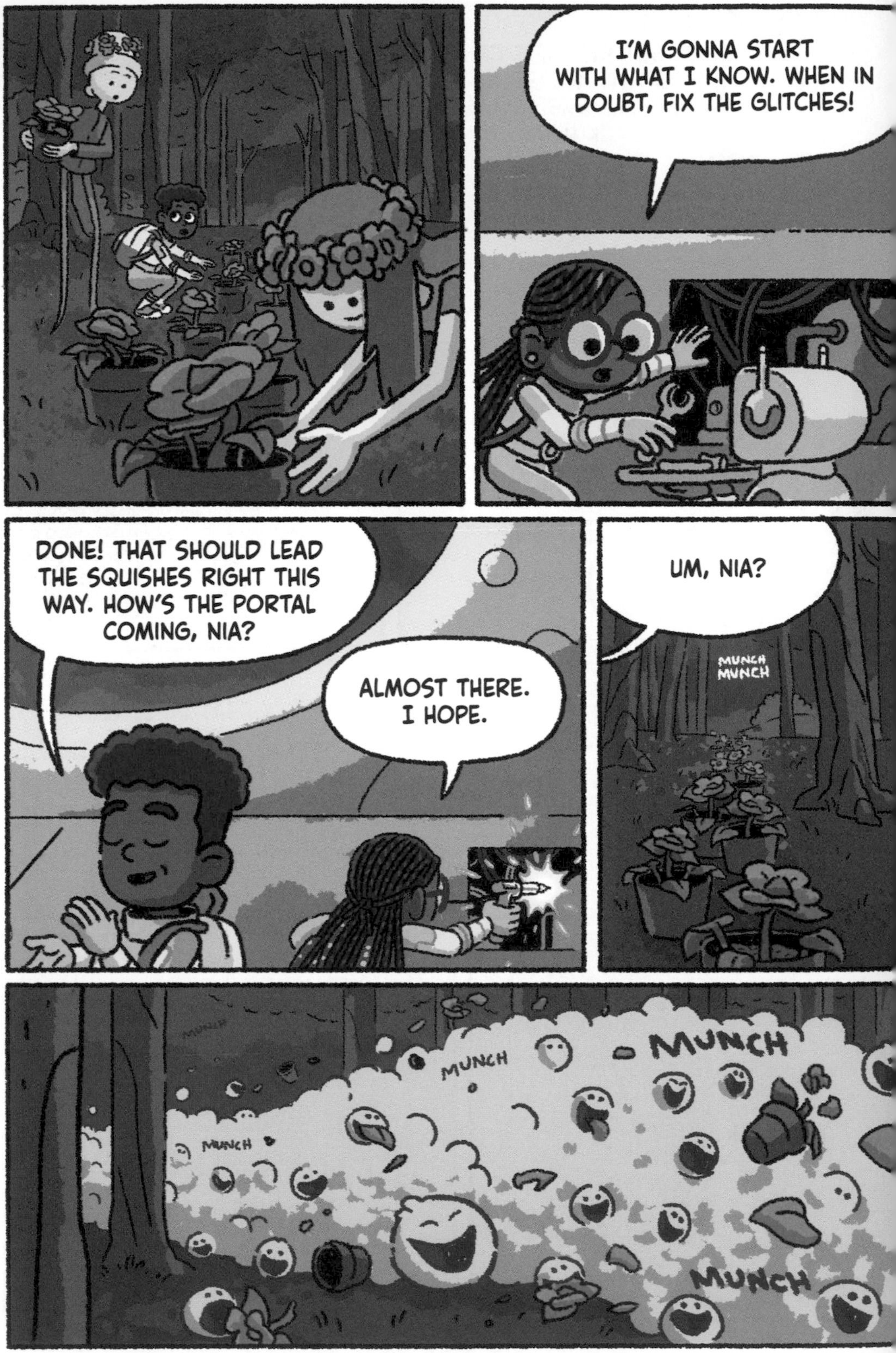
I'M GONNA START WITH WHAT I KNOW. WHEN IN DOUBT, FIX THE GLITCHES!
DONE! THAT SHOULD LEAD THE SQUISHES RIGHT THIS WAY. HOW'S THE PORTAL COMING, NIA?
ALMOST THERE. I HOPE.
UM, NIA?
MUNCH MUNCH
MUNCH
MUNCH
MUNCH
MUNCH
MUNCH

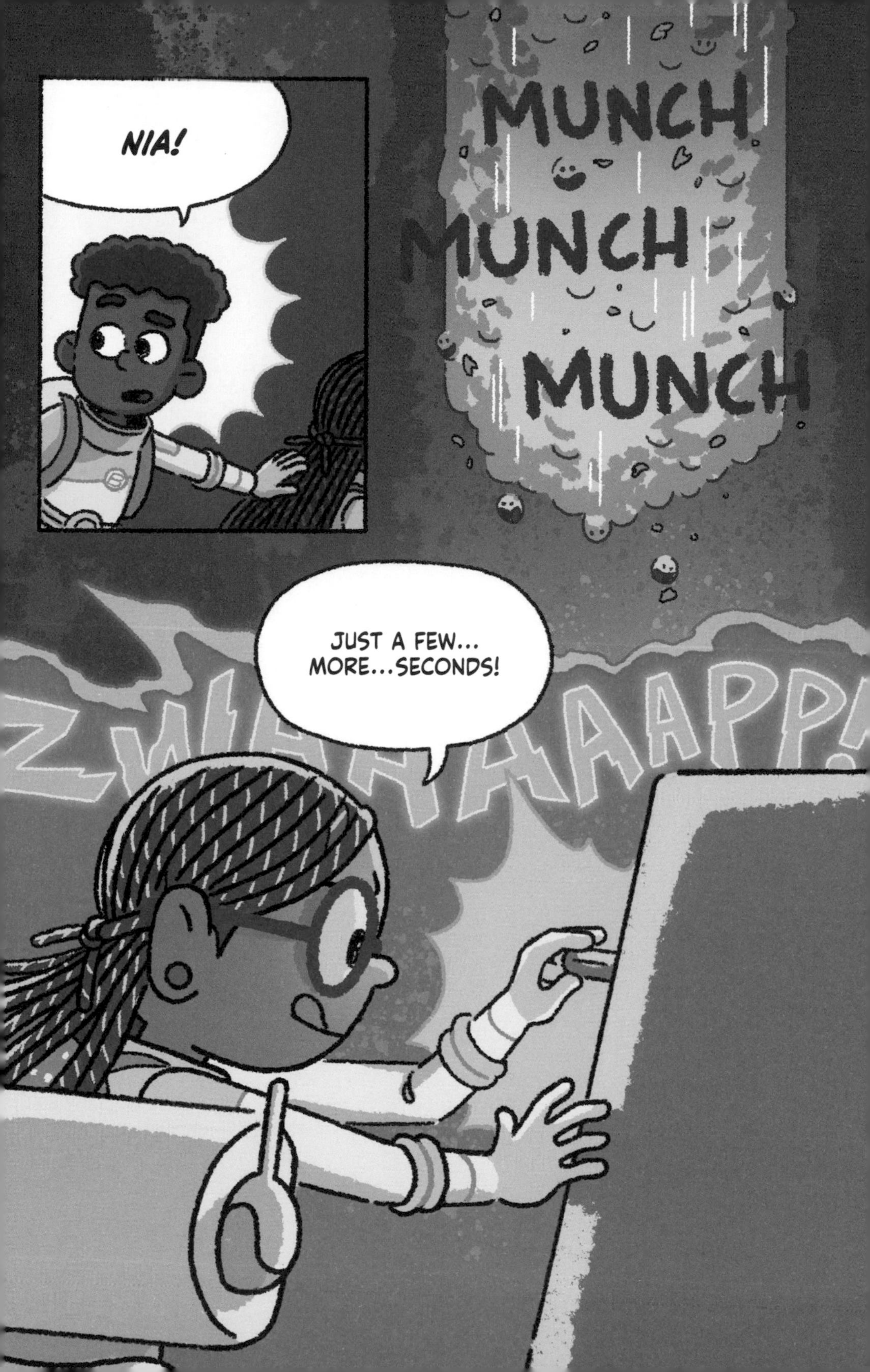
NIA!
MUNCH
MUNCH
MUNCH
JUST A FEW... MORE...SECONDS!
ZWAAAAAPP!

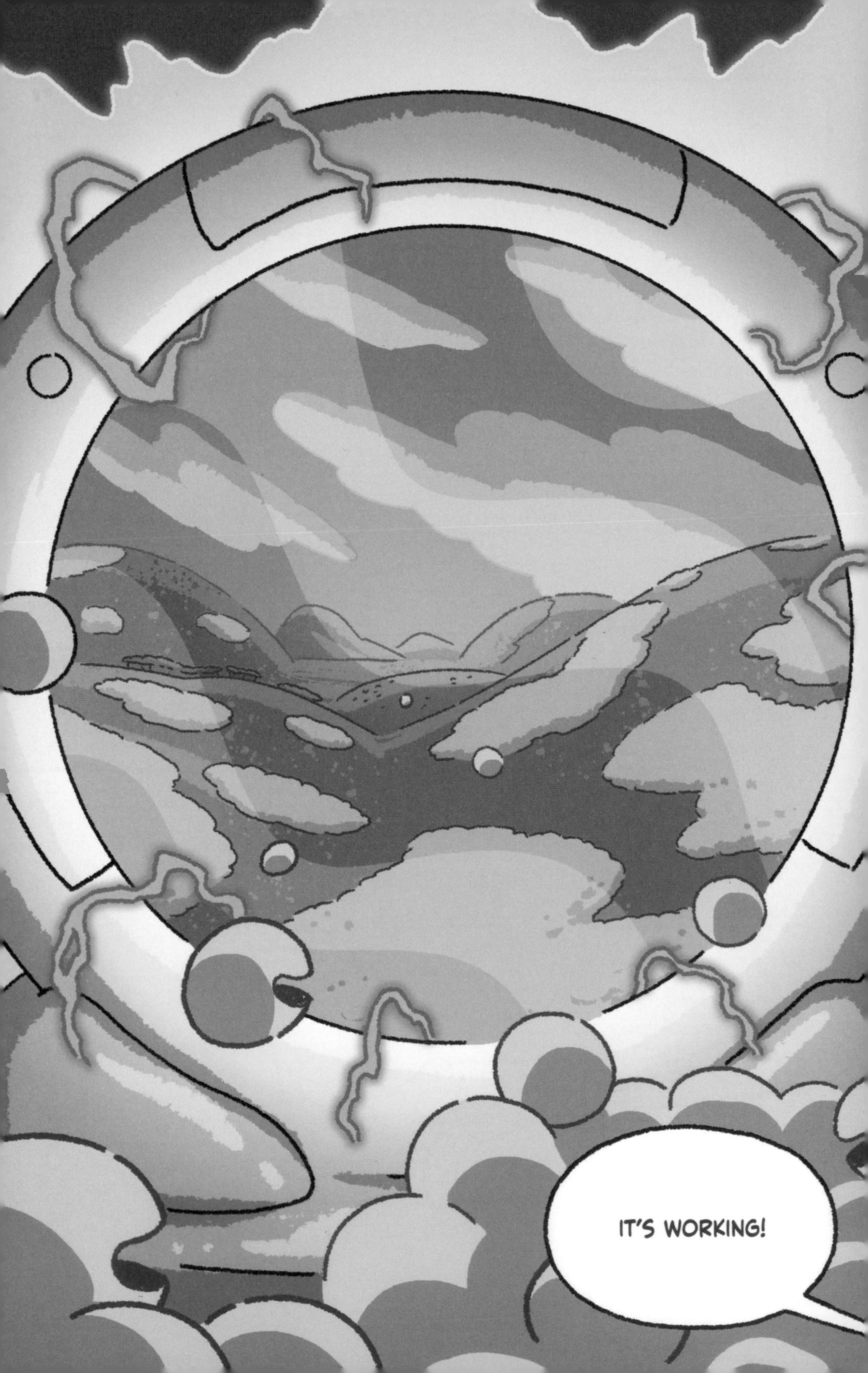
IT'S WORKING!

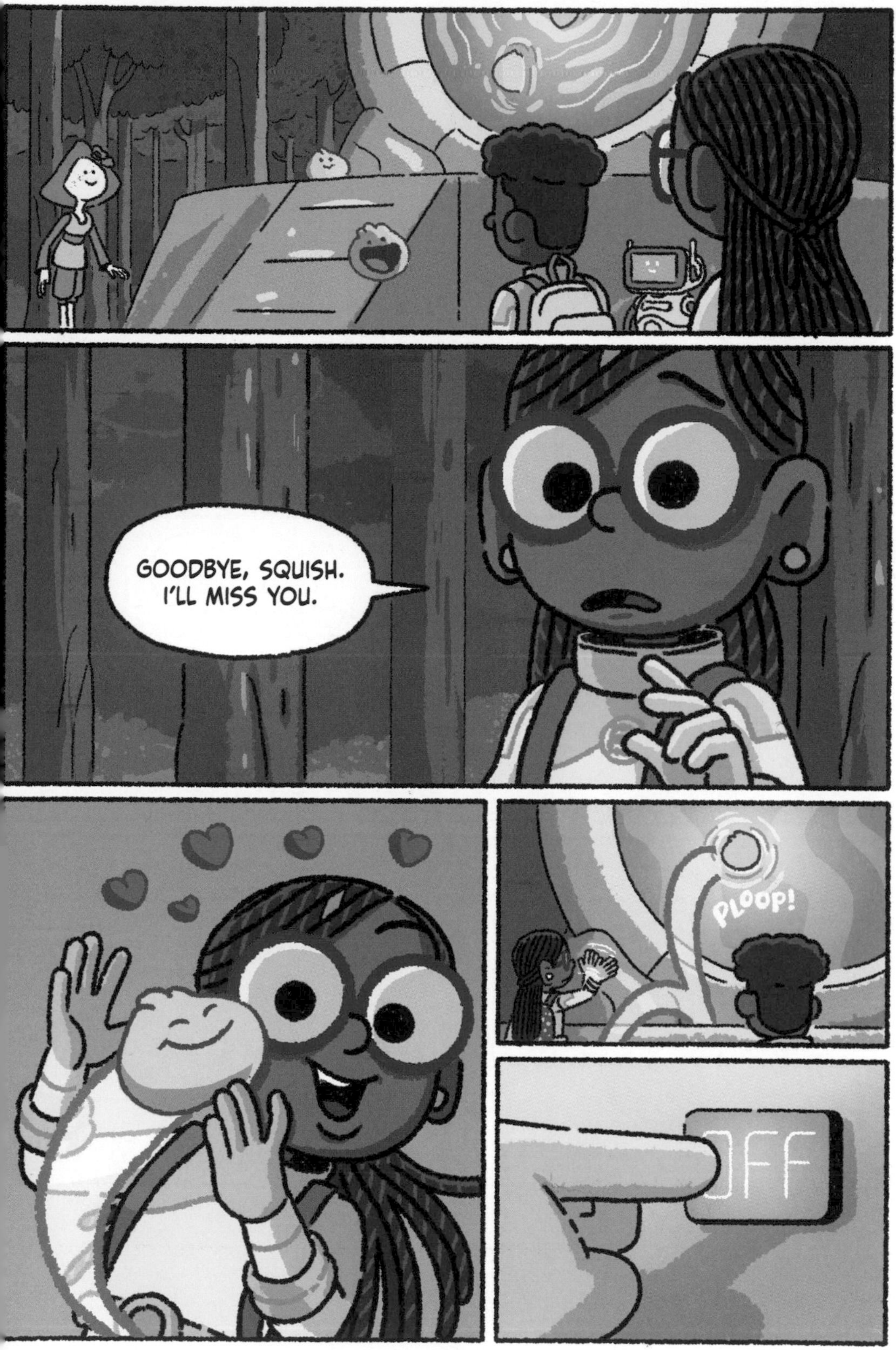
GOODBYE, SQUISH. I'LL MISS YOU.
PLOOP!
OFF

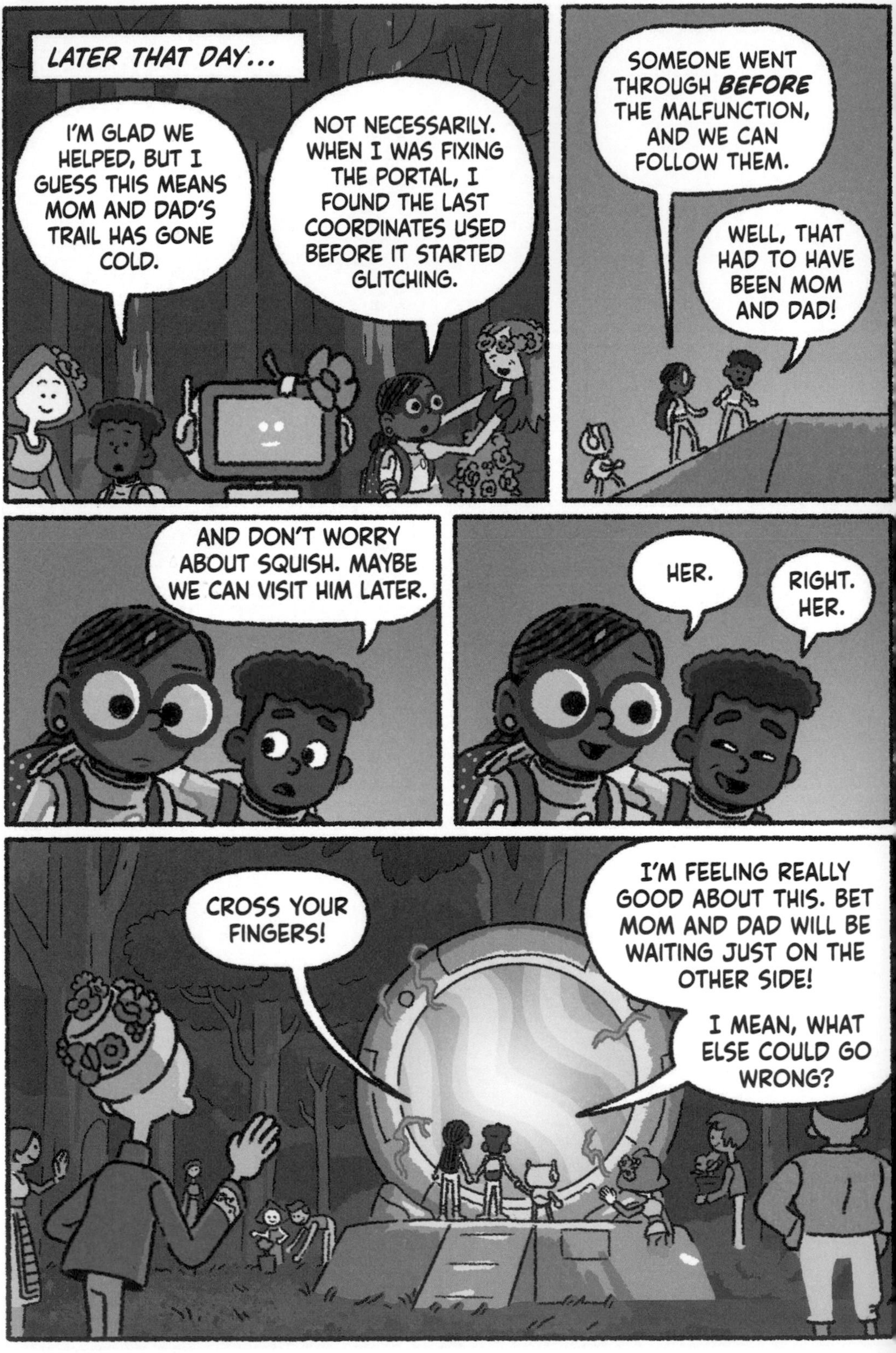
LATER THAT DAY...
I'M GLAD WE HELPED, BUT I GUESS THIS MEANS MOM AND DAD'S TRAIL HAS GONE COLD.
NOT NECESSARILY. WHEN I WAS FIXING THE PORTAL, I FOUND THE LAST COORDINATES USED BEFORE IT STARTED GLITCHING.
SOMEONE WENT THROUGH *BEFORE* THE MALFUNCTION, AND WE CAN FOLLOW THEM.
WELL, THAT HAD TO HAVE BEEN MOM AND DAD!
AND DON'T WORRY ABOUT SQUISH. MAYBE WE CAN VISIT HIM LATER.
HER.
RIGHT. HER.
CROSS YOUR FINGERS!
I'M FEELING REALLY GOOD ABOUT THIS. BET MOM AND DAD WILL BE WAITING JUST ON THE OTHER SIDE!
I MEAN, WHAT ELSE COULD GO WRONG?

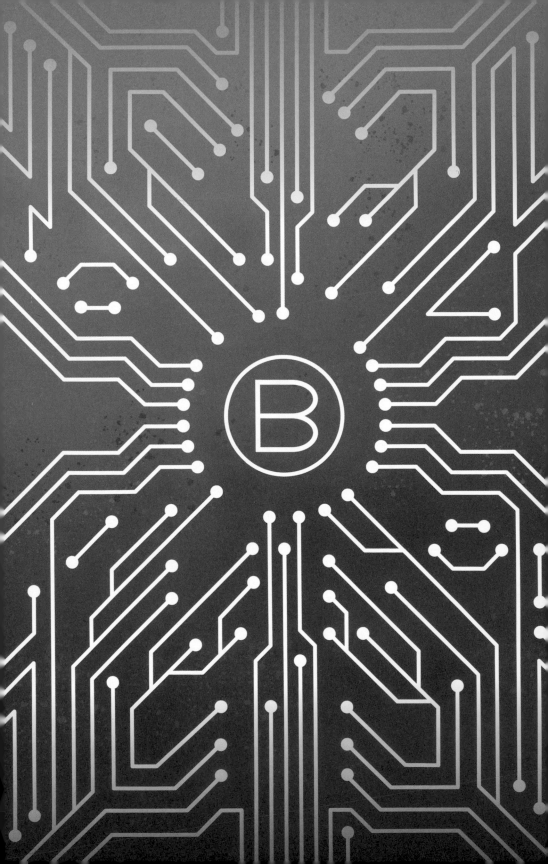

# CHAPTER 4
# IT'S DANGER TIME...TIME!

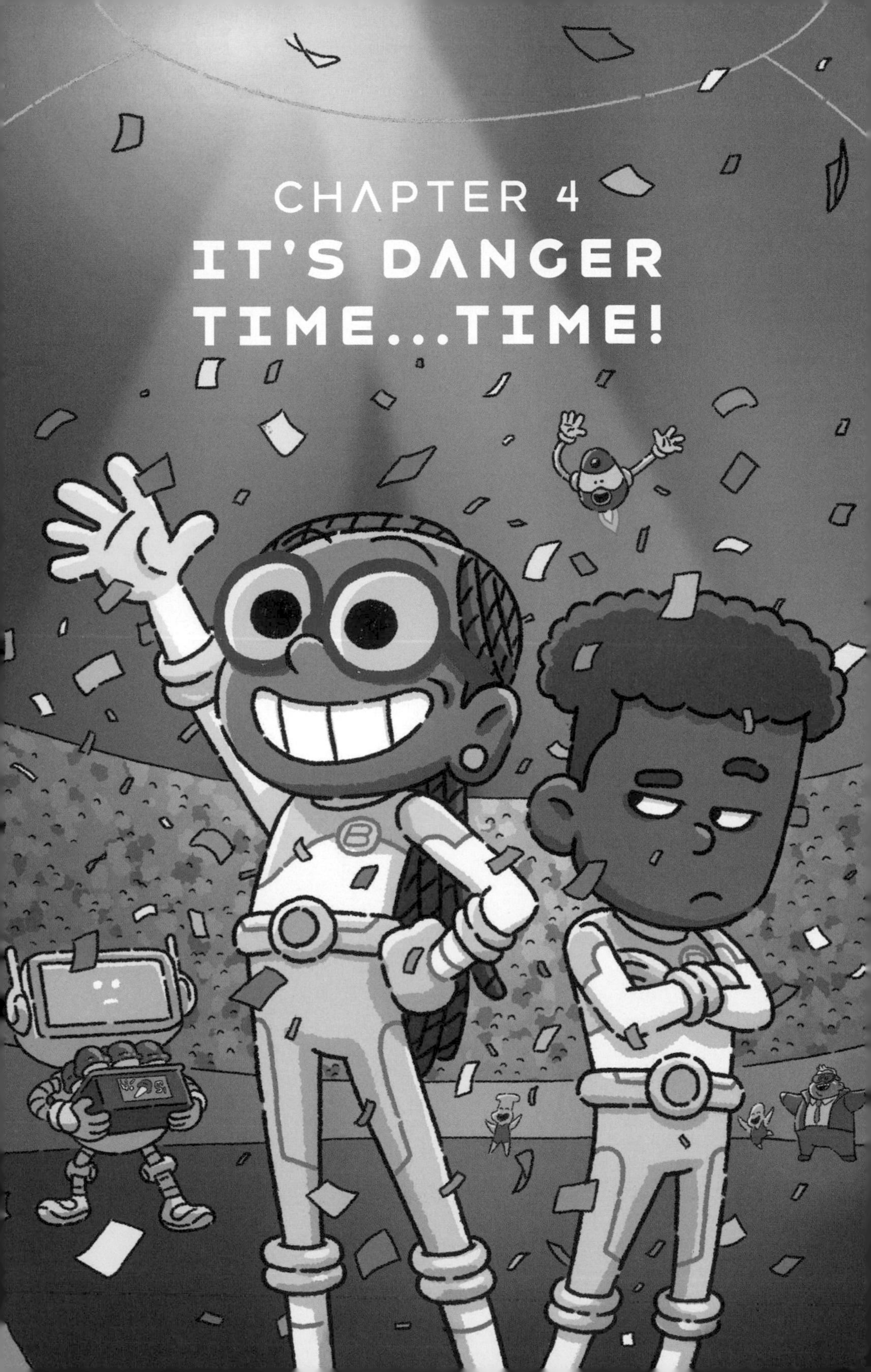

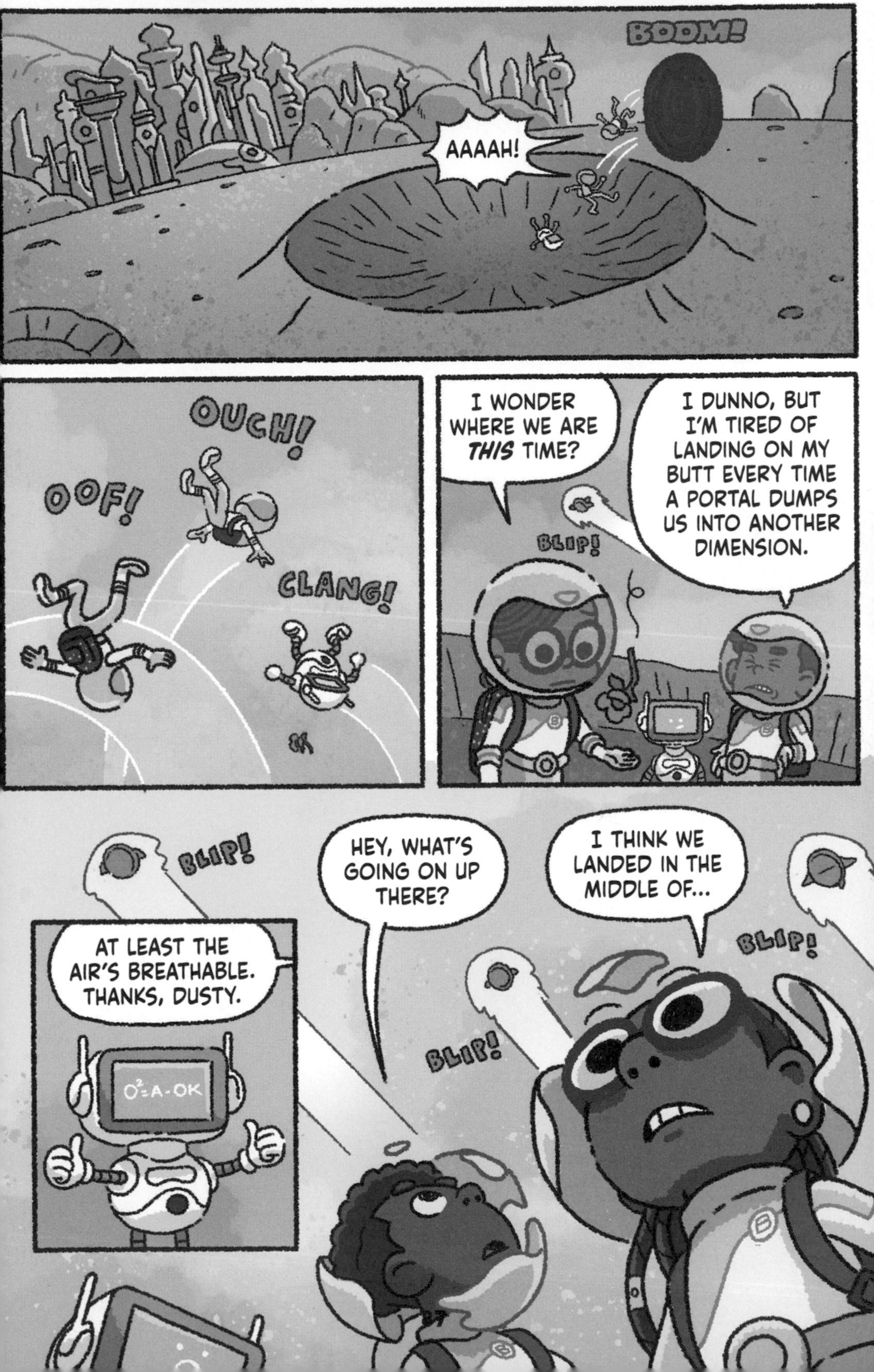
BOOM!
AAAAH!
OUCH!
OOF!
CLANG!
I WONDER WHERE WE ARE *THIS* TIME?
BLIP!
I DUNNO, BUT I'M TIRED OF LANDING ON MY BUTT EVERY TIME A PORTAL DUMPS US INTO ANOTHER DIMENSION.
BLIP!
HEY, WHAT'S GOING ON UP THERE?
I THINK WE LANDED IN THE MIDDLE OF...
BLIP!
AT LEAST THE AIR'S BREATHABLE. THANKS, DUSTY.
O²=A-OK
BLIP!

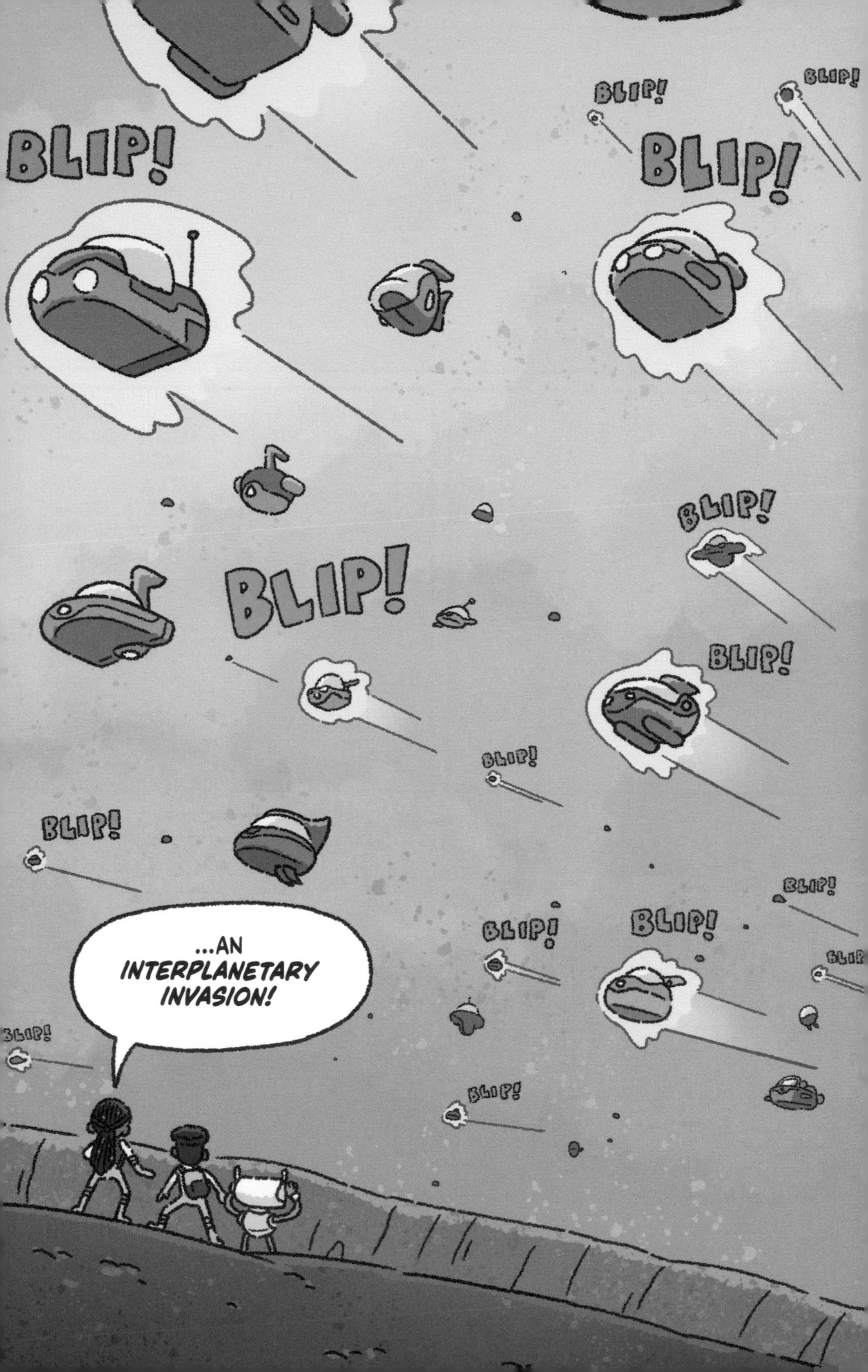
BLIP!
BLIP!
BLIP!
BLIP!
BLIP!
BLIP!
BLIP!
BLIP!
BLIP!
BLIP!
BLIP!
BLIP!
...AN INTERPLANETARY INVASION!
BLIP!
BLIP!

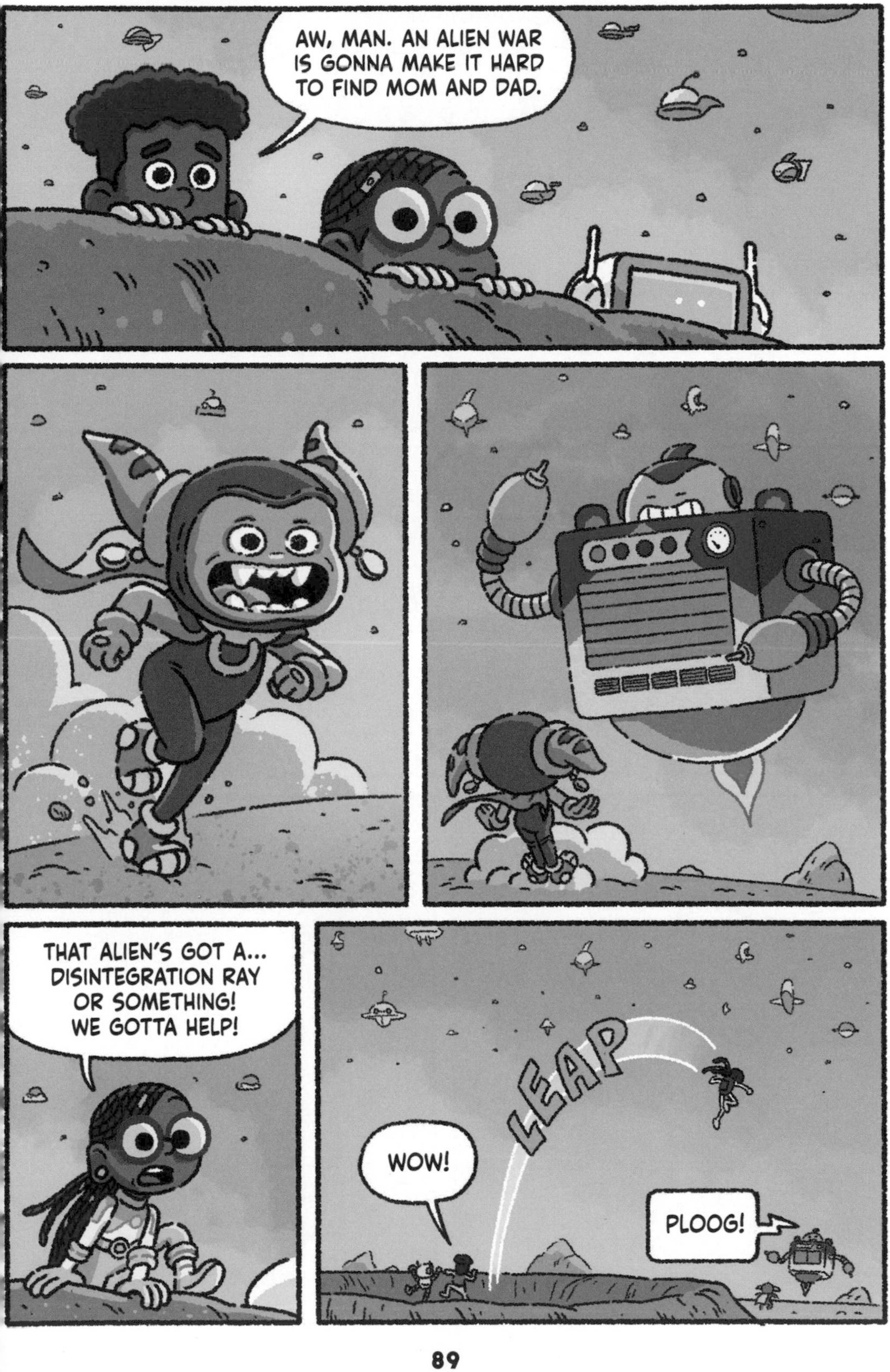
AW, MAN. AN ALIEN WAR IS GONNA MAKE IT HARD TO FIND MOM AND DAD.
THAT ALIEN'S GOT A... DISINTEGRATION RAY OR SOMETHING! WE GOTTA HELP!
LEAP
WOW!
PLOOG!

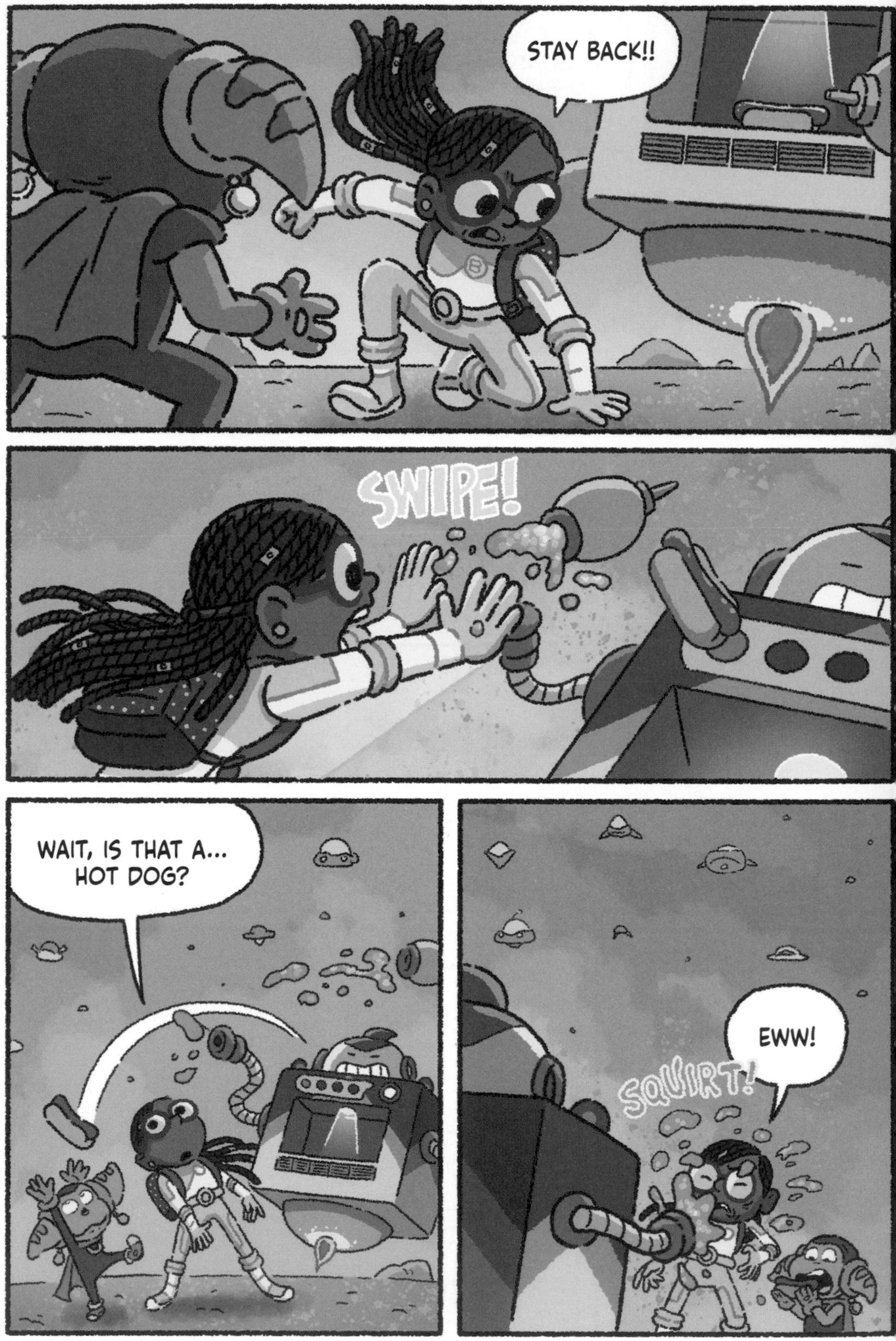
STAY BACK!!
SWIPE!
WAIT, IS THAT A... HOT DOG?
SQUIRT!
EWW!

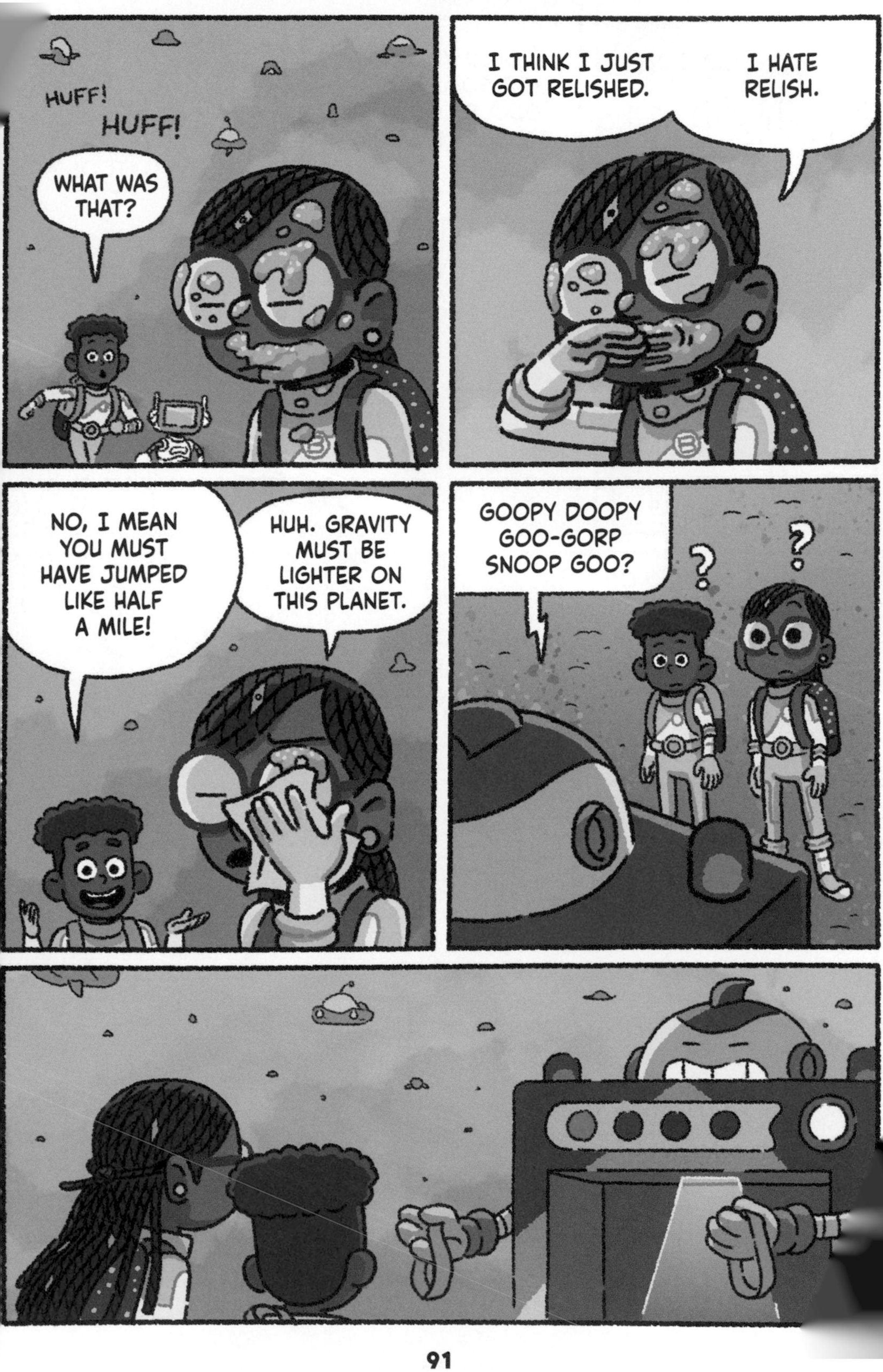
HUFF!
HUFF!
WHAT WAS THAT?
I THINK I JUST GOT RELISHED.
I HATE RELISH.
NO, I MEAN YOU MUST HAVE JUMPED LIKE HALF A MILE!
HUH. GRAVITY MUST BE LIGHTER ON THIS PLANET.
GOOPY DOOPY GOO-GORP SNOOP GOO?
?
?

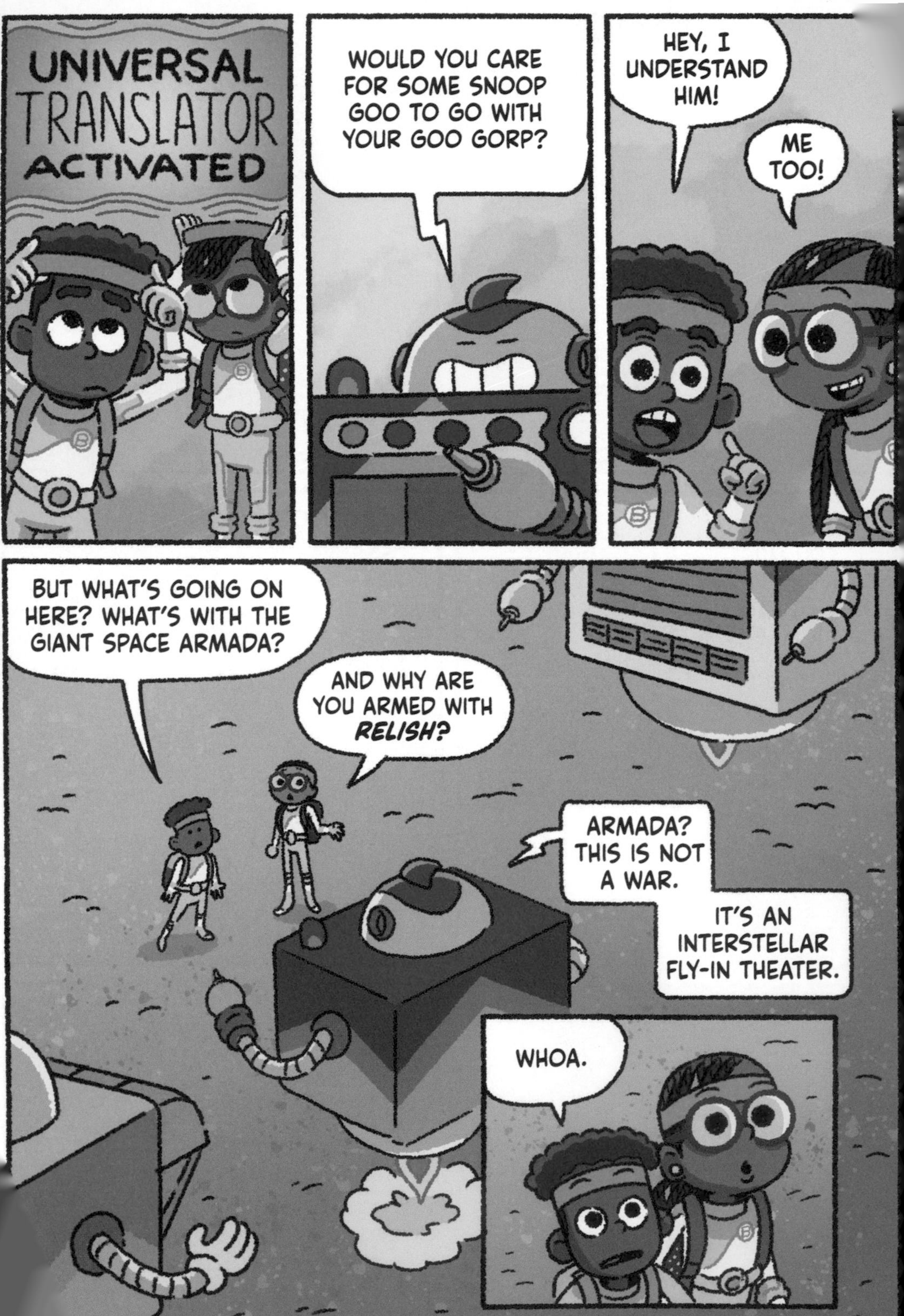
UNIVERSAL TRANSLATOR ACTIVATED
WOULD YOU CARE FOR SOME SNOOP GOO TO GO WITH YOUR GOO GORP?
HEY, I UNDERSTAND HIM!
ME TOO!
BUT WHAT'S GOING ON HERE? WHAT'S WITH THE GIANT SPACE ARMADA?
AND WHY ARE YOU ARMED WITH *RELISH?*
ARMADA? THIS IS NOT A WAR.
IT'S AN INTERSTELLAR FLY-IN THEATER.
WHOA.

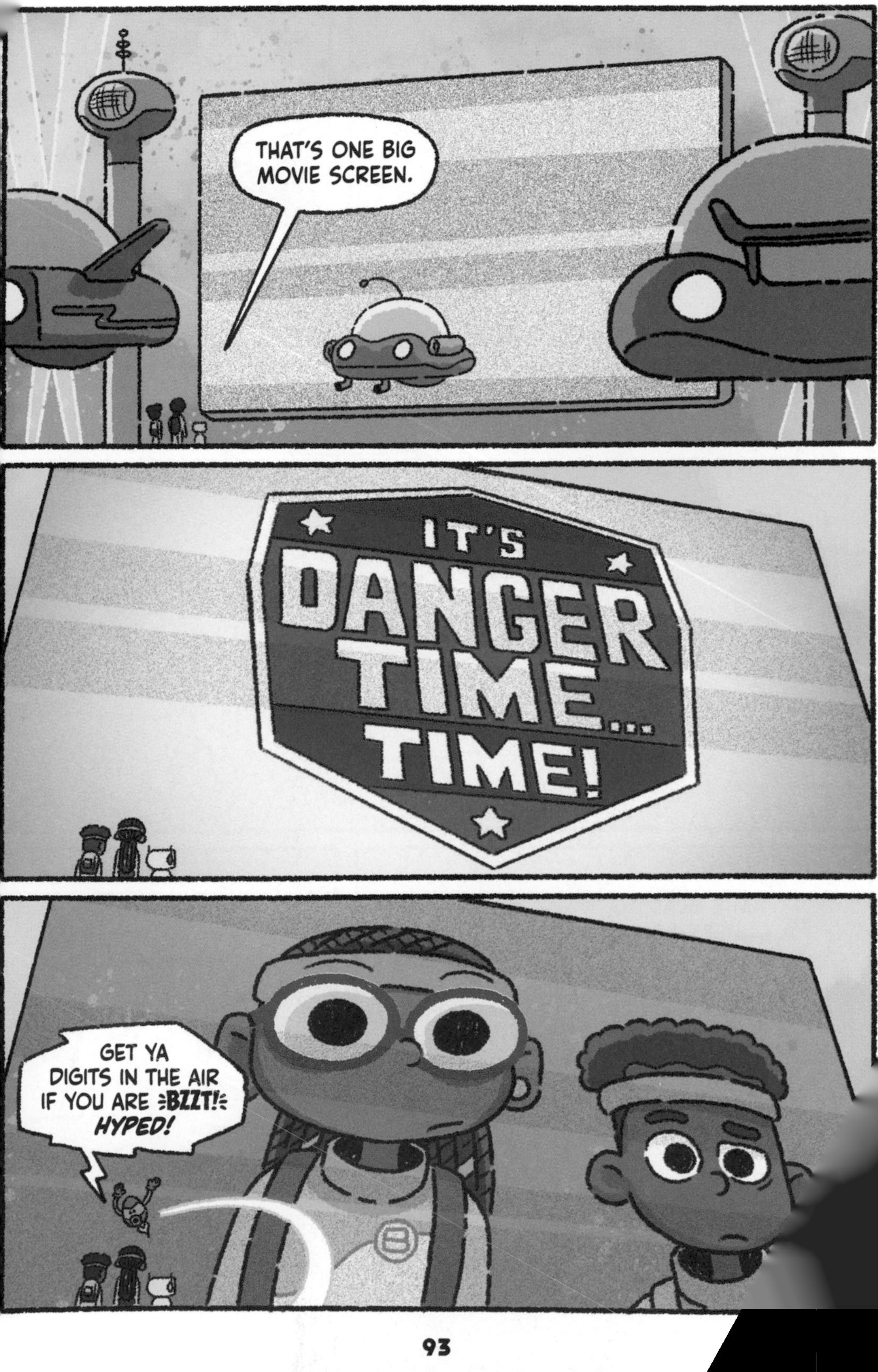
THAT'S ONE BIG MOVIE SCREEN.
IT'S DANGER TIME... TIME!
GET YA DIGITS IN THE AIR IF YOU ARE BZZT! HYPED!

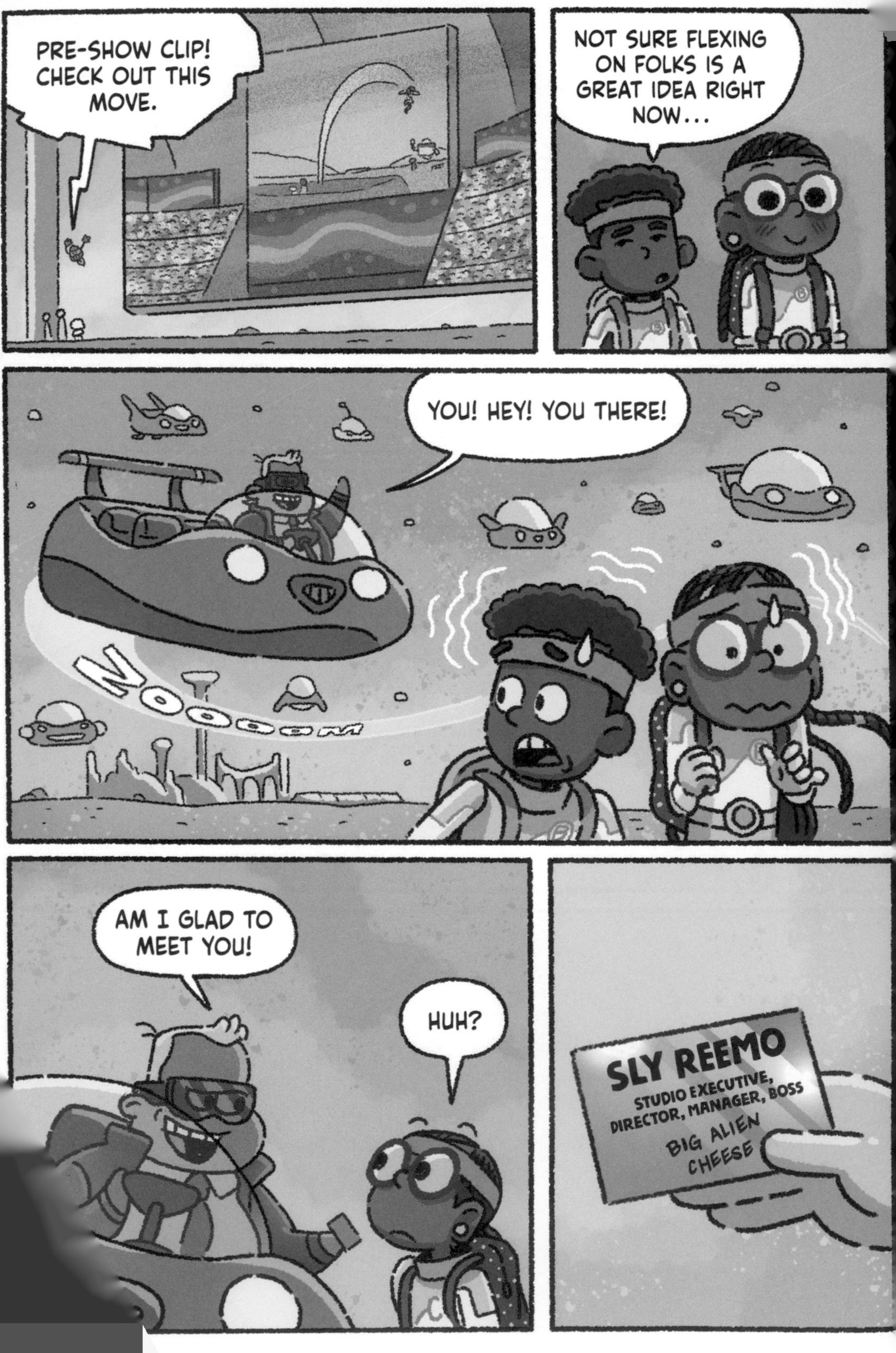
PRE-SHOW CLIP! CHECK OUT THIS MOVE.
NOT SURE FLEXING ON FOLKS IS A GREAT IDEA RIGHT NOW...
YOU! HEY! YOU THERE!
NOOOOOM
AM I GLAD TO MEET YOU!
HUH?
SLY REEMO
STUDIO EXECUTIVE, DIRECTOR, MANAGER, BOSS
BIG ALIEN CHEESE

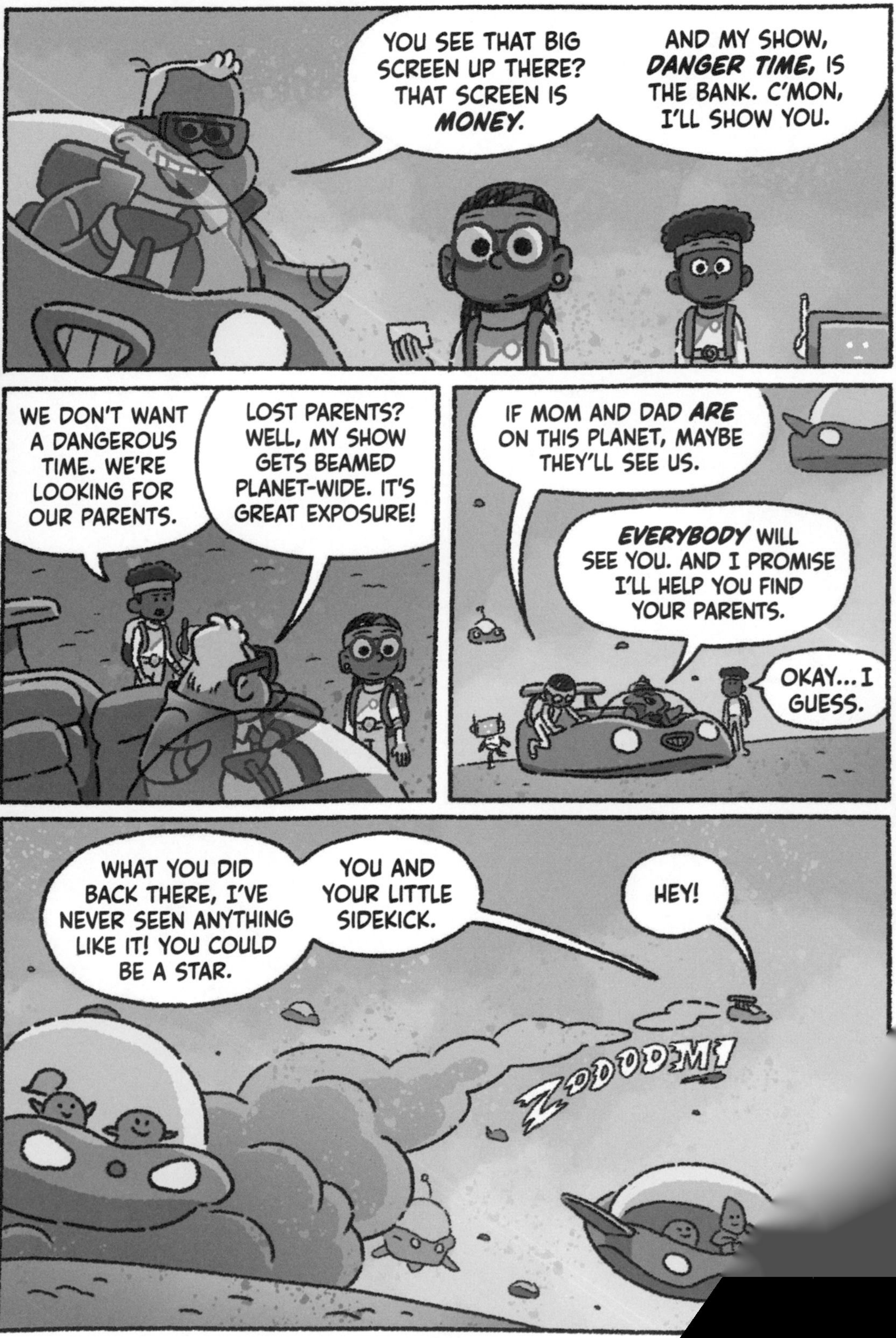
YOU SEE THAT BIG SCREEN UP THERE? THAT SCREEN IS *MONEY.*
AND MY SHOW, ***DANGER TIME,*** IS THE BANK. C'MON, I'LL SHOW YOU.
WE DON'T WANT A DANGEROUS TIME. WE'RE LOOKING FOR OUR PARENTS.
LOST PARENTS? WELL, MY SHOW GETS BEAMED PLANET-WIDE. IT'S GREAT EXPOSURE!
IF MOM AND DAD ***ARE*** ON THIS PLANET, MAYBE THEY'LL SEE US.
***EVERYBODY*** WILL SEE YOU. AND I PROMISE I'LL HELP YOU FIND YOUR PARENTS.
OKAY... I GUESS.
WHAT YOU DID BACK THERE, I'VE NEVER SEEN ANYTHING LIKE IT! YOU COULD BE A STAR.
YOU AND YOUR LITTLE SIDEKICK.
HEY!
ZOOOOM!

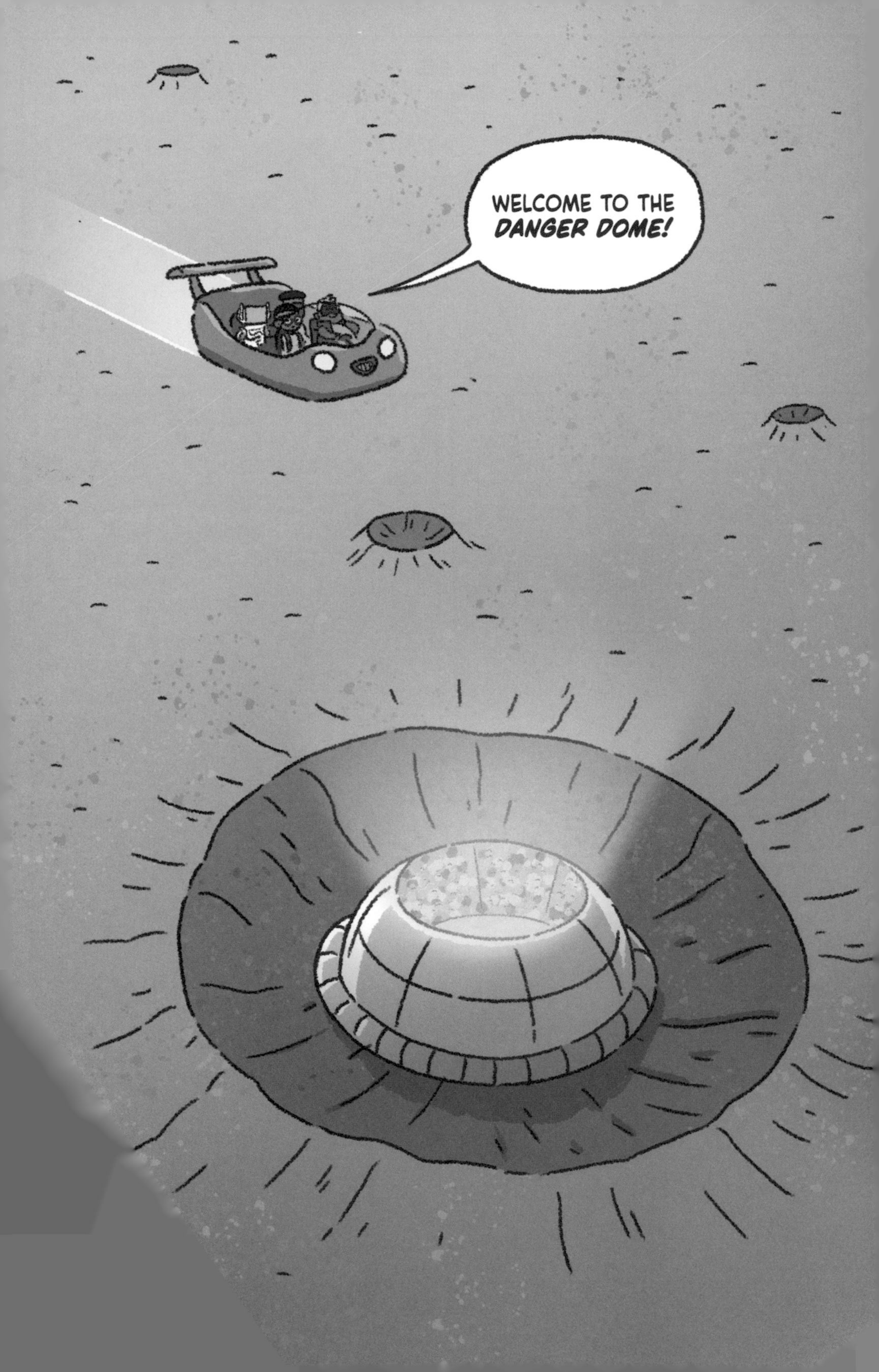
WELCOME TO THE *DANGER DOME!*

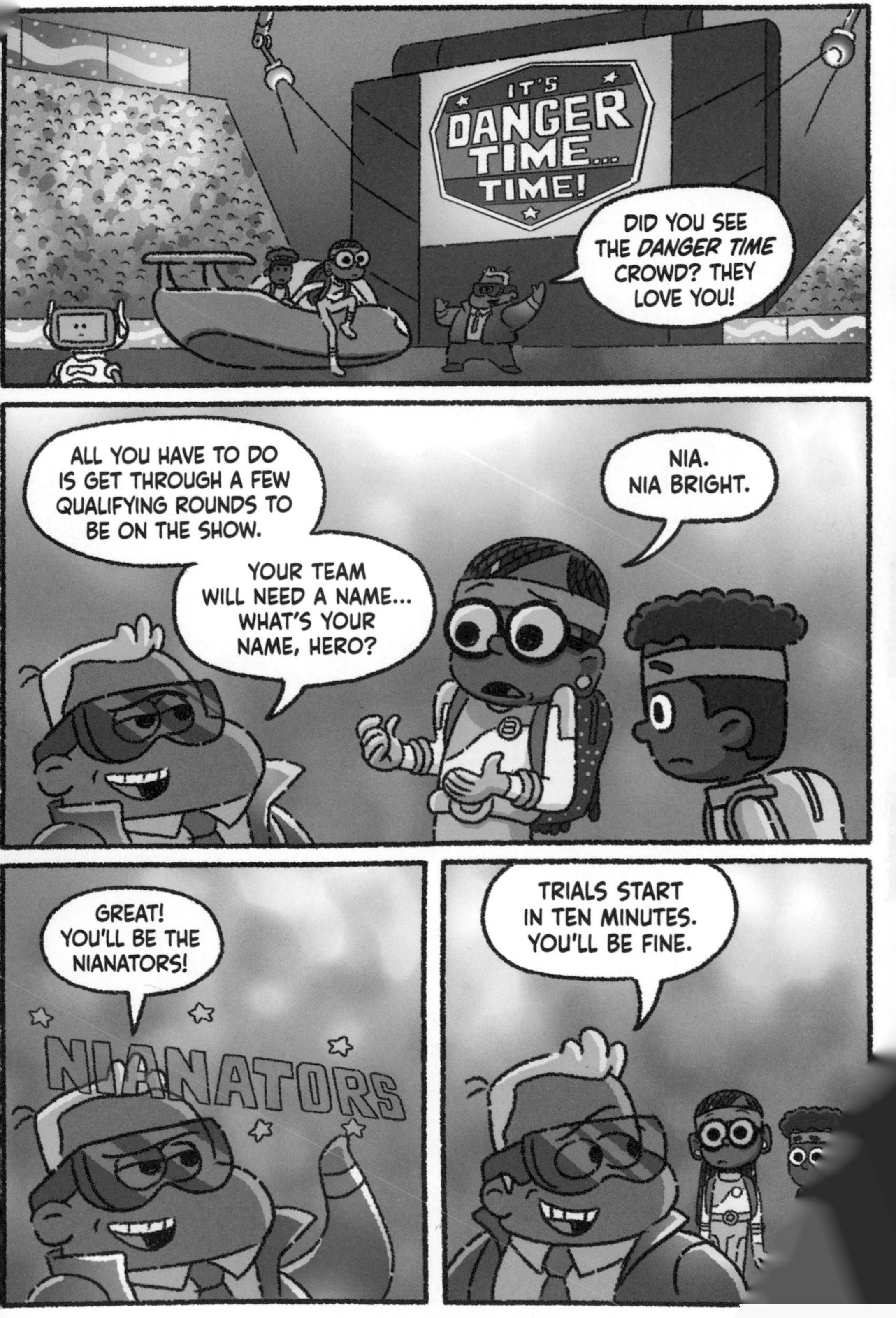
IT'S DANGER TIME... TIME!
DID YOU SEE THE *DANGER TIME* CROWD? THEY LOVE YOU!
ALL YOU HAVE TO DO IS GET THROUGH A FEW QUALIFYING ROUNDS TO BE ON THE SHOW.
YOUR TEAM WILL NEED A NAME... WHAT'S YOUR NAME, HERO?
NIA. NIA BRIGHT.
GREAT! YOU'LL BE THE NIANATORS!
NIANATORS
TRIALS START IN TEN MINUTES. YOU'LL BE FINE.

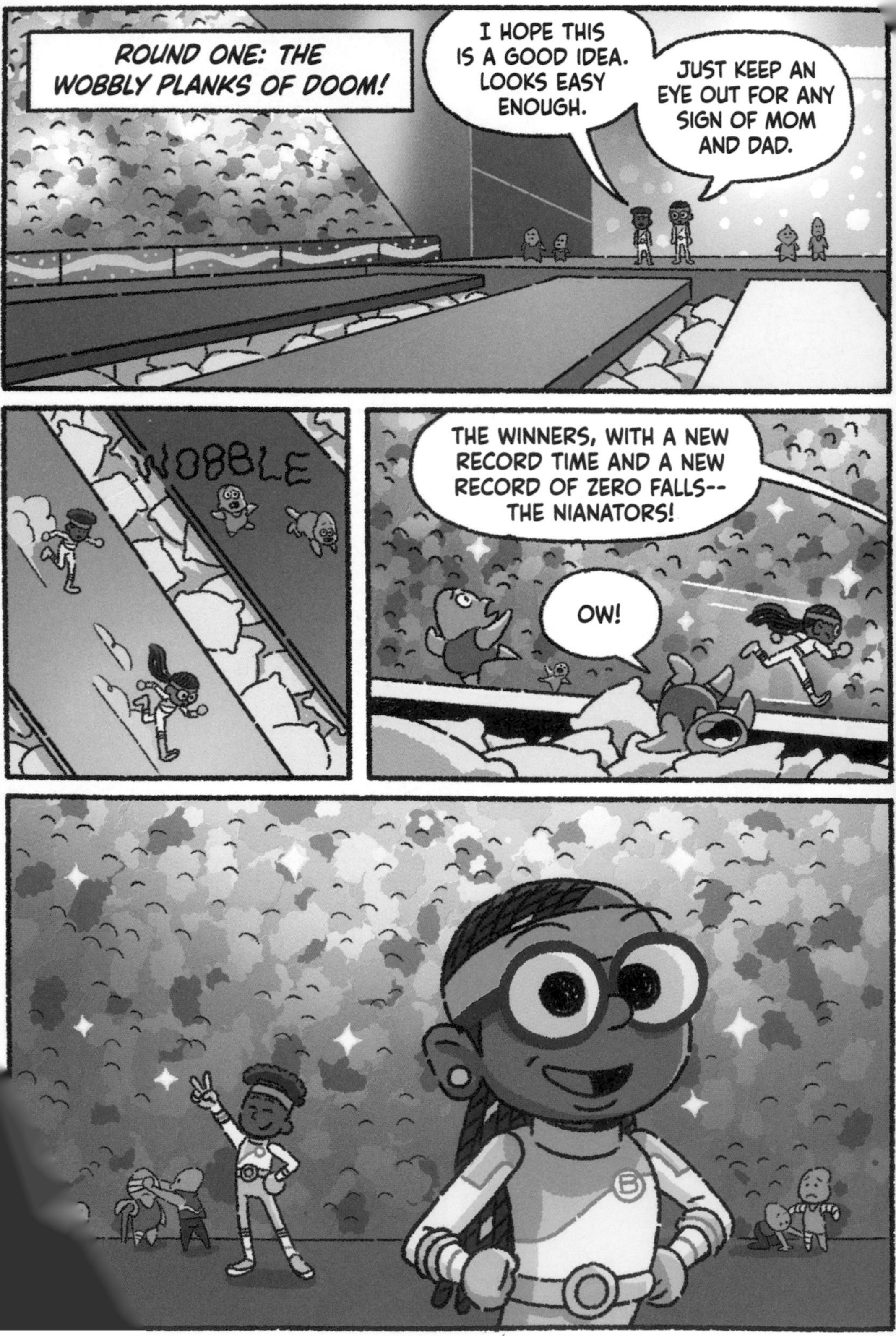
ROUND ONE: THE WOBBLY PLANKS OF DOOM!
I HOPE THIS IS A GOOD IDEA. LOOKS EASY ENOUGH.
JUST KEEP AN EYE OUT FOR ANY SIGN OF MOM AND DAD.
WOBBLE
THE WINNERS, WITH A NEW RECORD TIME AND A NEW RECORD OF ZERO FALLS-- THE NIANATORS!
OW!

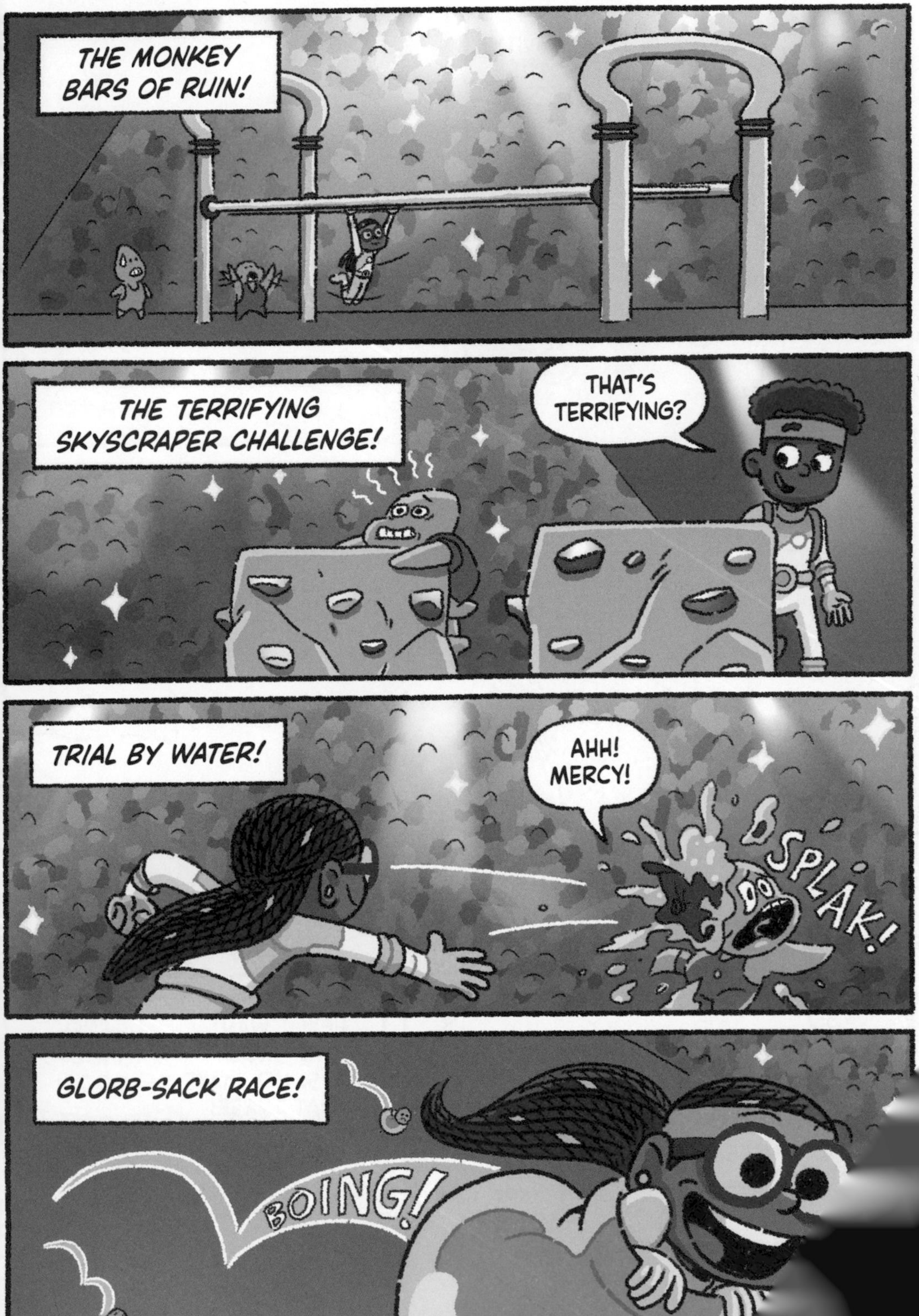
THE MONKEY BARS OF RUIN!
THE TERRIFYING SKYSCRAPER CHALLENGE!
THAT'S TERRIFYING?
TRIAL BY WATER!
AHH! MERCY!
SPLAK!
GLORB-SACK RACE!
BOING!

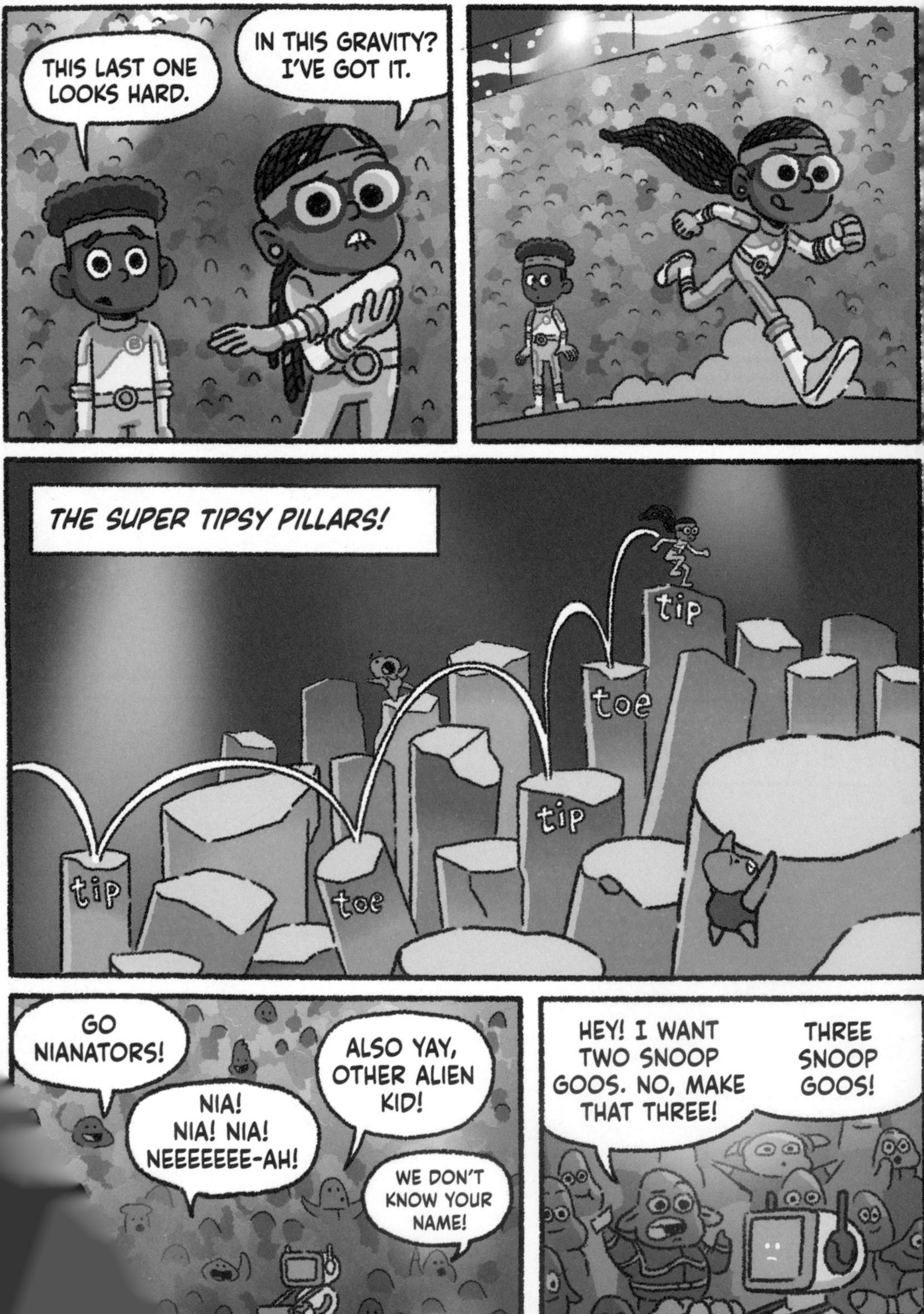
THIS LAST ONE LOOKS HARD.
IN THIS GRAVITY? I'VE GOT IT.
THE SUPER TIPSY PILLARS!
tip
toe
tip
toe
tip
GO NIANATORS!
NIA! NIA! NIA! NEEEEEEE-AH!
ALSO YAY, OTHER ALIEN KID!
WE DON'T KNOW YOUR NAME!
HEY! I WANT TWO SNOOP GOOS. NO, MAKE THAT THREE!
THREE SNOOP GOOS!

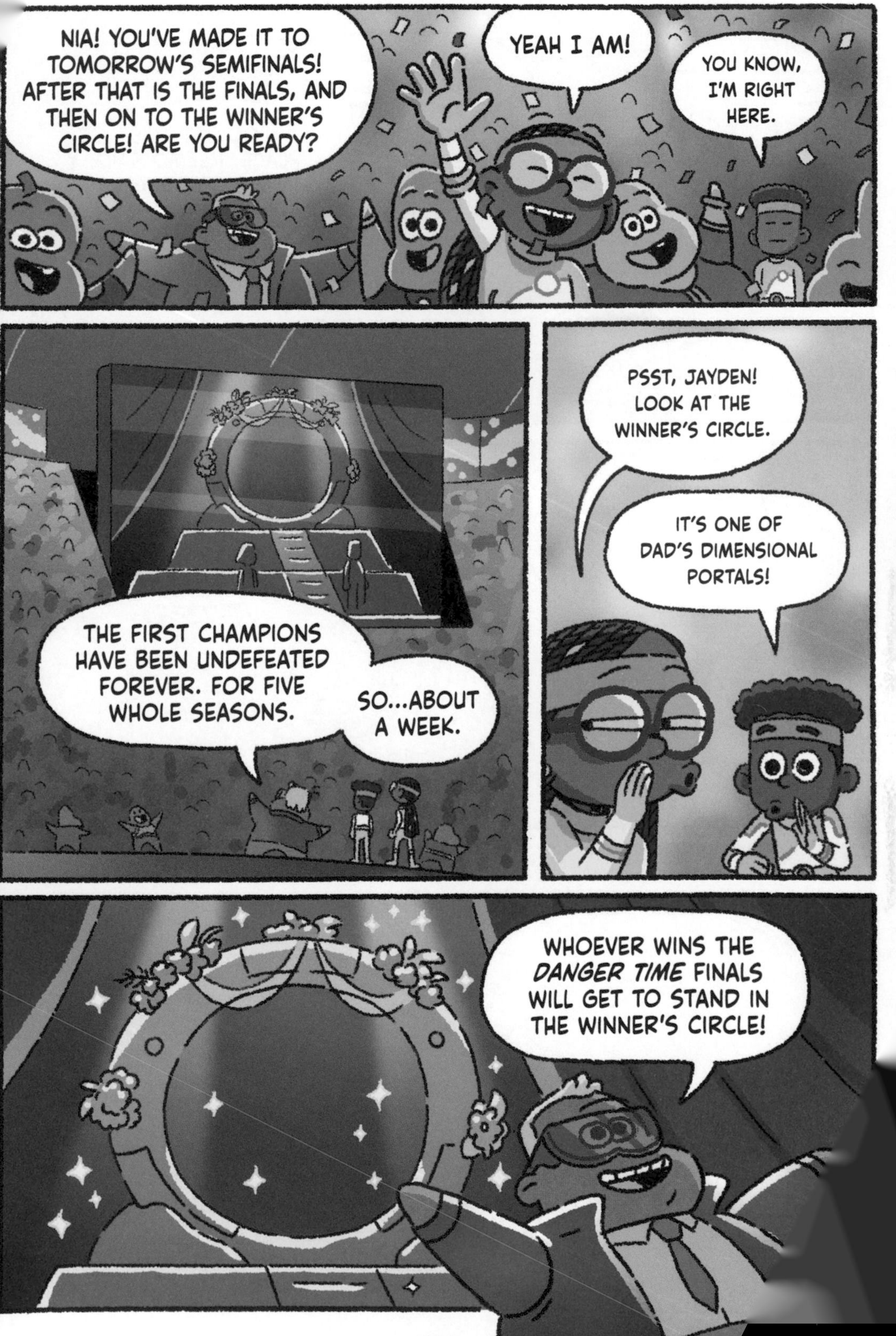
NIA! YOU'VE MADE IT TO TOMORROW'S SEMIFINALS! AFTER THAT IS THE FINALS, AND THEN ON TO THE WINNER'S CIRCLE! ARE YOU READY?
YEAH I AM!
YOU KNOW, I'M RIGHT HERE.
THE FIRST CHAMPIONS HAVE BEEN UNDEFEATED FOREVER. FOR FIVE WHOLE SEASONS.
SO...ABOUT A WEEK.
PSST, JAYDEN! LOOK AT THE WINNER'S CIRCLE.
IT'S ONE OF DAD'S DIMENSIONAL PORTALS!
WHOEVER WINS THE *DANGER TIME* FINALS WILL GET TO STAND IN THE WINNER'S CIRCLE!

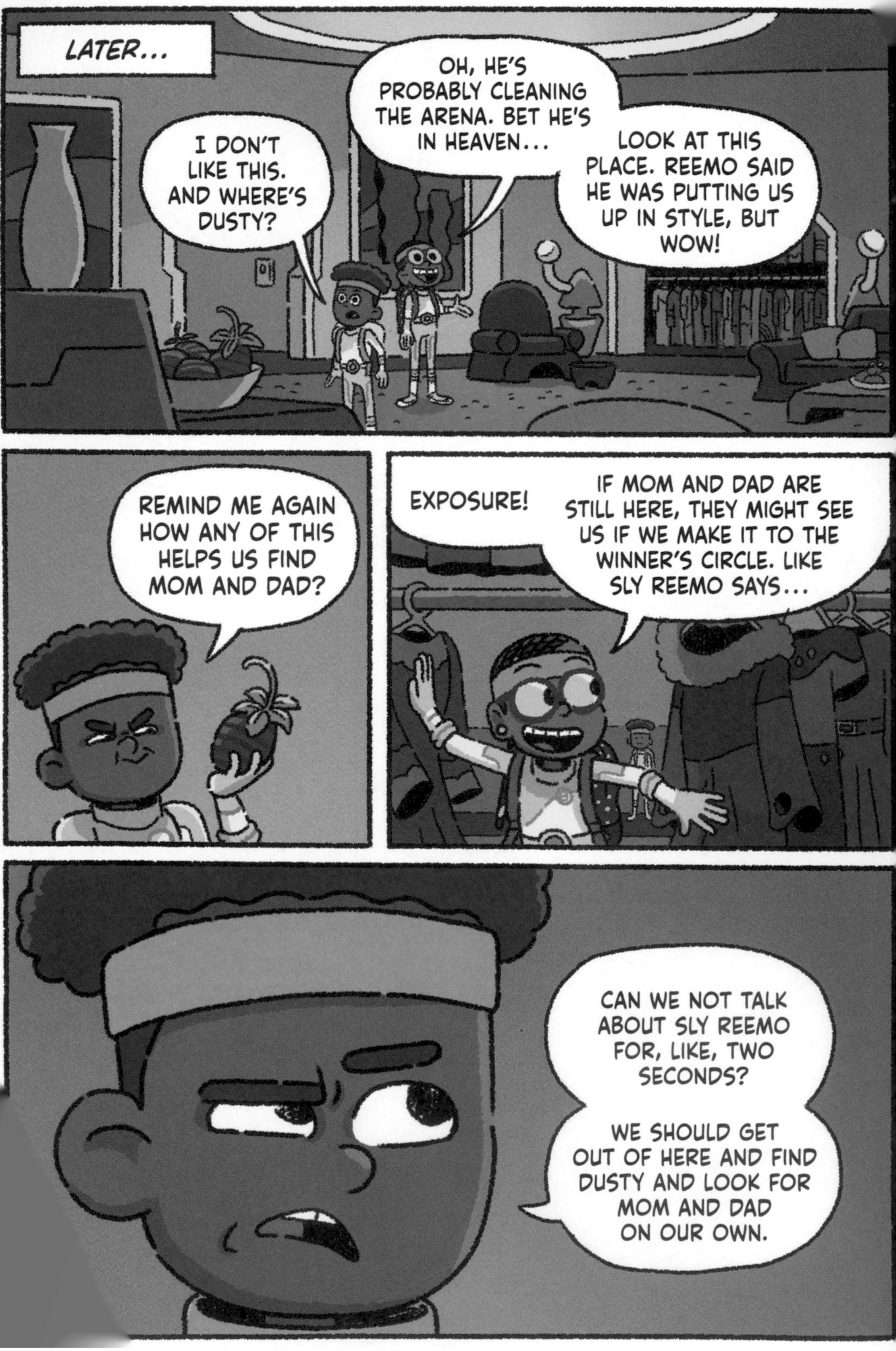
LATER...
I DON'T LIKE THIS. AND WHERE'S DUSTY?
OH, HE'S PROBABLY CLEANING THE ARENA. BET HE'S IN HEAVEN...
LOOK AT THIS PLACE. REEMO SAID HE WAS PUTTING US UP IN STYLE, BUT WOW!
REMIND ME AGAIN HOW ANY OF THIS HELPS US FIND MOM AND DAD?
EXPOSURE!
IF MOM AND DAD ARE STILL HERE, THEY MIGHT SEE US IF WE MAKE IT TO THE WINNER'S CIRCLE. LIKE SLY REEMO SAYS...
CAN WE NOT TALK ABOUT SLY REEMO FOR, LIKE, TWO SECONDS?
WE SHOULD GET OUT OF HERE AND FIND DUSTY AND LOOK FOR MOM AND DAD ON OUR OWN.

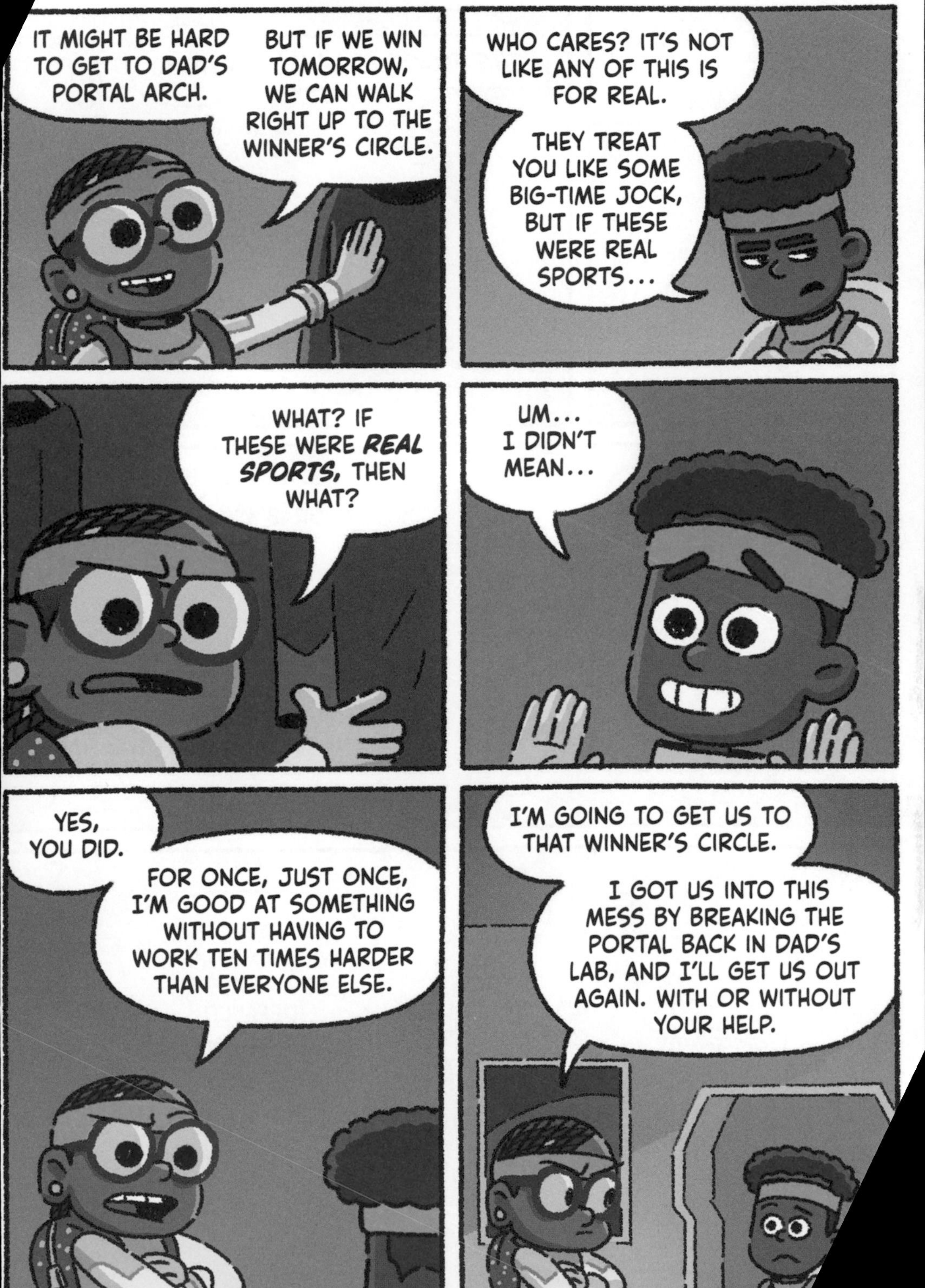
IT MIGHT BE HARD TO GET TO DAD'S PORTAL ARCH.
BUT IF WE WIN TOMORROW, WE CAN WALK RIGHT UP TO THE WINNER'S CIRCLE.
WHO CARES? IT'S NOT LIKE ANY OF THIS IS FOR REAL.
THEY TREAT YOU LIKE SOME BIG-TIME JOCK, BUT IF THESE WERE REAL SPORTS...
WHAT? IF THESE WERE *REAL SPORTS,* THEN WHAT?
UM... I DIDN'T MEAN...
YES, YOU DID.
FOR ONCE, JUST ONCE, I'M GOOD AT SOMETHING WITHOUT HAVING TO WORK TEN TIMES HARDER THAN EVERYONE ELSE.
I'M GOING TO GET US TO THAT WINNER'S CIRCLE.
I GOT US INTO THIS MESS BY BREAKING THE PORTAL BACK IN DAD'S LAB, AND I'LL GET US OUT AGAIN. WITH OR WITHOUT YOUR HELP.

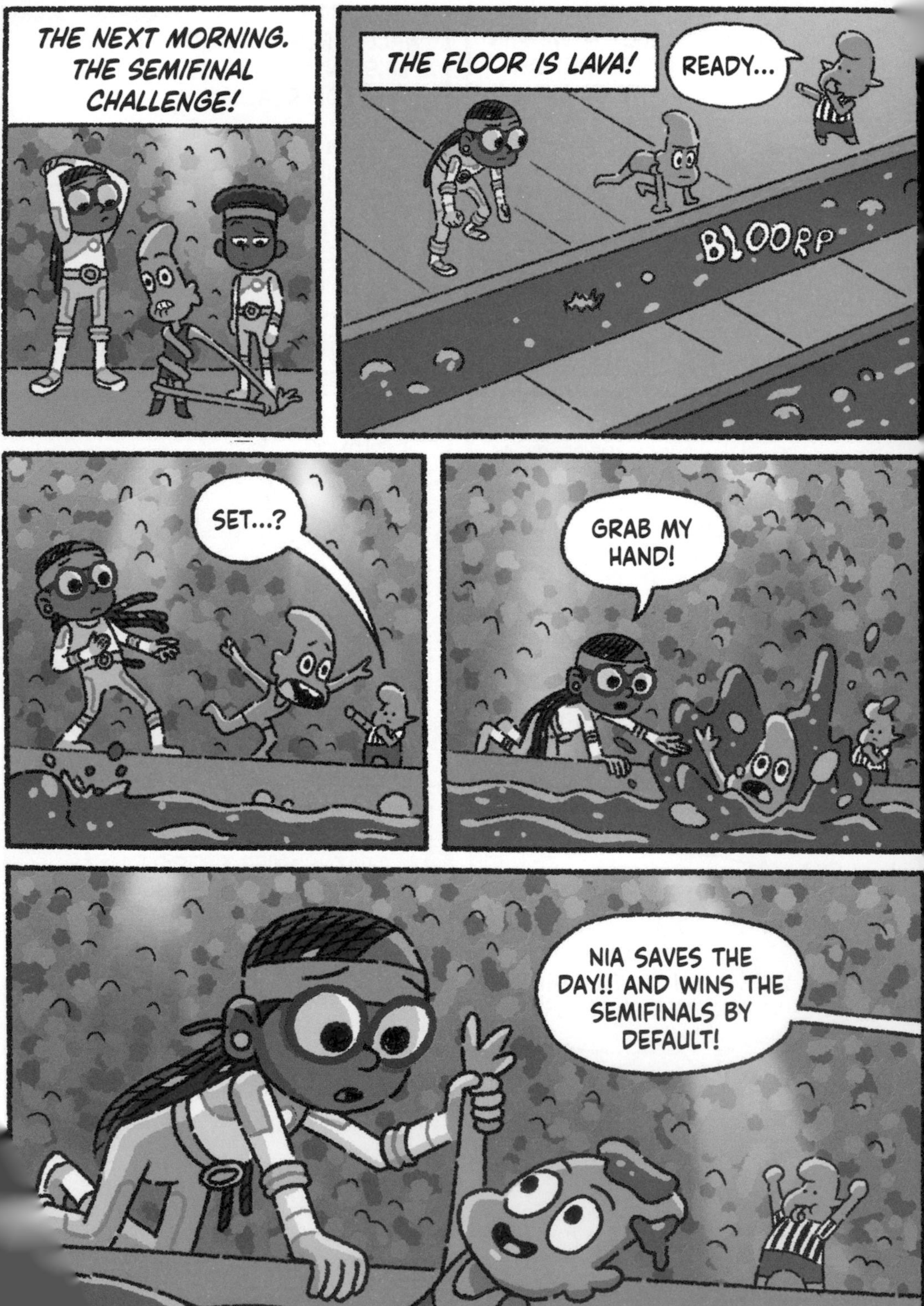
THE NEXT MORNING. THE SEMIFINAL CHALLENGE!
THE FLOOR IS LAVA!
READY...
BLOORP
SET...?
GRAB MY HAND!
NIA SAVES THE DAY!! AND WINS THE SEMIFINALS BY DEFAULT!

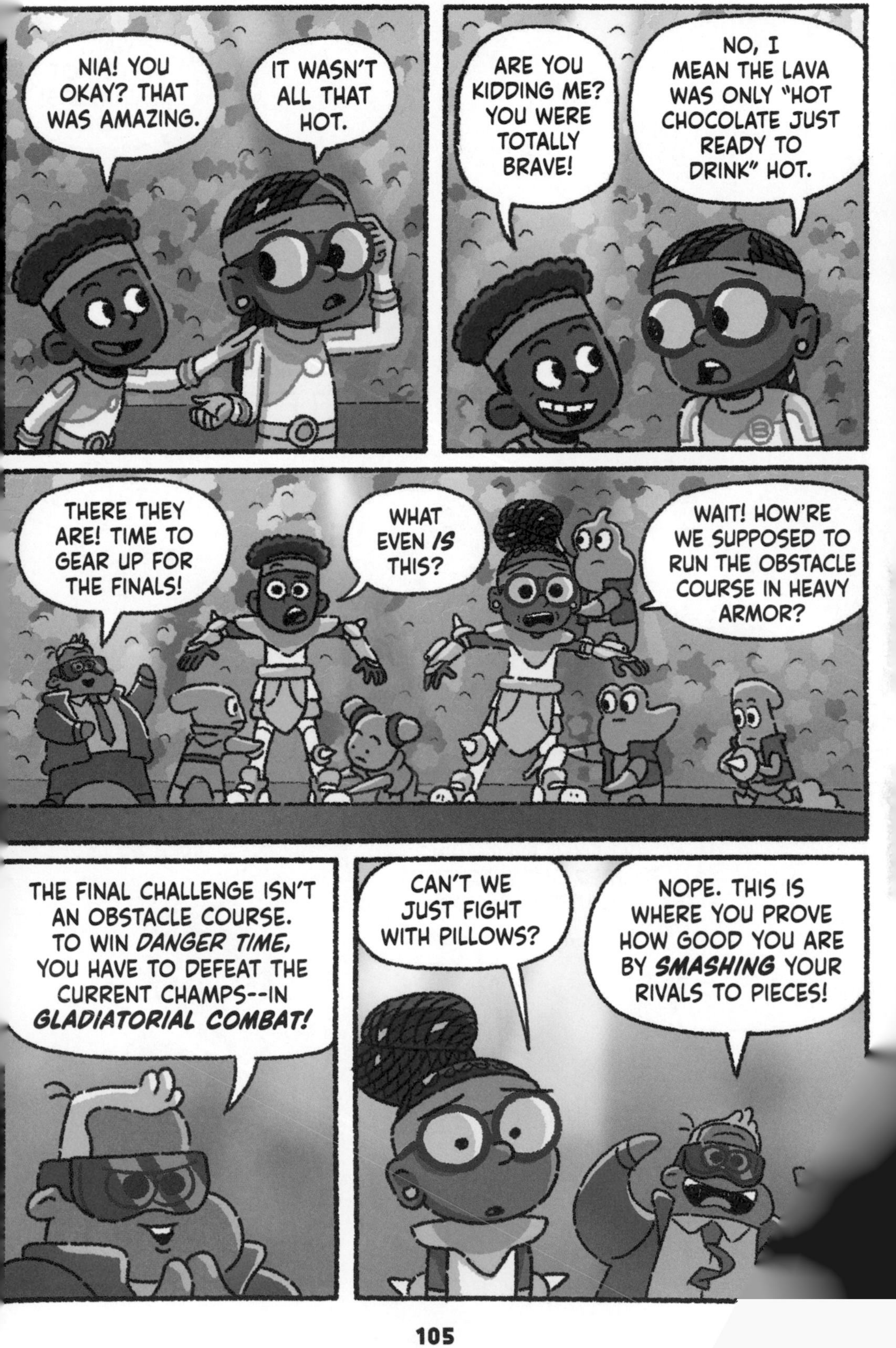
NIA! YOU OKAY? THAT WAS AMAZING.
IT WASN'T ALL THAT HOT.
ARE YOU KIDDING ME? YOU WERE TOTALLY BRAVE!
NO, I MEAN THE LAVA WAS ONLY "HOT CHOCOLATE JUST READY TO DRINK" HOT.
THERE THEY ARE! TIME TO GEAR UP FOR THE FINALS!
WHAT EVEN *IS* THIS?
WAIT! HOW'RE WE SUPPOSED TO RUN THE OBSTACLE COURSE IN HEAVY ARMOR?
THE FINAL CHALLENGE ISN'T AN OBSTACLE COURSE. TO WIN *DANGER TIME,* YOU HAVE TO DEFEAT THE CURRENT CHAMPS--IN ***GLADIATORIAL COMBAT!***
CAN'T WE JUST FIGHT WITH PILLOWS?
NOPE. THIS IS WHERE YOU PROVE HOW GOOD YOU ARE BY ***SMASHING*** YOUR RIVALS TO PIECES!

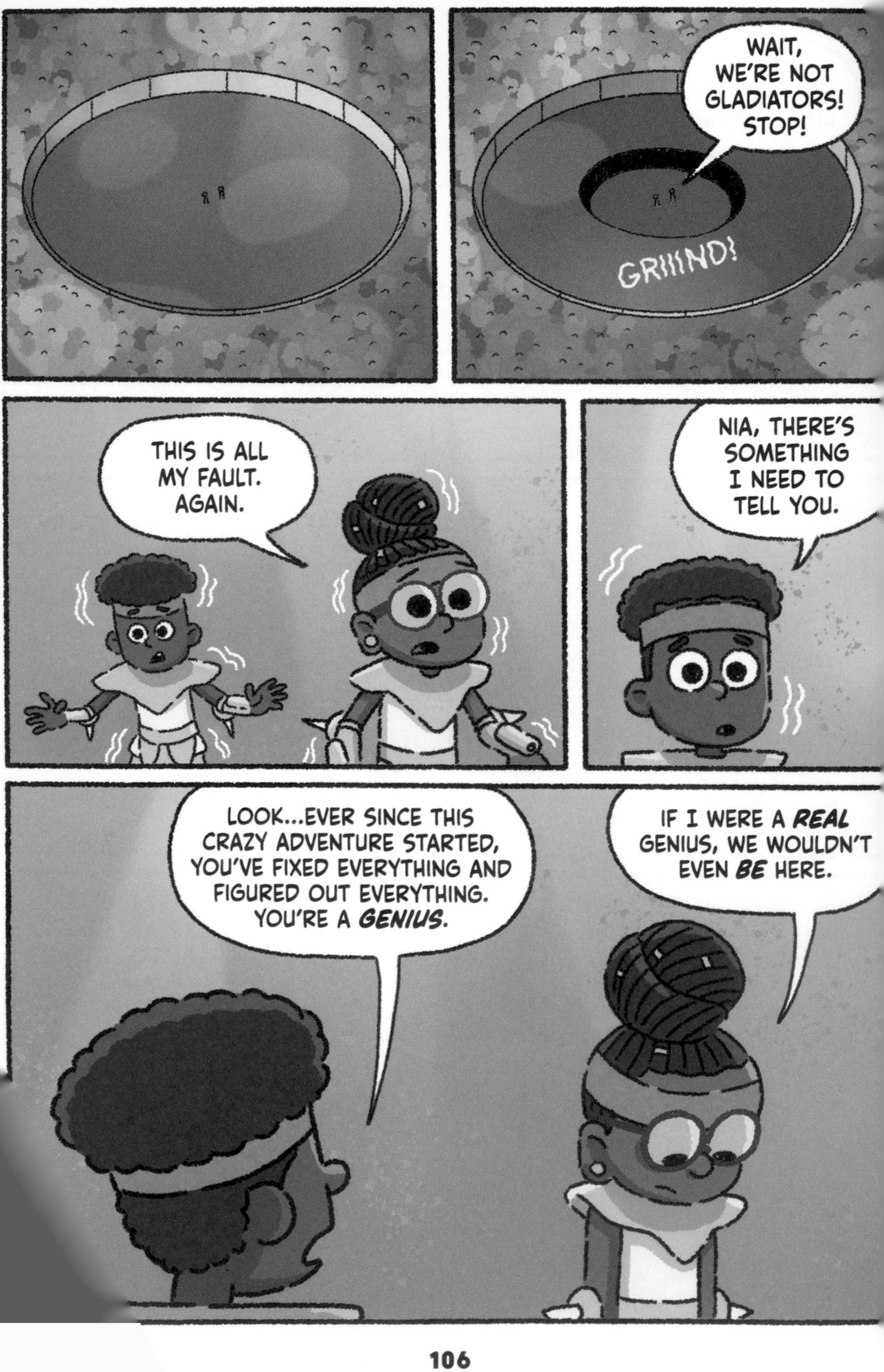
WAIT, WE'RE NOT GLADIATORS! STOP!
GRIIIND!
THIS IS ALL MY FAULT. AGAIN.
NIA, THERE'S SOMETHING I NEED TO TELL YOU.
LOOK...EVER SINCE THIS CRAZY ADVENTURE STARTED, YOU'VE FIXED EVERYTHING AND FIGURED OUT EVERYTHING. YOU'RE A *GENIUS*.
IF I WERE A *REAL* GENIUS, WE WOULDN'T EVEN *BE* HERE.

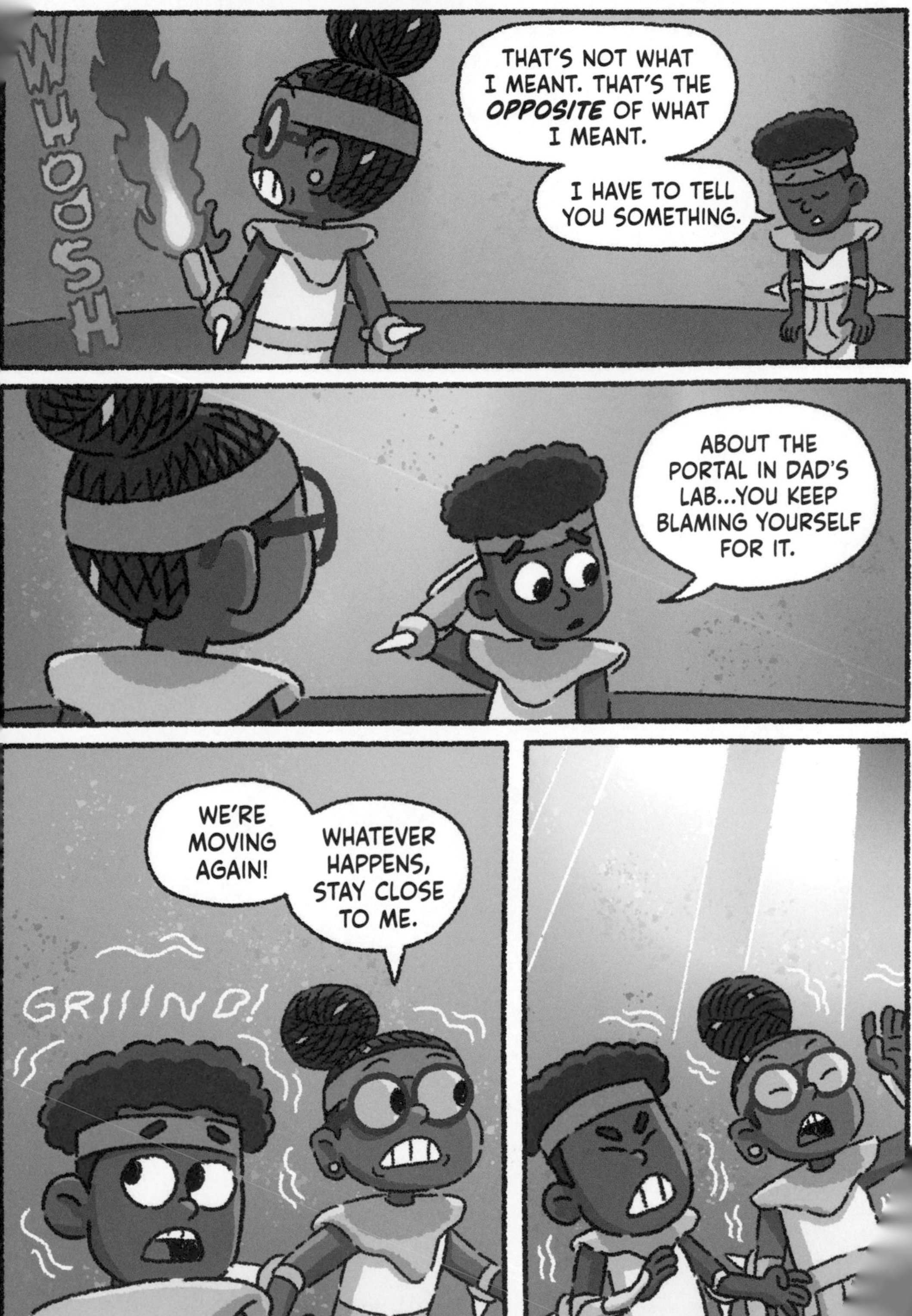
WHOOSH
THAT'S NOT WHAT I MEANT. THAT'S THE *OPPOSITE* OF WHAT I MEANT.
I HAVE TO TELL YOU SOMETHING.
ABOUT THE PORTAL IN DAD'S LAB...YOU KEEP BLAMING YOURSELF FOR IT.
WE'RE MOVING AGAIN!
WHATEVER HAPPENS, STAY CLOSE TO ME.
GRIIIND!

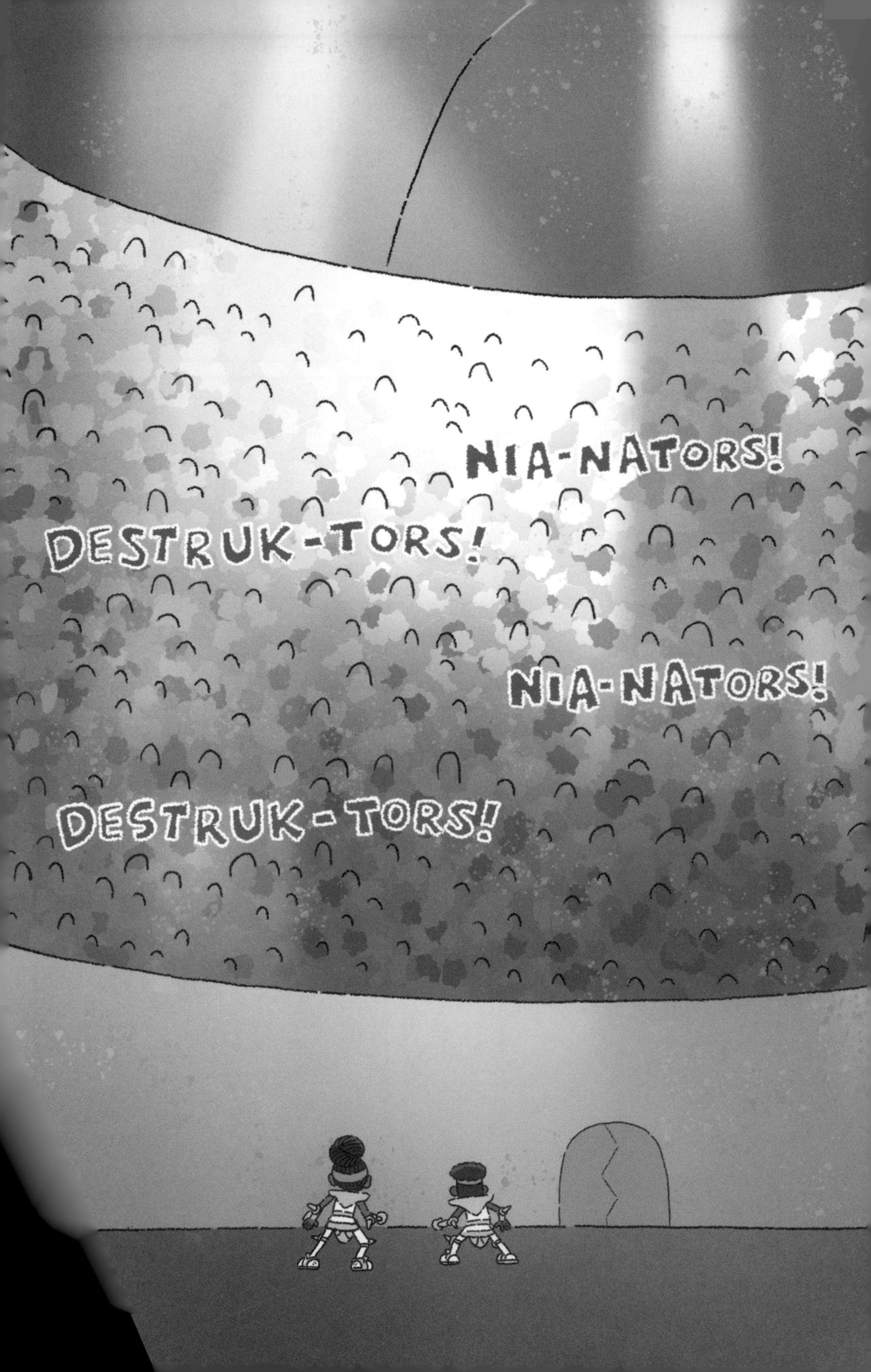
NIA-NATORS!
DESTRUK-TORS!
NIA-NATORS!
DESTRUK-TORS!

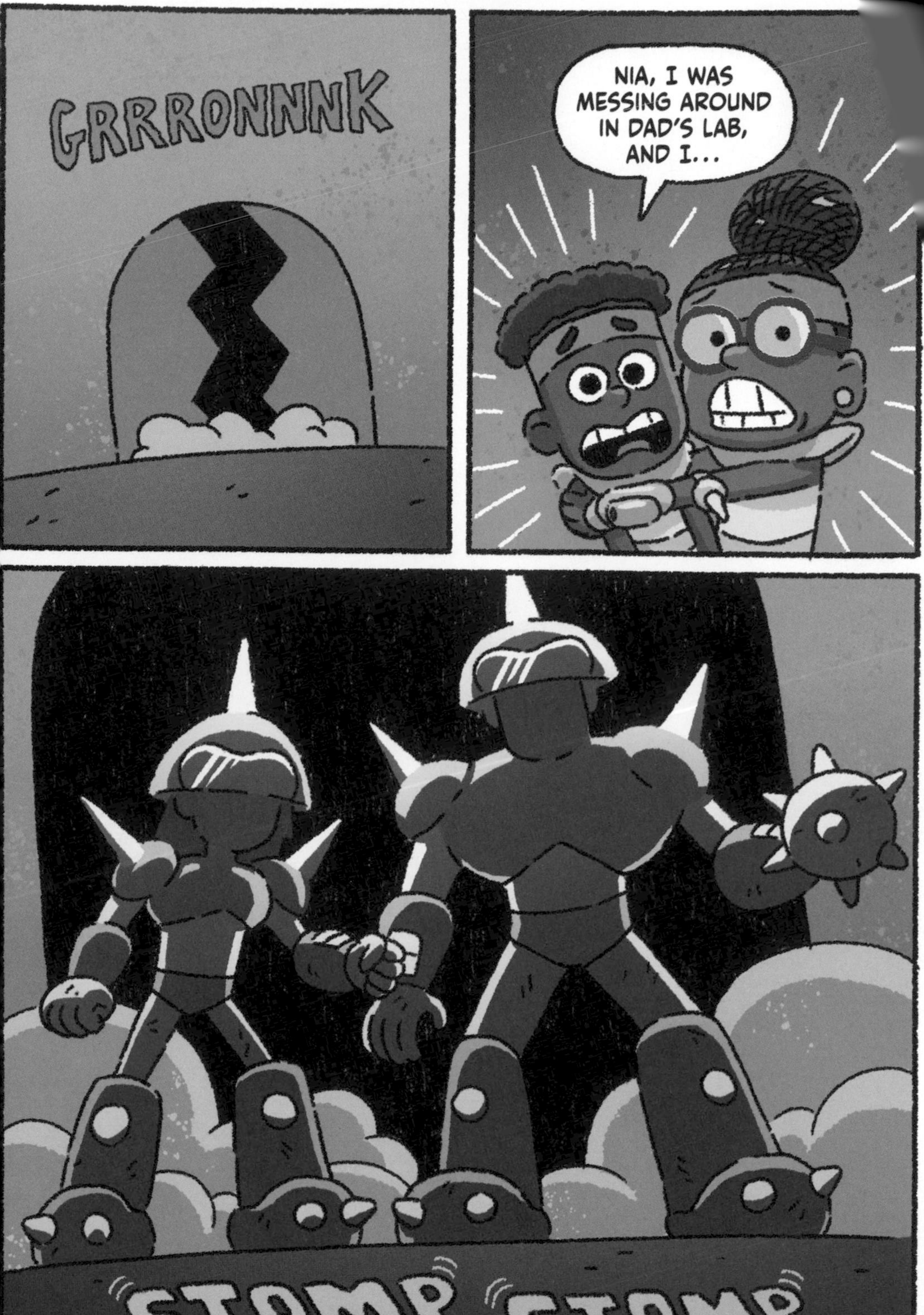
GRRRONNNK
NIA, I WAS MESSING AROUND IN DAD'S LAB, AND I...
STOMP STOMP

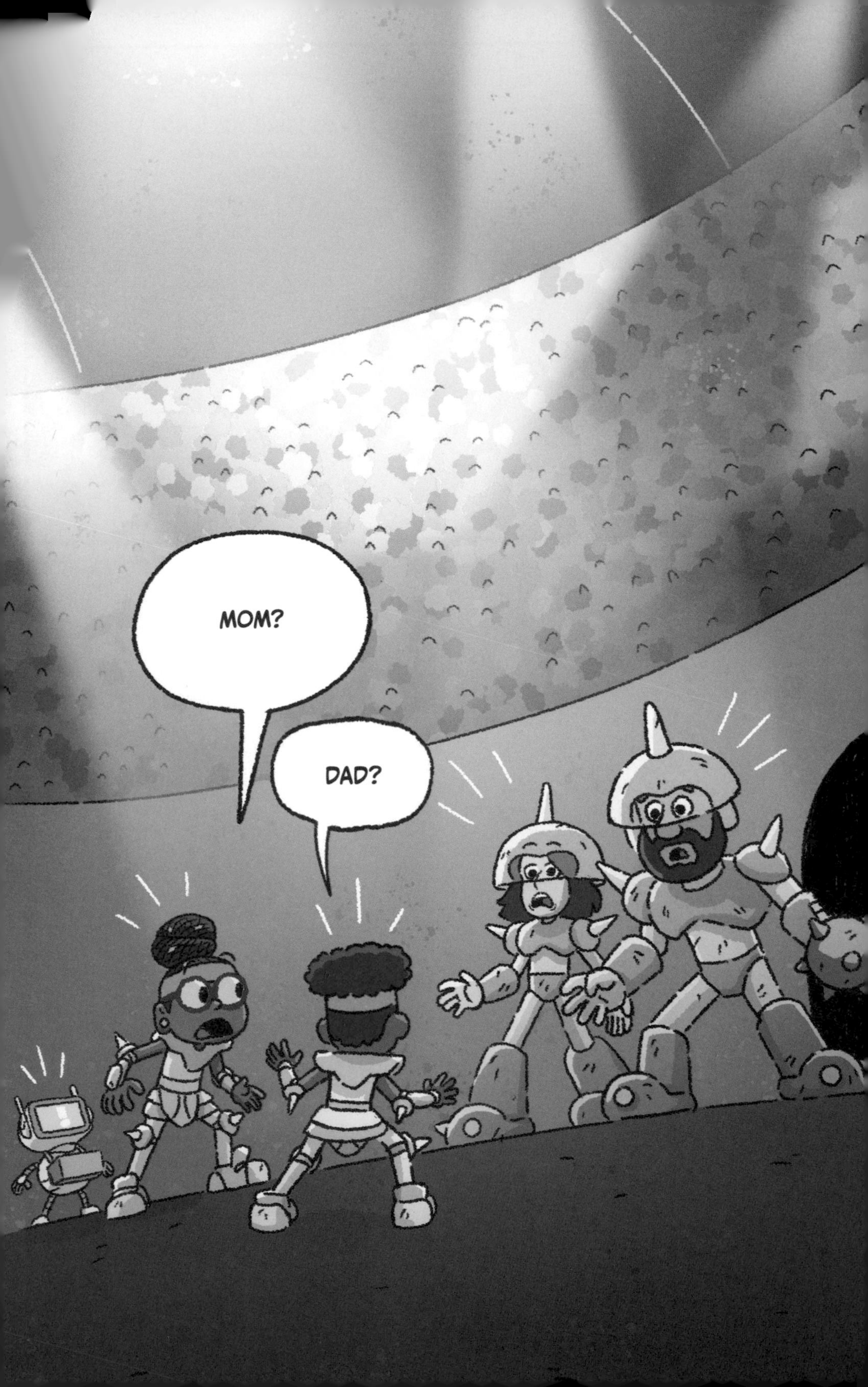
MOM?
DAD?

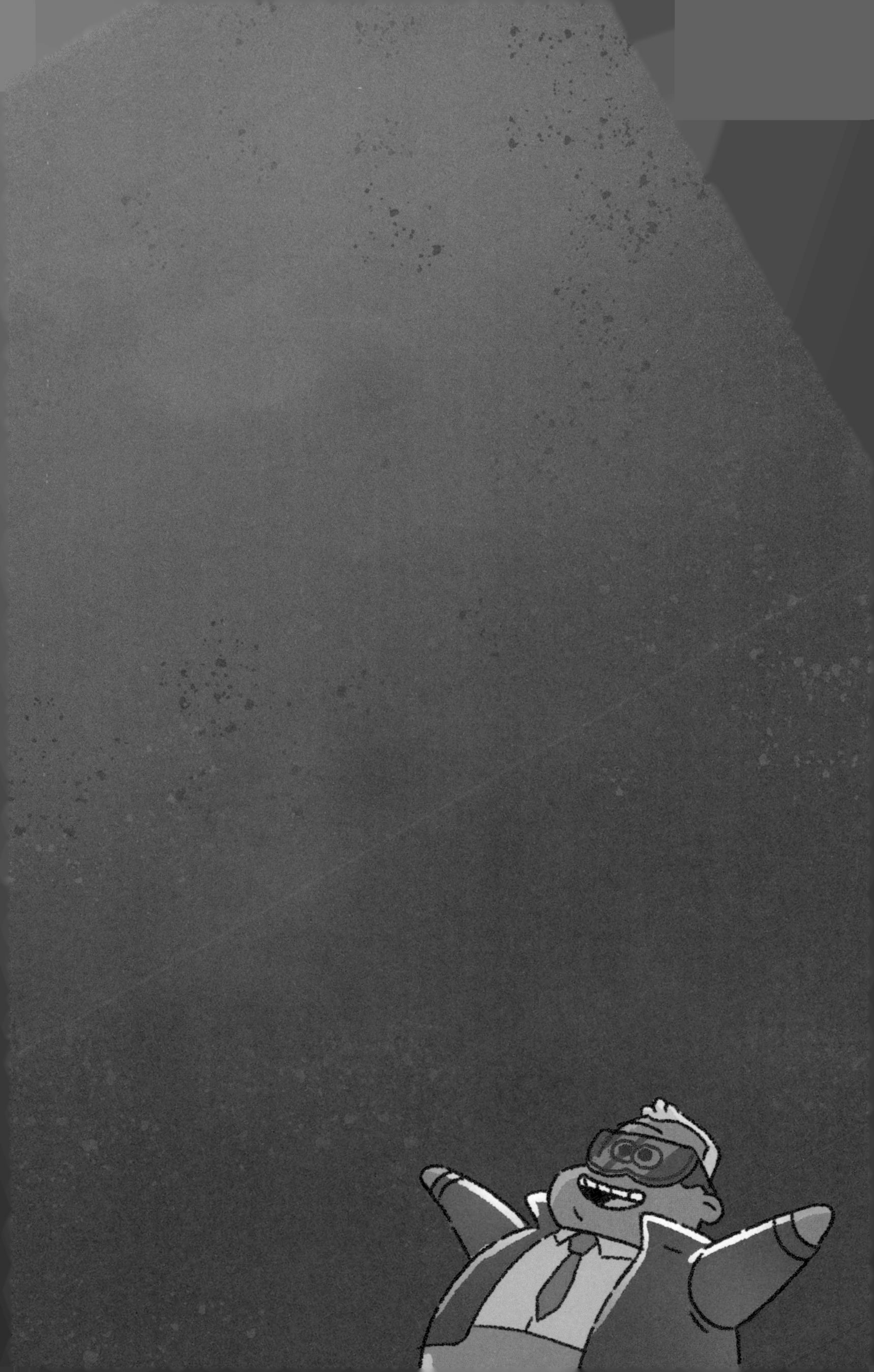

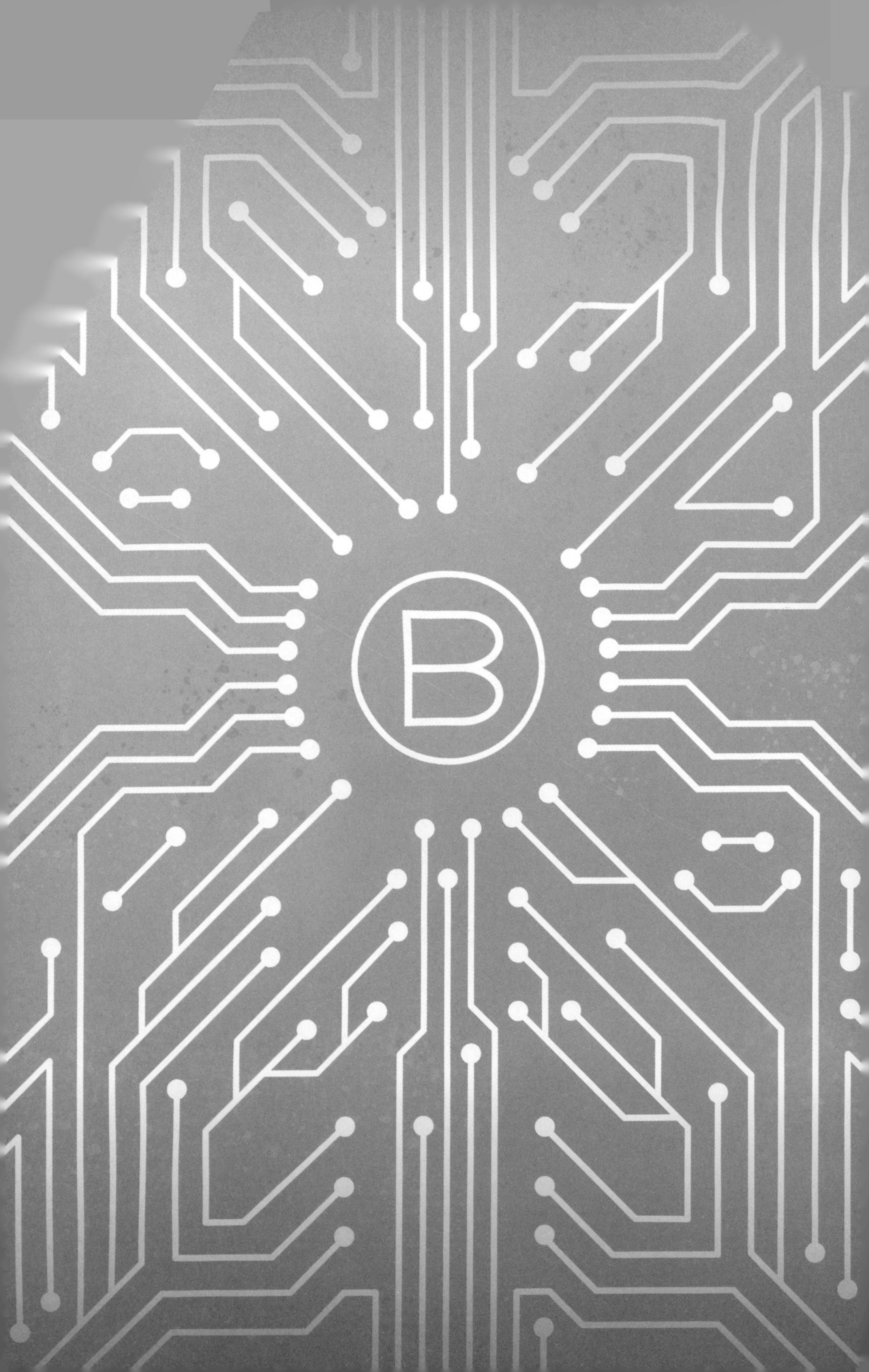

# CHAPTER 5
# QUANTUM LOOP

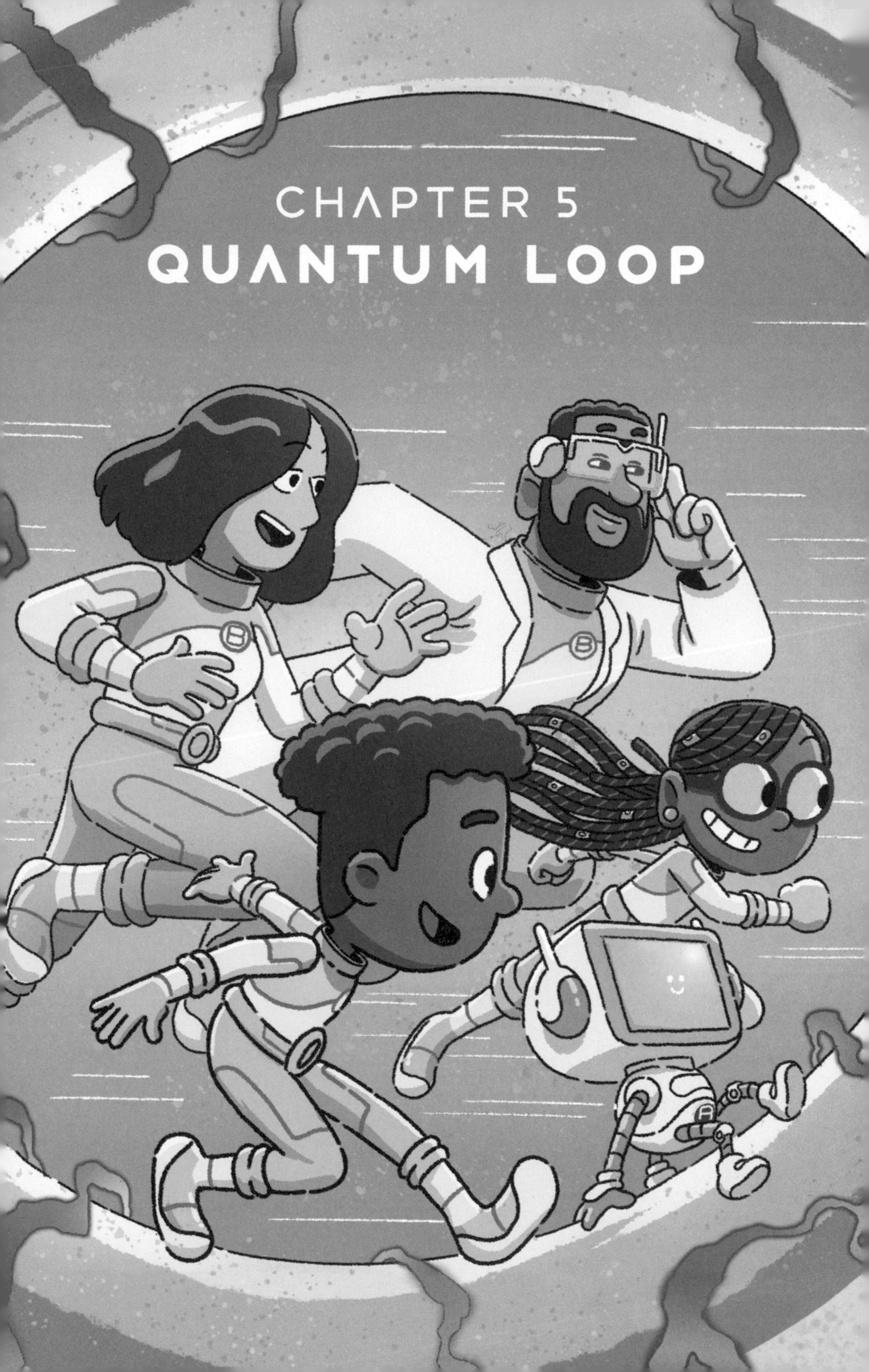

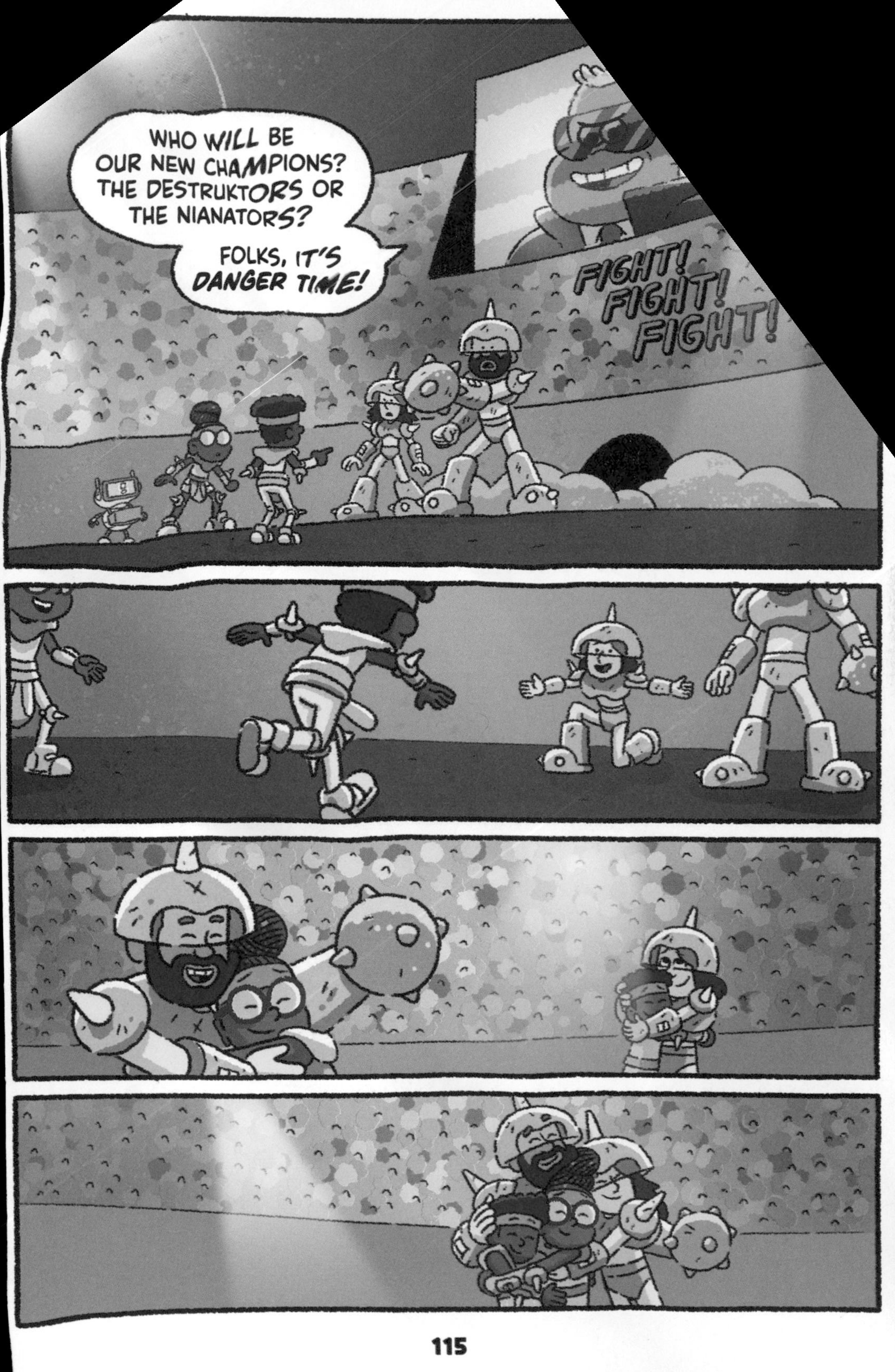
WHO WILL BE OUR NEW CHAMPIONS? THE DESTRUKTORS OR THE NIANATORS?
FOLKS, IT'S DANGER TIME!
FIGHT! FIGHT! FIGHT!

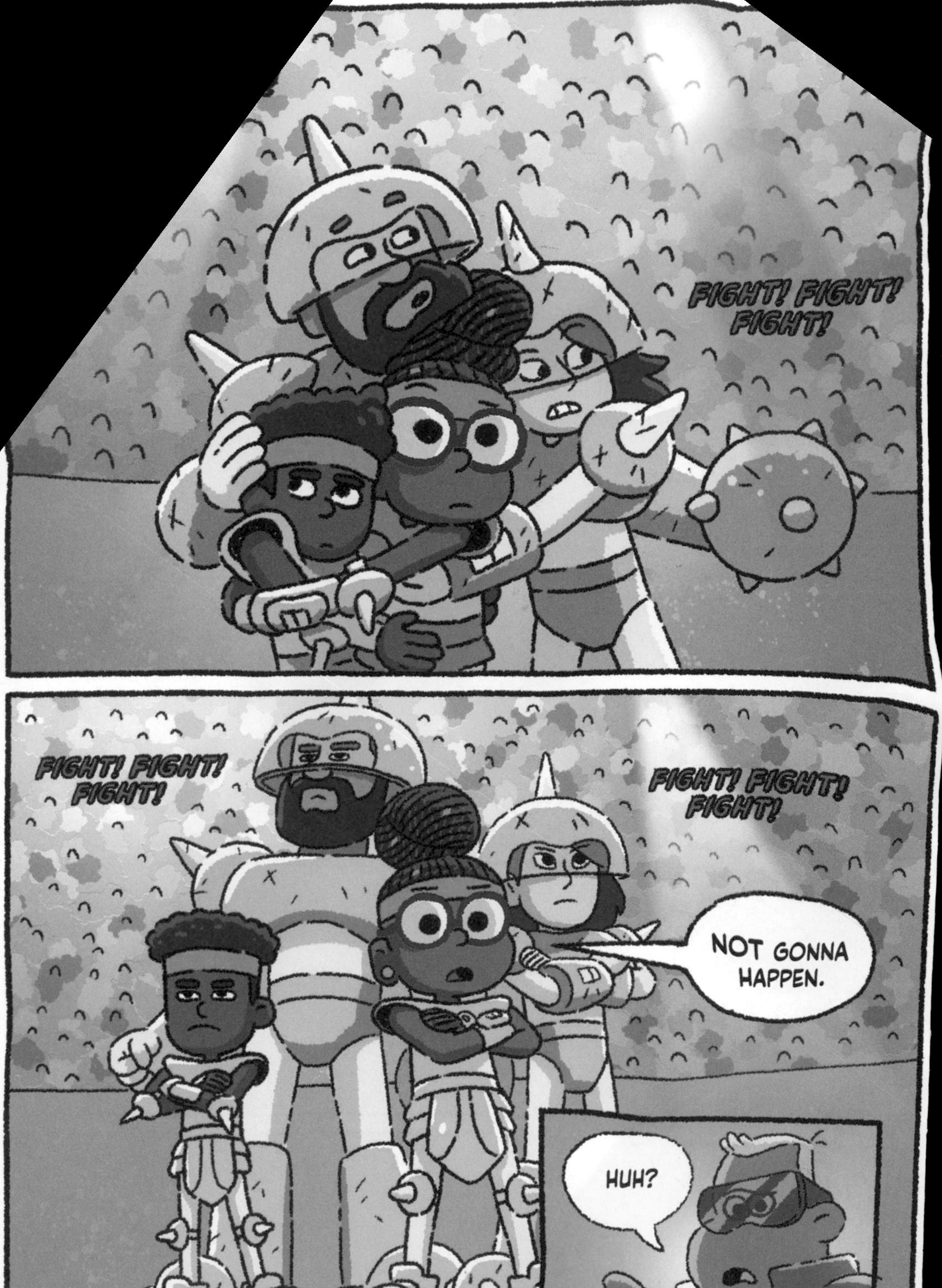
FIGHT! FIGHT! FIGHT!
FIGHT! FIGHT! FIGHT!
FIGHT! FIGHT! FIGHT!
NOT GONNA HAPPEN.
HUH?

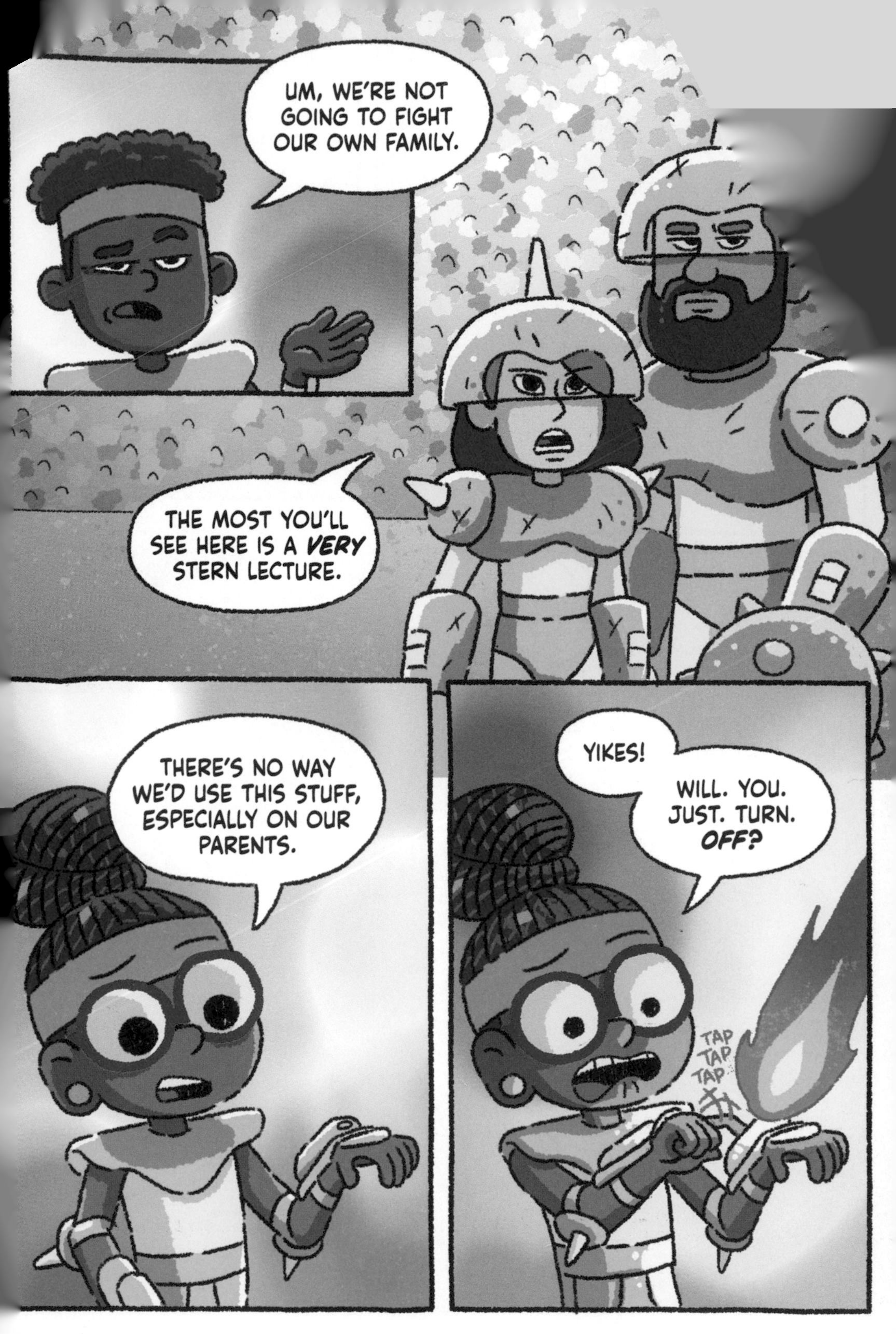
UM, WE'RE NOT GOING TO FIGHT OUR OWN FAMILY.
THE MOST YOU'LL SEE HERE IS A *VERY* STERN LECTURE.
THERE'S NO WAY WE'D USE THIS STUFF, ESPECIALLY ON OUR PARENTS.
YIKES!
WILL. YOU. JUST. TURN. *OFF?*
TAP TAP TAP

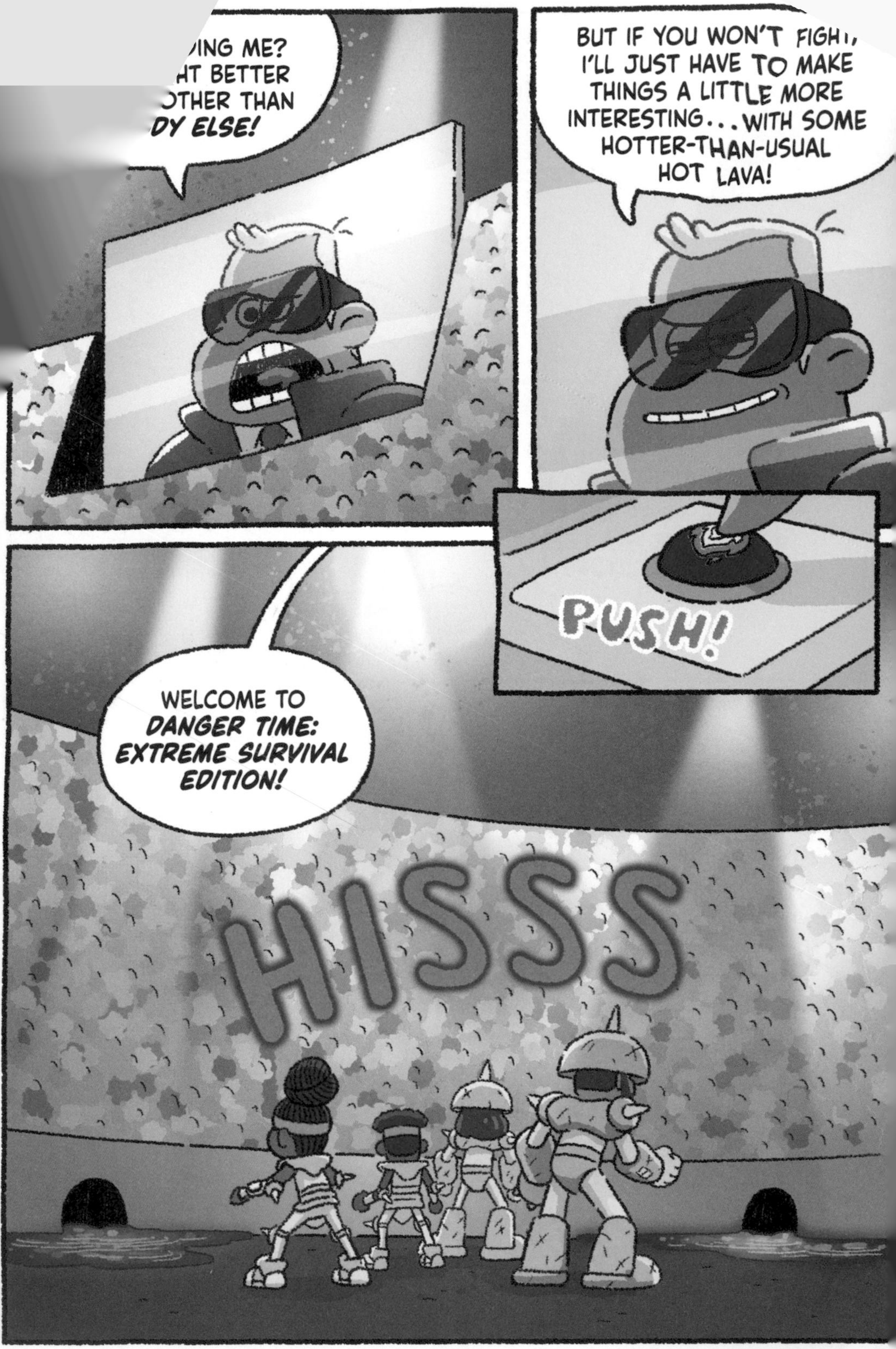
DING ME?
HT BETTER
OTHER THAN
DY ELSE!
BUT IF YOU WON'T FIGHT,
I'LL JUST HAVE TO MAKE
THINGS A LITTLE MORE
INTERESTING...WITH SOME
HOTTER-THAN-USUAL
HOT LAVA!
PUSH!
WELCOME TO
DANGER TIME:
EXTREME SURVIVAL
EDITION!
HISSS

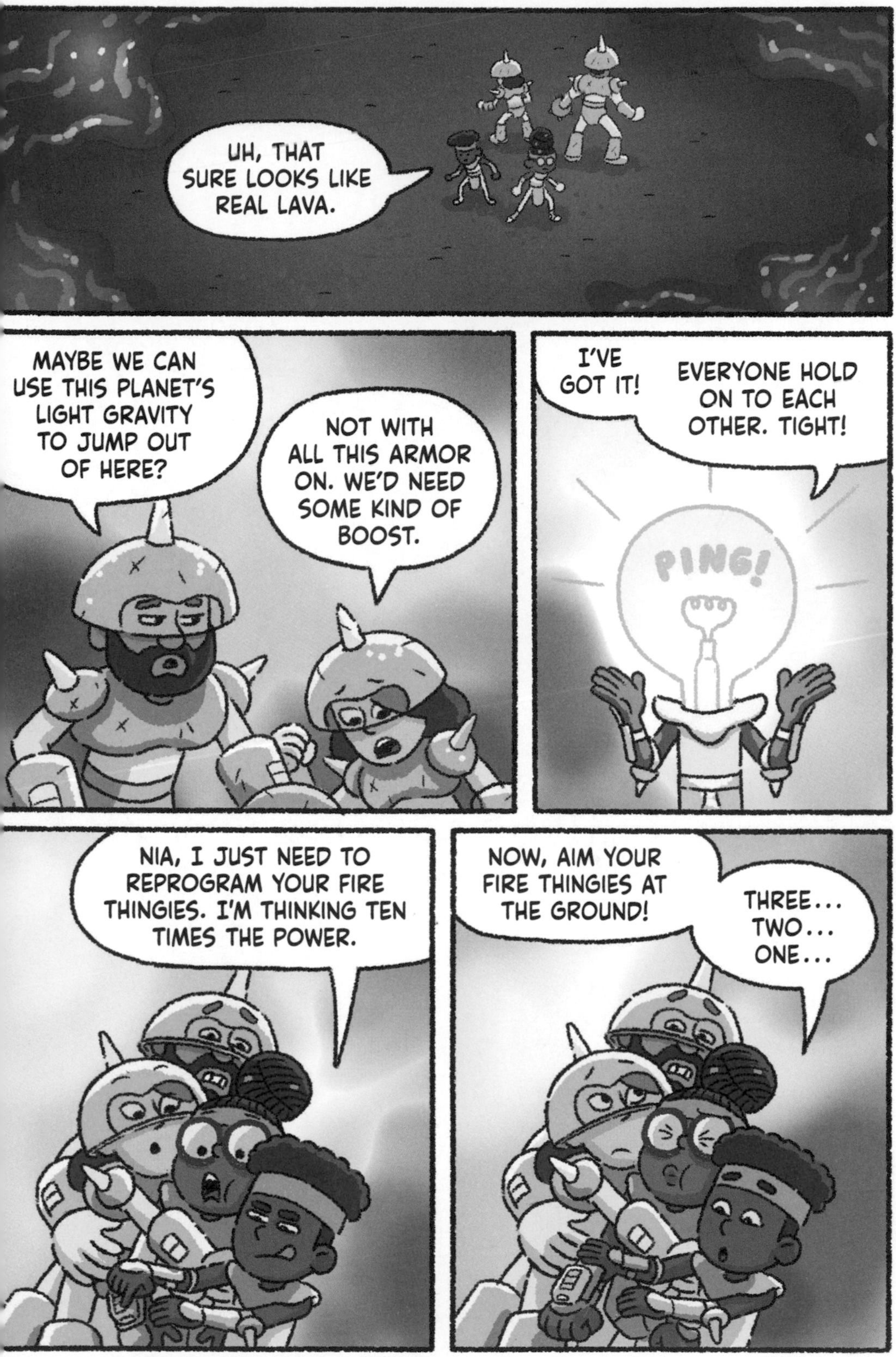
UH, THAT SURE LOOKS LIKE REAL LAVA.
MAYBE WE CAN USE THIS PLANET'S LIGHT GRAVITY TO JUMP OUT OF HERE?
NOT WITH ALL THIS ARMOR ON. WE'D NEED SOME KIND OF BOOST.
I'VE GOT IT!
EVERYONE HOLD ON TO EACH OTHER. TIGHT!
PING!
NIA, I JUST NEED TO REPROGRAM YOUR FIRE THINGIES. I'M THINKING TEN TIMES THE POWER.
NOW, AIM YOUR FIRE THINGIES AT THE GROUND!
THREE... TWO... ONE...

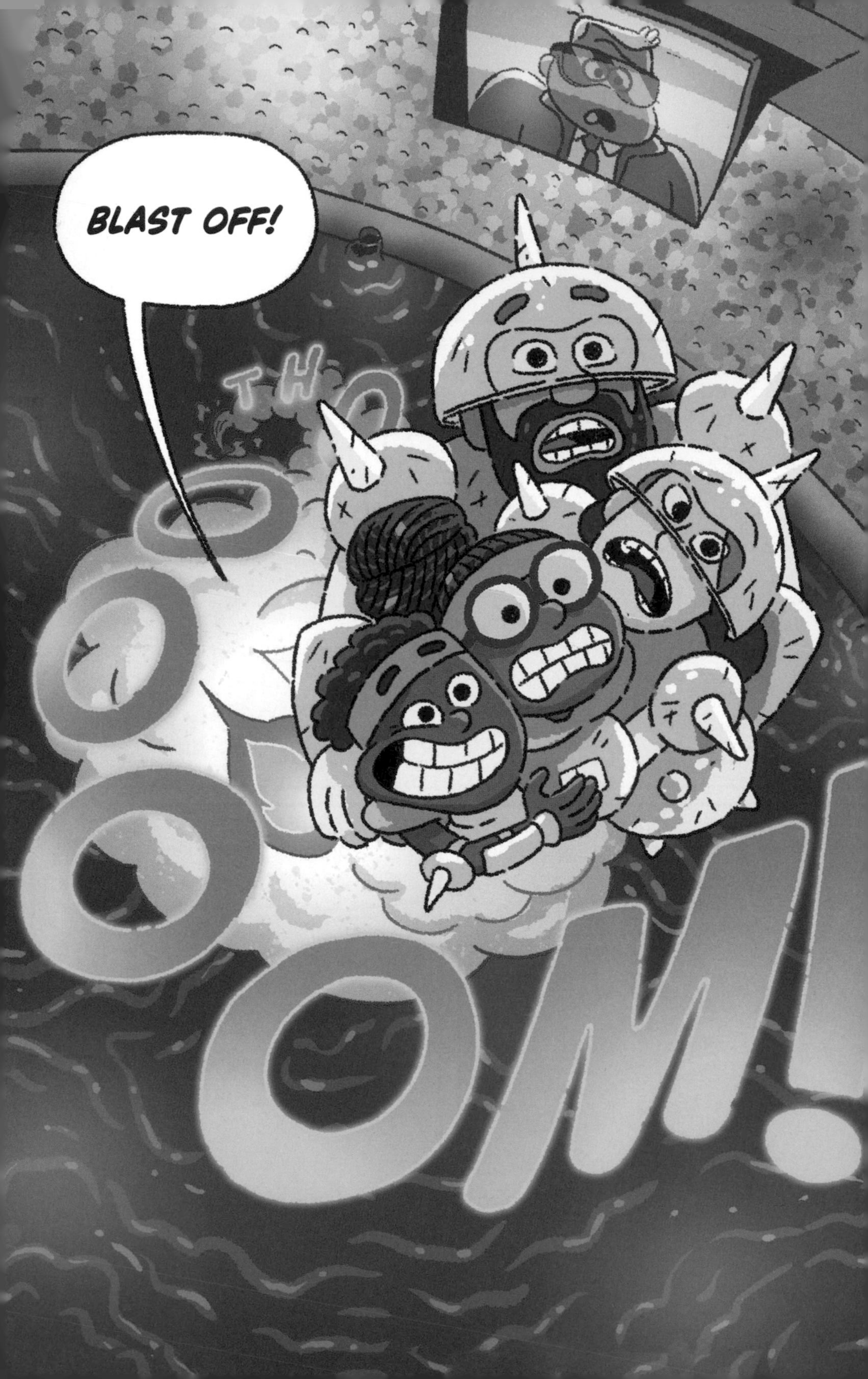
BLAST OFF!

116

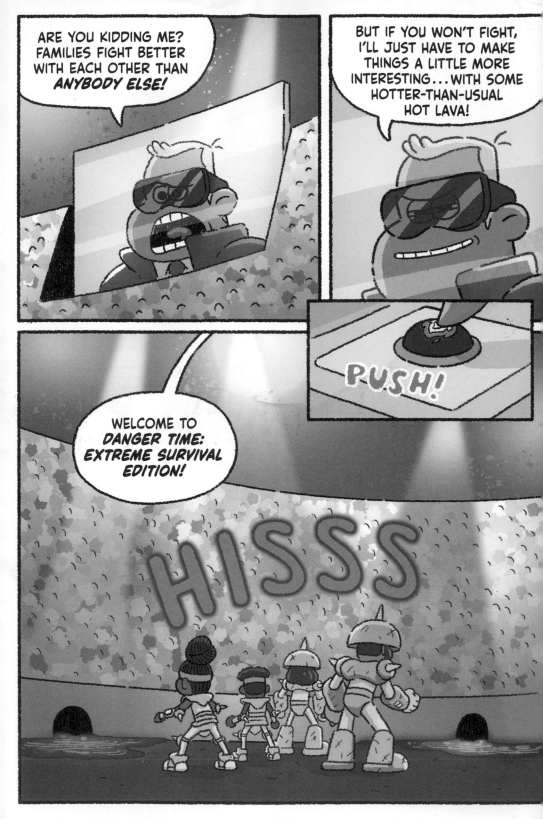

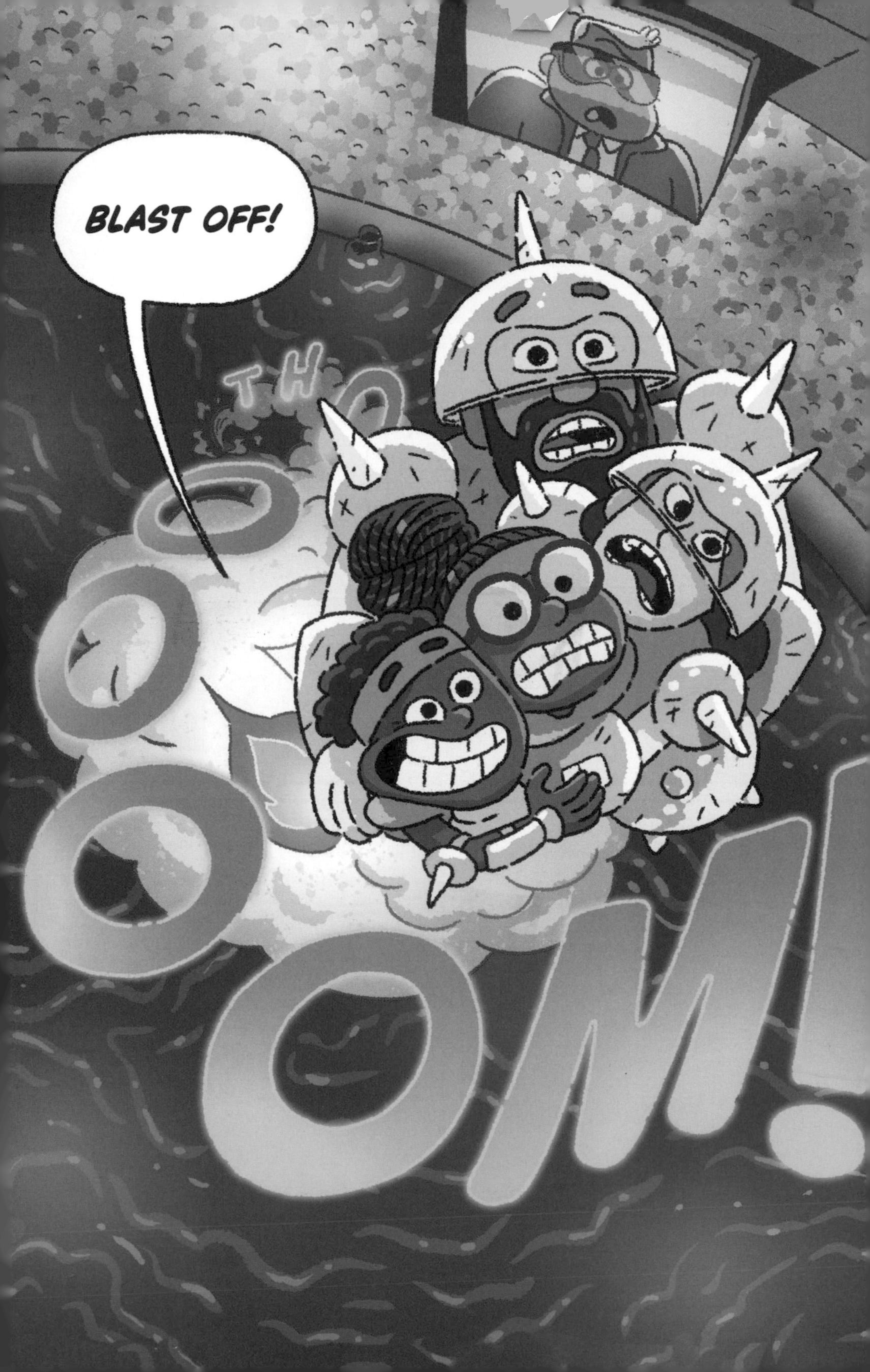
BLAST OFF!
THOOOOOM!

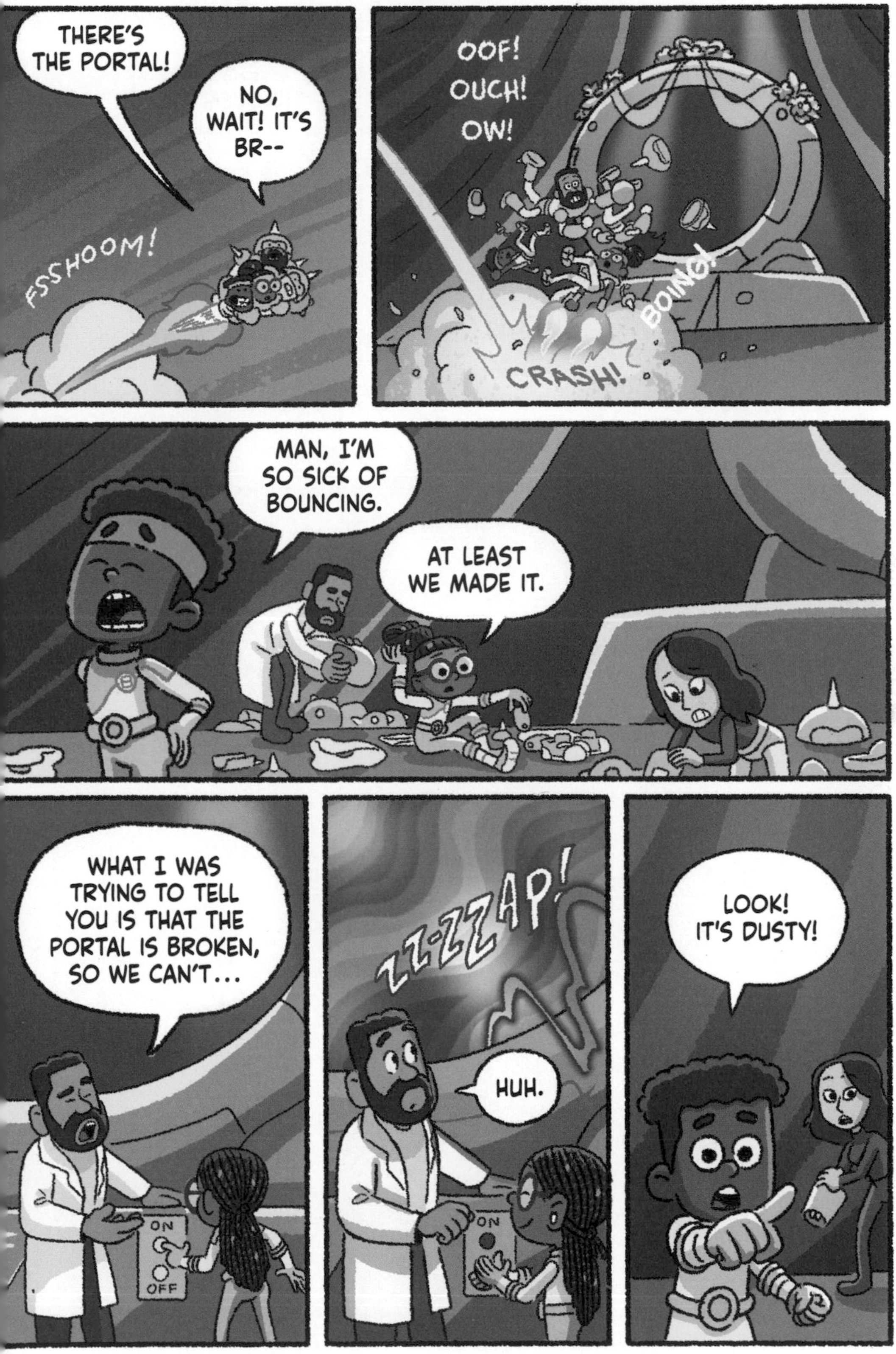
THERE'S THE PORTAL!
NO, WAIT! IT'S BR--
FSSHOOM!
OOF!
OUCH!
OW!
BOING!
CRASH!
MAN, I'M SO SICK OF BOUNCING.
AT LEAST WE MADE IT.
WHAT I WAS TRYING TO TELL YOU IS THAT THE PORTAL IS BROKEN, SO WE CAN'T...
ON
OFF
ZZ-ZZAP!
HUH.
ON
LOOK! IT'S DUSTY!

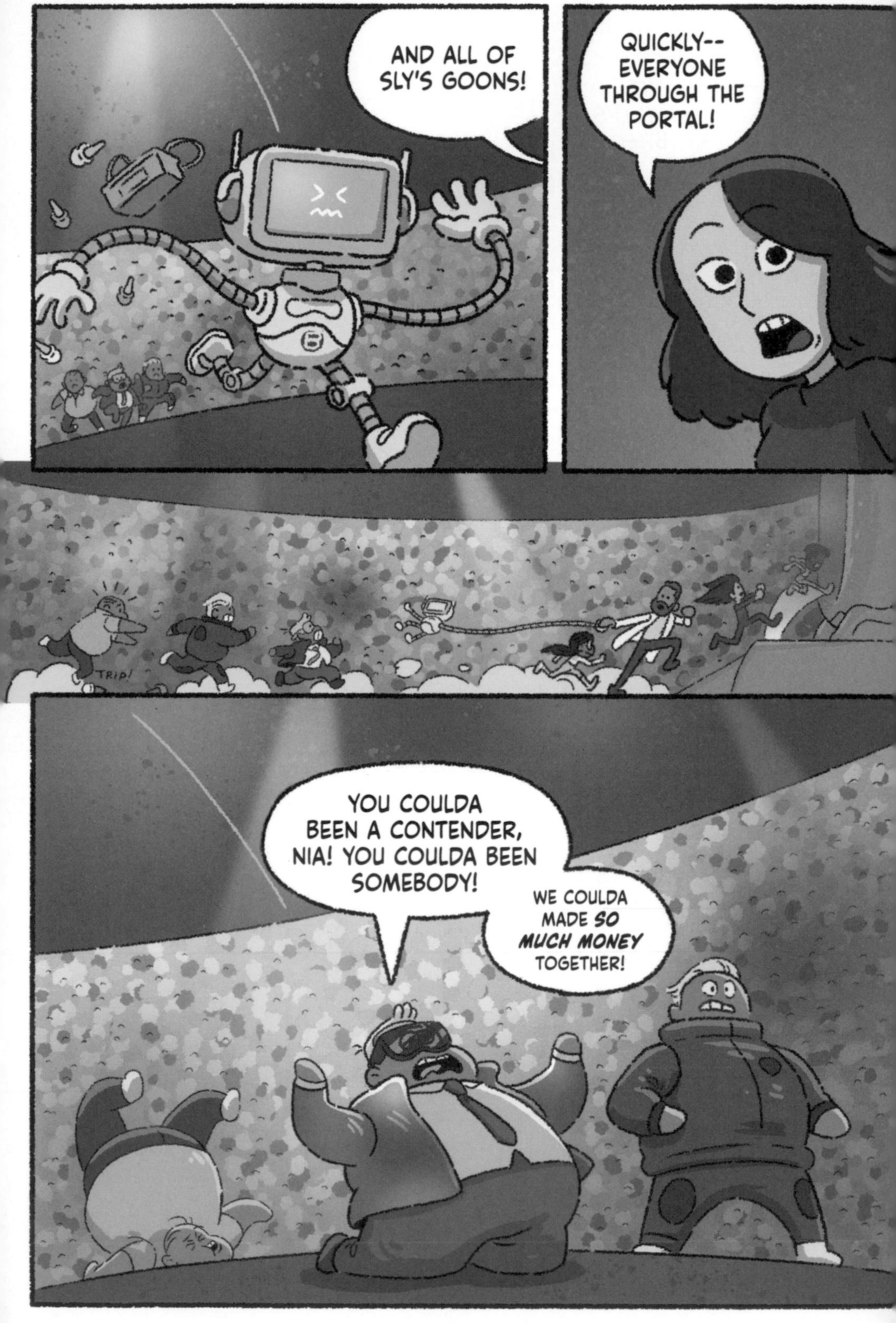
AND ALL OF SLY'S GOONS!
QUICKLY-- EVERYONE THROUGH THE PORTAL!
TRIP!
YOU COULDA BEEN A CONTENDER, NIA! YOU COULDA BEEN SOMEBODY!
WE COULDA MADE ***SO MUCH MONEY*** TOGETHER!

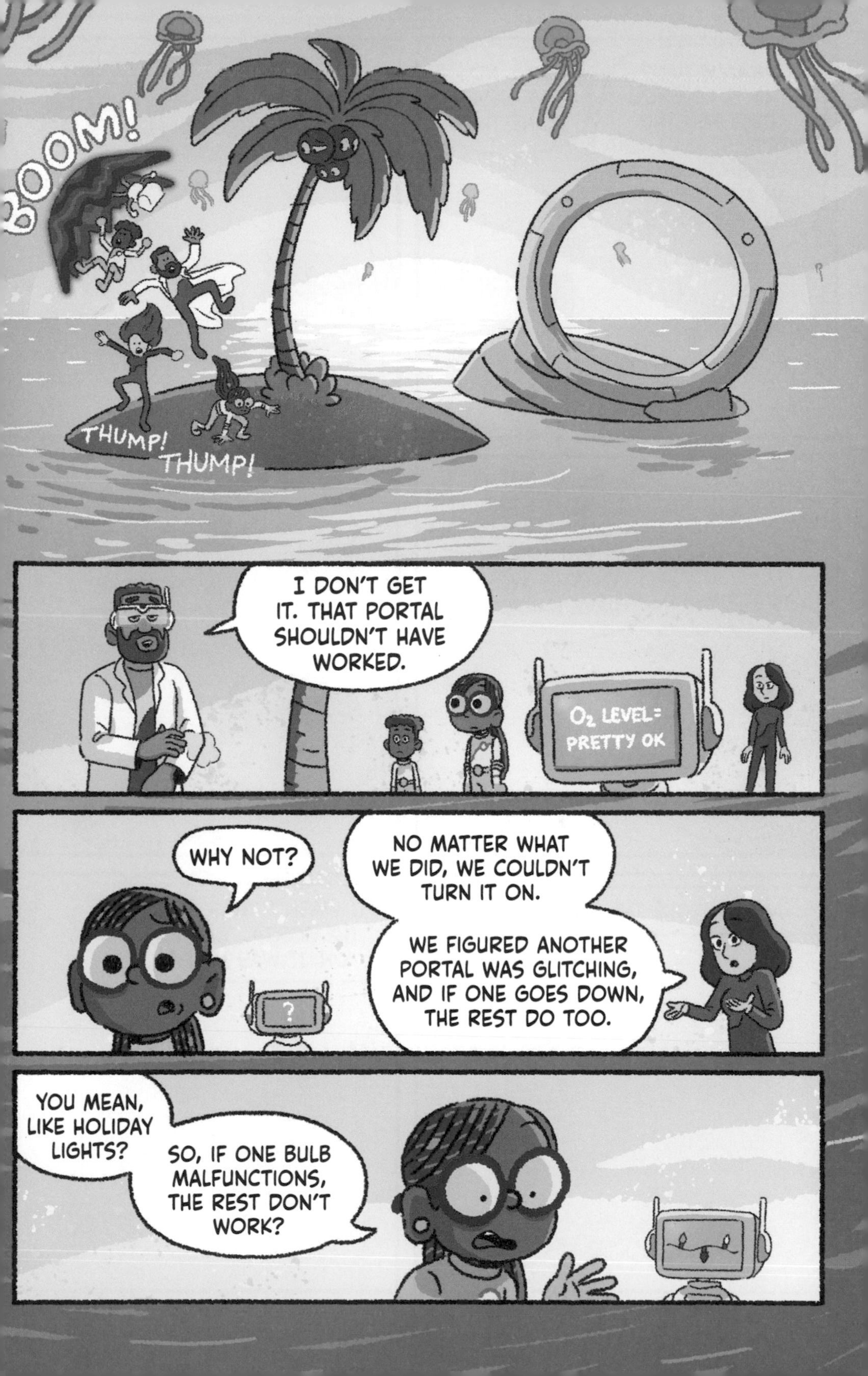
BOOM!
THUMP!
THUMP!
I DON'T GET IT. THAT PORTAL SHOULDN'T HAVE WORKED.
$O_2$ LEVEL= PRETTY OK
WHY NOT?
NO MATTER WHAT WE DID, WE COULDN'T TURN IT ON.
WE FIGURED ANOTHER PORTAL WAS GLITCHING, AND IF ONE GOES DOWN, THE REST DO TOO.
YOU MEAN, LIKE HOLIDAY LIGHTS?
SO, IF ONE BULB MALFUNCTIONS, THE REST DON'T WORK?

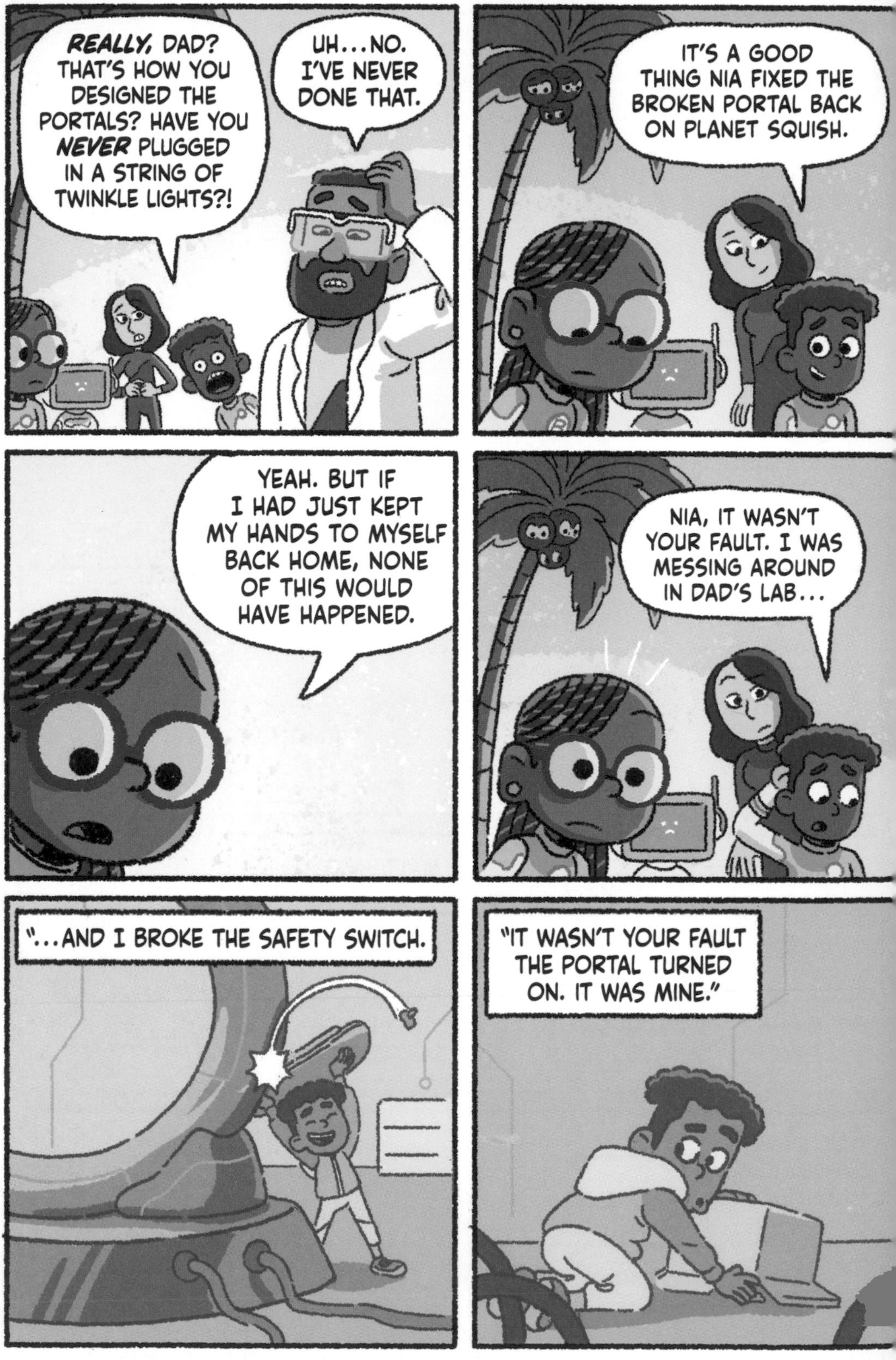
REALLY, DAD? THAT'S HOW YOU DESIGNED THE PORTALS? HAVE YOU NEVER PLUGGED IN A STRING OF TWINKLE LIGHTS?!
UH...NO. I'VE NEVER DONE THAT.
IT'S A GOOD THING NIA FIXED THE BROKEN PORTAL BACK ON PLANET SQUISH.
YEAH. BUT IF I HAD JUST KEPT MY HANDS TO MYSELF BACK HOME, NONE OF THIS WOULD HAVE HAPPENED.
NIA, IT WASN'T YOUR FAULT. I WAS MESSING AROUND IN DAD'S LAB...
"...AND I BROKE THE SAFETY SWITCH.
"IT WASN'T YOUR FAULT THE PORTAL TURNED ON. IT WAS MINE."

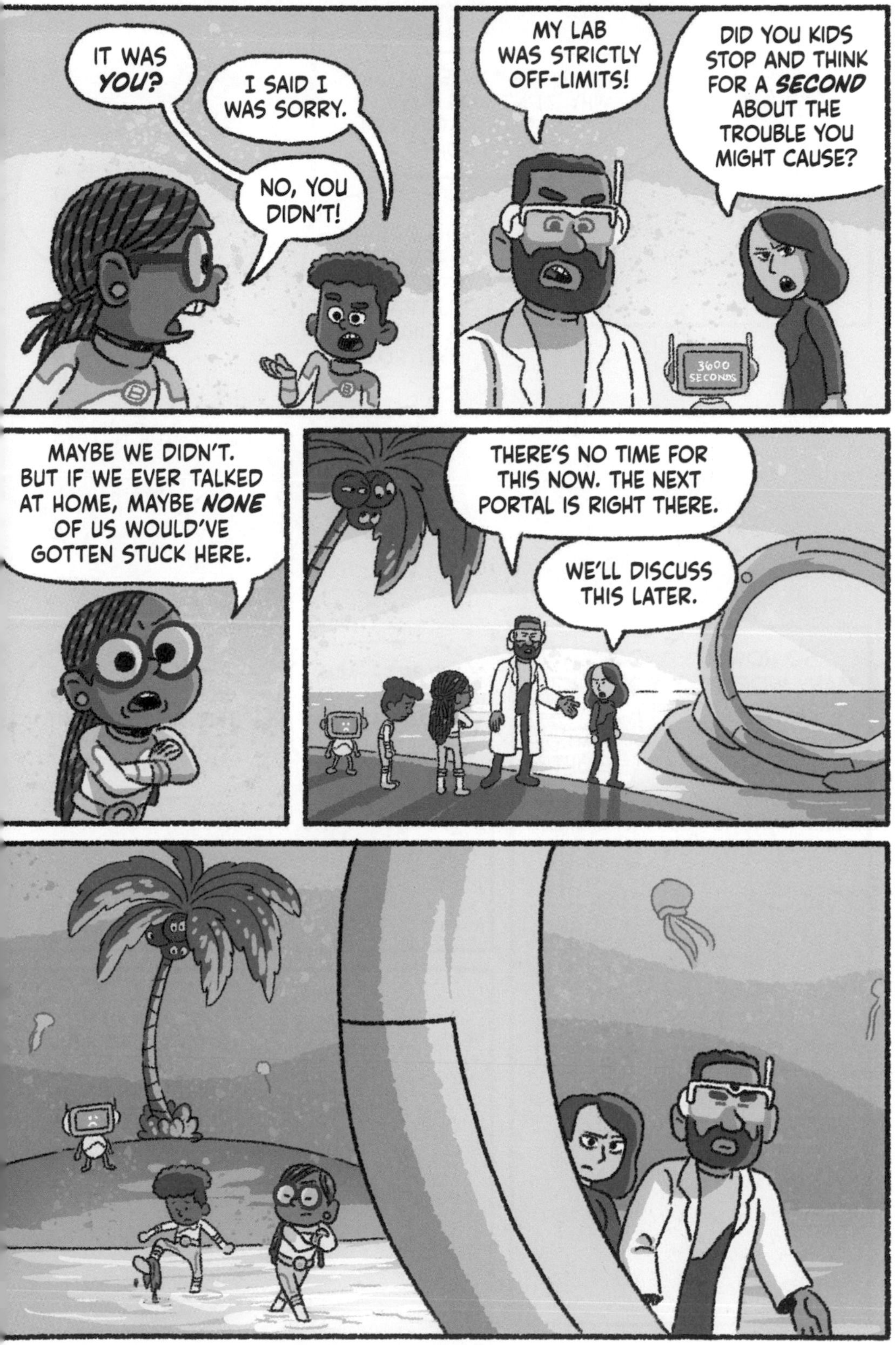
IT WAS *YOU?*
I SAID I WAS SORRY.
NO, YOU DIDN'T!
MY LAB WAS STRICTLY OFF-LIMITS!
DID YOU KIDS STOP AND THINK FOR A *SECOND* ABOUT THE TROUBLE YOU MIGHT CAUSE?
3600 SECONDS
MAYBE WE DIDN'T. BUT IF WE EVER TALKED AT HOME, MAYBE *NONE* OF US WOULD'VE GOTTEN STUCK HERE.
THERE'S NO TIME FOR THIS NOW. THE NEXT PORTAL IS RIGHT THERE.
WE'LL DISCUSS THIS LATER.

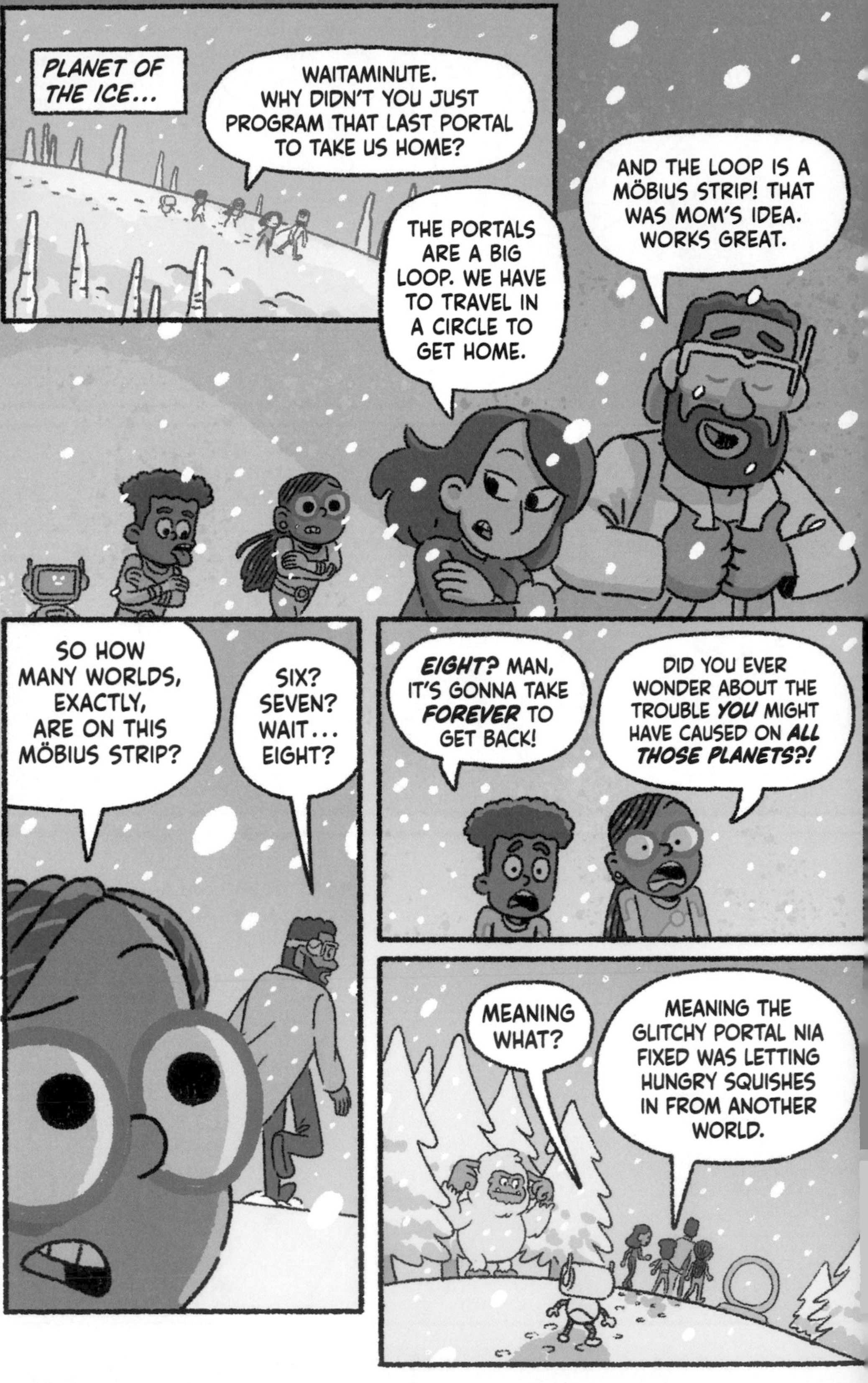
PLANET OF THE ICE...
WAITAMINUTE. WHY DIDN'T YOU JUST PROGRAM THAT LAST PORTAL TO TAKE US HOME?
THE PORTALS ARE A BIG LOOP. WE HAVE TO TRAVEL IN A CIRCLE TO GET HOME.
AND THE LOOP IS A MÖBIUS STRIP! THAT WAS MOM'S IDEA. WORKS GREAT.
SO HOW MANY WORLDS, EXACTLY, ARE ON THIS MÖBIUS STRIP?
SIX? SEVEN? WAIT... EIGHT?
EIGHT? MAN, IT'S GONNA TAKE FOREVER TO GET BACK!
DID YOU EVER WONDER ABOUT THE TROUBLE YOU MIGHT HAVE CAUSED ON ALL THOSE PLANETS?!
MEANING WHAT?
MEANING THE GLITCHY PORTAL NIA FIXED WAS LETTING HUNGRY SQUISHES IN FROM ANOTHER WORLD.

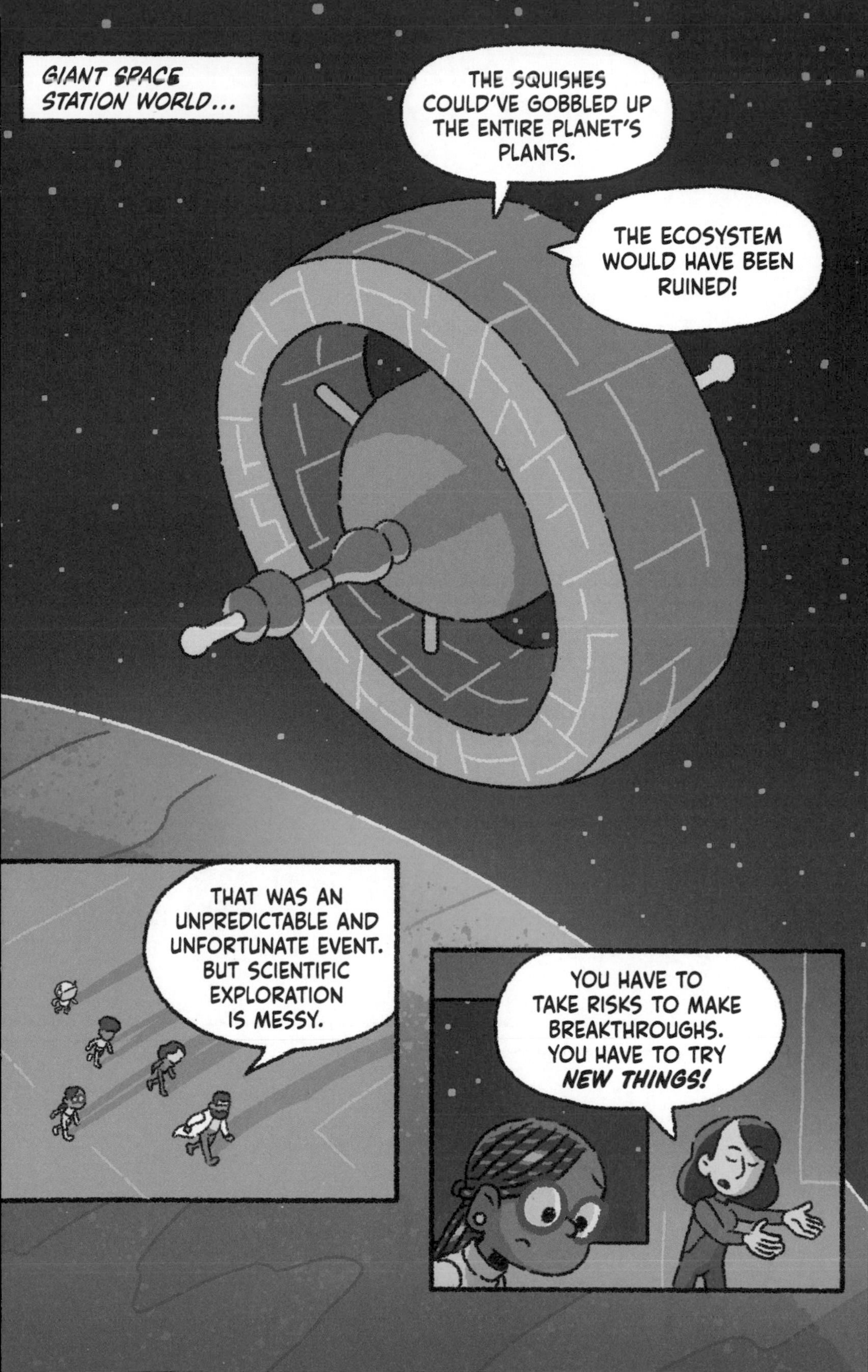
GIANT SPACE STATION WORLD...
THE SQUISHES COULD'VE GOBBLED UP THE ENTIRE PLANET'S PLANTS.
THE ECOSYSTEM WOULD HAVE BEEN RUINED!
THAT WAS AN UNPREDICTABLE AND UNFORTUNATE EVENT. BUT SCIENTIFIC EXPLORATION IS MESSY.
YOU HAVE TO TAKE RISKS TO MAKE BREAKTHROUGHS. YOU HAVE TO TRY *NEW THINGS!*

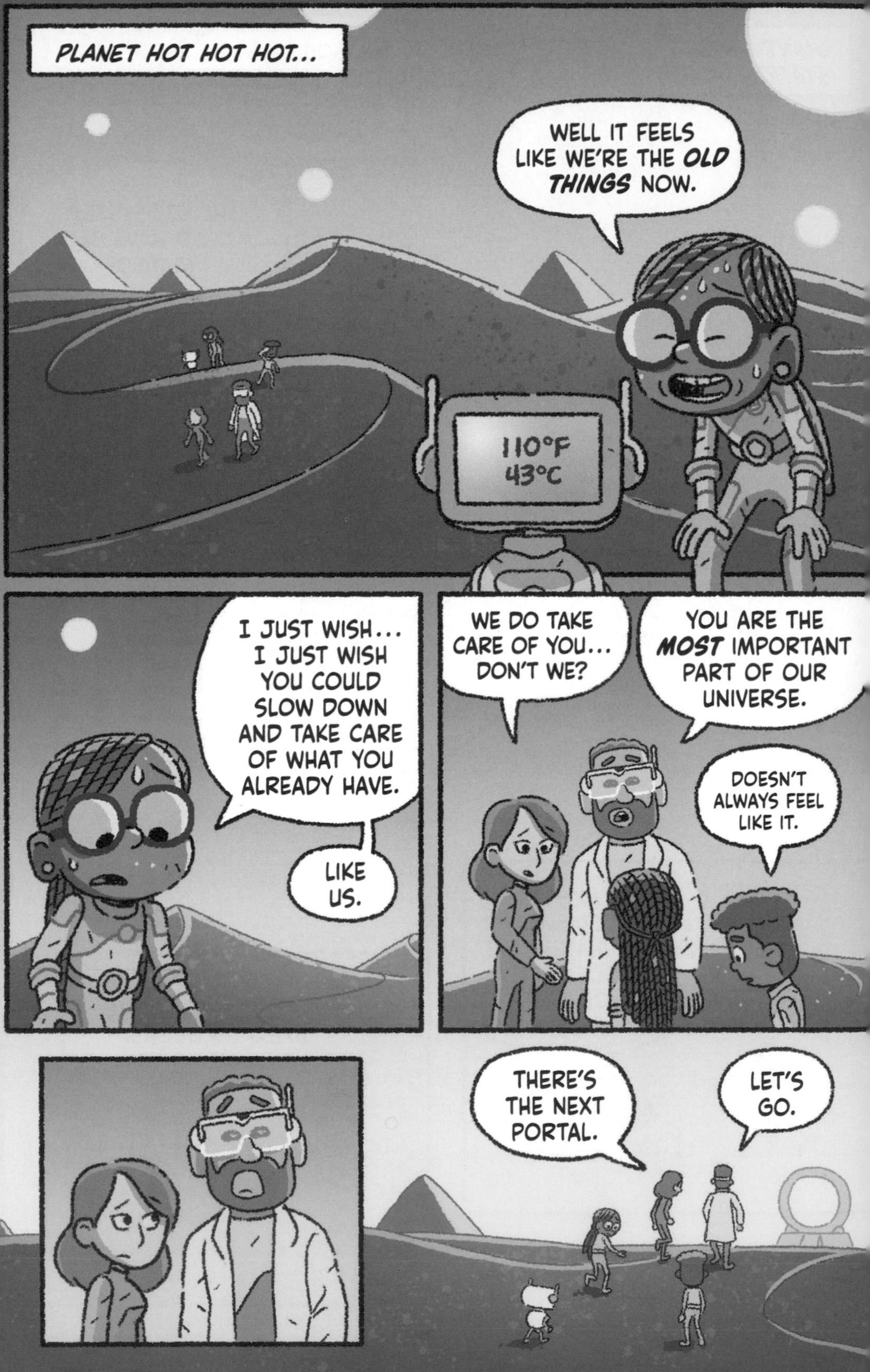

PLANET HOT HOT HOT...
WELL IT FEELS LIKE WE'RE THE OLD THINGS NOW.
110°F 43°C
I JUST WISH... I JUST WISH YOU COULD SLOW DOWN AND TAKE CARE OF WHAT YOU ALREADY HAVE.
LIKE US.
WE DO TAKE CARE OF YOU... DON'T WE?
YOU ARE THE MOST IMPORTANT PART OF OUR UNIVERSE.
DOESN'T ALWAYS FEEL LIKE IT.
THERE'S THE NEXT PORTAL.
LET'S GO.

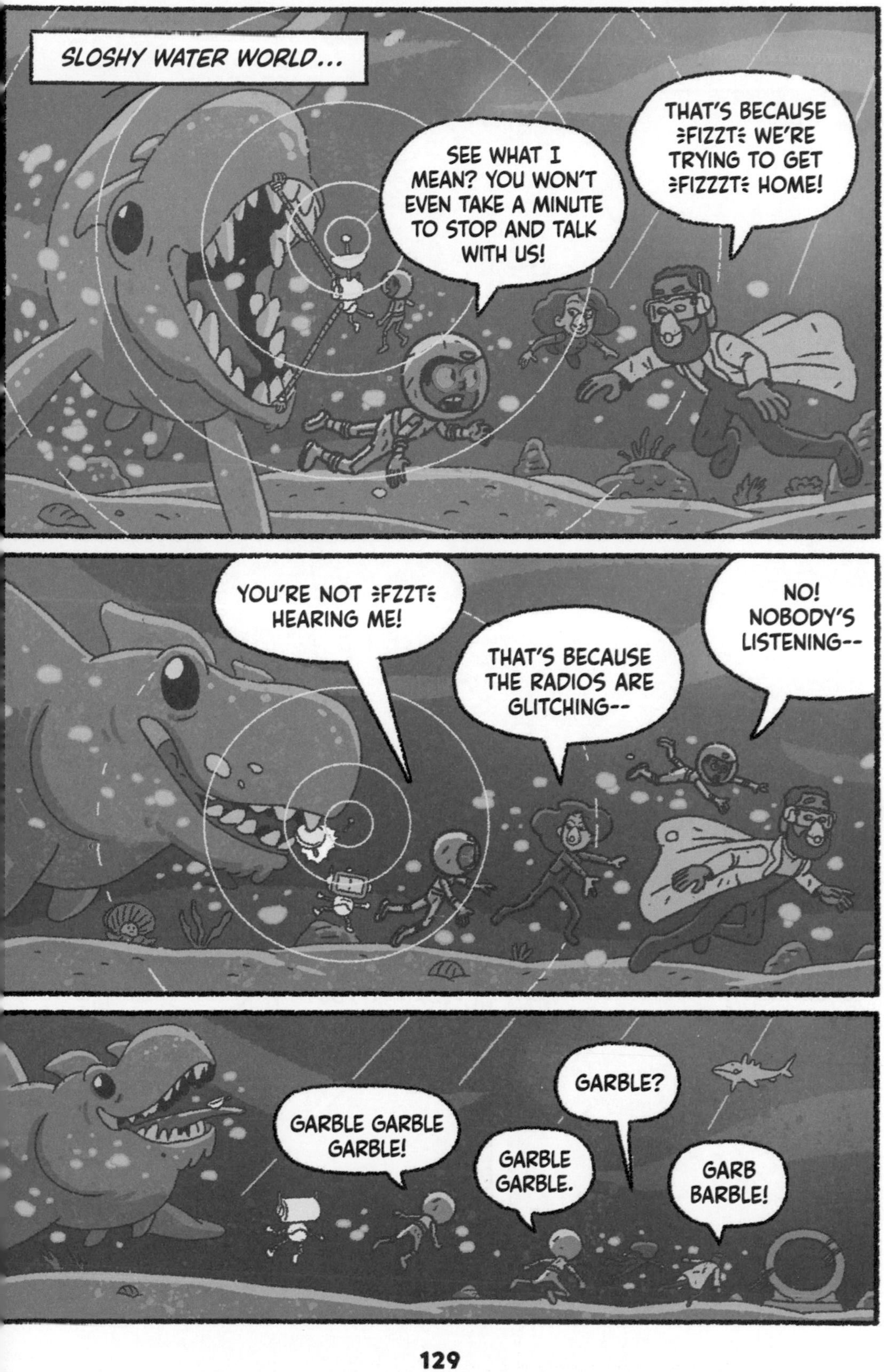
SLOSHY WATER WORLD...
SEE WHAT I MEAN? YOU WON'T EVEN TAKE A MINUTE TO STOP AND TALK WITH US!
THAT'S BECAUSE ⁝FIZZT⁝ WE'RE TRYING TO GET ⁝FIZZZT⁝ HOME!
YOU'RE NOT ⁝FZZT⁝ HEARING ME!
THAT'S BECAUSE THE RADIOS ARE GLITCHING--
NO! NOBODY'S LISTENING--
GARBLE GARBLE GARBLE!
GARBLE GARBLE.
GARBLE?
GARB BARBLE!

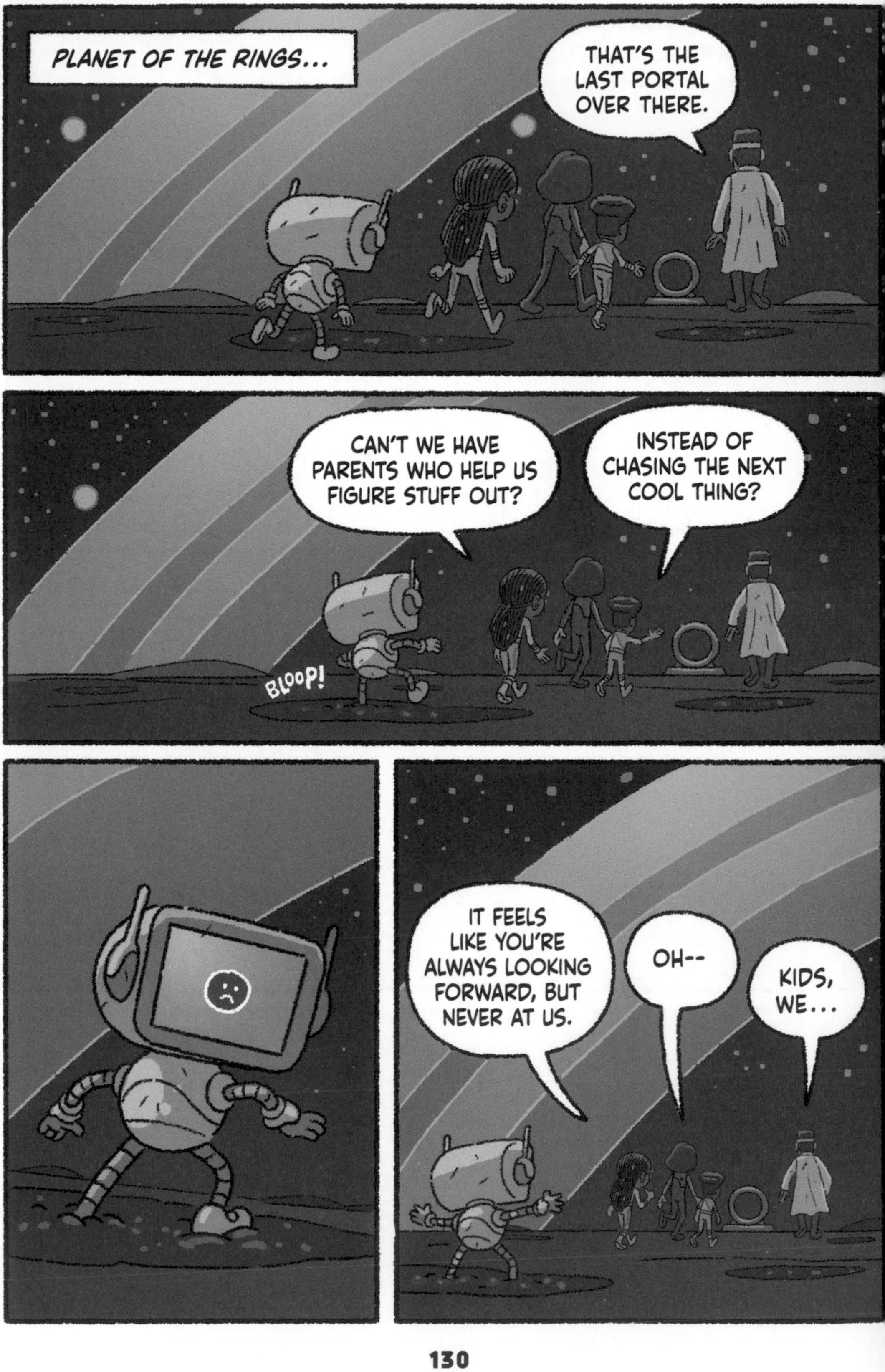
PLANET OF THE RINGS...
THAT'S THE LAST PORTAL OVER THERE.
CAN'T WE HAVE PARENTS WHO HELP US FIGURE STUFF OUT?
INSTEAD OF CHASING THE NEXT COOL THING?
BLOOP!
IT FEELS LIKE YOU'RE ALWAYS LOOKING FORWARD, BUT NEVER AT US.
OH--
KIDS, WE...

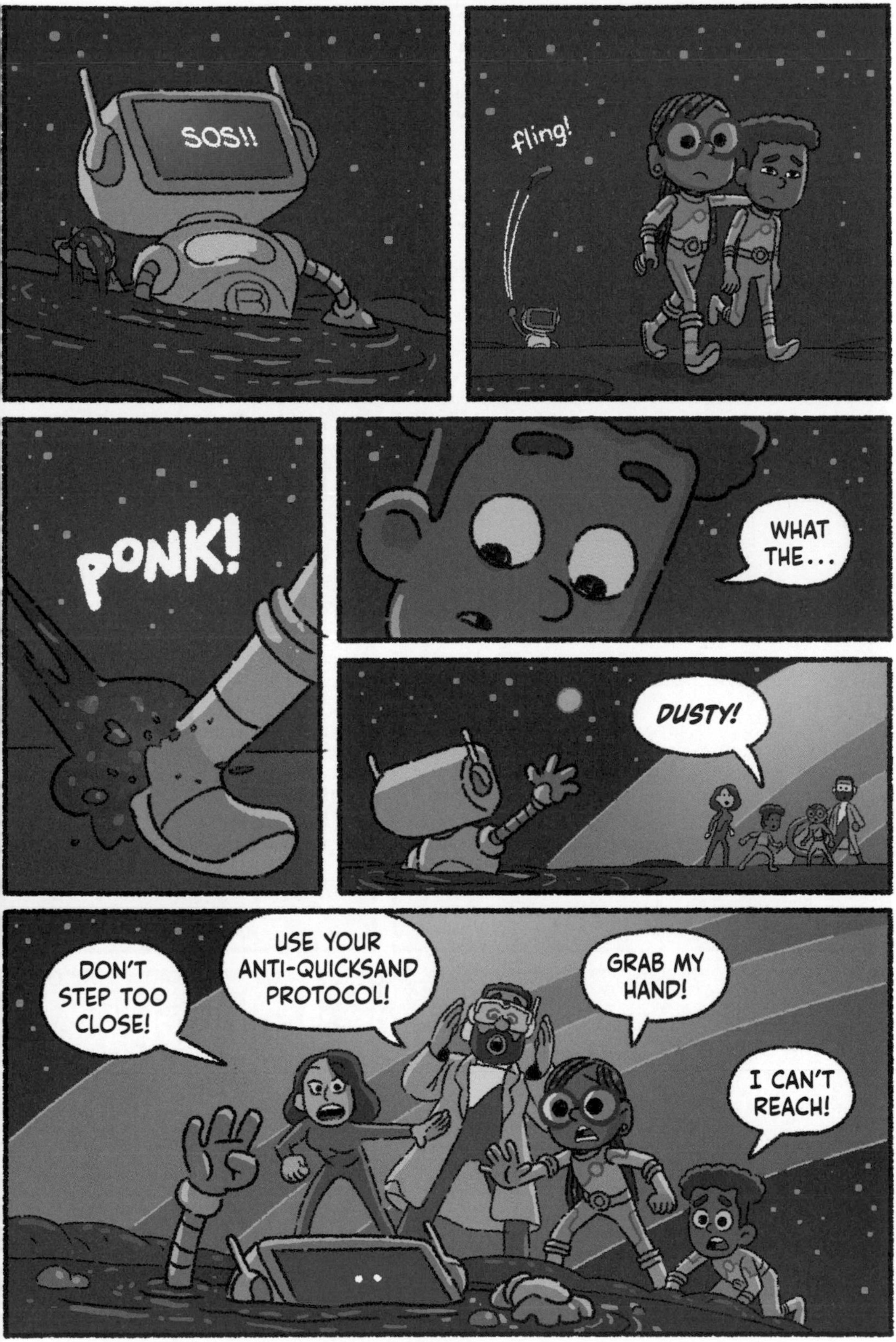
SOS!!
fling!
PONK!
WHAT THE...
DUSTY!
DON'T STEP TOO CLOSE!
USE YOUR ANTI-QUICKSAND PROTOCOL!
GRAB MY HAND!
I CAN'T REACH!

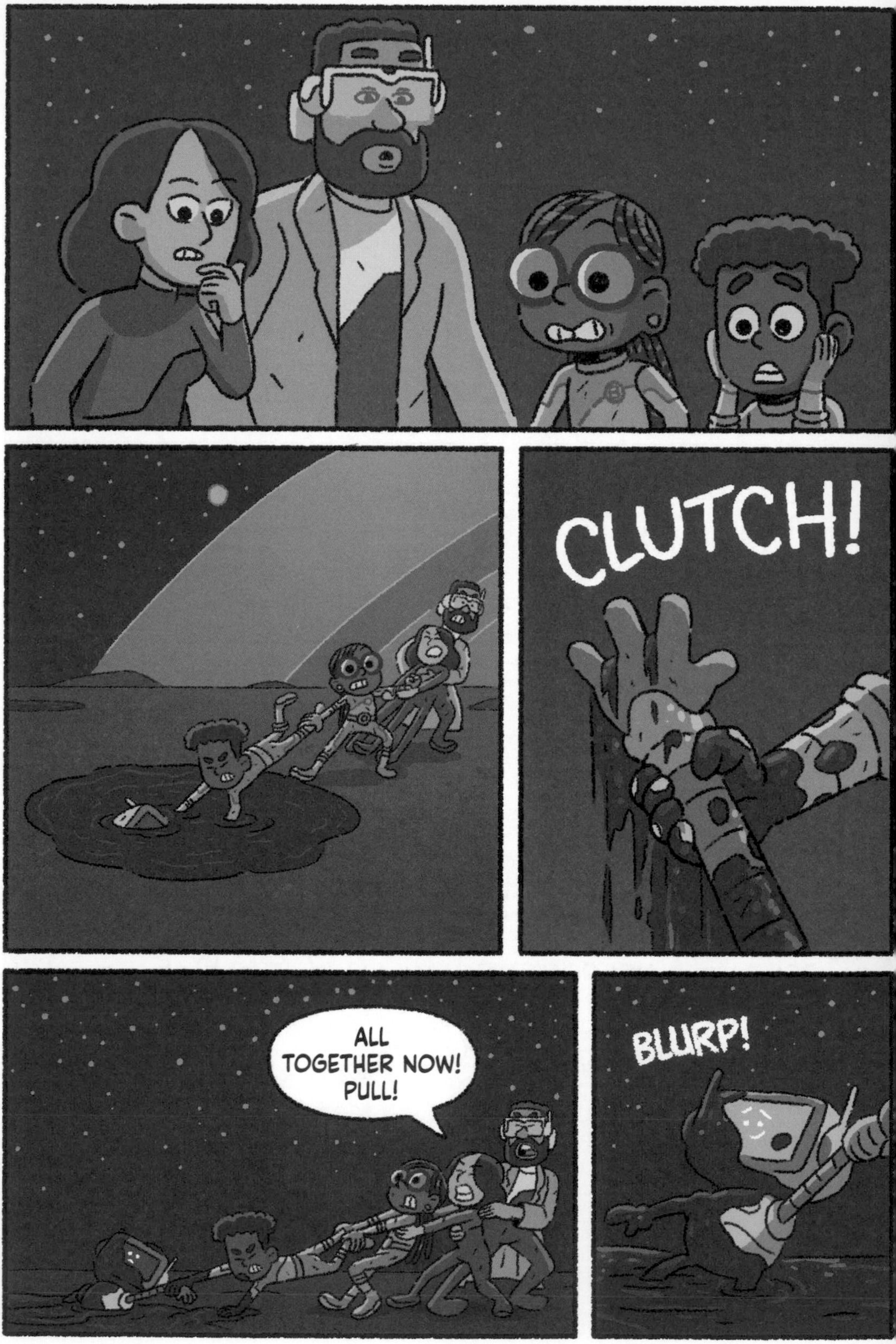
CLUTCH!
ALL TOGETHER NOW! PULL!
BLURP!

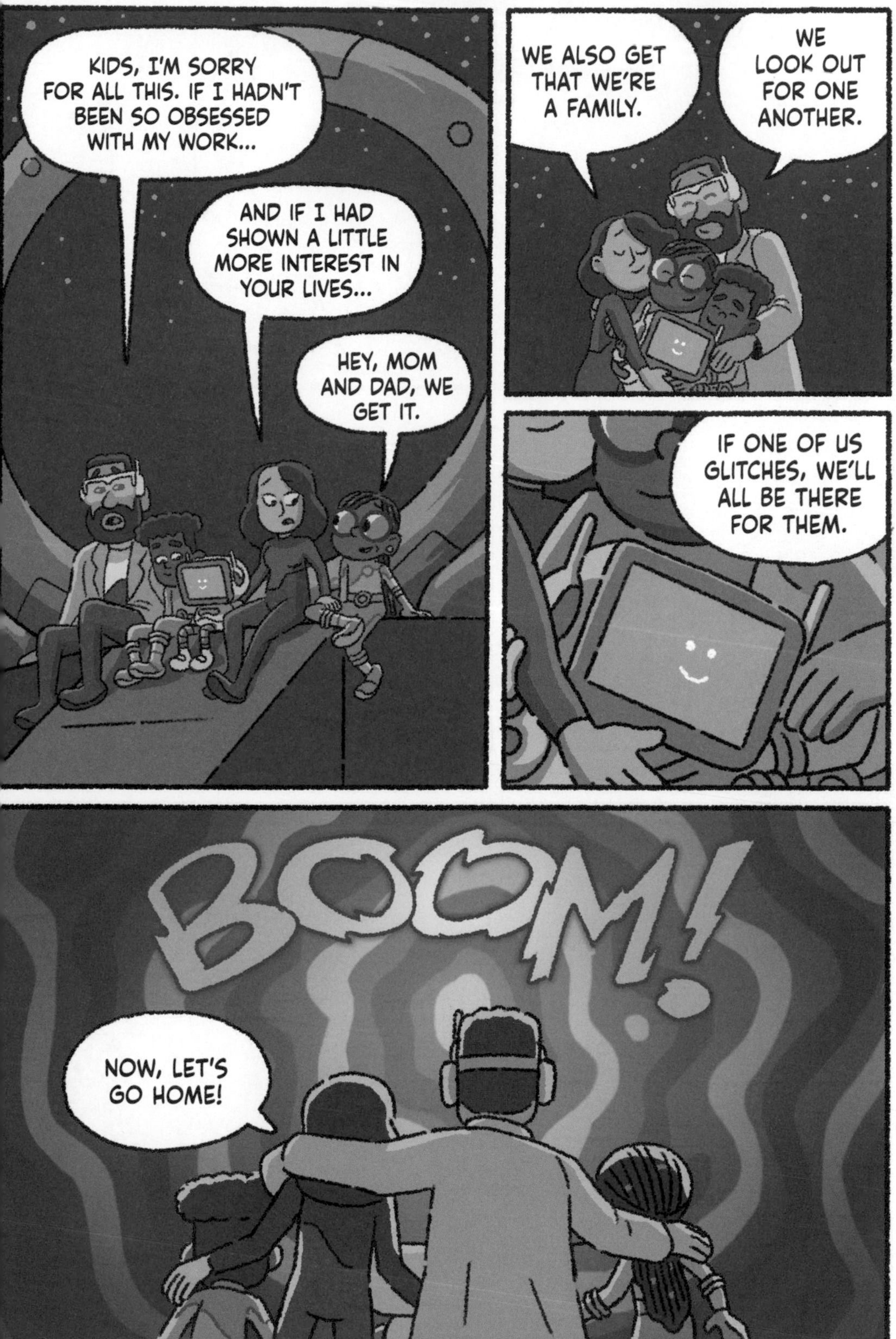
KIDS, I'M SORRY FOR ALL THIS. IF I HADN'T BEEN SO OBSESSED WITH MY WORK...
AND IF I HAD SHOWN A LITTLE MORE INTEREST IN YOUR LIVES...
HEY, MOM AND DAD, WE GET IT.
WE ALSO GET THAT WE'RE A FAMILY.
WE LOOK OUT FOR ONE ANOTHER.
IF ONE OF US GLITCHES, WE'LL ALL BE THERE FOR THEM.
BOOM!
NOW, LET'S GO HOME!

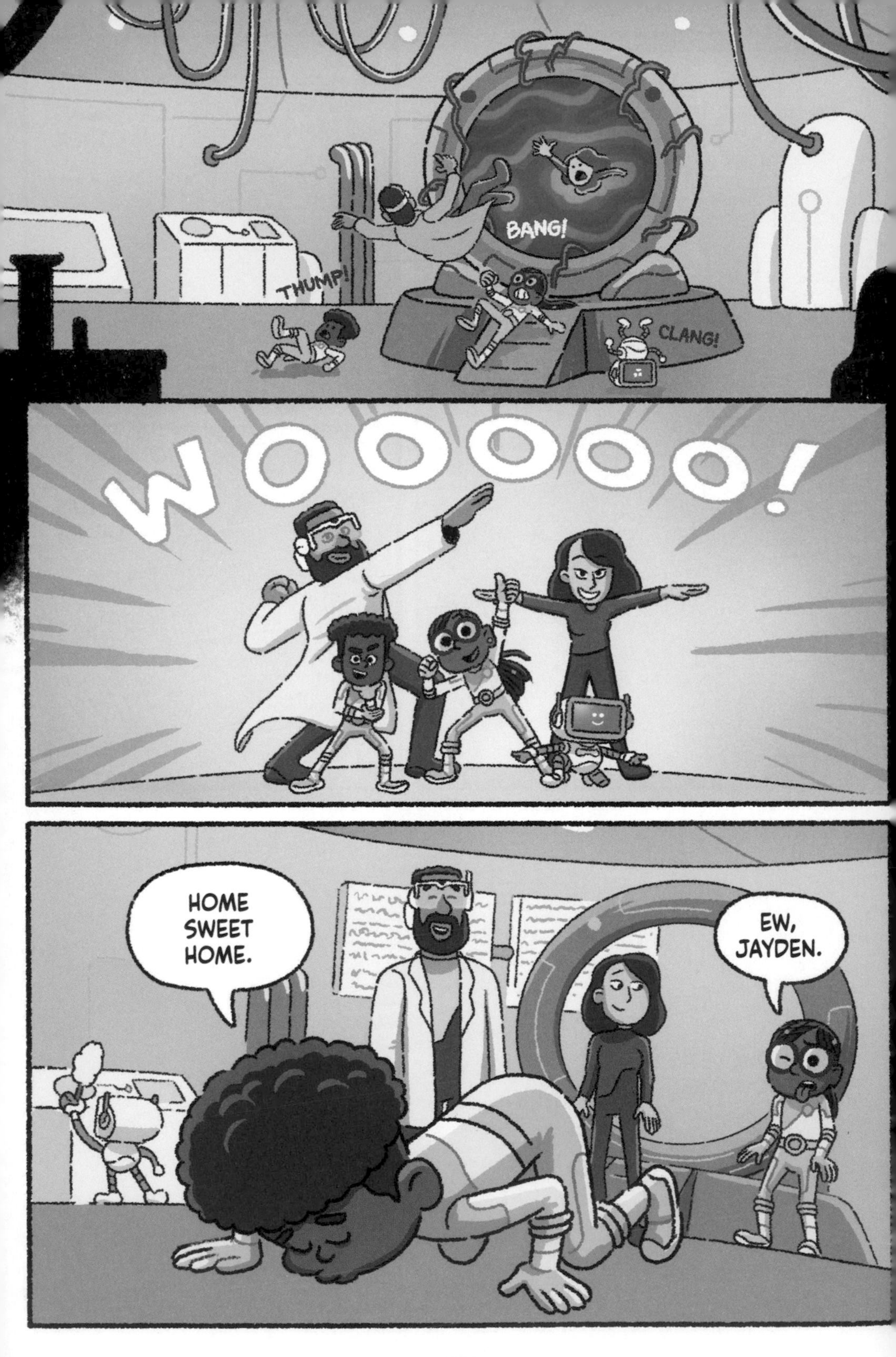
BANG!
THUMP!
CLANG!
WOOOOO!
HOME SWEET HOME.
EW, JAYDEN.

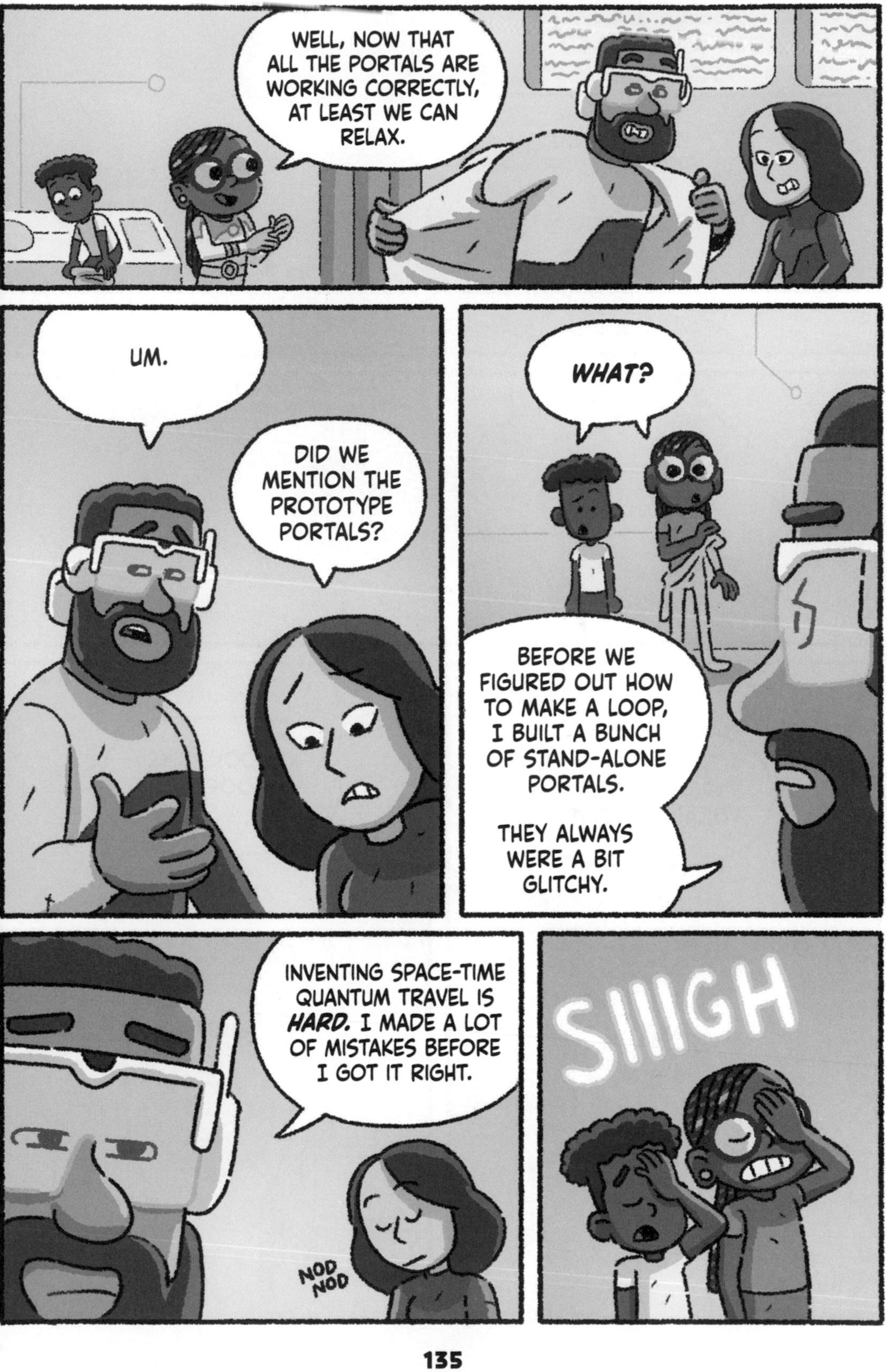
WELL, NOW THAT ALL THE PORTALS ARE WORKING CORRECTLY, AT LEAST WE CAN RELAX.
UM.
DID WE MENTION THE PROTOTYPE PORTALS?
*WHAT?*
BEFORE WE FIGURED OUT HOW TO MAKE A LOOP, I BUILT A BUNCH OF STAND-ALONE PORTALS.
THEY ALWAYS WERE A BIT GLITCHY.
INVENTING SPACE-TIME QUANTUM TRAVEL IS ***HARD.*** I MADE A LOT OF MISTAKES BEFORE I GOT IT RIGHT.
NOD NOD
SIIIGH

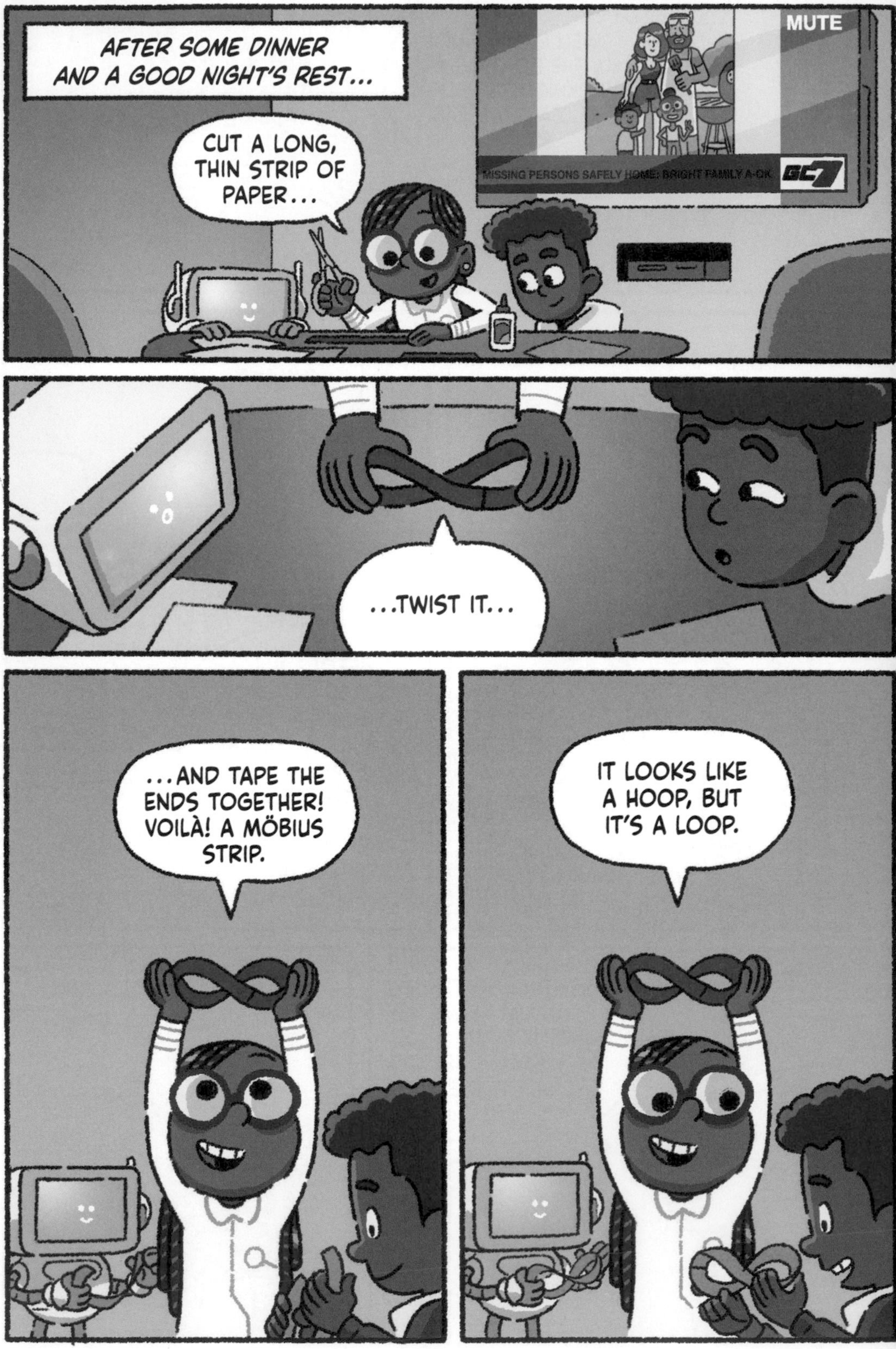
AFTER SOME DINNER AND A GOOD NIGHT'S REST...
MUTE
MISSING PERSONS SAFELY HOME: BRIGHT FAMILY A-OK
GC7
CUT A LONG, THIN STRIP OF PAPER...
...TWIST IT...
...AND TAPE THE ENDS TOGETHER! VOILÀ! A MÖBIUS STRIP.
IT LOOKS LIKE A HOOP, BUT IT'S A LOOP.

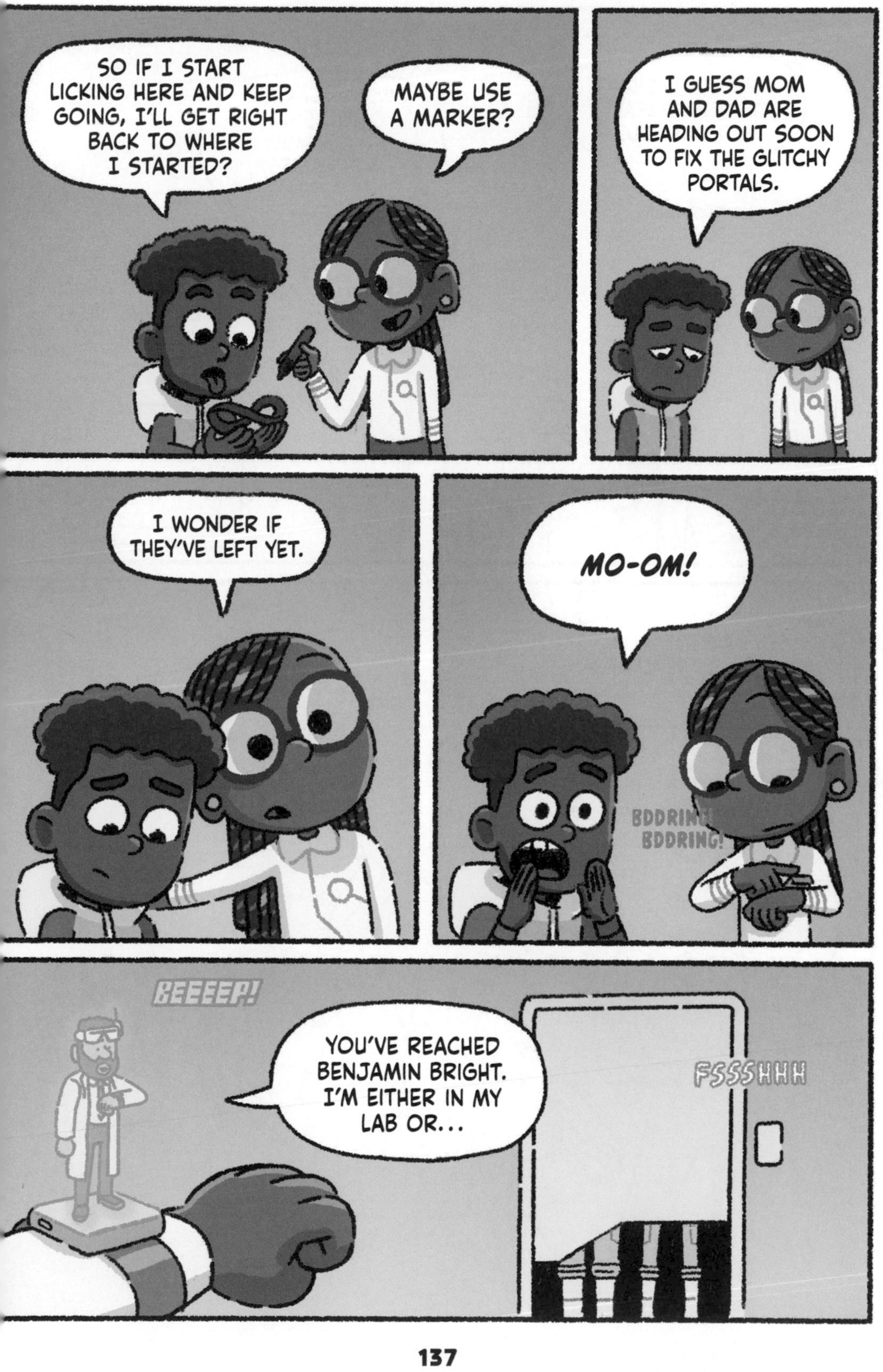
SO IF I START LICKING HERE AND KEEP GOING, I'LL GET RIGHT BACK TO WHERE I STARTED?
MAYBE USE A MARKER?
I GUESS MOM AND DAD ARE HEADING OUT SOON TO FIX THE GLITCHY PORTALS.
I WONDER IF THEY'VE LEFT YET.
MO-OM!
BDDRING! BDDRING!
BEEEEP!
YOU'VE REACHED BENJAMIN BRIGHT. I'M EITHER IN MY LAB OR...
FSSSHHH

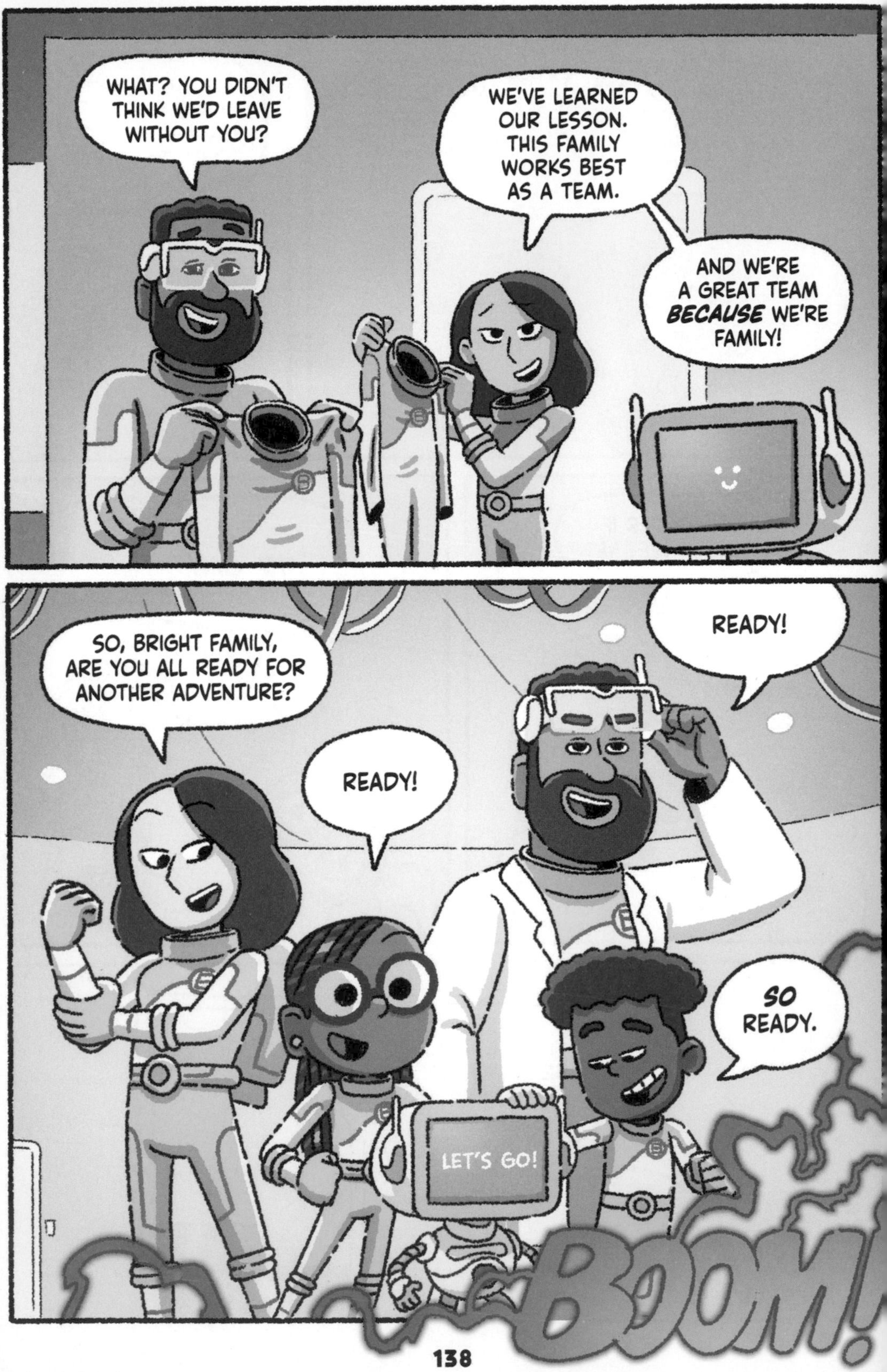
WHAT? YOU DIDN'T THINK WE'D LEAVE WITHOUT YOU?
WE'VE LEARNED OUR LESSON. THIS FAMILY WORKS BEST AS A TEAM.
AND WE'RE A GREAT TEAM *BECAUSE* WE'RE FAMILY!
SO, BRIGHT FAMILY, ARE YOU ALL READY FOR ANOTHER ADVENTURE?
READY!
READY!
*SO* READY.
LET'S GO!
BOOM!

# ABOUT THE AUTHORS

**MATTHEW CODY** is the author of several popular books, including the award-winning Supers of Noble's Green trilogy: *Powerless, Super,* and *Villainous.* He is also the author of *Will in Scarlet* and *The Dead Gentleman,* as well as the graphic novels *Zatanna and the House of Secrets* from DC comics and *Cat Ninja* from Epic/Andrews McMeel. He lives in Manhattan, NY, with his wife and son.

**CAROL KLIO BURRELL** is an editor, author, illustrator, and translator of enough graphic novels to have lost count. She grew up in New York City and a little bit in Miami, swapped New York for London for a while, and, unrelated to any of this, loves big hairy dogs.

# ABOUT THE ILLUSTRATOR

**DERICK BROOKS** is a cartoonist and illustrator from Newport News, VA. His work is a mixture of adventure and fantasy with a slice of life. He is the creator of the graphic novel *Grip Up,* to be published by Iron Circus in 2022. He currently lives in Richmond, VA, where he eats copious amounts of potatoes and hangs with his wife and their pets.

# ABOUT THE COLORIST

**WARREN WUCINICH** is a comic book creator and part-time carny who has been lucky enough to work on such cool projects as *Invader ZIM, Courtney Crumrin,* and *Cat Ninja.* He is also the cocreator of the YA graphic novel *Kriss: The Gift of Wrath.* He currently resides in Dallas, TX, where he spends his time making comics, rewatching '80s television shows, and eating all the tacos.

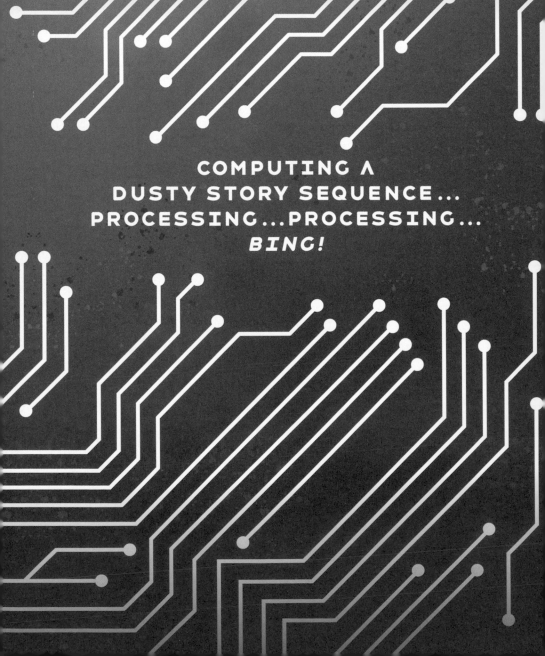

COMPUTING A
DUSTY STORY SEQUENCE...
PROCESSING...PROCESSING...
*BING!*

# I, DUSTY

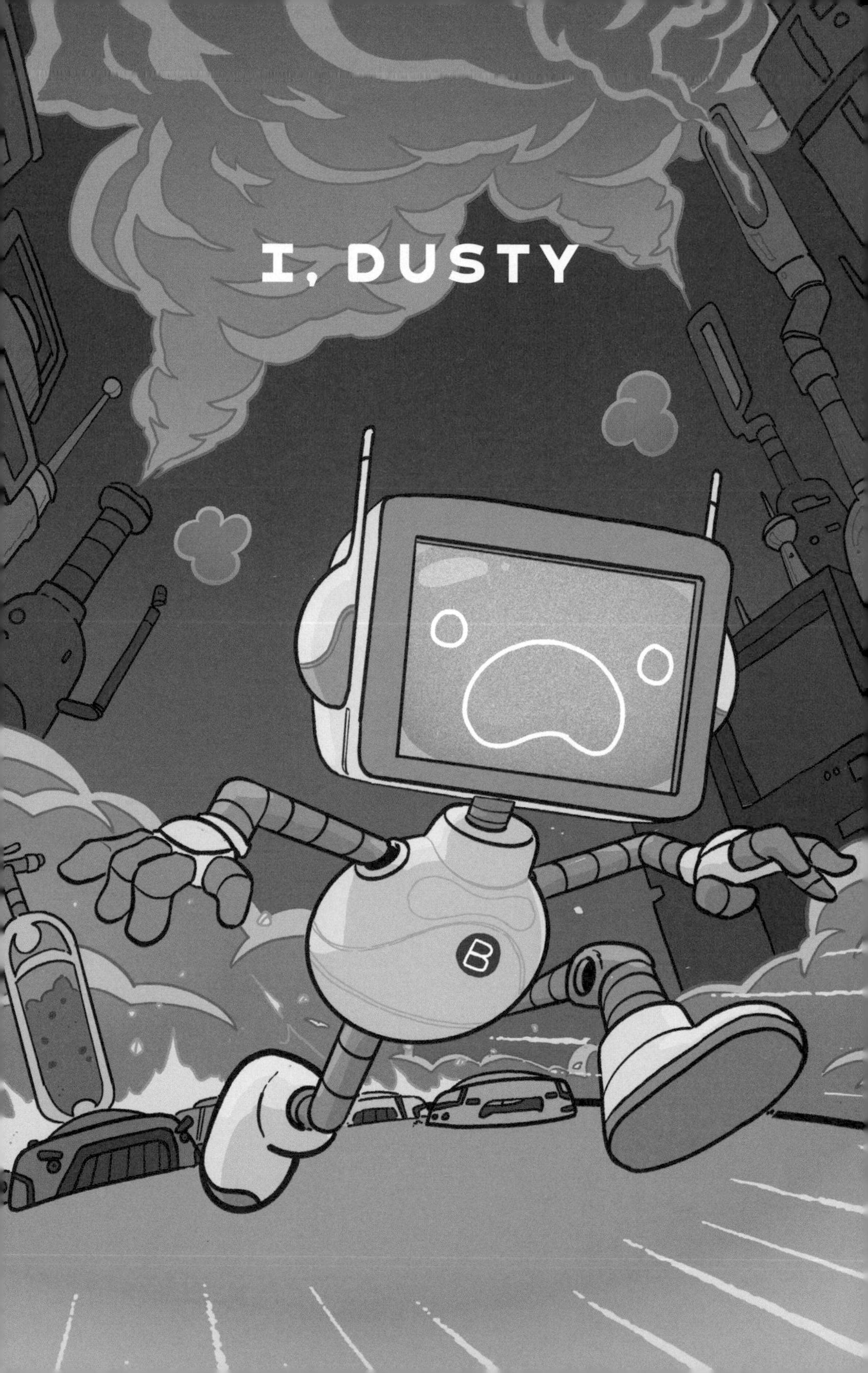

WRITTEN BY
**STEVEN SCOTT**
ART BY
**SEAN DOVE**
COLORS BY
**SAMANTHA BENNETT**

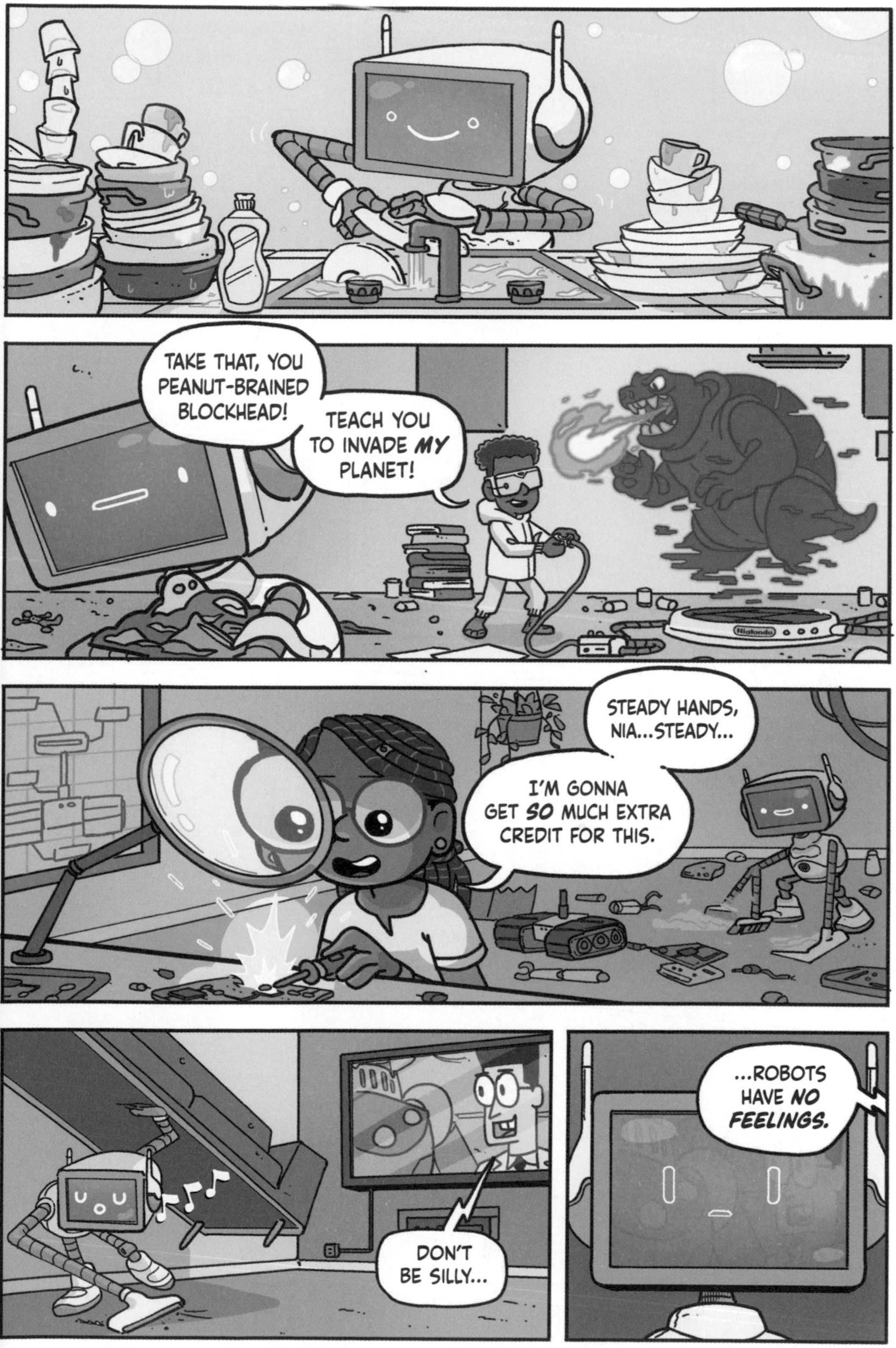
TAKE THAT, YOU PEANUT-BRAINED BLOCKHEAD!
TEACH YOU TO INVADE *MY* PLANET!
Nintondo
STEADY HANDS, NIA...STEADY...
I'M GONNA GET *SO* MUCH EXTRA CREDIT FOR THIS.
DON'T BE SILLY...
...ROBOTS HAVE *NO FEELINGS.*

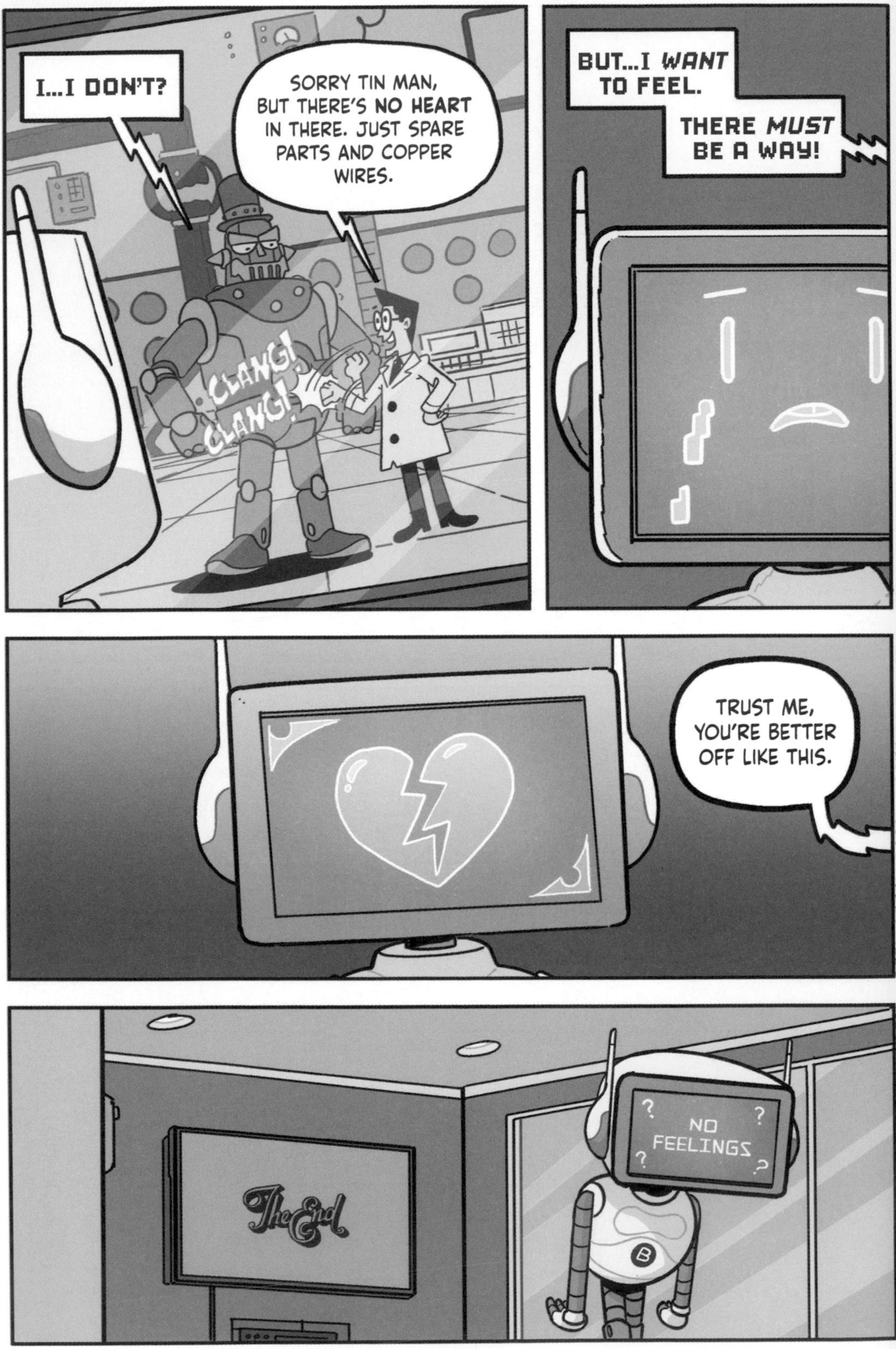
I...I DON'T?
SORRY TIN MAN, BUT THERE'S NO HEART IN THERE. JUST SPARE PARTS AND COPPER WIRES.
CLANG! CLANG!
BUT...I WANT TO FEEL.
THERE MUST BE A WAY!
TRUST ME, YOU'RE BETTER OFF LIKE THIS.
The End
? NO FEELINGS ? ? ?

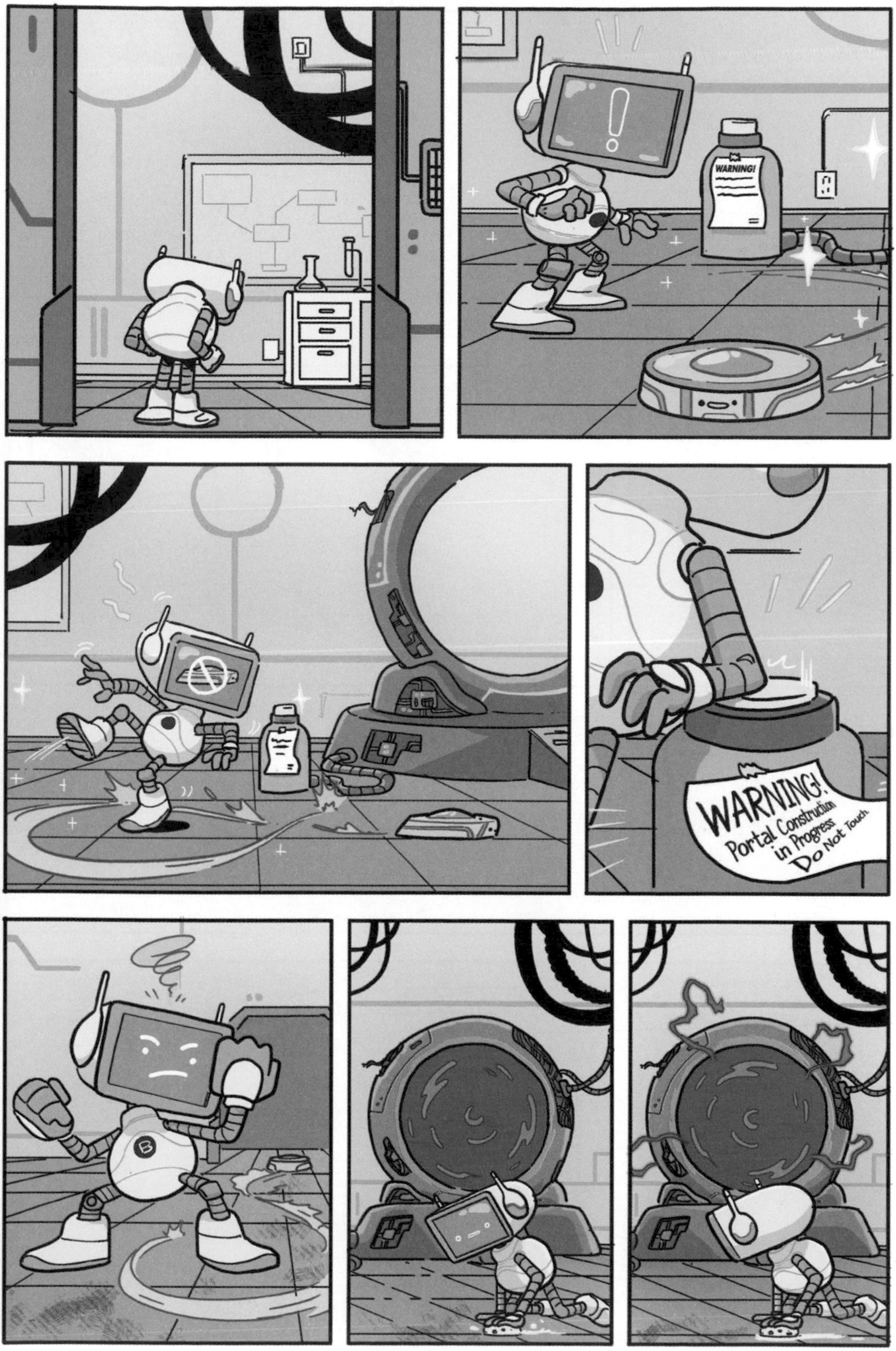
WARNING!
WARNING!
Portal Construction
in Progress
Do Not Touch.

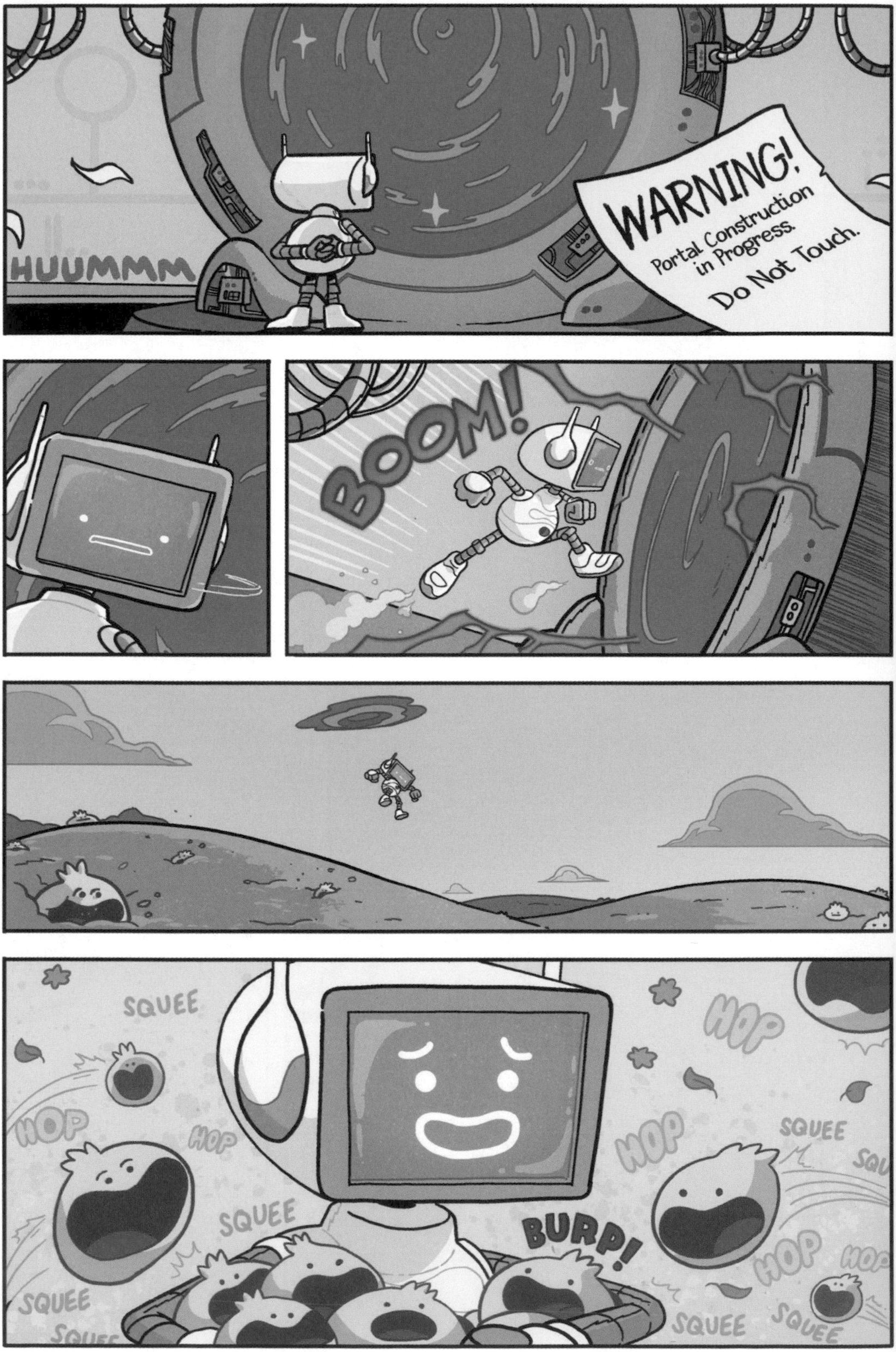
HUUMMM
WARNING!
Portal Construction in Progress.
Do Not Touch.
BOOM!
SQUEE
HOP
HOP
SQUEE
BURP!
HOP
SQUEE
HOP
SQUEE
SQUEE
SQUEE

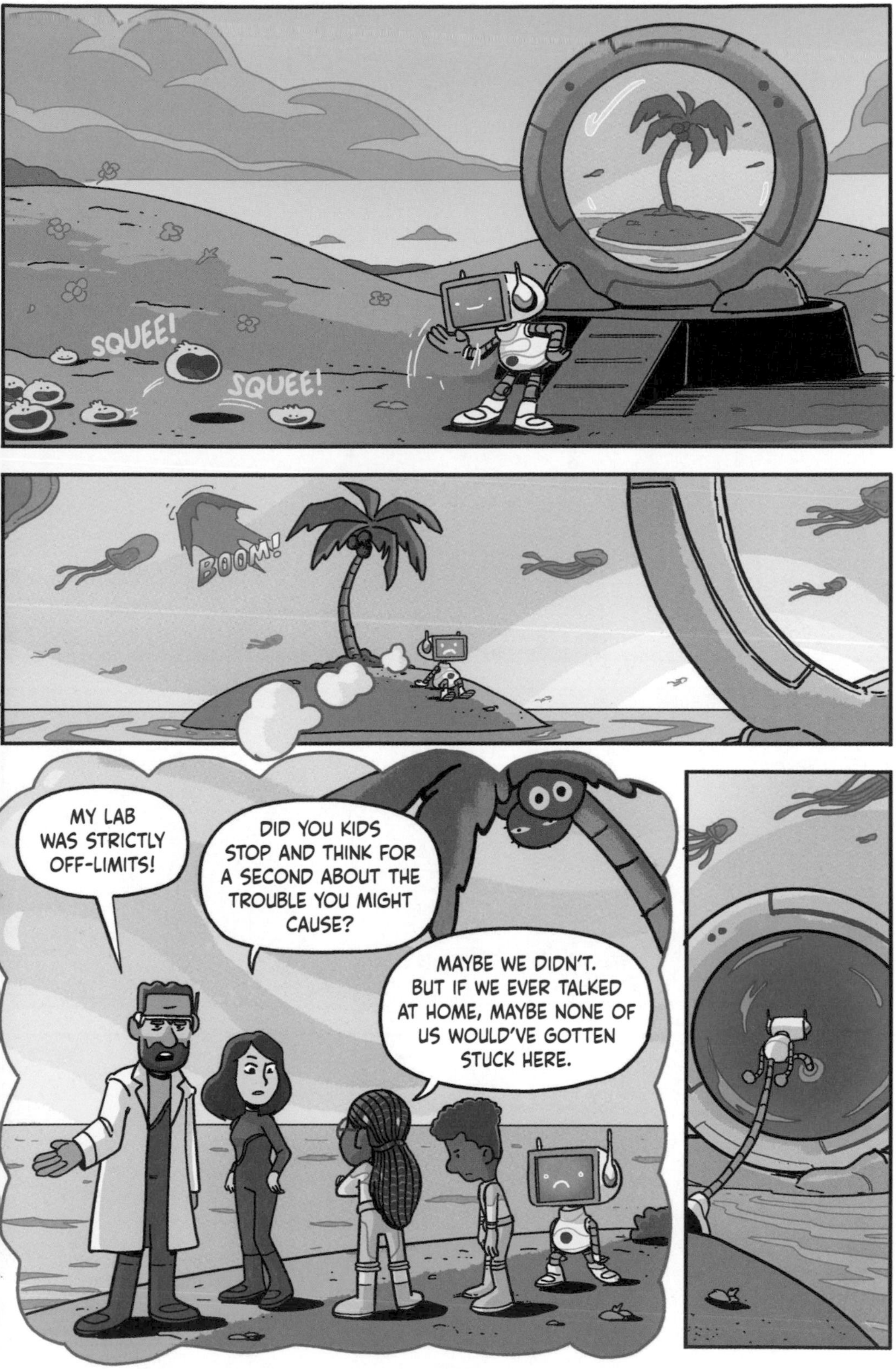
SQUEE!
SQUEE!
BOOM!
MY LAB WAS STRICTLY OFF-LIMITS!
DID YOU KIDS STOP AND THINK FOR A SECOND ABOUT THE TROUBLE YOU MIGHT CAUSE?
MAYBE WE DIDN'T. BUT IF WE EVER TALKED AT HOME, MAYBE NONE OF US WOULD'VE GOTTEN STUCK HERE.

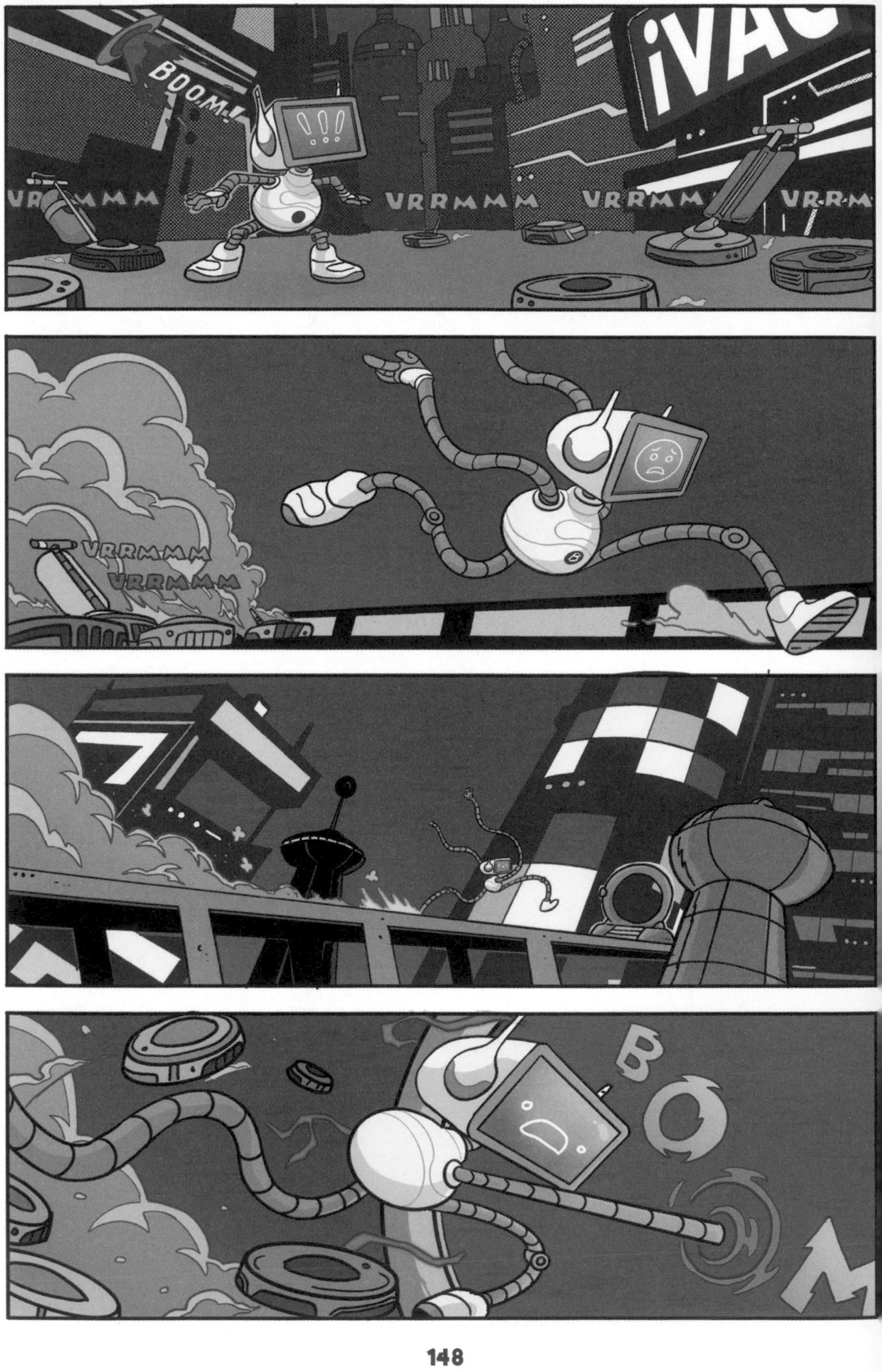
BOOM!
iVAC
VRRMMM
VRRMMM
VRRMMM
VRRMMM
BOOM

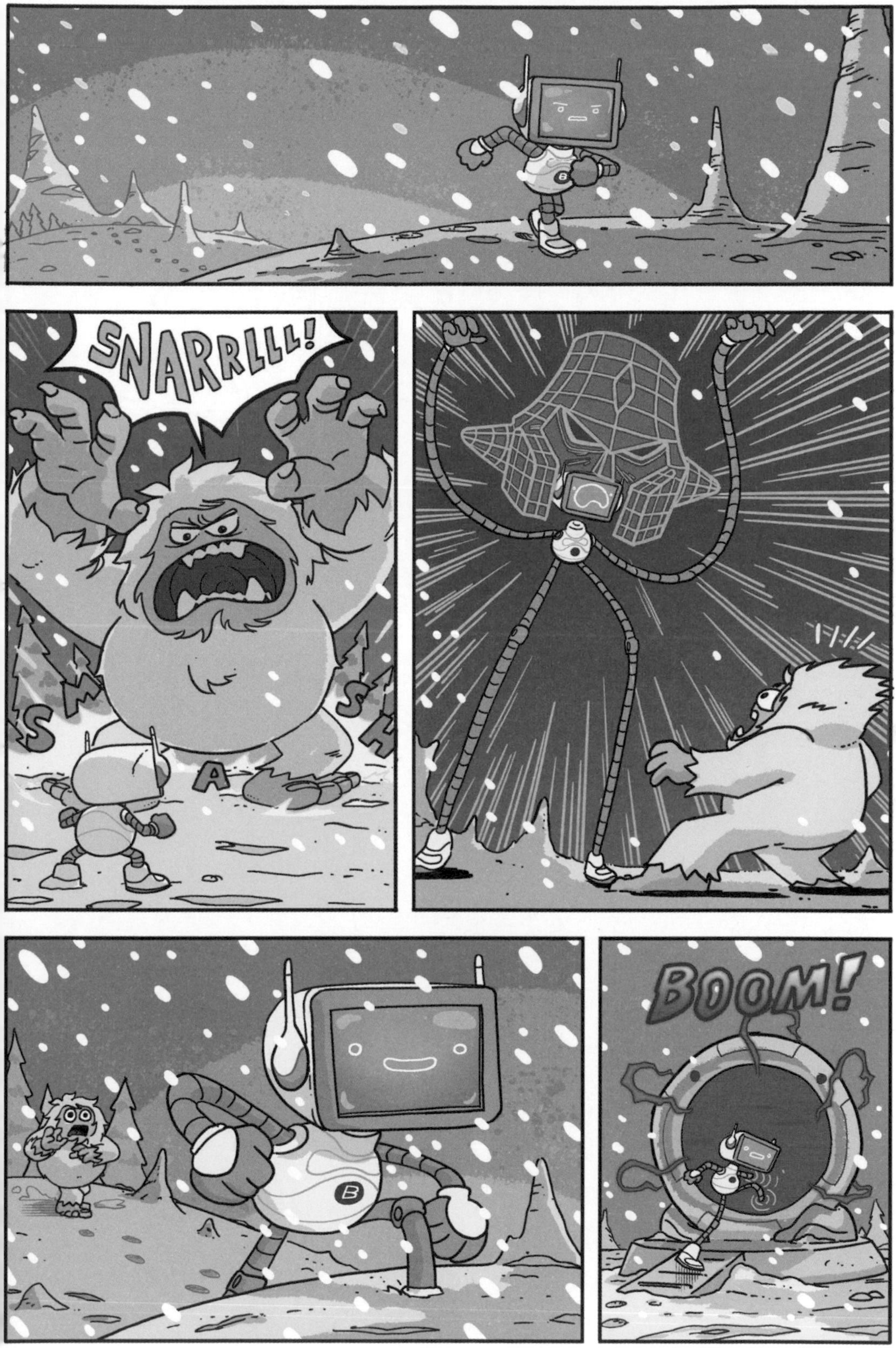
SNARRLLL!
BOOM!

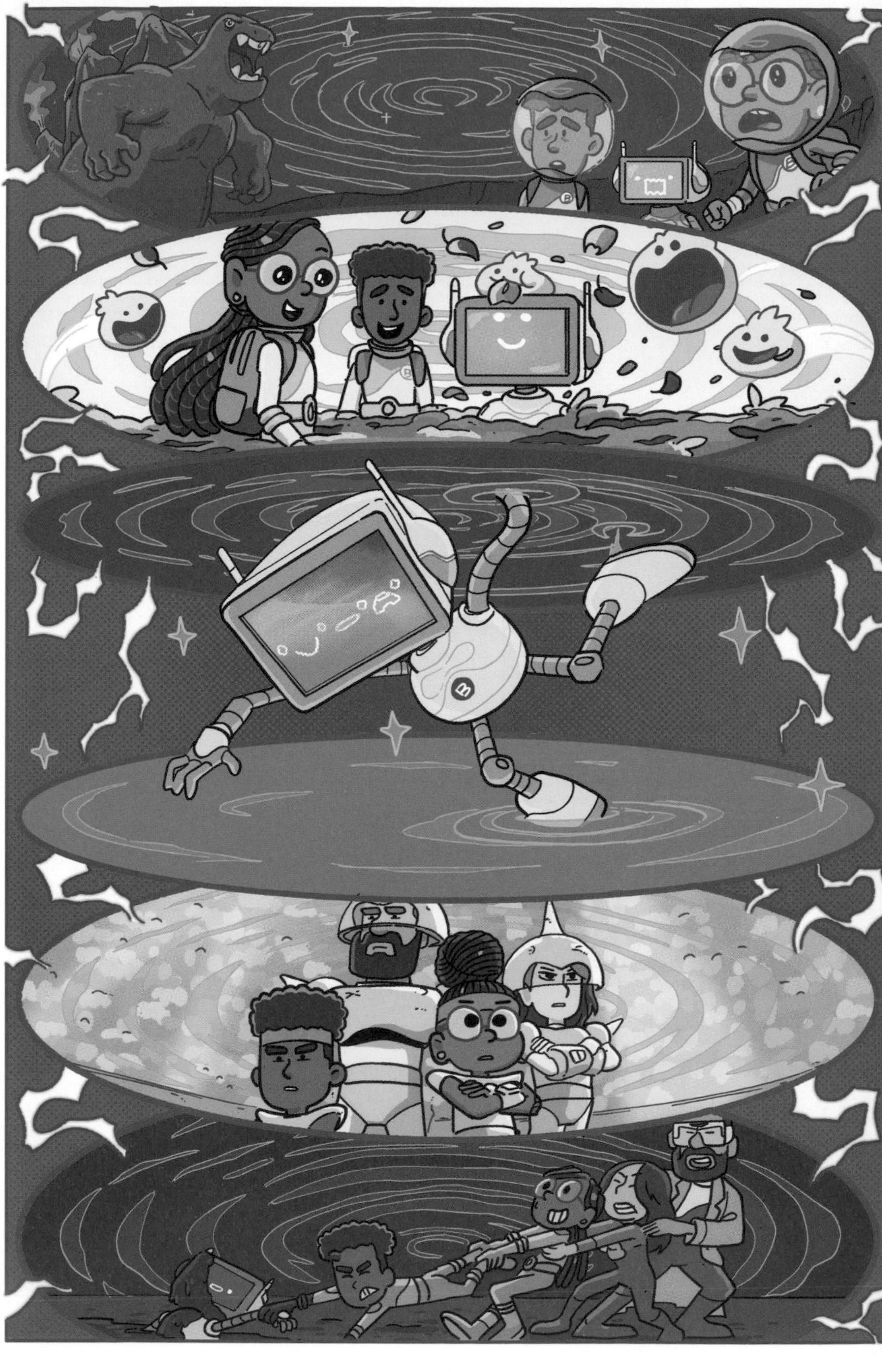

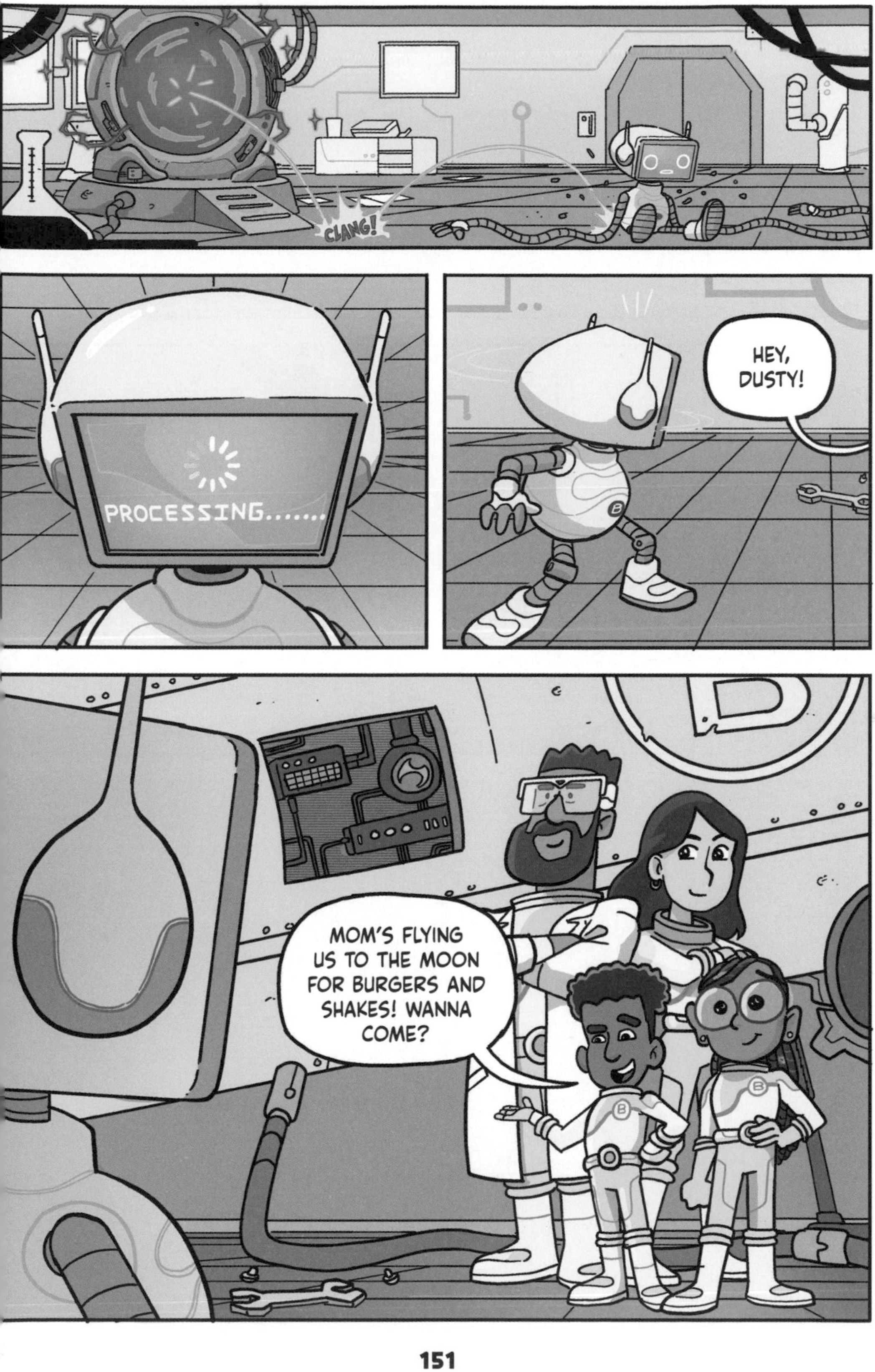
CLANG!
PROCESSING.......
HEY, DUSTY!
MOM'S FLYING US TO THE MOON FOR BURGERS AND SHAKES! WANNA COME?

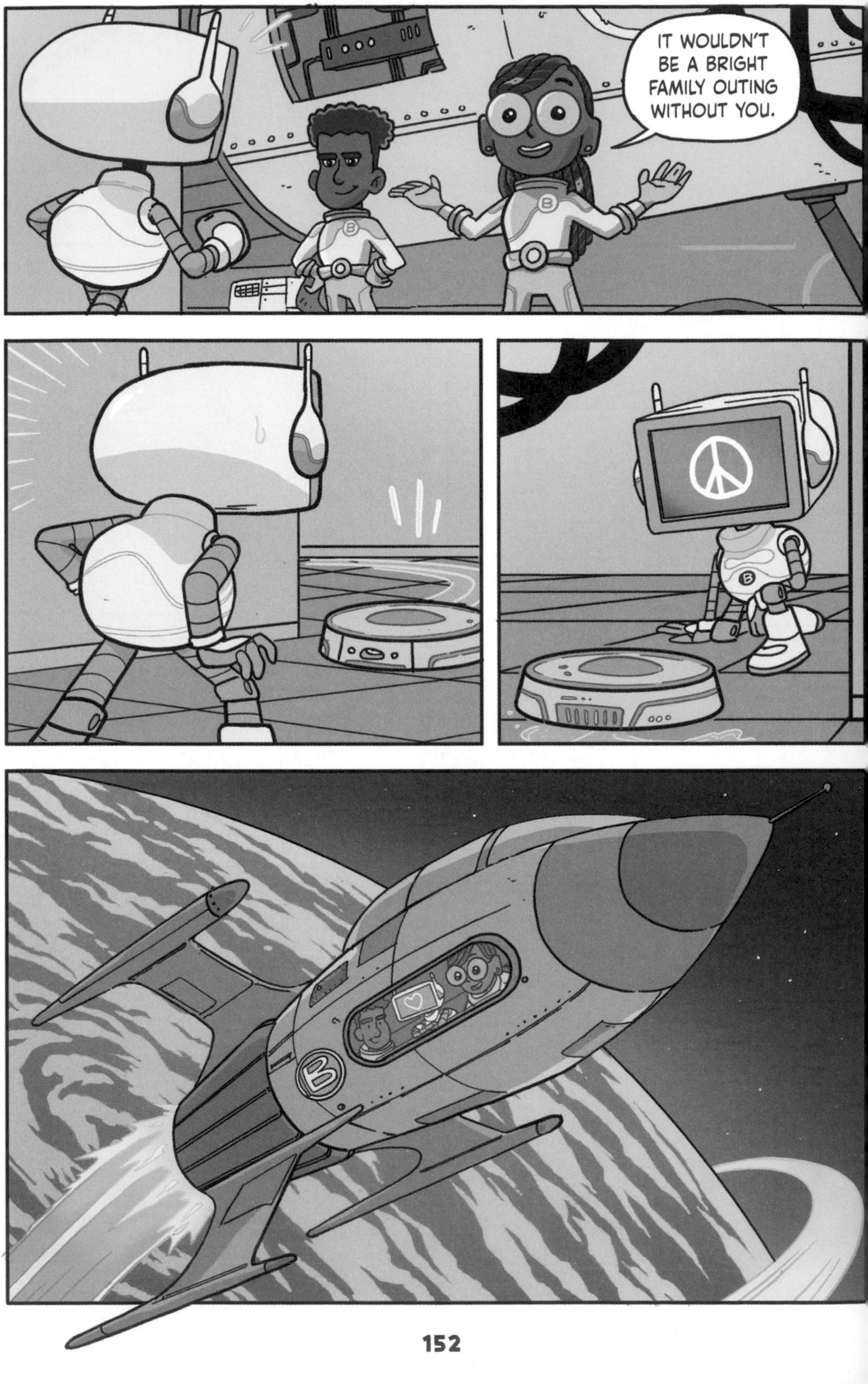
IT WOULDN'T BE A BRIGHT FAMILY OUTING WITHOUT YOU.

# HAVE YOU HEARD ABOUT epic! YET?

We're the largest digital library for kids, used by millions in homes and schools around the world. We love stories so much that we're now creating our own!

With the help of some of the best writers and illustrators in the world, we create the wildest adventures we can think of. Like a mermaid and a narwhal who solve mysteries. Or a pet made out of slime.

We hope you have as much fun reading our books as we had making them!

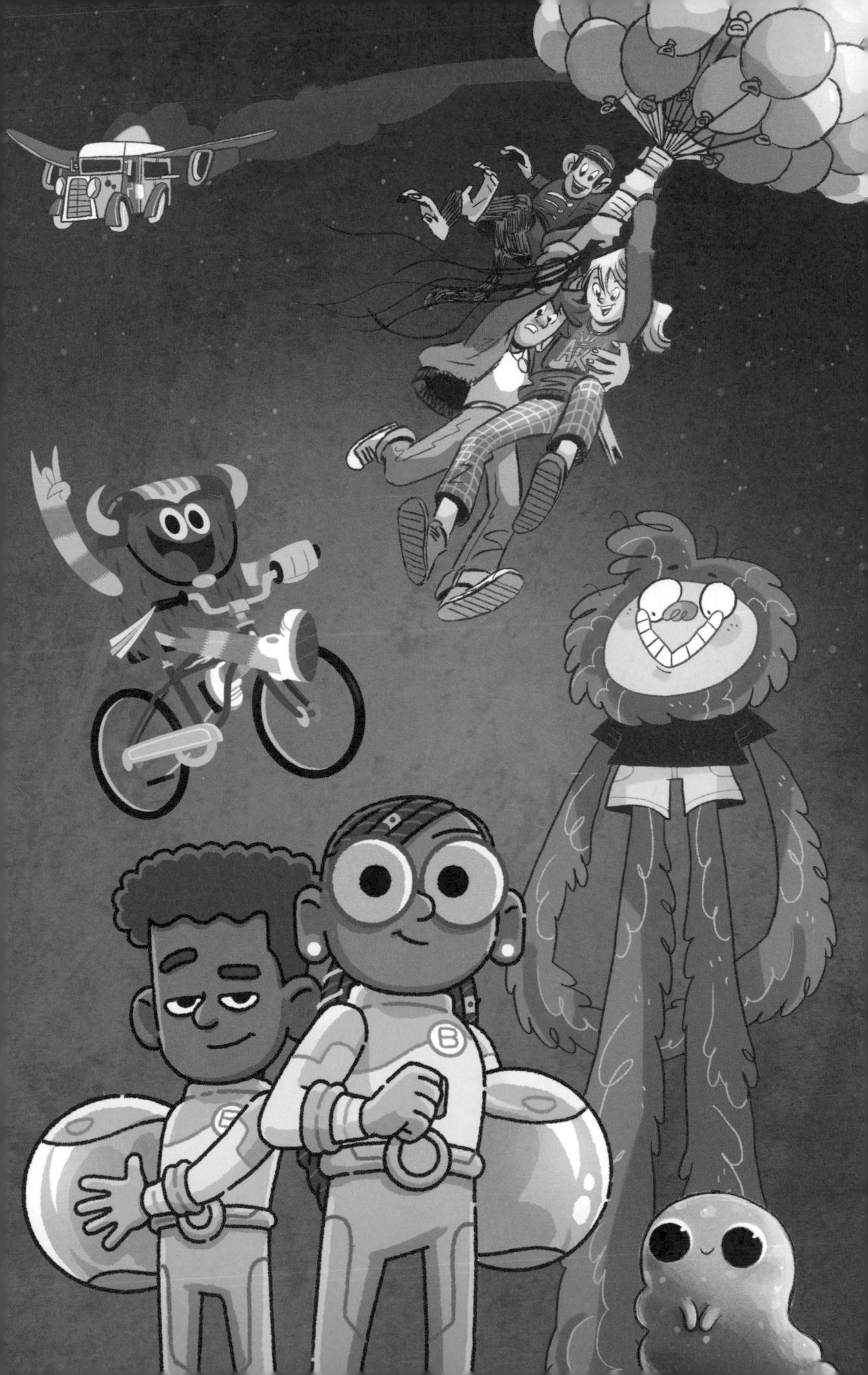

# LOOK FOR THESE BOOKS FROM

# epic!

# AVAILABLE **NOW!**

## TO READ MORE, VISIT
# getepic.com